The Young Shall Endure

Aerolan Saga: Book 2

By

Larry W. Crow

The Young Shall Endure

Aerolan Saga: Book 2

Published by: CrowsToes, USA

Printed in the USA.

Cover Template by: CreateSpace Cover Creator

Interior Maps by: Larry W. Crow

First Printing
0 9 8 7 6 5 4 3 2 1

ISBN10: 0-9744042-4-1
ISBN13: 978-0-9744042-4-0

Table of Contents

Dedicated to:

All the authors who bounded their way through the fantastic worlds of magic, dragons, elves, dwarfs, giants, trolls and all the mystical wonders as yet not real. They have blessed us all with that ridiculously wondrous otherworld that lives in their heads – and thankfully welcome us to visit.

I suppose one has to begin with those from our past: Edgar Rice Burroughs, Jules Verne, J.R.R. Tolkien and, lately, J.K. Rowling for what they have given to our lives through their vivid imaginations and that nth degree of sly humor.

Dome of Eternal Ice

Nortor'o Sea

Straits of Garnin'a

Xari'e Island

Eveto's

Ravelan

Agino'n Ocean

Hamero Levy

Ravelan

Mavelan'g

Maa'n Gulf

Alist'a

Garol'x

Etoron'h

Burs'e

Kalen'r

The Wastelands

Kenu'x

Habenlein

Well of O'Faz'n

Ranome

Barnota

Andreu's Wall

Musrag'y

Garut'x

Voravia's Castle

Tynoc'l

Pillar of Don'n

Isle of Hanet'x

Corothe'a

Aerolan

Litley

Ofan'n

Jareut's

Vargil

Caliste

Craylock

Ohel'd Bay

Isle of Garn'o

Beyond'n Sea

Dutlin's

Carties

TrailEnd

Coma't

Seam'a

Bay

Enspree

Farl's

Valnonal

Safe Inlet

Straits of Anden'o

Ransea

Hang'm

Urca'l Bay

Southern Sea

Varspree

Tayrun

Freiz'n

Pull'r

Amelas's

Avilan

CrossPoint

Larilla

Meruo'a

Tariny

Passg'n

Bran'n Gulf

Roahan

NoBend

Marn't Sound

Norts'a Reach

Rallf'r Castle

Graac'a Inle

Calm'n Gul

Peetle

Bottom of the World

Farsea

Welnon Sea

5

PROLOGUE

He ran as fast as he could, his breath rasping with each step. Tripping, he stumbled and fell into a small ditch, plowing into the dirt with his face.

I can hide.

But, he knew he couldn't stop. They were coming for him. He jumped up, brushed his hand across his face and started running again.

I can reach the river before they can catch me.

He twisted from side to side through the underbrush, avoiding contact with the bushes and hoping he could last until he was safely beyond their grasp

Soon he recognized the low shrub growing close to the water's edge. As he ran, they ripped at his clothing, already in tatters from the horrible attack on his village. He remembered the way they ravaged his village, taking lives at will, not stopping nor accepting surrender.

Thinking he gained ground, he stopped, breathing so deeply he placed his hands on his knees while he gasped. He looked back toward the forest.

Then he saw them, closer than before. Quickly realizing his mistake, he bolted and ran even harder toward the water.

Where is it? The river never seemed this far from home before.

He stumbled and fell. This time he crushed his chest on a stump of a tree, cut long ago by his people. He couldn't catch his breath. He strained to get off the ground, but his breath wouldn't come. Finally, he drew in one deep breath and forced himself to stand.

Stunned, he turned back to look back down the path behind him. He couldn't see them. He only sensed they were following him.

Then they appeared. They were almost upon him. He turned back toward the river and stumbled along, running as best he could.

Why can't I go any faster? Where's the river?

Suddenly he pushed through the bushes into the open, the river was in front of him. He could see the water through the low reeds along the banks. He kept going. Encouraged, he felt he was gaining speed. He believed now he was going to make it.

There were only a few more feet to go, when something struck him from behind.

His eyes widened with surprise. His body arched backward and he lost his footing, tumbled through the underbrush and slid down the riverbank. He jumped up, wobbling, unable to stand and fell back onto the bare bank of the river. He slid further, almost reaching the water.

He lay there, unable to move, unable to see, pain holding him to the ground.

Why am I not in the water? What happened?

He heard the soldiers sliding down the bank toward him, chattering gibberish as they came. He felt one of them grab his shoulder and hair.

They tossed him up the bank a short distance. He fell on his back, opened his eyes and only saw the sky. The puffed clouds floated slowly by. The smoke, the smoke from his village floated unevenly above him, mingled with the clouds. He closed his eyes, tears forming.

Something hard touched him.

Maybe a weapon?

He clinched his eyes not wanting to see.

Then it struck his ribs. He heard them crack.

He opened his eyes, startled. Then he screamed.

Lonl'a woke. He was lying on his back. Looking around he

7

realized he was a captive in a rather large wooden cage. There were several others in the cage with him.

As his vision cleared, he could see other cages, spaced around a large clearing in the forest, with other men and boys, sitting and waiting.

On the other side of his cage, he could see an encampment. Tents were everywhere though placed in an orderly group across the middle of the meadow.

His ribs hurt when he moved. There was still mud on him from his slide down the riverbank. He rolled over and lay on his stomach, trying to determine where he was.

Soldiers were walking back and forth, going about their business. He thought they might be preparing for war. But he knew nothing of a war in Aerolan. This was stranger than he expected.

The sun was fairly high now and it was terribly hot out in the open. He could see some of the cages were in the trees.

Those captives, at least, have some shade.

He wondered who his captors were and where they were from.

Why have they invaded my village? Or other villages? Why are they taking prisoners?

Looking at the soldiers more closely, they all seemed very strange. He had never seen any soldiers in his life. There was never a need, as far as he knew. Lord Hart'l, a rich man who ran his businesses from Safe Inlet, usually kept a small group of men patrolling the eastern shore, and the surrounding middle country, for troublemakers. They did a good job of taking care of any disturbance shortly after it happened.

So why are these soldiers here? What are they doing here? Why was I taken?

Something was odd about these soldiers. He watched them going back and forth in the camp. They seemed not to notice anything around them as they walked. They weren't speaking to each other, as far as he could tell. He saw none of them relaxing or talking to any of the other soldiers. They seemed to always

8

walk about at attention. They were very concentrated and stiff. They were huge. Most of them easily towered over him.

Something was wrong about them but he couldn't really tell what from where he was.

No wonder I didn't get away. What kind of men are they?

He decided he couldn't determine anything from his vantage point, so he sat up, his side rippling with pain and turned back to look at those in the cage with him.

All were men, many young men like himself, crushed together in a small space. A few were older and others seemed very young. Some injured, as he was, and others just tired and sick. All waiting.

He wondered why there were so many men taken. He looked around at some of the other cages to see if there were any with women. He could only see one, sitting in the shade and pulled away from the others. He was too far away to recognize any of them. They too were crushed together so it would have been difficult to identify anyone anyway. But they all seemed to be quite young.

What happened to the women of my village? What about my mother and sister? Where are they?

It bothered him he didn't know what happened to his family. He held his head in his hand and brooded for a while, wondering. Finally, realizing he could determine nothing by worrying about something he had no way to change, he relaxed and began to study the area more thoroughly.

Maybe I can discover a way to escape. If I can escape, I need to go back home and determine what happened and see if I can help in any way.

As he finished his survey, he noticed a raised platform near the center of the camp. There were village men standing on it, looking around at the soldiers watching them. He could tell, despite the distance, the villagers were frightened.

There was activity and conversation among those soldiers, standing in front of and near the platform as they inspected each

9

villagers brought onto the platform. Most of the soldiers near the platform seem to have better uniforms than the men wandering around the camp. Occasionally one, or two, of the soldiers raised their voice, or their hand, and the villager of interest would be led to the side of the platform. It seemed there was an auction.

Those bidding must be officers. What kind of auction is this? I see no cattle or any other livestock. So what are they bidding for? Are they actually bidding on those village men? Choosing the ones they each want. But for what?

Then the auction proceedings were suddenly completed.

The officers gathered at the bottom of the steps and, as the villagers were led off the platform, they instructed their soldiers, pointing fingers at each villager as he walked down the exit, to take the selected captives from the group as they approached. Each officer gathered several victims.

Those men, the villagers chosen, are slaves now. They're not just prisoners any longer.

When the platform was empty, the smaller groups of prisoners then followed the officer and his men. Almost all the groups walked in a direction away from where Lonl'a sat and disappeared behind a grove of trees.

But one of the smaller groups of slaves approached a tent near the meadow where Lonl'a's cage sat. He decided all those locked in a cage were actually slaves, including him, and what he was watching predicted his, and their, future. Any man taken in a bid by the officers wasn't going to easily escape, even if he tried. Lonl'a wasn't certain what happened to the women, but he could guess.

He continued to follow the closer group as they neared the tent. He recognized no one from his village, but it was still difficult for him to tell. The group disappeared into the larger of two tents. Guards stood silently and motionless at the entrances, both in the front and back.

While Lonl'a watched, one of the slaves walked out the back

of the tent, pushed along by a guard toward the smaller one. The man, and the soldier guarding him, disappeared inside.

There was a long pause. Nothing was happening.

They're probably questioning him? But about what?

Lonl'a turned away from watching the strange activity at the tents to see what else was going on around the camp. One thing he observed was a small corral built into the woods on the far side of the camp. There were a small number of prisoners standing around, talking to each other.

Probably wondering, like me, what's going on?

Then suddenly a piercing scream erupted from the smaller tent he was watching earlier. There was a pause then another scream of pain, shorter this time. Then there was, what seemed to Lonl'a, a whimper, or a sigh, that followed. He wasn't able to tell which but it seemed to possess the sound of resignation, or bitter acceptance. Then all was quiet again.

After a moment, two soldiers left the small tent and walked to the larger one. The villager who was taken to the smaller tent didn't return. He wasn't taken away, as best as Lonl'a could see.

What is happening here? What happened to that man?

Then the guard pushed another man from the larger tent's rear exit and led him, like the last one, to the smaller tent. The sequence of the sounds from the smaller tent was repeated.

Lonl'a sat back, holding his head. He didn't understand this. The unusual process at the tents was a mystery.

"What's happening over there?" an older man, sitting on the floor of the cage and watching the tents, asked, "What's happening to those men?"

Lonl'a jumped when the old man spoke and jerked around looking for the speaker, fearing he was noticed by one of the guards. He looked down and saw the man was sitting on the floor of the cage, looking through the bars.

The old man had a slight accent. He sounded like most of the people Lonl'a knew but there was a strange lilt with certain

11

words. Lonl'a decided the man must be from a region just a bit further down the coast from where he lived.

"I don't know, sir. I was wondering the same thing?" Lonl'a answered. He looked back toward the tents.

Again two soldiers left the smaller tent and there was no evidence the villager left it at all. Then he turned back to the old man.

"What do you think? What are they doing to those men?" he asked.

"Don't know. But I believe those fellows are gone, either killed, or hidden or something. I just don't know," the old man said slowly, shaking his head, as though he couldn't believe what he was watching.

Then from the larger tent, a guard ushered a man out of the front entrance, pushing the man ahead of him. The man was taken to the corral Lonl'a saw earlier. The gate opened and the man was thrown inside, tumbling across the ground with the force of the toss. The gates slammed shut. The guard then returned to the tents, walking methodically across the compound, never looking from side to side. It seemed he was unaware there were others around.

Back at the tent area, the cycle of taking men to the smaller tent continued into the early hours of dusk. Just at dark, a small group of soldiers was escorted from the larger tent and marched to the center of the encampment. Another officer at that site took command of the group, led them away and out of sight.

Darkness settled over the area. Lonl'a and his new friend sat looking at the tents until the light faded.

"I don't know what's goin' on," the old man muttered.

Lonl'a shook his head, knowing the old man couldn't see him.

"Me neither. It's all too strange. Doesn't make any sense," he mumbled.

They sat in silence for a while. The old man finally lay down near the side of the cage, close enough to the bars so he wouldn't get stepped on, and fell asleep.

Lonl'a stared up at the night and the stars and wondered why his world was falling apart.

The next morning, soldiers who spoke no more than necessary woke everyone in Lonl'a's cage. These were regular soldiers, obviously different than the larger ones. They handed out bowls of barely edible mush and a cup of water.

They commanded everyone to eat and drink. They also told them they each were responsible for the bowl and cup. If those were lost, no food or drink. Then the soldiers left and went to the next cage.

Everyone ate quietly. They wiped the containers as clean as possible when they finished eating, wrapped them and shoved them into their shirt. No one was concerned another would steal anything, certainly not a cup and plate.

The days passed. Lonl'a tired of watching the activity around the tents and tried to sleep, even when the sun beat down on him. He and Runf'a, the old man, spent time talking about their separate villages, their lives there and how surprised everyone was when these soldiers attacked and began gathering the men and boys – no matter what age.

"Wonder why they took old men, like me?" Runf'a pondered. "Don't make any sense. We sit here and watch this strange parade of men into those tents that are never seen again. I still can't figure out where all these soldiers come from that leave the large tent at night. Curiouser and curiouser, I'd say."

"You got that right. Where do they come from? There must be another entrance on the side we can't see. Maybe that's how the lost men leave the smaller tent. I don't know, but I'm getting tired of sitting in this sun all day," Lonl'a added.

While they waited to see what might happen to them, the cages in front of them were shuffled forward in line as each group of men went through the same procedure as the first – the auction for the larger group, the small groups taken to separate

13

tents and the cycle of the small tent repeated until each cage was emptied. The cage, next in line, was raised and brought forward with the rest each night. This procedure repeated itself over and over.

Lonl'a thought each of the emptied cages was taken to the back of the long line and refilled with new captives. Looking back along the line that disappeared into the forest, he could see no end to the cages.

He and the old man watched, out of fear, more intently as their cage drew closer to the encampment and the platform. They still weren't certain what was happening. But Lonl'a thought his auction idea was true and he tried to prepare himself for it.

Finally, the day came for them to be next on the platform.

"I guess we're gonna find out what's happening soon enough," Runf'a spoke under his breath.

The guards hadn't warned them to be quiet, but the old man was taking no chances. One of these strange guards might hit him if he spoke too loudly.

Lonl'a was still having trouble with his ribs. He originally wrapped some cloth around himself he borrowed from one of the other men in the cage, but the pain still came if Lonl'a moved the wrong way, or strained his muscles at all.

As the day wore on, all seemed quiet. He and Runf'a were trying to nap, when the cage door yanked open violently. One of the guards grabbed one of the men near the door and practically threw him out.

Lonl'a and his friend said nothing but both stood, trying to make their exit from the cage more pleasant than what they witnessed, though they still suffered being thrown forward into the dirt. They rose from their tumble and tried to stand.

Runf'a wasn't quite as quick as most of the others and the guard grabbed him so tightly he broke Runf'a's arm, but still threw the old man toward the steps. Lonl'a move forward quickly, reached and helped the old man rise and walked toward the steps supporting him. Both now were battered from the harsh treatment.

Lonl'a decided he didn't need to be pulled around too much, so he moved himself and Runf'a from their original position in line and walked closely behind one of the other men and waited quietly.

After all the prisoners were out of the cage, a guard at the steps motioned for them to climb the step. It was intended the villagers should, and must, go onto the platform.

They shuffled slowly onto the stage and huddled near the center. There was a standing area, just in front of the stage, for the officers attending this bidding session.

The first bidder raised his hand and pointed to a man on the front row and barked out something Lonl'a didn't understand.

A guard walked to the prisoner. He grabbed the man's arms and held them aloft and then he pushed the arms down and turned him slowly. The man tried to resist, but he wasn't strong enough to change anything. He soon allowed the guard to push him about as he wished.

There were several bids for the prisoner. He was of medium height and somewhat muscular, so a potentially strong candidate if slavery was intended.

The bidding became a little livelier with some of the officers actually growling when they were outbid. But finally, there was a bid no one else wanted to exceed and the man was sold to the last bidder. The guard pointed toward the bidder and indicated to the villager he should go stand near his buyer.

Lonl'a assumed the villager knew he needed to follow the instructions, but the man apparently thought otherwise. When he walked to the steps, the guard released his hold on the man's arm. The prisoner, believing this an opportunity, broke away and leaped down the steps, blasted his way through the first ring of bidders and began running away from the crowd. He seemed to break free. But suddenly a hand thrown weapon – somewhat oblong and thin – floated through the air, hitting the man in the back and he fell, plowing some dirt from the ground as he slid to a halt.

The prisoner's new owner came over and kicked him, but not hard enough to break anything. The man was already unconscious and his body rolled over helplessly. The officer then motioned to his personal guard to bring the man along and place him in the area intended for his collection.

The result of the episode provided an understanding for the rest of the villagers on the platform. They needed to remain quiet and should obey the orders or run the risk of being injured, or killed.

The bidding continued for some time, each man – young and old – forced to stand and be judged for worthiness.

Lonl'a's friend, Runf'a, stood, his arm hanging limp. When the guard grabbed the old man's arm, he screamed out in pain and fainted, crumpling on the platform. The bidding stopped and no one picked it up again. The last bidder was asked a question and he shook his head.

Runf'a was lifted then and taken to the side of the stage away from the steps and dumped over the edge. He cried out when he hit the ground, but afterward, he laid still and wasn't noticed again except when he gave an occasional cry of pain. This drew the attention of some of the odd looking soldiers standing nearby, but for only a glance. There were several of the older men and other weaker ones who were not chosen and were delegated to the group with Runf'a.

Lonl'a saw no way he could ever help the old man relieve his pain. He never saw Runf'a again after that.

Lonl'a's time came. He was young, relatively strong and certainly seemed healthy, so the bidding was vigorous. When the guard reached for his arms, he raised them both himself to avoid the jerking motion the guard used. His ribs were painful enough; his injury didn't need to be aggravated anymore.

16

Soon the bidding for him was complete and his new owner was pointed out. The guard escorted him to the steps and watched while he walked down and around to stand in the bidder's group of previous purchases.

When the auction finally ended, each officer took his own group to a large command tent such as the one Lonl'a and Runf'a watched all those days from their cage. The tent that was so mysterious they never understood what was happening inside.

I suppose I'll learn soon enough what happens.

He watched as one of the men ahead of him was taken out the rear of the large tent. Lonl'a could see, not far away, the small tent, its sides billowing in the wind, sitting silently in the trees.

Then the same agonized cries came briefly from the small tent, a pattern he was already familiar with. The wait was agonizing.

What is happening in that tent?

As though hearing Lonl'a thoughts, the man sitting next to him asked him a question, aloud

"What's happening over there?"

Lonl'a remembered the man from earlier at the platform but knew he wasn't from his village.

Suddenly the man was lying on the ground holding his head in his hands. Struck from behind by one of the guards who didn't try to be gentle, the man screamed in pain.

Lonl'a stepped away from him, watching the man's agony and looking briefly at the guard. The guard showed no emotion but just stood and waited. He wanted this man to be quiet. Apparently, he wanted all of them to keep their silence. The man's head and one of his ears was bleeding a great deal as he rolled around on the ground, holding his hands over his wounds, obviously in pain.

The guard did nothing for a while then leaned over and hit the man on the head with his weapon and knocked him unconscious. The prisoner lay on the ground; no one around attempted to help him. When the time came, he was picked up and taken to the small tent. There was a long silence and then the same agonizing cries Lonl'a expected came from the tent. Then there was quiet again.

Everyone in Lonl'a's group was now looking at each other. Lonl'a avoided looking around too much. He realized it only brought attention to him.

Finally, his turn came. He stood and walked, without being forced, to the small tent. His curiosity almost overcame his fear. When he entered, he saw a small man sitting in the middle of the tent with a low, small table next to him. On the table was nothing but a stone of unusual grain and color – almost black -- radiating a misty, shadowy light.

The small man, sitting at the table, was wrapped in long robes and obviously wasn't a member of the military. He seemed to be a doctor attending patients. He had long dark hair draped down his back and peered oddly at Lonl'a as he walked in.

"Rather young, I see," the man replayed. "I want you to keep silent unless I ask you a question. I'm about to perform a procedure on you. You'll not like it, but, if you do not resist, there will be less pain. You will be different when you awake; you'll look different. You will have changed in other ways, but you'll still understand others and me. You will know what is going on around you, but you'll react only to those things important to you and important to your commander.

Those are things that will happen. Are you prepared for this?"

"As much as I'll ever be, I imagine," Lonl'a answered. "I doubt I have a choice, if I'm not mistaken."

The small man turned his head, "Hm-m-m. Brighter than most. I'll commend you to your commander afterward."

Then the small man placed his hand on the stone on the table and motioned with his other one for Lonl'a to come closer. Lonl'a stepped forward and stopped in front of the man. The other reached out and clasped Lonl'a's arm.

The sky exploded. A light flashed across Lonl'a face and

18

whipped back into his awareness. He couldn't remember where he was or what was happening to him. He thought he remembered moaning, but knew he didn't scream as he heard others do in one of these tents.

He felt his body and mind changing, not necessarily an unpleasant feeling, but strange and oddly relaxing. Then it was finished. He opened his eyes slowly and realized, for the first time, why the other villagers never returned from the small tent.

All the others, were, and now he was, a soldier of the new army.

The small man spoke some alien language to the Lonl'a's guard. Lonl'a realized he understood it. The small man told the guard that Lonl'a was safe and could be returned to the larger tent.

Then the little man, obviously a wizard, or a priest, nodded his head and waved them away. But before they left the wizard gave additional instructions to the guard.

"Tell Tern'a this one is a good match for a personal guard," the wizard said. "He'll want to know that."

The guard, in turn, nodded his head and motioned for Lonl'a to follow him and they walked back to the large tent together.

Lonl'a knew what was happening. He knew his ribs were healed. He knew he would never be the same. He knew he would obey his commander and be extremely obedient. He knew his old life, which he vaguely remembered, was gone. He recognized his differences.

But one thing significant had changed besides all those things and he saw it as odd and alien.

He no longer cared.

VORAVIA

Let us continue our story of fear and tenacity. Our three young people have endured a battle, small but relevant. They have proven to themselves they are, at least, capable of protecting themselves and Narhtrae from some of the evils brought to this world. Though only having to face two of Baalsa'n's children, they won the day and diverted an attack that could have set the world into a tailspin toward disaster.

An ending must have a beginning, some stories though may have many endings. Of this story there is to be more; for it's about the good in man and we have come only a short way on our journey. There may be other stories to tell with other beginnings.

But, I digress. We now have brought our story to the point where almost all of those who have desired to protect, or destroy the Ahar'n, are present in one time and place.

There have been too many paths taken, too many opportunities lost. We must improve our effectiveness in our dealings with our children over those past instances.

We have not affected a way to provide a better world to these children. We who wish for there to be peace and harmony are no longer willing to lay down and lose what we have worked for so long without fighting to save it.

There is a moment when one has to ask why there must be war before there is peace. War comes about by the recognition that there is an element within a culture that does not consider the welfare of the community as a whole.

So, there is war . . .

Voravia bounced off a wall, a chain clinked in the darkness. She couldn't be certain where she was except the place smelled of a cave. There were no lights to show her whereabouts, but her vision slowly adjusted.

Finally she realized she was in a cell, behind bars, leaning against large chains bolted firmly to the wall above. She was sitting in a corner and looking out into a larger cavern that somehow seemed familiar.

The door to the cell stood open though the area seemed to have been used recently. The bracelets at the end of the chains had been torn apart by something, or someone, with massive strength; they hung, twisted into uselessness.

There was a small bunk, a bowl in another corner. The whole reeked of human excrement.

She jumped up quickly, brushed her free of the refuse and straw that covered the floor and stepped through the doorway, turned and recognized where she was. Somehow she stood in the caverns below her own castle near the black stone tower. She turned and looked back at the cell.

That is where I thought I could capture, and destroy, the new Guardian of the Ahar'n. Apparently I was wrong and was too late to stop him from gaining his powers.

She grinned, turned and walked to the familiar steps leading up to her chambers. On one of the landings, she was halted by a disturbance.

Looking up she saw her servants tumbling down, attempting, in their ridiculous way, to protect her castle from intruders. They had come prepared, or so they thought, to do battle with any interlopers.

Their efforts however were, at best, not very well organized and possibly humorous to another observing them. Voravia did not find their actions laughable however and now she vented her anger at them.

"You idiots! What do you think you're doing?! Get away from me! Get out of my way! I must get to my room immediately. *Get out of my way!*" She screamed at them again.

They tumbled, stood and dropped their weapons. They would stop, pick up the weapons, try to run and bang against each other, and then drop the weapons again. There was bedlam and error in everything they did.

Voravia had enough. She threw out her hands, glared and the whole stupid mess disappeared.

"Good, now I can make more of these idiots, maybe a little smarter the next time," she snapped, as she proceeded up the steps to the great hall above, never looking back, nor wondering where the dullards went. She was unconcerned.

When she walked through the door at the top, her servant, Mord, came running to her. Half of his last few steps where actually taken on his knees. He slid to a stop just in front of her.

"Oh, mistress. Pleaz. Wes wuz scared when yous go. Wes not knows yous come back. Wes not know what is to do, and not know where wes can go," he bowed his head to the ground.

He was afraid, but strangely relieved. Voravia had returned. He had no way of knowing whether he should be happy or frightened. His mind weakly pursued many avenues of thought but uncertainty reigned.

He drooled on the floor in his agitation.

"Get up, you moron! If you've allowed this palace to be damaged in any way, you shall rue the day I made you," she remarked snappily, looking down on this creature of her making and kicked him in the side. "Get up from the floor, bring me food in my room. I've much work to do."

Voravia swirled away and stomped along the hallway to her room, entered and went to the window from which the fugitive young people had escaped, reached out, grabbed the casements and slammed the window shut. She stood satisfied with herself, turned to go to her closet to change her clothing.

Feeling a tension in the air, she turned back into the room and stopped, surprised.

A man stood just beyond the table where Anisah and the young wizard were standing before Rab'k tried to torture them. He wore black clothing; his hair flowed over his shoulder and framed a handsome face. He was obviously strong physically, but there was a certain air about him that revealed he would seldom have need for such strength.

"Sister, you seem a bit distressed. Have you not had a good afternoon?" the man smiled and gestured with a flip of his hand. He walked to the chair by the table and sat down, "Surely, you remember me, do you not?"

Voravia startled at first sight of the man; now scowled at him.

"Mano'n, where have you been? I thought you were dead, and so did our young brother, Rab'k. Rena'x told him he thought you had angered Baalsa'n."

"We have a young brother? Must have been that young upstart at our last meeting. How enchanting. Apparently Baalsa'n has not given up all his pleasures despite his sudden urgency to destroy this fragile planet. Besides, he's always angry at me," he gestured again, waving his hand as though dismissing the world as he saw it.

"As for my disappearance, I was a bit busy with certain personal matters. Besides, it obviously wasn't time to dispose of all this." He waved his hand nonchalantly again. A mannerism that was beginning to annoy Voravia.

"His urgency happens to have justification. There is a new order of wizardry, I believe. I don't know how, but all of them are very young and have gained tremendous powers in a very short time," Voravia retorted.

She hadn't seen her brother in all the years since their arrival in the southern world. As children, though knowing nothing of each other, they had learned about the ways of the harsh life, about power, and about whom they were to become. Now their time had arrived and she hardly knew him at all. At the moment, she thought him to be a pompous ass.

"Not very flattering, my kind sister. One has to have a certain sense of finery when given the opportunity. Besides, I have looked about the country, in my way, and I still believe the time is right for the great changes Baalsa'n wants. Besides what can these young pups do we cannot?" Mano'n interrupted her thoughts, revealing to her he could read them.

"Possibly, you shouldn't be so self-assured, dear brother," she answered sarcastically, noticing and pleased he reacted.

"If you are reading my thoughts then perhaps you see the image of the young girl who is with these new wizards. It seems to me she bares a strong resemblance to you."

"Anisah! How is it she is with this rabble?" Mano'n asked, surprisingly changing his previous demeanor. "Are you certain this was the girl?"

"Curious are you? Anisah, I do believe that was her name. How do you know her? Where have you met her?" Voravia suddenly was enjoying the direction the conversation was taking.

"Is it possible, brother, you pursued a bit of dalliance of your own?" Voravia was almost ecstatic inside, but showing a very calm and serious visage to her brother.

"Shut up, Voravia. Yes. Yes, I have an interest in the welfare of the girl." Mano'n answered brusquely, "and yes, she's my daughter."

Voravia sneered at him, "You thought this trivial thing would not be noticed if you hid away. Do you think Baalsa'n is a fool? How could you do this?"

"Very easily, as it turns out. Strangely I've always felt a certain responsibility for her welfare. I have been watching her in her recent adventures and actually had taken a bit of pride in her progress. I haven't seen her though since she left Tariny several days ago. How did you meet her?" Mano'n inquired, surprised more than curious.

"She visited , I suppose you could call it a visit. She was here, just this morning, with her two friends. The cataclysm happened. Of course, you missed it. There now is a known division between these miserable beings in the southern land and us. You surely noticed there was a change," she snarled at him.

24

"Yes, I knew. That is the reason I'm here. But I was unaware of these new wizards. I thought Kalbr'an had something to do with starting the conflict. But three young people? What is he planning by using the young?" Mano'n was meandering; his thoughts were rummaging through what he knew of the old legends about the gods.

"Well, whatever. One of the new wizards is, in fact, this daughter of yours," Voravia spoke bluntly, hoping for the shock she got from her brother the effect was satisfying.

Mano'n stared at her for a moment without speaking. He obviously no longer pretended to affect the air of impunity.

He was actually surprised. He lost contact with his daughter and was unaware of the changes in her. He saw a delightful rebelliousness in his daughter. He enjoyed that. He felt certain, with all he saw earlier of her discovering her talents, she would someday become a great contributor to their fight for Baalsa'n. That she had now risen as companion to wizards who would try to prevent this happening was not something he foresaw.

"Since you seem to be able to find me easily enough, where is this Anisah now?" Voravia asked, relishing this entire scene. "Perhaps you should pay her a little visit and bring her into the fold of our cause sooner than later, if you can."

"If I can? Of course, I can. You're correct. I think I should go now and help her make this transition," Mano'n answered, paused for a moment, turning his head slightly as though sensing the motion of the air about him.

"She's returned to the village where she was born. I'll return shortly and bring her back with me." He disappeared as suddenly as he had appeared.

Voravia waited for (omit) some time; she was busy straightening her affairs before the massive war she knew was soon to begin and gave no more thought to her brother and his difficulty.

Later though quite busy with her plans, she noticed a great deal of time had passed and no brother, or niece, had returned.

25

"I believe I should go work on this problem, too. Something about this incident is obviously unpredictable," she looked about her home, satisfied all was well, smoothed down her gown, and disappeared.

ANGER

Baalsa'n was not happy; he raged because of the failure of his children.

"Mano'n wasn't there. Where was he?" he stormed, slamming about his suite.

He forced them to wait, wait until the time was ripe for a quick conquest. It should have been a simple task; all was in order.

But, what of these three new problems? Who were they and where had they been hiding? There is something important I'm not seeing about the girl. Why is she somehow relevant? There have been no traces of magical occurrences anywhere, prior to the incidents of yesterday.

These three have set my plans back. I must prepare an event to reset the balance in my favor.

Are the Al-Esfer'n helping somehow? Are they aware I've returned? If so, what are they planning?

But then it makes no difference, I shall crush them as I have before. My armies are too strong, too large, and too mobile. They have never tasted defeat.

Slowly, he calmed himself; concentrating on Ravelan in the far north, beyond Aerolan.

A country of warlike people, limited by the great seas surrounding them, possessing many candidates for armies he could use. Strongly tribal people and lovers of war, they slaughtered each other constantly, but Baalsa'n could steal away many of their strongest to fight in his new war.

Yes, there are plenty of recruits there. With my modification, I should have an unbeatable force. But, I must trust at least one of my children with this new plan. Which? I feel I can no longer trust Mano'n, what happened to him? But whom do I trust? Maybe Voravia.

Voravia. It must be her. She has proven to be more dependable than the other two. She continues to provide strength to the cause and was the most evident in the first battle.

He turned, left his suite and marched to the outer entrance of Esclare'. All those who saw him striding their way quickly decided they had urgent business somewhere else. He reached the doors, signaling to the guards to open one of them as he approached.

The door eased open just enough for him to exit and, as he whipped into the burning desert air, he called back. "Leave it open. I'll only be a moment!" He walked to the edge of the plateau, stood looking over the desert and down at Tynoc'l below.

Even this place has grown some since I first started this campaign. Good, the more angry people who wish to worship me the better.

Then he took a stance and peered into the skies toward the distance north. He drew the earth's strength into himself. The winds began to swirl upward, shielding him within the dusty wall of the vortex. But he didn't extend it beyond what was necessary to accomplish his task.

Suddenly, a vision of a man became clear to him. He paused until he had the man's attention.

"Drang'm, I have need of your services," he announced. The other only bowed toward him.

"I will need an army, ten thousand strong, to battle in Aerolan. I must have your best. The Al-Esfer'n have infiltrated the minds of the people there and a small group of natives seemed to be attentive to their ridiculous promises. I wish to destroy them now and replace them with good, and loyal, people."

Drang'm remained on Narhtrae when Baalsa'n left after their first visit. He waited for the wave of Om-Esfer'ns who quietly returned to this Al-Esfer'n world. He originated and instituted a plan to gather captive subjects and undermine the authority of any enemy that might revive itself with this new invasion. All of Baalsa'n's people knew the importance of destroying this world.

More importantly, through Drang'm's efforts, the people of

Narhtrae began to forget the Al-Esfer'n ever existed. Centuries passed after the first invasion failed. Drang'm stayed behind to begin his program of undermining the trust within the lives of all the inhabitants of Narhtrae on the first days after Baalsa'n's retreat.

Drang'm was dramatically successful. Most of the lands, except Aerolan, had succumbed to his efforts quite readily. The people in those other nations were easily led by greed and power. He managed to deceive them quickly. He pressed the tribes into fighting, almost continuously, with each other. It was a self-destructive mode, but each nation thought itself correct.

This plan was less militarily oriented than previous attacks on defeated planets, but Baalsa'n suspected the Al-Esfer'n were probably more cautious than most others The leaders of Aerolan, in particular, might actually be able to gather a force to defeat him again, if memory of the first instance remained. Now, after a millennium of deception, there was less danger and potentially a quicker, and less damaging, victory awaiting him.

"I want Monsh'a, with his Maah'e elite, to lead," he added. "He is to report to Voravia."

"It will be done, sir," Drang'm replied, bowing again. "Very quickly." Drang'm's image faded.

Baalsa'n stopped the vortex spinning around him and looked about. Then he turned and walked back to his enclave. Once inside, he went directly to his suite, not speaking to anyone along the way. His anger was dangerous at any time, but especially now. Any failure, any delay would cost someone today. Baalsa'n did not accept failure.

He initiated contact with Voravia. She responded quickly.

"I'm bringing troops, from Mavelan'g, in through Magin'n Gulf. These are trained warriors, not the rabble your inventions have become.

A strong man will lead this army I've ordered to come. His name is Monsh'a, he needs only to talk to you, and doesn't need your help. In fact, you should turn over all your little people, except servants you wish to keep, to him. He will not follow any orders but mine, but he will be very effective in reforming your group. See to it you follow his suggestions!

Now, enough of this! Where is Mano'n? Where is Rab'k?" he stormed at her.

Voravia stood for a moment, unable to respond. But knowing the silence wouldn't last much longer, spoke, "I've no idea where Rab'k is. He may be nearer you than me. We all disappeared from the plateau at the same time. Mano'n did come later; but he wasn't at the battle. He seems to be having trouble with his daughter. I had her trapped here, but she was able to get away," Voravia fought through her fear and was, she thought, unusually calm, considering.

"Baalsa'n, the girl is dangerous. I'm not certain where her strength comes from nor how she has achieved it without training, but she is very powerful and has no love for us. Fortunately, she's new to her magic. And worse, she's Mano'n's daughter." Voravia was searching for a way to have Baalsa'n's anger turned away from her. She chose her brother.

"I warned Mano'n! I warned him about controlling the girl! Maybe, I have to intercede in this training," he paused, looking into the distance a moment. "I'll look into this, but you must meet the commander of these new troops," Baalsa'n added. "Provide all Monsh'a's needs to develop a true attack, along many borders, and end this war quickly.

It will become your responsibility to complete what I have commanded of you from the beginning. No person from the Aerolan natives must discover the Ahar'n nor, if they have, learn to use it. There must be no Guardian!"

Voravia only nodded, trying to prove her compliance with Baalsa'n's wishes. But, her fear ran deeply now.

The outcome of sweeping the Aerolan people from this planet, if what Baalsa'n states must come to pass, was not so certain, even after all these years of working for this end. Our lives are in danger. I've told him about the girl, but I dare not tell him about the boy. I dare not reveal the Guardian roams the land already.

She looked across at Baalsa'n, glaring at her.

I can only hope he is not able to read my thoughts from this distance.

Baalsa'n was looking away from her and seemed deep in thought. Then the vision dimmed and closed with a snap.

Voravia looked around her private room, then out her window overlooking the darkened land. She pondered the importance of this fearsome conversation with Baalsa'n.

That was not a good ending for me. Not a good omen at all.

ACRON'N

On the day after Pet'r left him, Acron'n looked out to determine whether he could travel southward from the mountains. The densely falling snow outside his small refuge dissuaded him from continuing his trip on that day. The snow was deeper here than any he had ever seen in this area. So, he lingered in his makeshift home above the Vranilla River valley. He saw no reason to try to push through the snow, especially since he had given his snowshoes to Pet'r.

He waited and inspected the snowfall each day before determining whether he should continue down or not. He needed to get his messages to Lord Garv'n but he didn't need to fight this intense cold and freeze to death before he could complete the mission.

My mission. Now I wonder whether I will be able to get to Garv'n and report soon enough to avoid the trouble I think is coming.

He spied on the people of the badlands for several months; relying on their general goodwill to roam between villages, taking part in the daily activities without being too obvious. He often lingered where the men – the leaders of the villages – sat and talked during the heat of the day.

There normally, in midday, was little activity in the lives of these desert people because of the intensity of the desert. So, there were often gatherings in the larger pavilions scattered about a village. The pungent aroma under the huge tents was ripe with the smells of meat cooking over small grills, fresh roots and vegetables gathered from the nearby foothills added their own distinct and delicate smells especially because of small amounts of water sprayed over them as they simmered. Flowers and other items also brought in from the mountains, hand-made clothing from different regions of the desert provided brilliant colors to the bustling marketplaces.

The people were trying to adjust to the migration. So many arriving in one place, and at the same time, was crowding the people together and causing shortages of water, food and other necessities.

The men, particularly talked of politics, as most men did everywhere. With his observations during his meanderings through the crowds, Acron'n maintained certain closeness to the center of all this activity and gained valuable information about several things he thought were suspicious.

The people talked about the mountain. One of the oddest things was the continuous trail of people flowing up the mountainside to a new shrine recently erected above the plain. He wasn't certain why it was there, or how it appeared so suddenly. The worst part, he didn't know who the shrine was dedicated to.

Why were the villages gathering near the central mountains and, more strangely, around Tynoc'l? Had Rena'x requested these people come for some reason? What and, maybe, whom was the shrine built for? What has changed? Why all this sudden activity?

Acron'n finally left the village, but he felt a sense of foreboding about Tynoc'l and the activities there. He needed to inform Garv'n and do so quickly.

Unfortunately, he was unaware he too drew attention during his visit.

When he was safely back in the mountains, he mulled over what he discovered and tried to determine what these things might mean for those in Aerolan. He was concerned his deductions were going to be true – he was afraid there was to be war.

A few days later, the snows slowed and an early morning fog crept over the white, leaving a light crust of ice over it all. Acron'n decided, after making a quick inspection, the crust was probably strong enough for him to travel on top of the snow.

So he gathered his belongings, wrapped his feet and legs with

33

some spare woolen items, and worked his way down to where the path normally meandered to the valleys below.

The path wasn't visible, but the way it wound down the mountainside was. So he determined, by following the depression, where he could walk safely. But the way was still difficult because of the slippery surface. Occasionally he had to sit and slide over areas that didn't allow good footholds.

The journey took him hours. He began to concern himself about shelter. If this slow pace continued into the night, he would be in danger from the cold. It was difficult to tell whether some of the recesses he saw, along the way, were deep enough to take shelter. But each time he hesitated, he checked the position of the sun by observing the shadows on the snow and, as best he could, looked further along the path for any distinctly hazardous areas and continued.

Once he hesitated when he heard a low growling of an animal on the other side of the valley. He stopped and lowered himself, as best he could without slipping on the ice, drew his fighting knife from his boot, and waited.

Fortunately, the animal apparently didn't catch his scent and moved on. Whatever it was, it didn't come into sight. Acron'n waited a moment longer then began to edge his way further down the path, trying to be as quiet as possible.

As the day slowly edged toward dusk, he could tell the snow wasn't as deep as before though still deep enough. He decided he needed to make camp. He was tired from the constant tension caused by trudging through the snow.

Finally he chose a likely spot just above the trail and on the west side of the ravine. Since he needed to proceed as early as possible the next day, and knowing the sun would strike the western ridge first the next morning and wake him, he found a way and climbed the western slope for several feet above the path. Tomorrow, if no more snow fell, he should break onto more solid ground early and gain a clearer path then.

He reached the spot he had chosen and dug a small cave into the snow. He made the opening as small as possible, climbed into the small pocket he gouged and began to scrap his temporary cave walls and placed the extra snow around the opening.

The snow cave soon was large enough for him to drag his belongings inside and, pushing more snow from around himself, he closed the opening except for a small breathing hole. Soon his body heat had rounded the cave and, by laying where he planned to sleep, the snow formed to his body in the floor.

After resting for a while, he thought a bit more about his stay in the desert and decided the urgency of the information about his discoveries warranted this trip down the mountain – even through all the snow.

Just as he lay down to get much needed sleep, he heard a night bird's scream echo across the silent blanket lying in white folds of nature's cold night. He smiled and fell asleep.

The next morning, he awoke and noticed the early light of dawn through the snow at the opening of his shelter. He rose but decided to wait until daylight helped clear his path going down. The early sun warmed the shelter and the ice began to melt rapidly from around him.

For some reason, the clouds previously hurdling over the mountains abated for a short time and the land was absorbing the warmth.

He punched out the rest of the opening, put his belongings just outside, climbed out, stood and stretched. The sun was warm on his face and he felt much better. He looked further down the mountain from this vantage point and saw that some of the path surface was visible through snow patches below.

Eager to continue, he hoisted his pack on his back, turned to work his way down to the path. He descended from the slope by walking backward. With each step downward, he pushed his toes into the snow, and then by leaning over with his hands on the snow, he was able to maintain a steady and careful pace. He worked his way down to the clearer path quickly.

Reaching the spot where he stopped the night before, he turned and walked down the ridge. It wasn't long before he reached some of those bare patches he noticed when further up and his pace began to increase.

He finally reached a point where there was almost no snow though he marveled at how far down into the valley it had fallen. He often traveled these mountains, when he and his brother roamed here and he had never seen it this far down before. Growing up in the area, he and Jond'r often wandered , camped, and hunted the forest and valley in this region.

Jond'r and he had been fortunate. They grew up in the area in the small town just to the east of the path, just up the river. Ofan'n was a good town for the young. The people watched over the children, cared for them, and let them grow by allowing, and encouraging, their independence. A good home.

Wish I could stop on the way through, but I've got to get to Garv'n.

He wandered casually to the river where the snow ended. He hoped to make good time today. He arrived at the Vranilla River in mid-morning and pushed his way through the shallow ford to the other side and walked a short distance to the edge of the forest. The day was going very well for him so he stopped to rest a moment. He lay in the high grass beside the river and listened to it murmur its way toward the west.

Suddenly he heard a crackling sound as though leaves, or fallen branches, were being crushed. It wasn't a sudden sound a falling branch might make. He leaned backwards and lowered his body to lay on his back so he might see all about without turning his head too much. When he noticed other movement directly be-hind him, he decided it wasn't an animal.

He slowly retrieved his hunting knife from his boot, moving as little as necessary. His clothing and light-colored hair blended with the new fallen leaves, making him almost invisible. But he was uncertain whether he had been seen or not.

The person moving was making no effort to hide and seemed intent on getting to the ford to cross into the mountains, or, at least, to the other side and apparently hadn't notice him as yet. Acron'n decided it was a soldier and wondered why it was here. He lay still when he saw it was passing without discovering him.

As soon as the soldier passed, Acron'n could hear voices approaching and he decided to lay as he was until the group passed. When they came into view, he noticed most of the marchers seemed to be prisoners while the guards around them held weapons. He decided there were too many for him to try to fight so he remained still. When the entire group was in the river, he rose slowly, planning to crawl into the concealment of the trees.

As he watched the group finish their crossing, he noticed something very odd. Some of the soldiers were not totally human but some sort of large and malformed beings.

Just as Acron'n turned to escape, he noticed the legs of another, possibly a scout, only a few meters away from him. Acron'n froze, holding himself as still as possible.

The scout was watching the trail, looking for any other who might be following his squad. Satisfied the trail was clear, he turned to cross the river and saw Acron'n lying on the ground. He yelled and charged Acron'n, raising a great club into the air intending to smash Acron'n to kill him quickly.

Waiting for the soldier to commit totally to his attack, Acron'n, realizing the being was going to run over him, waited until the last moment then leaped into the air, rolling under the club as it swung down, his knife slicing the air and the body of the scout.

The scout stalled, dropped his club and turned to see Acron'n standing before him. He looked down, grabbed his midriff to stop his intestines from flowing onto the ground. He looked up again at Acron'n and was going to shout, or scream, when Acron'n sliced his throat open and leaped back. The man made no sound, his eyes glazed and he fell forward into the grass.

Acron'n ducked low and began to run into the forest, not taking time to look back. He covered ground swiftly with skills learned as a child, dodging and weaving through the trees almost soundlessly. He ran for several minutes then leaped over a small hummock and slid to a stop. He paused to catch his breath, then rolled himself onto his knees and peered out and back along his path.

Not following yet. Who. . . No, what were those creatures? Had to be Voravia's, but what are they doing here in Doom's Woods? They've never roamed this far from her castle before. Something isn't right, there is trouble here. Must be some advance troops for a large movement. Got to go. They'll discover that scout is missing at any moment.

He rose to continue his run, heading slightly toward the west. In the distance behind, he heard soldiers shouting to one another, following him and, he noticed, gaining on him.

If they come for me, I'll soon have disappeared. I just need to catch the road over that next hill and head south, they probably won't follow me once I've done that.

He ran, skipping on top of the larger rocks, walking slowly through any streams he came to. He wanted to conceal his path as best he could. He traveled to the top of the hill and saw the road below.

He turned to look back and a squad of the marauders was there, closer than he hoped. He tried to keep aware of the pursuers as he ran, so he checked fairly often, but these creatures caught him more quickly than he thought possible.

Where did they come from? The forest must be filled with them. Why are they here?

They raised their weapons. Some had long throwing clubs and were launching them.

He turned and took a few steps down the hill when a weapon hit him. He tumbled forward and rolled into a large rotting log, and fell unconscious. The last thing he remembered were the soldiers standing around him, some threatening to pierce him with their spears. He remembered thinking how strangely large some of them were.

Later when he woke, he was bouncing around in the bottom of a small wooden cage, being carried without effort, by four of the creatures he saw before. His side was bleeding where the spear struck him. Someone or something, wrapped a cloth around him, but the jostling about opened the wound again. He wasn't too worried about it and the pain wasn't too great, so he let it be.

He looked about as best he could without moving too much, checked quickly and realized they were taking him westward along one of the northern paths of the Forest of Galyd'n, near the mountains. Apparently they had already crossed the Vranilla at the ford where it continued its journey southward.

Why am I still alive? Why did they create this cage and carry me all this way? Probably taking me to a major encampment. Just have to ride it out.

He looked back down the path and saw other cages, like the one he was trapped in, following.

They're kidnapping people, wonder if it's only men, or are there women also? Can't tell from here, just have to wait until tonight.

Near the road to Coma't, they came over a small ridge. In the valley below, there were hundreds of tents spread for almost a kilometer toward the north and west.

The encampment bustled with activity, some of the monstrous soldiers ran about on errands, troops were practicing battle tactics and hand-to-hand combat methods on the northern end. On the slope of the hill above the practice area, and set back into the forest, was a high fenced corral with a large group of guards surrounding it.

Prisoners, no doubt.

There were a few tents, near the middle of the camp, belonging obviously to the officers. In front of these was an open arena with a small platform in the middle.

Selection block? Probably.

Acron'n knew he was headed there. When he reached the area

near the platform, he was dumped from his small cage onto the ground. He jumped to his feet and stood in swirls of dust stirred by the troops as they deposited all the other captives. He could see most of the victims were men, some few were boys, no girls, and, surprisingly, there seemed to be only three, or four, women. He didn't want to think about why the last were there.

As they all stood in the heat, he saw the officers walking from their tent. These men were obviously stronger and more ugly than some of Voravia's odd men. Great heads, massive upper bodies and a savage look about them that showed in their squinting eyes. They didn't falter as they came; they were seemingly more intelligent than the smaller beings of Voravia. They pushed aside the lesser ones who clamored for attention.

They were only interested in what they might find in this new prisoner group. Acron'n decided they were obviously looking for new recruits. Any who failed to reach expectations were probably expendable. The outcome of this selection process was a life of unknown circumstances, or certain death.

The officers pushed their way through the group of prisoners, checking the bodies, limbs, eyes and teeth of each person they thought interesting. Those they were not satisfied with were sent to the smaller corral in the woods near the western boundary of the gathering area.

As they found possible candidates, the officers had their personal guards take each one chosen to the platform where the captives just stood waiting in a huddle. Acron'n was placed in that group.

"What ish yous name?" A burly officer stood looking Acron'n over. The creature seemed more brutish than the others. He reached and pushed Acron'n, trying to knock him off balance.

Acron'n was prepared for the move, having watched the process for the other prisoners. He only stepped back a small amount and kept his eyes fastened on the officer's. He said nothing.

40

The officer hit Acron'n solidly in the chest. Acron'n seeing the punch coming, jumped back simultaneously, avoiding most of the impact of the jarring blow. It still stunned him how strong the man was.

"Name!" the officer bent down, placed his face up to Acron'n's. "Now!"

Acron'n pulled his face away, but looked back into the beast's face and smiled. The beast raised his arm to backhand Acron'n. But, before he could swing, another officer grabbed the aggressor's arm and stopped the blow.

"What yous do?" this officer spoke calmly, towering over Acron'n's attacker. He stood looking down at both. The most remarkable thing for Acron'n was the realization this monstrous man had walked up to them and he didn't hear him coming.

The attacker backed away a step, turned to strike at the one who interfered, with malice in his eyes. But instead of fighting, he, realizing who stopped him, quickly began to back away, bowing and whining, as though he was an animal.

The colossus watched this display only a moment and turned back to Acron'n.

"Yous want to die?" he asked.

"Not particularly," Acron'n answered. The officer looked at him for a moment then he chuckled. Not what Acron'n expected. "But the possible life offered here doesn't appeal to me either."

The officer chuckled again.

"My names is Monsh'a. I am the leader the Maah'e," he spoke then paused a moment, "and of Voravia's forces."

He spoke without forcefulness then smiled at Acron'n, "It seems you do not like my offer."

"So you do understand," Acron'n answered, with a sharp tone.

Back at the auction, one of the chosen captives, a young man, decided to run. He was followed by several of the Maah'e. Quickly, they ran him down and dragged him back to the platform.

41

Monsh'a and Acron'n watched the skirmish, then turned back to each other.

"Yous have no options better then hims," he nodded his head toward the returned captive. "Hes destinies are sealed." He turned and walked away.

Maybe. There is always a way. Always.

The guards surrounded those still standing in the original group. Acron'n figured he, with the others, was headed to the corralled prison with them.

But just as the group started moving, Acron'n was pulled away and led to the platform to wait alone. Soon, a number of the officers arrived, milled around and kept looking at him but none approached.

Soon, Monsh'a strode through the officer's group, stepped onto the platform and motioned to the guards to have Acron'n brought to him. Acron'n resisted but was forcefully placed beside Monsh'a.

"Dis mans believes he cans escape from here," Monsh'a addressed the group, pointing at Acron'n. "Hes probably a soldier froms some wars somewheres; hes believes hes has the answers.

But, I tell yous he hasn't the powers to escape me, nor our Lady Voravia. Hes only a man, with no powers. So I offer hims a chance to proves me wrong. But I'm telling all yous he cannots escapes for hes soon will be ones like yous. Hes cannots escape, or some of yous will die."

Acron'n stood listening, he tried to show no expression to indicate what he thought about the speech. He tried to show no emotion. He already understood he was to be *converted* to be like one of the men in this group. It seemed Monsh'a had decided he was officer material. But this speech did surprise him.

What is he talking about? Is he actually going to let me try to escape just to show his power, or Voravia's? Why would he do that? Does Monsh'a have problems within his officer ranks? Is he trying to rid himself of someone, or several?

Monsh'a continued, "Tomorrows I wills let hims go. But hes will not escape or someones here will suffer." He pointed at the officers. They all turned to look at each other. They seemed confused, wondering why Monsh'a was doing this.

"I have believes at least a few of yous is not working hard enoughs for Lady Voravia. But, I ams a fair man. You will haves an alarm when this man runs for his life. So bes prepared. But, I warns you alls, hes is not to be killed."

Monsh'a turned and walked off the stage, motioning for his guards to bring Acron'n and follow him. He strode toward the larger tent, separated from the others. When he reached the tent, he had the guards cut Acron'n's bindings. He opened the tent flap and held it back for Acron'n to enter, raised his hands to stop the guards, then entered the tent. He walked around Acron'n, who was as yet unable to decide what was happening.

"Yous, like my officers, probably is wondering at mys purposes," Monsh'a started and moved behind a low table, sat down on the blankets piled behind it, picked up a small knife and, turning it in his hand, was inspecting it closely. After a moment, he looked up, waited a moment to make certain Acron'n was listening.

"It is simples. I needs to knows who, of all mys officers and people, cans do the jobs assigned. Yous escaped from thems, more than once even if yous didn't knows this. I cannots have that happenings in my armys. I believe yous will be a greats officer when I have yous changed, but I intend to determine mys peoples weaknesses first.

Tomorrow yous will be released just befores dawns. I suspects you knows this areas very well; it will be a good tests." he said, rose, walked around the table and looked down at Acron'n for a moment.

"I don't expects yous to get very fars, but, if yous do, I will have learns much — about mys people and about yours. I am not from this lands. I' from across a sea. But, my Lady Voravia, has

43

mades me her army's commanders. I do nots intend to fail."

"Guards!" he suddenly shouted.

"Yous will be readys early." He placed his huge hand on Acron'n's chest then removed it when the guards entered. They stood on each side of Acron'n, prepared to grab him if he moved at all. Monsh'a waved them away and looked out the back of his tent at the forest. "Takes hims to middle quarters, put into a tent and place guards around."

Acron'n was taken to a tent in the center of the complex and placed in one of the troop tents where the Ravelan soldiers slept when not on duty. Two of the cots were occupied. There were other cots inside, so he assumed he'd have other company, unwanted but there all the same.

Now. This was an interesting turn of events. I need to decide how to use the opportunity. What must I do to survive this? The alternative is not inviting. Regardless, I need to rest now, more than anything. I know they'll not care for my wounds, so I'll have to deal with that myself. Monsh'a understood I knew this area, and I'll need to use that to my advantage. Not his.

Monsh'a also stated he was from 'across a sea'. From where? Is it possible these arrived by using Magin'n Gulf, or Beyhon'd Sea, and marched across the northern part of Voravia'a lands? That would be likely. So the north knows little about the lands; even the Wastelands are not so familiar to us.

The first thing to consider, if I escape, is how all of these invaders arrived here without being noticed by someone. Were Garv'n's people asleep? One possibility is this army, and these creatures, came from the north and somehow were able to do so quietly.

Acron'n lay down in a corner cot. He not only needed to escape the encampment and this area, but he needed to be going someplace to reach safety among his own as quickly as he could.

Where can I run to and gain safety? Coma't. The people there are probably not aware of this camp, but there are huntsmen there with skills that would be a problem for Monsh'a if they were to learn he's nearby. Maybe I can help change that too, as well as get away cleanly. But Monsh'a will ex-

pect me to go there; I have to determine how to trick his people about my direction and lose them before I'm captured.

Not concerned with any other preparation, he rolled toward the tent wall and soon fell asleep.

Just before dawn, someone, and he couldn't tell whom, shook him awake and quickly disappeared from the tent.

He rose slowly looking about to make certain the soldiers were all still asleep. He walked quietly to the tent flap and peered out to determine where the guards were. None were about. He checked his wound that had closed overnight.

Not to worry about that. Got to prepare to escape.

He turned back, noticing a knife on a sword belt, he slid it quietly from its scabbard. There were heavier weapons available lying on the ground next to his cot. He decided against taking the sword, or the club. He took the knife instead, thinking the other items would only encumber him.

He crept outside, staying low. He looked toward the south, then turned and headed toward the mountains, passing the corralled enclosure.

I need to go north, cross the roadway to Coma't and travel toward the west before heading south, probably would be good to cut through the forest to Trail's End, then double back to Coma't.

He looked at all the obstacles he could see on the northern end of the camp, ducked his head to conceal his light skin and ran in spurts, hiding behind various obstacles, until he passed the corral. Then he broke into a strong, but relaxed, lope through the forest beyond.

He traversed a small creek not far from the end of the encampment, then turned sharply up the hill and then, checking the shadows for his direction, headed directly west, running strongly. He soon left the camp far behind.

When he crested the second hill, he heard the horns sounding an alert for his escape. He diverted more toward the north for a

45

few miles, then turned westward again, hoping to throw any following him off his trail. Dawn was breaking, it would be light soon.

Hopefully, my unusual direction will confuse them for a while.

He turned back to his task and began to run as fast as he could. He rested once after climbing two more hills, caught his breath, listened and couldn't hear any sounds of pursuit.

He only paused long enough to cut himself a small sapling to make a staff. He didn't want it to be too heavy but did want it strong enough to help in a hand-to-hand conflict. As he turned, he heard them coming. He started running again, hoping to reach the road soon.

Well, it seemed like a good plan. Maybe Monsh'a's people are a little smarter than I thought. At least, I know they have to capture me alive which always gives me a fighting chance.

He wasn't particularly winded from the run but he knew he had to push to reach the road, cross it and enter into the forest on the other side. He tried to run harder, not concerned with any concealment now.

He reached the road, near where he saw a side road, not often used, that ran through the foothills to Voravia's castle. Acron'n inwardly chuckled.

Maybe I should go there and hide.

He stopped for a moment, looked both ways, crossed the road and immediately entered the dense forest on the other side. He decided to run westward a few miles then south to the town.

But suddenly his forest cover dissipated and then vanished. All that was left were stark trunks of deadened trees, stumps of others cut to the ground and no low vegetation at all. There was only a burnt land as far as he could see. He could even see the towers of Voravia's castle.

He stopped stunned. Then realizing he couldn't cross this and stay concealed, he turned back to the edge of the forest and began to run in a southerly direction but eastward to angle back toward the road while staying under cover.

He'd lost track of where the road might be. Then suddenly he stumbled up the bank and stood on it. He could see no one following him so he ran across and down the other embankment. Then he turned southward trying to parallel the road.

Now he was just in a hurry.

They surprised him. Several soldiers, obviously the elite guards, suddenly were running along beside him. As they ran, they eased ahead of him, swords drawn. It was as though they knew where he was going.

He finally decided he couldn't outrun them. He slid to a stop and raised his staff, preparing for a fight. The officer with them reminded the men they were not to kill him, but the punishment for allowing him to escape would be severe. The soldiers put away their swords and closed in on him.

He was able to ward off most of the early blows, but he was not able to stop them all and soon the battering began to wear him down. He knew he wouldn't be able to endure much more.

He fell, then struggled upright. The soldiers, realizing they were now winning the fight, didn't risk themselves too often. When one did, Acron'n cracked his head with his staff, then quickly braced against the staff to right him and waited. The others drew back a bit and came to rest. The officer started walking toward him.

Acron'n raised his staff with difficulty. He would fight until he couldn't, but he knew he was finished.

ANISAH

If evil gains control, there will be many lives lost and life itself will become a misery. We gods who wish to avoid such a life for these children have now brought together those who can attain the strength to defeat such an element.

These young people chosen will fight this war There is now a belief among us they will defeat the evil lurking and will win a victory to lead this world to achieve this hoped-for life.

There will be great battles and a war fought. It has begun. Those who now stand on each side are chosen, both good and evil. We must go forward to see if the plan that provides hope for the people will come to fruition . . .

Anisah hit the ground and rolled through the lush grass, bumping gently against a large tree trunk. She lay there for a moment looking up through the tree limbs and was surprised by the lights shining through the leaves overhead. Memories of her childhood rushed back to her.

She smiled and relaxed. She rubbed her hand over her neck, trying to determine whether the rope, recently around it, had bruised her. It hadn't.

She rose, straightened her gown, making certain nothing was torn and walked toward the sounds she heard in the distance.

Through the trees came the sound of children playing -- children with familiar voices somehow. Anisah walked in the direction of the voices, cautiously peering through the tall grass in the meadow where she found herself. After pushing through the underbrush a while, she saw her brother and sister, both a little older now, playing with each other near a stream she recognized.

Her mother was sitting in the shade, stitching some clothes, glancing at the children occasionally. Anisah frowned remembering Braex, but she didn't see him anywhere.

It was as though she had never left.

Deciding she needed to talk to her mother, she stepped out of the grass and walked to where her mother was sitting, unaware of her presence. As Anisah approached, she suddenly felt agitated and her heart suddenly pulsed to that pull. She stopped and looked around her slowly but saw nothing.

Just nervous. My god, what a horrible experience. Where are Pet'r and Geth'n? How did I get here? Voravia — who is that woman? My aunt?

"Strange you should be thinking of my sister," a voice behind her suddenly interrupted her thoughts.

Anisah jumped sideways several feet, spinning in the air as she moved, landing solidly and facing in the direction of the voice.

There was no one there.

"You seem to be a bit more wary than when I last saw you," the voice came again. From where she stood the undergrowth limited her view, but she glimpsed an image of someone just before it disappeared. She was certain her newly acquired powers were responsible for catching that glimpse.

Newly acquired powers? What am I thinking?

"You surmise correctly, my dear. You now seem to have new and possibly curious powers that place you beyond that little girl who grew into a young woman here in this village," the beggar, Old Bas stepped from behind a tree not fifteen feet from Anisah, held his hand toward her in a peaceful gesture, "I have watched you grow now for these many years," he said.

Watched me grow? Why would this old man have such an interest?

Anisah was concentrating on what the old beggar was saying, but her thoughts raced.

In my old village? Caliste? Why am I here?

She learned extreme caution from her recent experience. She didn't respond, just listened and watched closely.

I have possibly two ways to escape, as I remember. Think, Anisah.

"You don't have to concern yourself with escape, my child,"

49

the old beggar began to walk toward her. As he continued; her immediate reaction was to retreat as many steps. "Come, let's just talk."

"Though I remember you, sir, I've no recollection we had anything to discuss other than the cost of your pots and pans," Anisah spoke slowly, watching every move the old man made.

"I remember we talked of many things, of ships and the sea, of far distant lands, of the stone about your neck, and of . . ., let's see if I remember correctly, a healing college in Tariny," he looked at her now, a twinkle of glee in his eye.

Anisah was surprised, taken back by this last, she had forgotten those long talks.

"Maybe you're right about that, but why are you here in this glade now?" she asked.

She looked around. She felt uneasy. She sensed there was some sort of evil near her but couldn't determine where.

Suddenly, the man's image began to change, shimmering in the air, appearing from nowhere, different than before and from this there came a younger man, a man who looked like Voravia, except for the color of the hair.

Anisah stepped back several more steps, partly in astonishment and partly to consider her defenses, for now she was very suspicious and tensed for a battle.

Who can this be? He looks too much like Voravia to trust? What happened to the old beggar?

"Let me introduce myself. Please relax. I mean you no harm," the man held his hand up again, palm toward her as he spoke quietly.

"I want, no, have wanted, to talk to you for a very long time. But you certainly have been too busy for me to interrupt your new adventures." he pointed toward the skies casually.

Anisah looked up slightly at his motion, but didn't take her eyes from the man.

"Sir, who are you?" she asked, knowing there was something

about this man she should know.

She had no need to stand and talk to this man who obviously possessed some magical powers. She already realized he was reading her thoughts and he looked too much like Voravia to suit her.

"Voravia again. Apparently my sister made a strong impression on you, Anisah," he said, looked behind him, waved his hand with a slight movement. A stool appeared behind him and he sat down, "I must insist we talk now, for I have much to say to you."

"I repeat, sir. Who are you?" Anisah asked again, stubbornly holding her position.

"I am your father." He spoke calmly, as though he was talking about the clouds.

Anisah's heart seemed to stop. "You are not my father! You cannot be my father! My father is dead; he died horribly before I left this place! How dare you!" she was screaming at this horrid man. Tears filled her eyes and flowed down her face. Now she was angry.

She wiped the tears away with the back of her hand, but to no avail. The sorrow welled up from inside her and would not let her grief stop. Through her tears, Anisah could see the man sitting, waiting.

Eventually, he waved his hand slightly and she could feel her grief slowly pass away, her tears stopped. Anisah felt certain contentment and she knew her father would always be there. She felt she shouldn't grieve anymore.

Through the leaves and brush stepped Anisah's mother. "Anisah, where have you been?" Her mother ran to her, held her close and wouldn't let her go.

Anisah returned the embrace, but continued to watch this man who claimed to be her father. She felt there was danger here and she was not going to be deceived.

"I wanted to go to Tariny to the healing college and I did, but things have changed since then." She looked directly into the man's eyes when she said the last, noting a small smile cross his face.

"Mother, I've been many places, but I'm fine. But I must leave again soon for there is a great deal more I must do and I need to prepare myself," Anisah held her mother at arm's length and smiled at her.

"I'm so glad to see you and so sorry you felt you had to leave. Are you doing well?" her mother, hugging her again, whispered in her ear then released her. "You know, Braex died. So you might come back home now. Why don't you come and play with the children?" Her mother stepped back and turned toward the field where the children were playing when she saw the man. She stopped, stunned and only stared.

"Hello, Callex, it has been awhile," the man spoke casually to Anisah's mother.

Callex gasped, held her hand to her chest as though she couldn't breathe, seem to stagger from the shock of seeing this man. Anisah looked at her mother's face and realized her mother not only knew this man but their association had been more than just a casual one.

Anisah turned back to the man. He had one eyebrow raised and that smile still held his face in a position, a smirk that irritated Anisah.

"Mano'n, why have you come?" Anisah's mother blurted out, "Where did you go?" She was angry and started to approach the man, but Anisah held her shoulders and wouldn't let her. "How can you come here now, after all these years. What do you want?"

"I came for my daughter," he spoke quietly to Callex. He did not seem concerned about her anger. He pointed his clasped hand at Anisah.

"You want what?" Callex was screaming at him now. "You fiend, how could you come here wanting her? How dare you make such an arrogant and stupid statement!"

Anisah was holding her mother who was sobbing uncontrollably.

Callex pulled away and continued her rampage against the man, "You, who deserted us, who left us destitute, who had to go attend to more worldly things. You come now; wanting her."

Now her mother stood defiantly, holding Anisah as though protecting her.

Anisah couldn't believe what she was hearing. She was stunned beyond belief. Her mother knew this man, knew him intimately.

What does this mean? Is this man my father? What about the man I have always believed to be my father?

"Actually, my dear, that man was more of a father to you than I ever was, but it is now time for you to seek your true and chosen path. I have come to help you along the way," Mano'n answered her thoughts again.

Anisah now was angrier than she could remember. "I haven't asked you to help me do anything," she said, with a venomous reply.

Mano'n smiled again. "Actually, I'm not asking you, my child. I'm telling you," he said pointedly.

Anisah pushed her mother gently away from her embrace, turned and faced him, and stood waiting for him to move.

"I have learned a few things on my own, since you've been gone. I think I will choose what my life will be like. I am no young girl. I've grown a bit without your help and I'll not admit to being your daughter."

Anisah tensed as another ripple disturbed the air behind her. Another voice rose, softer, "Well now, my young niece, we meet again so soon."

Anisah spun about and Voravia was standing only a few paces away. Anisah grabbed her mother's shoulders tightly and began to back toward the glade where the children were playing.

"I find your defiance enthralling. You are learning well and I'm proud of your courage. But, I believe we certainly have the upper hand here." Mano'n was being very nonchalant. It was obvious he was confident he had control.

53

Anisah turned back to him. He was standing now, arms crossed over his chest; the smirk still on his face.

She turned to her mother and asked, "Is all this true, mother?" Her mother looked through her tears with fear in her eyes.

"Yes, yes, yes, it is. Oh, Anisah, I'm so sorry I never told you. I was so afraid; this man is evil. I'm so sorry I can't change this. Please forgive me."

Anisah pulled her mother close again, "It's going to be all right, mother. I believe everything will work out. I don't blame you for what I've learned here today. Don't worry, I shall always love you and hold you dear to me. Do not forget that. Ever."

"Please now, for me, return to my brother and sister and care for them. I will attend to this problem." She held her mother from her a moment, then hugged her again, released her and motioned toward the glade.

"Good-bye, Anisah. May you know happiness. Please come back to me." her mother offered and turned away. Her head hung low, sobbing; she walked into the sunshine and disappeared.

Anisah watched her mother then turned back to look straight into Mano'n's eyes.

"Now, Anisah, you've said your farewells, it's time for us to go. You have much to learn," Mano'n said, stepping forward.

"You and I share something, as I remember," Anisah growled, reaching into her dress and drawing forth the black stone chip that always lay between her breasts.

It began to glow. Mano'n reached up and touched his chest, feeling the warmth of the stone on his chest reacting to hers.

"Yes, you're correct. So you do remember," Mano'n smiled, wondering where Anisah was going with the statement.

"Oh, I remember. The day I discovered you had the other half of this," she started, "other things happened. Important things I didn't understand at the time. But now I believe I do," she smiled back at him.

She pondered the feelings welling up inside her. She marveled

54

at how easy those past incidences had been. At the time, she was surprised and overwhelmed by the strangeness.

But now, she felt the inner burning, and recognized it for what it could be. She had felt pain and had struggled with her new life, but now she understood some of what she could do and be.

I've no reason to fear these two. I've no reason to care about them or about what happens to them. I can hate them for no other reason than they are trying to destroy my life. This was what Brae'x wanted; to rule over my life. I will not have this.

Anisah became quiet, a smile crossed her face, but her look showed vehemence.

Mano'n's brow wrinkled, puzzled. He hadn't expected Anisah's smile.

"What might that have been?" he asked, not comprehending.

"This." Anisah didn't shout, but her voice filled the forest glade. Mano'n covered his ears. Voravia staggered backwards in surprise.

Anisah raised her hand from her side, only a small way, just to her waist. Trees and boulders began to rip from the ground in the glade behind the other two. The objects rose quickly above the glade, lingering, swaying there and waiting.

Mano'n and Voravia turned and looked upward at what hovered over them, overwhelmed by the brute power it took to perform this act.

"What are you doing?" Voravia shouted. "You can't do this. You have no power to do this."

Mano'n turned around to stare at Anisah, frowned and shook his head. He remembered another day when Anisah was much younger. A day he had never mentioned.

Turning back to look at Anisah, he saw determination and rage. He knew he had to do something to stop this. He had to do it quickly.

This has gone beyond what I ever expected. This has gone too far. Baalsa'n will discover too much. I must stop this.

55

He raised his hand in front of himself, prepared to stop his daughter's act. But suddenly found his intent beyond what he was able to do.

Anisah had placed some sort of force around him; he was ensorcelled. He was unable to act.

Voravia raised her hands to strike the girl down. But, she tumbled backwards, falling to the ground, accomplishing nothing.

Anisah step to one side and turned to view both.

"Do not attempt to hinder me," She almost snarled, the look of dominance filled her eyes. "You would not survive."

She pulled her hand back to her side. The trees and boulders, being held aloft, came crashing down around the other two. They dodged and moved to avoid being crushed.

Mano'n attempted to rush at Anisah but found his forward motion was stopped. Disbelief crossed his face. It was obvious he hadn't expected to stop. He looked down and tried to move again but to no avail.

Behind Anisah, Voravia started to sneak forward, but she too halted abruptly.

"What do you think you are doing, you ingrate?" Voravia shouted at Anisah.

Anisah turned slowly and smiled, a smile not unlike her father's.

"You will come with us now, or suffer for not doing so!" Voravia was ranting now.

"I doubt you are able to bring harm to me, my dear aunt." Anisah spoke, smiling again.

She made no obvious move to change the situation, no motion to bring magic into play, but she now controlled both of them.

"I think you should return to your beautiful home," Anisah raised her right hand only slightly and Voravia vanished.

Anisah turned to the man she now knew as her father.

"So why did you leave my mother and me? Was there no reason to have fathered me?" she asked, her eyes smoldering. "Was your task to set this upon the world?" She motioned with her left hand and the sky darkened overhead.

The sun was still shining brightly over the glade, but above Anisah and her father the clouds swirled violently. Anisah dropped her hand, and the clouds disappeared

"How do you know these things?" Mano'n asked, astonished.

Anisah only smiled about his confusion, "I believe, Father. Our meeting is at an end."

She lifted her left hand slightly and vanished.

Mano'n stood, stunned now by what he just witnessed. He never realized the girl's power had grown to such an extent. His thoughts raced. His fear mounted in concern for his daughter. His apprehension rose about Baalsa'n's reaction when he discovered the truth about his granddaughter.

There are now other plans to make; there is now another power in the world.

When Anisah reappeared, she stood in the alcove of the healing college. She glanced around, glad to see the entry where she felt her life was going to become what it should. She bowed her head slightly and could not help feeling a certain remorse for all she just discovered.

Would things have been different had I known I was a witch, like Voravia? Will I be different now? Life is so sudden.

She knew there wasn't soon going to be a beautiful ending to her story. Her dream of healing others must wait a while longer.

So now she needed to find her friends, Pet'r and Geth'n, for they had to work together for the greater task before them. She didn't weep, only sighed, looking around again at the one place she had so wanted to be.

Then she vanished again.

PET'R

Pet'r landed, hitting the surface hard, and rolled. He jumped to his feet but crouched, one hand on the Ahar'n still about his neck, and the other held out, in front of his chest, to defend himself.

He looked around slowly, wondering what happened to everyone else involved in the short battle. He was somewhere he hadn't expected to be. He stood beside a small stream, flowing through a great cavern. He turned, looked about to survey the area and realized he was back in the cave of Areb'l. He was surprised but not displeased. He could think of no better place to be.

He relaxed, sat down on a small outcropping of rock near the inset where he found the Ahar'n the day he was captured by Voravia's odd men. He turned and looked down the darkened corridor through which he had tried to escape and smiled to himself.

"It's always interesting when surprises turn for the good. Don't you think?" A deep, velvet voice filled the cave.

Pet'r leaped from his seat, spun around to determine the source of the voice and stood looking at a man standing only a few feet away, smiling at him. Pet'r didn't hear the man arrive nor see him before he spoke.

Tall and striking, the man wore a long robe, its color difficult to determine. Looking at the garment gave the impression of looking into the night sky. He had pale blue eyes, golden hair hanging below his shoulders. He was still smiling, amused probably by the surprised look on Pet'r's face.

"How did you get in here?" Pet'r blurted out, still defiant and protective of the Ahar'n. He immediately clasped it and took a few steps back until he touched the cave wall behind him. His day was too full of surprises for him. He would rather things became a bit more predictable.

"The same way you did. I'm just here." the man spoke calmly, looked behind himself, walked to a nearby outcropping similar to the one Pet'r had been sitting on earlier, and sat down. "Perhaps, I should introduce myself."

"That would help, I think. Who are you?" Pet'r still stood tensely, waiting for something to happen, looking obliquely for some means of escape.

"I am Kalbr'an, perhaps you have heard of me?" the man told him nonchalantly, still smiling but now with a look of curiosity.

"Kalbr'an? What? I'm sorry, but you don't exist except in fables and legends. Kalbr'an was of the first family and one of the protectors of the Ahar'n, according to those stories."

"Nevertheless, I'm here now, fable or not," the older man responded. He looked about the cave, pausing a moment to observe the shrine now emptied of its treasure.

Pet'r was astonished, he never really believed those fables and now this man was claiming to be that person.

Pet'r stood, looked around again. Worrying about a trap, he began to pace and walked a little further away from this stranger claiming to be a god. "That doesn't actually seem real, or true."

"Actually, you have every reason to disbelieve me," Kalbr'an offered. "We haven't helped the people of this world as much as we should have, I fear. There was, and is, suffering because of that decision made too many years ago.

It's obvious the people have largely forgotten us, not only here in this land, but on this entire world. Now those of us who believe Narhtrae bears promise should not abandon it. So we have decided it is time to fight back," Kalbr'an talked calmly but expressed his conviction with certainty.

He watched Pet'r as he talked, trying to determine what the young man was thinking, and how he was responding to this revealing information.

He felt Pet'r, as one of those who needed to know of the past, probably had little trust in this new reality. What Pet'r was being told was certainly beyond belief and he had no reason to accept. The boy was now only slightly aware of his own changes.

It was Kalbr'an's decision to approach Pet'r first because Pet'r was the first to receive the new powers for defense of the Ahar'n. Kalbr'an felt Pet'r would be the quickest to respond to what he had to tell him, having experienced some of the magic inherently felt as the Guardian.

Kalbr'an began the tale of the battle for a world of peace.

"Please sit and I'll tell you our history and the reason we, and all the people of Narhtrae, are here. So I can reveal the danger that now threatens to engulf us all.

Today I've come to reveal myself, inform you of the Esfer'n people – both the good and the bad-- and to tell you of this world and tell you about the war that, unfortunately, must be fought here.

There have been many wars between those of my kind, whether for political reasons in our domain or simply out of jealously. The reasons no longer matter. All happened before this world came to be. These were wars fought between us, terrible wars and entire worlds were destroyed. Now, I fear, I must reveal there is another war coming, to be fought here.

We tried to protect Narhtrae from any outside intrusion, but have failed.

Once many centuries ago when the first man to wear the Ahar'n lived here, there was a terrible war and the people survived and sent the Esfer'n villain away.

We Al-Esfer'n who survived wanted to avoid another incident at all cost. We now believe we cannot prevent it," Kalbra'n stopped and watched the young man for a reaction.

Pet'r had continued pacing back and forth as Kalbr'an told his story. The young man, who reminded Kalbr'an of Areb'l, turned to his previous seat, sat and waited to listen to the rest of the story.

"The costs will be great when this occurs. We have no champions. You, in fact, admit you haven't believed, but only thought of us as fables," Kalbra'n continued.

The Al-Esfer'n are real, all of us. Though we do not exists as you do. We live in the spirit world and the Ahar'n is our only place of existence. The stories and legends, as in most cases, contain a large portion of the truth. Unfortunately, the stories often aggrandized us and made us gods. We are magically powerful and immortal, but we aren't gods and can't interact directly with the people of Narhtrae, or on any other world.

Kalbr'an continued to relate his message, "We aren't capable of preventing what is to come. We do recognize that it eventually will. We are trying to devise a way to lessen the impact when this does occur. For that reason, we have come asking for help."

Pet'r was transfixed, his astonishment total. The air in the great cavern seemed to hold life in suspension, no movement occurred. The only sound, other than Kalbr'an's soft voice, was the gurgling of the branch flowing across the cavern floor.

"Now we, who tried to defend, have decided some of our descendants and the descendants of those who knew us and protected those things most precious to us, must be called on to fight this battle.

You, Pet'r, and your two friends, Geth'n and Anisah, are those chosen," Kalbr'an stopped for a moment to let the young man absorb this news.

Pet'r waited. He sat quietly, listening. He knew somehow what he was being told was of greater consequence than what he felt about it.

"There is an enemy. Let's say he is a fallen angel. He has followers – the Om-Esfer'n. His name is Baalsa'n, one of us, but he lives a mortal life too. He has determined we, who now call ourselves the Al-Esfer'n, are wrong and he wishes to destroy all

61

we've created on this world and on other worlds. He would just as soon destroy us as well," Kalbra'n revealed. "He doesn't understand, nor wants to, why we wish to create these worlds and provide people all in our image more or less, to inhabit them.

Maybe we don't understand why we want this either, but we've found pleasure in the making of something beyond ourselves. As I mentioned there have been many wars, almost all of them started by Baalsa'n, on each of the planets we have created and many of those worlds have been destroyed.

Baalsa'n had allies within our ranks, enough to have a force powerful enough to overcome us. We failed to recognize the danger signs and never prepared the people of each world for what was to come. This time we've decided we must act, and to react more quickly to provide the answers for saving what we did," Kalbr'an finished, standing as he did.

He strolled across the floor, almost floating. It was obvious he was concentrating on what he should mention next. He stroked his chin as though pondering the import of his next statements.

"During the last war, the Varkanian, almost all Al-Esfer'n were destroyed. There was no way to save our physical being. So we can't interact with you, or anyone, with our physical presence. We are limited in what we can do. Any exchange between the Al-Esfer'n and the people must be a spiritual, or magical.

We did this because we hoped not all would be lost and possibly someday, another miracle may come about that would release us. I, too, entered it at the last. Only Areb'l, a human I befriended when we lived on Varkan, survived those days. He alone wanted to help us. So we gave him the gift of immortality and he survived all those centuries until he came to Narhtrae as part of Baalsa'n's entourage. Only he would be able to save us after we placed our spiritual being into an amulet."

That vessel, my young friend, hangs about your neck," Kalbr'an stopped, turned and watched Pet'r.

Pet'r instinctively reached for the Ahar'n and grasped it firmly.

It glowed in response. He noticed he was holding his breath as the tale was told and, only when he had to, did he softly take another.

"During the time before we entered the Ahar'n, we were here, creating this world," Kalbr'an continued. "Baalsa'n attacked Varkan with full force. He viciously ripped that world apart, even killing his own followers in the devastation.

We returned to Varkan, attempting to save it but our effort was much too late and we lost dearly. Only the souls of those who did not die were added to the Ahar'n. I, and any of us, can only appeared to you, and other humans, in a spirit form.

Baalsa'n, mimicked our effort, capturing the souls he didn't want to lose in the dark crystal you saw today. Both can be used as a force for great magical presence. So now we have these two icons, precious to the Esfer'n that hold those we would wish to bring back, both ourselves and Baalsa'n's followers – the survivors. Loss of either one destroys that possibility," Kalbr'an explained. He was pacing now.

"These things have no great value to the inhabitants of any of the remaining worlds except they are now the reason for which new battles and wars are fought. As more on those worlds die, the Ahar'n, and the Dark Crystal, become more precious," Kalbr'an paused, and absently looked around the cavern.

"Why must we, your only descendants, be involved in these wars? We are your children," Pet'r asked. The idea that these wars were fought only for the god's benefit didn't sit well with him.

"We are your survivors. Your immortality is with us regardless of these stones. Why must these wars be fought on the planets where there are people, surely there are empty planets that would serve."

"Good questions. Reasonable ones. Unfortunately we, both Baalsa'n and those of our group, are forbidden to battle with each other. So we must recruit. The people of the planets involved become those volunteers. Those, like myself, have never wanted these great wars, but they all occur because Baalsa'n and the others spread their destruction on the people and worlds with a voracity we can't stop because of this limitation.

We don't start these wars but we tried to protect the people. As I mentioned before, we were often too late because we never planned for what was to come. We were complacent and our failures show our mistakes," Kalbr'an turned to talk directly to Pet'r with this last.

"There is no apology for such travesty and yet once again we are going to war. This time, however, we intend to involve ourselves, in ways we are able, to save the people on this planet. Therefore, you, Anisah and Geth'n are our first recruits." Kalbr'an finished, stopped, and sat down.

He waited a moment. "Do you have more questions?"

"Yes. You are saying we have no choice in these matters?" Pet'r asked forcefully. He was angry about what he was hearing. "The Esfer'n, whoever they might be, have no right to do these things."

"I'm telling you this because you and yours are even now under attack, whether we, the Al-Esfer'n started it, or not. Only today, you were a participant in what was probably the first, but certainly not the only, battle to be fought," Kalbr'an was stating the truth, not trying to be tactful. He presented it without apology.

"So now there is a war on our world you people have started. You need humans you created, on any of your planets, to help defeat the evil ones. But why we three?" Pet'r insisted. He was stunned by what he was hearing.

"First, you. You are a direct descendant of Areb'l, the first Guardian of the Ahar'n. Areb'l was one of the human inhabitants of Varkan who survived the terrible ravaging of that poor place. His entire family was destroyed," Kalbr'an revealed.

"Geth'n, he curiously enough, is the offspring of those my love and I bore so many centuries ago; so he could be considered

64

one of my lineage," Kalbr'an explained, wanting to inform Pet'r fully and without fanfare.

"Anisah, strangely enough, is the child of one of the children of Baalsa'n," he continued.

"Wait. Wait. That can't be. She's so special. She fought against Voravia on the plateau. She can't be evil," Pet'r interrupted, standing in his anger. He began to pace. He couldn't believe Anisah was one of the aggressors. He stood looking down at Kalbr'an with malice in his eyes. He tried to control his anger, but it was difficult for him. "I don't believe that is true."

"But, my young friend, it is true. I did not say she is evil. We felt her heart was too pure and would be diminished had she followed her father's lead. So we've protected her and, in our way through dreams, we've taught her to detest evil."

Pet'r pacing stopped and he sat, waiting.

"Her father, in fact, was born of a woman from this world, sired by Baalsa'n himself. He is a strong lieutenant of Baalsa'n's still. Anisah, though her father is evil, was born of a woman in the midlands, who was deserted by the father. She taught Anisah that the common good should be upheld," Kalbr'an added.

"The leadership of the Al-Esfer'n feels you three could be and, by our choice, will be the vanguard of the forces who will save Narhtrae. Possibly that places a great deal of pressure on your shoulders, but we considered many candidates. You were the best, and we know you each need the other. Without that recognition, you will not succeed."

Pet'r sat staring at Kalbr'an, unbelieving. He rose again, trying to think; trying to decide if he should be angry, or if he should recognize what was happening and join with the Al-Esfer'n in this holy war.

The past few weeks had passed quickly, but some portions had passed too slowly. The changes Pet'r had experienced now seemed beyond belief and to have taken years, but he knew all had occurred since the time he and Geth'n had decided to depart

Peetle. He now understood those days were encouraged by others.

"What do we do? How are we to know what to do and when? We all led simple lives. We are not warriors," Pet'r began to plead the obvious.

"We know those things; you'll not be left alone. We will be there to guide and teach so you three will be prepared when the time comes. The experience you had today was an example. Nothing occurred by chance. You three did very well," Kalbr'an added. "There will be more of these individual battles, so warn your friends."

"I cannot even consider what the possibilities are. I'm overwhelmed. I only hope your faith in us is not ill founded. I do believe in Anisah and Geth'n. Hopefully, we will do our best. But you and your people should understand. We are not willingly doing this. It's only because we wish to save our people from this stupid war. I think we all will fight when the time comes," Pet'r was confused by the enormity of what he had just been told. He had no great testimonies to make.

"I think we've chosen well. You've all already proven your intensity and your desire to do your best," Kalbr'an walked to Pet'r, resting his hand on the young man's shoulder. "You aren't aware yet, but both Geth'n and Anisah have accomplished a great deal in their individual situations. We are pleased. But now, you must rejoin your friends. Anisah and Geth'n are both in Tariny and you should go there also."

"It will take me many days to travel there . . ." Pet'r began but Kalbr'an raised his hand from Pet'r's shoulder and held it before him, requesting Pet'r to stop.

"No. You now have power to transcend what you were. Close your eyes and concentrate on where you must be," Kalbr'an interrupted and stepped back slightly.

Pet'r closed his eyes and thought again about parting from Anisah and Geth'n on the crossroads west of Varspree. They were going to Tariny, he to the Wastelands.

When he opened his eyes, he saw Kalbra'n fading away.

"Beware of dangers lurking in unlikely places and trust each other," the ghostlike image disappeared.

The wall of the mountain began to rumble and he remembered it opening for him the first time. He gazed out into the brightness, blinked a few times and stepped through the opening.

He thought a moment about what he needed to do, then began walking eastward. He traveled for several miles to relocate the road he had traveled from the Wastelands. He soon came to it and knew it was a road that would take him to Tariny.

He approached it slowly, investigating the area cautiously. When satisfied the way was clear, he stepped out onto the road and headed south.

As he walked, he was very wary, scanning the road as he walked. He was traveling through Voravia's lands and he didn't want to meet any of her odd little men wandering out of these woods.

He was considering the possibility of returning to Peetle, thinking Geth'n might have landed there after the battle. But Kalbr'an told him Anisah and Geth'n were both in Tariny already, so it would be better if he went there first. He and Geth'n needed to visit their home, but not immediately.

Suddenly, the sound of struggle came up from a small valley just west of the road. He was near Coma't and he thought this disruption could be dangerous. Voravia kept a close watch in this region; he knew that from experience.

He crept forward to look down into the forest below and saw a man being attacked, by what appeared to be, Voravia's men. The man looked familiar even at the distance to the bottom of the canyon. Pet'r decided he must help him. Wasting no more time, he stood, immediately jumped over the ridge and ran toward the fighting.

67

SURPRISE

Voravia felt herself being lifted away from the scene. It faded in a whirl of blackness she couldn't avoid.

She was prepared to ensorcel this young witch so she and Mano'n could take her back to the castle and begin her training. But now she was at a disadvantage and surprised. She could sense she was flying but had no idea why, nor where she was going.

She braced herself, preparing her body to avoid imminent damage. Suddenly she knew the ride was over, she plummeted. Just as she wrapped her arms about herself, she slammed into a table and lost consciousness.

Later, she awoke with a start and rolled off the table, hitting the floor with her head.

Now that's going to leave a bruise.

She rolled over onto her back and looked up. There was a ceiling so she knew she was in a building somewhere. She rolled her head to one side and then recognized where she was.

Anisah had launched Voravia and crashed her onto the very table Rab'k had placed Anisah when she was captured by Voravia's minions and him.

Voravia was in her own castle.

That little wench is playing games. This is deliberate. But the power she has, the power was beyond imagining. Wonder what Baalsa'n is going to do about this? I can certainly imagine he'll not be pleased.

She rolled and lifted herself from the floor and sat in the nearest chair.

Well, at least, I'm home. I'm going to hurt tomorrow. But, I believe, we must determine what should be done about Anisah.

She stretched her shoulders, flexed her arms and legs, reached up and lightly touched the area where her forehead hurt, then

69

held her head in her hands.

I thought the Guardian was going to be a problem. What is Mano'n going to do with his problem? Whatever he tries is going to be difficult for him. I've got to get busy. I've too much to do. My niece is Mano'n's problem — not mine.

I need to start rebuilding my "troops" into something more destructive than I originally envisioned. There has to be more evil in their make-up. Monsh'a has warned me and, I suspect, what he says is what Baalsa'n would insist on. At least, this Monsh'a seems to know what he's doing and was willing to take over the creation and training of these locals' troops. He got that off my back.

"Mord! Sesk! Where are you two," she shouted, rising stiffly but walking to the door as she screeched. "Get up here now."

Might as well start with these two. They're useless as servants.

She heard them scrambling up the long stairs, fighting each other to be first to please her. She realized she might use that jealousy to her advantage.

They rushed into her room, smashing against each other in their effort to be first. They slid to a stop when they reached her, brushed themselves off, and stood at attention waiting for Voravia.

She usually was infuriated by the idiotic way they conducted themselves, but today she had a plan she thought would please her, even if these two didn't like it. So she didn't yell at them as she usually did, she remained calm and deliberate.

Mord, nor Sesk, knew what to do under this circumstance, so they stood there and waited, silent for once.

"I've decided to give you two a small task, but it will require you to leave my castle and wander through the land. I need to find someone. This should be easy, but one never knows what excitement there might be," she spoke slowly so she wouldn't have to repeat it. She smiled all the while and finished without demanding anything of either one. They were obviously confused by this new approach toward them.

70

"Wheres do we go?" Mord asked. His hesitation evident, he was not accustomed to asking questions, just obeying screeching commands. "Whos do we looks for?"

"It's simple. Remember the girl and boy we captured before? Remember Rab'k brought them here from the caves?" she again was deliberate in her questioning. "Do you remember they ran away with another boy who helped them?"

Both were nodding their head, concentrating intensely.

Probably neither one of them remembers that. But it doesn't make any difference. The task serves other purposes.

"I need you to find her and kill her," Voravia added. She watched their reaction and it was as she expected. Killing the girl posed no problem for these two; they had no moral reason not to do so.

"If you find any girl who looks like that girl, with all red hair, like mine," she brushed her hair upward, causing it to bush out in a great fluff on top of her head. "Except me, you should kill her."

"But whys does shes need dead?" Sesk asked, curiosity filling his face.

"Because I have learned she wants to kill me," Voravia added, looking as sad and afraid as she could.

Mord and Sesk both stared at Voravia with widened eyes. The look of astonishment was obvious. They couldn't believe anyone would want to kill their mistress.

"Wes will do this. Wes will finds this bad girl and kills her," Mord spoke strongly, defiance filling his face. Sesk just stood nodding his head, enthusiastically.

"I'm so happy with you two. I always knew you cared about me," she spoke, trying to indicate how pleased she was. "You are truly my heroes. Maybe you can leave tomorrow. I believe she lives down the road toward Cartles, maybe farther.

You can just follow the roads looking for a girl that looks like me. Then you must kill her. But then maybe she isn't the girl who

71

was here and you have to keep looking until all the girls, who look like me, are dead. Then you can come home."

Voravia reached and touched their shoulders as she finished. Her hair fell back in place and she smiled as sweetly as she could.

"You boys should go and get ready now. I'll talk to you tomorrow before you leave," she said, patting their shoulders.

They spun around, bumping each other, banged against the door facings as they both tried to exit the room at the same time. Finally they got past the doors, bumped and clattered down the hallway.

Voravia reached for the door and slowly closed it. She wore a smile at once, both delightful and malicious. She went to a bowl of water sitting near the entry, washed her hands and wiped them dry on a towel hanging from the wash table. She looked in the mirror and grinned.

"This has enormous promise, I think. Now I need to find that map Rab'k brought from the caves and study it. He said the boy . . . Wasn't his name Geth'n? . . . revealed many things about the map in his conversation with my niece. Many things questioned for centuries in this god-forbidden country about where certain caves are and what their purpose is; where the passageways all go under the mountains and where they all lead," she mumbled a while about the possibilities.

"Wonder how the boy knew what the map meant?" she pondered. "Why didn't that idiot Rab'k grab the map and papers with it, when he brought the kids up? Is everyone an idiot? No wonder Baalsa'n is concerned about failure– my brothers are both stupid."

She turned, walked across the room and peered out the window, thinking about what was stated about the room where Rab'k had found the kids.

I believe there was some mention about them being there after coming through one of the caves normally used by her small beings when bringing taxes from across her area. I believe from those bits of information I know

72

where this map is. Since it was probably drawn by one of the Al-Esfer'n, it undoubtedly would prove to be valuable to the person who had possession of it.

Voravia believed she knew just which group of caves and what room the map was in. She had been there herself, looking through some of the older books. It never occurred to her to look for rolls of maps.

Well, that error can be resolved. I'll go recover those maps tomorrow after my two boys leave. Should be a fruitful day. Certainly a more promising one.

She stood a bit longer, looking out the window toward the Beyhon'd Sea, watching as the high tide beat against the cliffs; then turned, looking toward the south.

It seems, my pretty niece, I may wreak some havoc in your precarious life. You will be haunted by my two gremlins until you die.

GETH'N

Geth'n slammed through the ceiling, hit the floor with some force and tried to stand, staggered and slumped to the floor.

Lying on his stomach amid piles of papers and old books, he could see the floor was made of great stones laid end to end. The floor and the building were cold.

He groaned and rolled onto his back. He looked up at the drifting dust filtering through a small beam of light shining from high above him, casting a yellowish haze on everything around him. He thought it strange he could see no evidence of his entry in the ceiling.

Rolling his head on the floor, he peered to his side, he could see there were long rows of shelves stretching away into the darkness. Shaking himself a bit, he rolled onto his hands and knees, raised his head slowly and looked around.

He was in a large room where shelves extended into the darkness at both ends, some of the shelves were stacked high with books, but most of the books were scattered, in small piles, around the room. He had no idea where he was, but he noticed a certain familiar smell.

Pushing himself off the floor, he dusted himself off, feeling rumpled. His clothes were indeed dirty and wrinkled as though he had been lying on the floor for some time.

Have I been lying for a while, or did I just arrive from the plateau of battle?

He had no answer to his question. So he looked around some more and noticed there was a door on the far side of the room. He began to wade slowly through the books, not wanting to disturb them too much. Finally reaching the door, he found it locked and he couldn't budge it. He banged on the door, pushed on the latch, stopped and listened for any sounds. Hearing none, he banged on the door again. The door lock suddenly turned and clicked open.

Geth'n stepped back and waited for the door to open, but it didn't. He reached forward and pushed it gently. It swung open slowly and revealed another chamber that was in greater disarray than the one in which he stood. Stepping over a few more stacks of books, he moved into the room. It was larger, but darker. He could faintly see a staircase along the side of one wall.

Seeing no recourse, he pushed his way through stacks of paper, large boxes partially empty though containing mostly books, and old chairs piled at random in corners. He reached the stairs and noticed some light shining under the door at the top. He climbed the steps carefully, they were ancient and not as steady as he would have liked.

Finally reaching the door, he opened it slowly, but easily. There was no resistance, so he stepped through and into the library in Tariny.

Well, why not this place? Am I to learn more about this day here? Must I prepare for what is to come? If so, there is not a lot of time to be wasted on simple research. Now I must find the secret of the Ahar'n and that of the Black Stone, for that knowledge is now vital.

He walked along a few small hallways, toward what he thought was the entrance of the building, past a few more open hallways with steps leading to the great stacks above.

At last, he rounded a corner and recognized the front desk directly in front of him, he approached it and stood waiting for the young woman sitting there to notice him.

He had no idea whether the dust from the basement area was still on him, nor what he looked like. He did stop before he reached the desk, wiped his hand over his face and beat some of the more obvious dirt from his clothing.

My appearance, I suspect, isn't what it should be and how is anyone able to brush off their own back?

75

The young clerk looked up as he approached the desk hesitantly. She smiled, looked him up and down, and raised an eyebrow.

"May I help you, sir? Do you need assistance?" she asked, obviously trying not to embarrass him.

"Yes, I do. I'm looking for one of the attendants. His name is Ald'n, or Alt'an, or something like that. Do you know where he might be?" He asked, trying to be nonchalant but was still aware of the girl's reaction to his appearance. "I have need to speak with him, if I may."

"I suspect he's very busy today. There have been some thefts, with some of the items under his responsibility involved. I'm certain he's trying to determine what has been affected and may not be able to take time away from that," she offered. "But I can contact him and ask, if you would like to wait."

"Where is he, please? I've something vital to tell him that may be associated with the break-in. Could you please ask him if he will see me soon? What is his name again?" Geth'n blurted out. He was concerned about the break-in. He felt certain, on considering his previous day's events, he could offer some suggestions about who the thief might be.

"Well, sir. His name is Alt'n. But I'm not certain I can bother him at this time," she answered, moving away from this disheveled man who suddenly seemed to be someone who could start some trouble. "I can ask my supervisor, if you'll wait just a moment."

She stood and back away from her seat, turned and walked toward an older gentleman sitting in a small office behind her. She asked permission to interrupt the gentleman, walked in and began to whisper to him, looking in Geth'n's direction as she talked, then turned away.

The gentleman raised his head, adjusted his glasses, gazed at Geth'n and frowned. He turned back to the assistant and said something to her. He again looked at Geth'n and frowned. Then

76

he returned to studying the items on his desk. The girl just stood for a moment, staring at Geth'n.

Geth'n felt awkward. Both of these people were, by facial expressions, showing some disdain for him, his questions, his appearance and request.

The supervisor looked up at the girl again and waved her away. She walked back to her desk, stopped, and put her fingertips on the desk. She prepared to push away in case there was going to be trouble.

"Master Harn'a says I should bring Alt'n to you, if he's willing." she said. Geth'n could tell she still was uncertain she should be doing this.

"If you just wait here, I'll do that if I can. And as I said, he's been very busy analyzing his problem," she told him and smiled. "As a reference for Alt'n, might I ask your name, sir?"

" Certainly, my name is Geth'n. Alt'n and I have talked previously," Geth'n informed her.

Geth'n now knew one thing. Alt'n was the name he remembered from when he and Anisah had visited. Alt'n was in charge of keeping order in the area reserved for mythical history of Aerolan.

The girl walked around the desk and down the aisle to the stairs. Geth'n remembered those stairs led to the stacks upstairs where the prehistory information was stored. She turned, looked back at Geth'n and walked out of sight.

Geth'n waited for a while looking around the vestibule. He was still awestruck by the immensity of this ancient place. After a while he began to pace, anxious for the girl to return.

Where is she?

The thought was no sooner out than she turned the corner and walked toward him. He walked part of the way down the aisle to meet her.

She's pretty. Wonder what her name is?

"Sir, Alt'n says he can spare a minute. He thought he remembered you from another visit, but wasn't certain," she told him, smiling now that Geth'n had, more or less, been identified.

"Thanks, Miss . . . ," he started.

"Siarra," she filled in her name.

"Thank you, Siarra," he smiled back at her and felt himself blush. "I'm certain we'll meet again soon since I'll probably take residence here."

She laughed, lightly. "I hope so," she too blushed, then turned and quickly walked back to her desk. He watched her until she sat and looked back at him.

He waved and she returned it, then he turned and walked down the aisle and went up the stairs to the top floor.

As he followed the steps, catching glimpses of the lower floors at each landing, he did remember where he visited before; he knew to return to the third floor and go back into the Mythology section.

He arrived and opened the door carefully. What he saw inside the room appalled him. Books were scattered across the floor. Volumes were smashed against the wall, pages hanging twisted and torn. Loose pages, from unknown manuscripts, were laying about everywhere. Other books were strewn and lying in disheveled conditions everywhere.

Geth'n could see several people carefully stacking the books on the floor, trying to collect those not damaged into recognizable categories for shelving.

He stood shocked.

Who would do such a thing? Why would they do it?

One of the workers looked up and noticing him, walked to greet him. It was Alt'n. As he approached, he held out his hand in greeting. Geth'n grasped it and placed his other hand over Alt'n's.

"I'm so sorry. This has to be such a bitter thing for you. Can I help in any way?" he asked, offering the only thing he could think of.

"You can. I do remember you now. In fact, the area I remember you being the most concerned about was the worst vandalized. You, as I remembered, were studying the ancient references in an attempt to find some evidence about whether the . . . Ahar'n, was it?. . . existed," Alt'n responded calmly.

"Yes, that's what I wanted to research," Geth'n answered, still looking around the room. "How could anyone do this deliberately. There is information in these volumes that is irreplaceable."

"This vandalism is reprehensible and unforgivable. It may take us years to recover from this. Any help you might offer would be greatly appreciated," he waved his hand over the entire scene. "But why are you here? I remember you thought you'd be returning shortly after you left the last time. You, and a young woman, I believe. But it's been a while since then."

"You're correct. Our attention was diverted to a problem we didn't expect. Later, I'll relate the tale to you. I believe it will be historically significant. But that's finished for the moment, and I'd love to assist with this disaster here. We can talk later. Do you have any clues who may have done this?" Geth'n asked.

"Only one, a small one. Siarra - you met her downstairs - remembered a man in black asking about the area the day before this happened. She said the man was a gentleman and friendly to her. She gave him directions, as she does everyone; he thanked her and left. She thought it odd someone of that bearing would be so genteel," Alt'n related the story indicating he thought it suspicious also, it was rare for the rich to be courteous.

Rab'k? Maybe, but I think this isn't his area. Must be the other brother Voravia mentioned. Wonder where he is? Wonder how he's involved.

"That's interesting. I've just recently met someone who might give me a clue to this person's identity. But I'm not able to contact them just yet. Let me help here for a while, then I'll follow that clue for you. If that's acceptable," Geth'n offered.

"Thank you. That's the only thing we've remembered that comes close to helping. If you do determine the culprit, we can have him apprehended and brought to justice for this," Alt'n seemed encouraged by Geth'n's offer.

"Well, it may not be that easy. I'll not be able to do anything about that for a short time, but let's get back to straightening this mess. And I do have some investigating for my own research while I'm here," Geth'n said. He knew apprehending the man, if his assumption was correct, was out of the question because of the obvious – the ancient magic. Today he wanted to help, but he also needed to look for one answer.

There might be references about this Baalsa'n Voravia mentioned. Maybe there are answers about who these people are in one of these great volumes. There may be answers on how to fight back.

"Anyway, let me get started," Geth'n said and headed toward one of the largest mounds of books and paper he could see.

He worked hard for several hours and had, he thought, re-covered a few areas of books, laid neatly along one wall, alpha-betized by the authors, pages reinserted, to be repaired.

He had no idea where these volumes should be in the stacks and didn't even try. He decided Alt'n should handle that. But, as he shuffled through the books, he discovered some clues he thought he could use for further investigation.

After a while, Alt'n told him the rest were going to take a break, so Geth'n decided he might go downstairs and see if Siarra would like to sit and talk. If he could convince her, he would cer-tainly welcome having her go to lunch with him.

He returned to the downstairs area and walked to her desk. She looked up and smiled.

"I was thinking I haven't had lunch, would you like to take a walk with me?" he asked, only hoping for a possibility.

"Well, I think so, but let me make certain I have a replacement," she answered. Geth'n almost breathed a sigh. He was so tense about this, he could hardly breathe. She returned shortly, a smile on her face. "I'm ready if you are."

They walked out the front door and turned in the direction of the Healing College and strolled quietly along the streets. She told him she wasn't very hungry but she would just like to walk for a while. So they walked, making comments about the weather and the library, but there came a moment without either talking at all.

"Do you know Alt'n?" she broke the silence.

"I met him several months ago. At the library, of course. We have, as it turns out, similar interest and, at that time, we discovered that. So, when I arrived earlier today, I couldn't remember his name because we only met that one time," Geth'n answered, startled from deeper thoughts. The awkwardness returned for a moment.

This is not going well. I have to start talking.

"So, do you work at the library all the time? I don't remember you being there when I first came?" Geth'n asked.

"Well, I just started last week. Mr. Harn'a, Alt'n and the others have been very nice to me and help me while I struggle to learn what I'm supposed to do. Harn'a is a nice man, but he keeps to himself a lot," she answered turning to face him.

"I decided, long ago, a fishing village was not going to allow me to follow some of my dreams, so I came to the city to pursue something more. I love books so I tried the library for employment first. They hired me, almost immediately, to be an associate responsible for meeting and helping people when they first arrive. Not very exciting most of the time, but occasionally I meet someone of interest," she explained and gave him a big smile. He knew he blushed again, but could do nothing about it.

"Well . . . What town are you from? I'm from a fishing village myself so I understand some of the frustration of living in one," he asked.

"I'm from CrossPoint just up the coast from here, not too far really, but enough," she told him. "I'm not quite as brave as I'd like to be."

She stopped suddenly. Geth'n laughed softly when he noticed she wasn't beside him. She waited for him to walk back to her.

"Why are you so frumpy? You seem very nice, but, frankly,

you look like a man of the road, a hard traveler," she bluntly asked him.

He laughed again, louder this time, delighted by her frank questions.

"Actually, I can understand your curiosity. I must look terrible; I haven't, with all the activity upstairs, had time to look at myself in a mirror to know what you mean. And I suppose you're right. But there's a long story and a short one. The short one is I woke this morning and found myself in the basement of the library. I'm not at all certain why. But now, considering how well this day has gone, and is going, I'm glad. The long story is very complicated and would require me to explain more than I can on this walk. We'll probably need to make time to sit and discuss many things, if you'd like," he said and laughed again. "It will really be a long story."

She looked at him a moment then smiled again. He found her smile to be a rather special thing for him.

"Well, you should at least wash your face," she turned and began to walk again. He, a little stunned, ran quickly and caught her.

"Yes, Ma'm," he said, laughing again. He couldn't believe how much it meant to be with her. He wanted to laugh at everything. He realized things, in his life, were much more serious than these brief moments had been, but he found comfort in being with Siarra.

They walked around the area of the library, talking and enjoying being outdoors.

"I need to get back, I'm afraid," she said, looking up at him with that same smile. It seemed to him she did so hesitantly. He was pleased she wanted to be with him.

"Can we do this again?" she asked.

He knew he was beaming but couldn't stop himself.

"Yes. Yes, of course. I would like nothing better, but I too probably need to get back to my job upstairs. Do we have a date for a walk tomorrow; I'll try to clean up a bit?"

"Yes, we have a date," she answered, laughing at him now. "Don't worry about it. I'd walk with you anyway. Even if you do look like a vagabond," She laughed again.

As they came to the entry, they stopped for a moment and said nothing. Then she reached, touched his hand and held it a moment. Then, smiling again, walked toward the door and entered the building leaving him standing, stunned again.

He blinked. Twice. Shook his head, rushed to the door and swung it open, but she was already gone.

What is this feeling? I don't understand. Is this going to be a problem for me? Should I stop this now?

But, he knew he wouldn't.

He walked to the stairs leading upward, turned, saw Siarra sitting behind her desk, waved and returned to the business at hand.

Later, he thought they made considerable progress on the recovery and Alt'n agreed with him. There were still a few of the small volumes not collected and ordered, but the task certainly seemed less difficult.

The other workers had departed, so Geth'n and Alt'n sat on some of the stacks of books and talked.

"So, Geth'n, why are you here? I've actually wondered, several times, why you never returned before," Alt'n asked.

"I've been very busy over the last few weeks attempting to deal with a severe problem. But, I'm specifically here to research some more information on the subject I mentioned before – the Ahar'n, the mythical orb mentioned in so many texts. I've recently discovered other evidence, in another . . . well, let's call it . . . library, in a rather secret place and I wanted to determine if there were documents here that correlated with those," Geth'n told him.

He didn't know how to broach the subject openly, not knowing what Alt'n's responses might be and he wanted to feel certain Alt'n was protected from knowing too much, but he felt he could ask pertinent questions without going into depth about what he had learned.

How did I get here. I'll save that explanation. Somewhere, sometime soon, Anisah, Pet'r and I must include others into a group of trustworthy people who can be informed about what is happening and can be part of the solution. Right now, I'm not certain what is going on, certainly not enough to reveal relevant information. I need to find Pet'r and Anisah. Maybe, Anisah's here, at the Healers' College; I have to check on that tomorrow.

"Geth'n? Geth'n? Are you all right?" Alt'n was shaking Geth'n's shoulder. Geth'n, without realizing it, had fallen into a daydream of sorts, concentrating on what he must do.

"Oh. Yes. Yes, of course," Geth'n answered. "Just daydreaming at bit, I'm afraid. But I'm fine. Just tired, I think."

Just confused about what I need to do first actually. Then, there's Siarra too.

He shook his head, then chuckled.

Yes. Then there's Siarra.

"I'm fine. I think we should get back to work?" he smiled at Alt'n and shook his head again.

Alt'n shrugged his shoulders and stood. "Might as well. This mess won't straighten itself. You have any ideas who did this, or why it happened?"

"Actually, I do have some. I believe whoever did this was looking for the same information I am. Knowledge of the Ahar'n seems to be the driving factor. The person responsible obviously wasn't interested in preserving the past, but looking for something, I believe, that would lead him, or her, to a specific thing. I think that something would be the Ahar'n," Geth'n answered.

He wasn't totally aware of what happened on that plateau during the battle. He remembered vividly his fight with Voravia. But he didn't remember what Pet'r and Rab'k were doing, or how Pet'r was able to fight as he did.

Where did Pet'r achieve such strength and battle skills? How did he manage to protect them from Rab'k, both in the castle and during the small

84

battle. What sort of power was he using? What power did Anisah have to withstand Voravia's attacks? Why didn't she respond in kind? Too many questions. I need to go the Healer's College soon and talk to Anisah.

All that afternoon, he searched through the manuscripts he selected and kept apart from the rest. He did find mention of the caves beneath the mountain where he and Anisah had been looking for Pet'r. He found references on how to enter these areas, the Crystal Cave, meeting place of the Immortals, and others mentioned Cave of the Guardian. But no definite answer about the whereabouts of the orb itself.

All these caves are in those mountains. Maybe I need to be looking there? But there is obvious danger in that effort.

At the end of the day, Geth'n, discouraged, returned to the front entrance, looking for Siarra, but she wasn't there. He asked about her without any results and finally went to Harn'a 's office to ask. Harn'a told him Siarra had to leave early, something about her family. Geth'n was surprised she hadn't left him a message.

So, Geth'n, now disappointed he had accomplished nothing, walked out of the library. He stood for a moment, looking up and down the street.

I should go to the Healers' College and look for Anisah. Maybe, she'll be there.

He turned toward the west gate and trudged toward the college, totally frustrated. When he arrived, he knocked on the great door in front and waited. The young lady, Mira, he met when he was there before, answered the door.

"Hello, sir. May I help you?" she asked.

"Actually, I hoped to meet a friend here. She and I came by several weeks ago to ask about her entering the college and she was supposed to have returned. I thought I might find her here. Her name is Anisah," Geth'n answered.

"I'm sorry, sir. I don't remember you, or her. But, I can tell you no new visitors have been here in several days. We keep a log, if you like to see it, of all the visitors."

"No, I certainly believe you. Well, I'll just wait until later and maybe I can find her elsewhere," he said, wondering where that would be. He had no way to know Anisah's whereabouts.

The next day, he arrived at the library, looked for Siarra again, but she still wasn't there. He returned upstairs, helped a bit more with the refurbishing of some of the manuscripts that could be repaired. He began to feel he had wasted his time being here. His new friend wasn't here; he found nothing of interest in the books he thought might have information. He was becoming more downtrodden with each moment.

He opened one more page to meander listlessly through yet another manuscript and noticed a listing for an Areb'l who lived ages ago on the southern coast.

In Peetle.

He never heard of Areb'l in the village before now. The man was proclaimed to be a great warrior who helped strengthen the boundaries of Aerolan in those ancient times; it stated he was the Guardian of the Ahar'n. But that was so long ago and so vague, Geth'n understood why that legend was no longer remembered.

Still, why haven't I heard about this man? You would think such a man's legend would have been repeated over and over again at home. Why wasn't it? How did those stories disappear?

Geth'n shut the book quickly, rose, walked over to Alt'n to tell him he had to leave and probably wouldn't be back for a while. Then he quickly walked to the door and out.

Alt'n stood stunned by Geth'n's quick departure.

What could have triggered that sudden change? Maybe Siarra is aware. I'll check with her later.

Geth'n rushed down stairs and looked for Siarra again. She was nowhere to be found. So he left a note and placed it on her desk explaining he was sorry, but wouldn't be able to walk with her for a while.

He explained he would be back to make up for this sudden change, still wanted to see her, and hoped there was no problem with her family.

He told her he would come to Crosspoint to find her, if necessary, and meet her family. But he had some very urgent business to attend to and had to travel for a few days.

He walked out the library and out of the west gate. He walked over the small hill on the road he and Anisah had taken when they went looking for Pet'r before. He stopped, looked around to make certain he was alone. He concentrated and thought of the plateau where the first battle had taken place.

He was suddenly there.

He retreated quickly behind some boulders, surprised at how quickly he arrived. After surveying the surrounding area, he walked out onto the plateau and wandered around, avoiding the tower in the center. He was looking to determine whether any of the participants were still there, or if there was some sort of trail he might follow. He found no one and nothing to guide him in his search.

In the distance, he could see Voravia's castle and the sea beyond. But his attention was focused on the low hills he could see to the north.

The Cave of the Guardian? The Cave of Areb'l? These two names must reference the same man. From what I remember from the old map Anisah and I found in the caves beneath Voravia's castle, that cave should be in the mountains he could see.

The road through Valhonal and Coma't runs through that area and onward to a pass into the Wasteland. I should begin my search along that route. If I'm going to discover where the Ahar'n is, I believe that area is where I should begin.

He once again concentrated on his destination, considering Coma't a good starting point to search the low foothills. He would have to be careful and not suddenly appear in the town, but some where just north of it.

He closed his eyes, disappeared and landed near the town, just beyond a small farmhouse, on the road he remembered from when he and Anisah had passed this way looking for Pet'r. He could see, looking toward the south, smoke rising gently from some of the houses in the town. The town knew nothing of trouble. As yet.

He turned north, knowing he was headed in the right direction, began walking, studying the land around him for any clues, or paths to follow, that might lead him to Areb'l's cave.

As he left the plateau, there was a sudden magical entry by another.

Voravia, sensing Geth'n's power from his earlier arrival, had rushed to engage any one of the three who might be that close. But, he, or she, was gone when Voravia arrived, leaving no trail to follow.

So, my young friend, you have discovered the means to travel quickly. We'll meet again I suspect. You, and your little friends, will have the misfortune of meeting me when I'm prepared. Hopefully, when you are not aware.

She disappeared.

RAB'K

Always there are men of war. Men who would be at the forefront of the conflict. Some for their loyalty to their leaders; some who wish to kill; some who wish to die; some who believe they are right, but all willing to stand face-to-face in conflict with another and willing to take a life for his belief.

War has never proven anything. But there are those who do not want to fight themselves, but, for many reasons, wish to have a political, or economic, or physical will over others. These often send others to their deaths to achieve these ends; most with no conscientious concern they are doing any wrong.

The credo for this act becomes -- "the most powerful is the last one standing" . . . .

Rab'k awoke suddenly, swinging his great fist through the air, fighting off an unseen enemy. He jumped into a battle stance with his back to a wall he could sense but not see, drawing his sword, expecting an attack.

Flailing his sword in the area in front and leaping about to slice the air behind, he struck nothing. He paused, breathing as quietly as possible. He blinked once, adjusting his vision to the darkness, and waited. There was no one near.

He had no idea where he was. But he stood still, trying to recall what happened at the battle. Then he noticed a glow seeping from his pouch at his off-sword side. The light was hazy and pulsating.

With that dim light, he could see the interior of the cave around him, showing a smooth surface molded by men's hands. He opened his pouch and discovered the black crystal from the plateau.

Is Rena'x dead? Has my father died? If so, who is now the protector of this stone?

89

Holding the stone, he felt the great power the crystal had as it caressed his mind and heart with its dark silence. Rab'k, for the first time in his life, felt whole.

He looked around slowly and noticed a slot overhead with some light showing through. He moved below the light cautiously. He then noticed, just out of sight, a sharp turn to his right into a small cleft in the cave wall.

Strangely, his concern with being trapped, caused him to be unaware of a larger opening behind him. An opening leading to greater discoveries than he could have ever envisioned. Whatever lay in the darkness beyond that threshold, remained a mystery as he moved into the discovered cleft.

He moved slowly through the darkness, near the seam in the bluff, squeezed into the crevice, his sword at ready. He walked only a short distance, bumped into another wall, looked about and noticed a sharp left turn, yet another crease.

As he walked through the cavern, twisting and turning through each slit, he noticed the light intensity increasing with every turn.

At the last, a great rush of light struck his eyes, causing him to blink and stagger from the pain. When he could see again, he moved toward what obviously was the cave's mouth and carefully peered out.

Before him lay the great wasteland of his youth, he recognized it immediately. Carefully pushing his head forward to looked around the corners of the stone, he investigated each direction, both left and right, for an enemy, but the desert was empty. He stepped out into the great blast of light, the searing heat.

Home. But how did I get here?

Moving away from the mouth of the cave and walking a short distance toward his old village to the west, he turned and looked back, wondering how this cave came to be.

He had never noticed it before despite having traveled this way numerous times, but he recognized that the opening to the cave faced the mountains. Few traveled on the backside of the monolith because those passing this way for ages unknown had worn a natural path on the desert side of the great rock.

He was surprised and amused when he recognized the great stone obelisk that stood at the foot of the mountains, near the passage to the south.

No one, within my knowledge, has ever known that cave existed. Strange, indeed. I wonder if the cave goes deeper into the mountains? Maybe I will come here when this war is over and search for the answers to those questions But, I can't now, I need to get to Rena'x as soon as possible, so I best be on my way.

He, feeling a need to contact Rena'x, turned away toward the west and began to trot tirelessly toward Tynoc'l. He knew, at the speed he was traveling, the trip should only take until morning.

He relished the feeling of power as he ran; there was much he needed to do now.

As he thought, he arrived shortly after dawn and trotted past the guards and other observers, with ease.

That can't be a good sign, considering what has just happened.

He quickly found his father's tent. Walk to the entrance and, was stopped by guards who seemed not to recognize him.

"Halt, who goes there?" one of them called out.

"Rab'k!" he shouted back.

"You will hold, sir," the guard replied. "I must be able to see you before you may enter this area."

Rab'k walked slowly toward the guards, now suspicious. He knew no reason for this delay.

How long have I been gone? Is Rena'x not doing well? Has he lost his powers? What has happened?

As he walked nearer, he recognized none of these guards, or the colors flying above the green canopy.

The guards stopped him again.

"What is the meaning of this? Where are my father's tents?" he was adamant; he didn't understand. His father's tents stood on

91

this ground for years — never changing while Rab'k was in the south, nor later when he returned.

"Rena'x has moved his clan near the pass to the south, on the road to Ramone," the guard answered. "This is the abode of Nife'r, our master - Baalsa'n's favored. You must leave now and go in shame to your father's home," The guard pushed his spear into Rab'k's chest, pushing him away.

Rab'k staggered backward. He couldn't believe this change and was so astonished he didn't consider he could have destroyed this impudent guard, the tents of Nife'r and any of the area within sight. He couldn't believe this was happening.

I'm the bearer of the Black Crystal. These fools can't treat me like this.

He was angry; he wanted to destroy these people and return Rena'x to his proper place. He stood trembling, holding in the frustration.

Wait. Wait. I've more control than this. If I start something now, I'll be exposed. I suspect that isn't the smart thing to do here. I need to talk to Rena'x.

"Very well, I'll go to Rena'x camp," he said, turned, trotted out of the large encampment and began his run to the west. As he ran, he tried to remember what had happened at the plateau.

He knew, or thought he did, the one called Pet'r had obviously been prepared for the battle. Pet'r showed no hesitation in engaging him though he seemed to be the smaller and weaker. Rab'k also realized Pet'r never yielded.

There was more than just strength involved. Pet'r had special powers from some other source. *Maybe he had the Ahar'n with him, hung around his neck as I have the crystal. That would account for the help he received. This man must be the Guardian of the Ahar'n now. But how did Voravia capture him? How did he escape to attack in the upper room at her castle? His strength must be immense. But, if that's true, why didn't he simply kill me.*

Rab'k looked toward the sun. The heat, this early in the morning, was intense, more so than he remembered. He assumed this

92

change had to do with Baalsa'n's anger.

Too many questions need to be answered before we can defeat this Pet'r and his friends, who also revealed amazing abilities. Those three have found, or received, some additional help from others much stronger. Baalsa'n may have some answers, but I'm not certain he's willing to talk to us as yet. Voravia and I lost an opportunity on that plateau. Baalsa'n is undoubtedly angry.

He slowed his pace though he wasn't tired. He needed to think more clearly. He needed to change his tactics. These were not people who would be afraid of him; they had already proven that. He, and Rena'x, had to determine a more subtle way to entrap them.

Rena'x has been around since the split of the Esfer'n. He probably knows where the three new combatants attained such strength.

Satisfied with his conclusion, he increased his pace and soon arrived at the new encampment. There were tents, animals and people spread over a huge area just below the high mountain pass. Hawum Pass generally was too high and retained too much snow to be considered a good way to go through the mountains. Though He looked to the ridge and noticed there was less snow in the high peaks. He decided the warmer air he noticed earlier probably was melting it sooner this year.

Or maybe, Baalsa'n is effecting this change.

His survey of the camp showed Rena'x had actually increased the number of people who followed him. There were more tents.

Wonder what tribes have followed? No time to consider this now. I need to find Rena'x.

He searched through the myriad colors of the canopies, looking for Rena'x banner. He discovered it, boldly flying not too far from the rise in the land to the foothills. That position provided a means to overlook the other tents and banners of the various tribes and keep watch of activity throughout this new village.

Rab'k also noticed there was an ample water supply. This

93

wasn't normally true in this place but possibly with the increase in heat of the land, the glaciers above were yielding an abundance of water with the melting. This also would make the reaches above more passable, if it were necessary to cross the mountains through this pass.

A good position. If necessary, an army could go a bit further west and traverse the mountains into Voravia's territory with ease. *My father has done well.*

Rab'k still did not recognize Baalsa'n as his father though he would never mention that to Rena'x.

He relaxed, now he knew what had happened, and walked to the tents of Rena'x. He knew Rena'x would not be removed from this cause. The southerners would be destroyed if Rena'x had anything to do with it. Rab'k was proud of his father.

Later that evening, after a good feast and celebration of his return, he and Rena'x had a long discussion about what Rab'k had experienced. Rena'x didn't condemn him for the failure at the plateau. He understood the new tactics of the enemy. The presence of the unknown, with the inclusion of the three young combatants, had turned the advantage. He also knew who the enemy was.

Despite the history surrounding the Al-Esfer'n and their claimed lack of involvement in the past, they apparently were now going to present a defense of this planet. This was a new tactic that was inconsistent with the past. The Al-Esfer'n had never offered to fight back in all those past wars.

Rena'x knew the strongest leader of the Al-Esfer'n.

"Kalbra'n," he mentioned. "Our real enemy. He apparently has handed over the Ahar'n to the young people despite their inexperience and youth. That means the Al-Esfer'n are consistent. They are not to be directly involved, but they've built their plan around the strengths of these young people."

"You say there was a young girl Voravia identified as Mano'n's daughter?" Rena'x asked. "That is interesting. Wonder how, or more importantly, why Mano'n allowed his offspring enough freedom to make her own decisions. I wonder if he did that intentionally?

"The girl denied any relationship, but her resemblance to Voravia was striking," Rab'k added.

Rena'x nodded his head at this troubling information.

I wonder if Baalsa'n is aware of the girl. Or if he is does he believe Mano'n has her safely under his control. I would assume he knows about the girl, but the latter seems untrue. What I question is whether the girl has any power? If she does, this could be a serious problem. Considering we have never heard about her before, who is she with?

Rena'x told Rab'k more about the Al-Esfer'n and Kalbr'an, their leader. Rena'x had a low opinion of them for they never showed any drive, or willingness, to defend themselves on the many planets Baalsa'n's people attacked. He granted they were persistent but not aggressive enough to support that effort.

"It seems to me the recent battle bears consideration and is strong evidence there is a change in the attitude of the Al-Esfer'n. Possibly they're still not personally involved but maybe they've decided to retaliate through those they can train," Rab'k suggested, mentioning the obvious.

Rena'x was pleased with this analysis.

Rab'k's suggestions are valid and insightful, considering his personal experience with Pet'r.

"So you believe these young people you've met, and engaged in at least one battle, are a beginning of the vanguard for the Al-Esfer'n?" Rena'x asked.

Rab'k looked at his father's strong features, deep in thought and realized why he admired him so much.

"I do. Their concentration and aggression certainly had a higher level of intensity than I've ever seen from any other south-lander. These three escaped and were aggressive when confronted. And, admittedly, they didn't lose," Rab'k shrugged, looking at Rena'x with expectations of condemnation. But Rena'x did not

95

react at once to Rab'k's admission, except to remain silent for a longer moment before speaking.

Rena'x revealed he knew Rab'k now possessed the Black Crystal. He knew it had disappeared when the battle near Voravia's had climaxed. He assumed Baalsa'n had wanted to use it that day and was only able to save it because of Rab'k proximity to the stone.

"You should feel no shame, Rab'k, for what occurred," Rena'x explained. "I believe Baalsa'n knew you all were surprised by the outcome of that first meeting; just as he was. As far as I know, he wasn't aware of these three. He was more upset Mano'n wasn't there than that the first battle was lost.

Before the fighting began, Baalsa'n placed the stone on the great pillar, but because of the surprise at the plateau, he sent the stone with you for safety. "You say this Pet'r had almost unbelievable strength and was quick, even quicker than you?" he asked.

"Yes. That was the most surprising thing about him. I am bigger and seemingly stronger, but I couldn't grapple with him. Whenever I thought I had a good grip on him, he would move and easily break free," Rab'k answered. "More than once, he was able to hold me in a compromised position against all my efforts to break free."

"I remember a human, Areb'l, in our forces. He was like that. I often used him to train my men in hand-to-hand fighting. He, as best I remember, never lost. Wily and strong, he kept to himself. I actually often suspected he was helping the victims of those wars escape, but never caught him. He certainly would have been sympathetic. I think his family died on Varkan."

"Where was the Ahar'n?" Rab'k asked. "Where was the Guardian all those years?"

"I don't know the answers to those questions," Rena'x answered. "But I believe it was delivered to this planet. I can only assume the Al-Esfer'n were able to get it away from Varkan. We believed that was the place it was created but were never certain.

It appears it wasn't in use for several of the later worlds we destroyed."

"Could this Areb'l have been the Guardian?" Rab'k said, wondering why the fighting prowess of that man and that of Pet'r were apparently so alike.

And why is the power of the Ahar'n more than that of the Crystal I have at my chest?

"I'm not certain Areb'l was the Guardian. No one could ever get close enough to him, nor ever spoke to him in private, as far as I know," Rena'x answered. "Since he always won all the fights he was involved in, there was no reason to maltreat him, nor was there anyone, or even a group, we would have considered sacrificing to his skills to discover the truth.

As to the power of the Ahar'n, the Esfer'n originally created it as a sacred amulet, holding the power of both houses. The Crystal was created by Baalsa'n at a much later date, a date after he began to conquer the others," Rena'x continued, patiently explaining each of his answers to his son. "I must assume the power of the orb has something to do with that circumstance."

"Can we defeat the Aerolan if the Ahar'n has been discovered?" Rab'k asked bluntly. "Can we win this war?"

"I believe we can. Baalsa'n's never lost. He is powerful enough assuming he isn't delayed. If delayed, the Al-Esfer'n may be able to build forces strong enough to offset that power. Kalbra'n personally has always avoided engaging in a war, but, if he were to do so, he is probably as powerful as Baalsa'n. I suspect Baalsa'n is concerned about that, so he is trying to press the issue now. No doubt he's immediate concern would be that those three young people were able to thwart a first attempt. That had to upset him," Rena'x answered, with nothing to hide.

Rab'k and Rena'x talked on into the night.

"So, father, why are you here?" Rab'k pushed harder. "Why were you cast out of Tynoc'l; why were you sent here?"

"After you and Voravia couldn't establish a power stand near her castle, Baalsa'n decided we would have to use a more standard attack mode. So, he sent me here to begin preparations for another effort and didn't want that to be hindered by the childish political arena that now has taken over Tynoc'l. Just too many people with leaders who have too little experience to believe anything could be accomplished there.

I think Baalsa'n deduced the things you and I have been discussing tonight. Now he knows he must fight to overcome the preparations he believes the Al-Esfer'n have made," Rena'x explained his thoughts about the future calmly. He felt confident Baalsa'n's forces would win.

"So, how ready are we to launch an attack," Rab'k asked.

"I just received more information from Baalsa'n. He recruited outlander troops from Ravelan. A general named "Monsh'a", a full force of Ravelan and an elite Maah'e squadron, 10,000 strong, are already camped near Voravia's castle. They were with us during the first invasion.

"We have some 20,000 troops trained and ready to go anytime we chose, or are commanded to do so. Of that number we have some 10,000 cavalry elite," Rena'x told him. "I want you to lead these forces over this pass and join with the Ravelan group. Then the combined force should be 40-50,000 strong. I believe there's no way for anyone to stand against that. But, if we wait too much longer, the Al-Esfer'n may be able to gather a like number of people. Though I believe none will have the skills of the Monsh'a's forces."

"But, sir, will Baalsa'n allow me to do this?" Rab'k puzzled, thinking of his recent failure. "He surely has no reason to trust me. I would be proud to lead this force. I've longed for this all my life but he may not allow it."

"I've already informed him I want you," Rena'x looked over at his son now pacing about the tent. "I still have an influence with him. He's angry, but you are his son and he wishes you to lead."

Rab'k whirled about, eyes flaring. "I'm not his son," he raised his voice, but didn't shout. He would never consider being disrespectful to Rena'x. "You are."

"I thank you, my son. But we both know the truth. You would be unwise to persist with your anger over this. Let's win this war and then it may be we can still be together. I've always hoped you would one day lead our tribe. Let's work toward that end," Rena'x admonished. "Anger, at this point, doesn't serve us well."

Rab'k turned about, almost lost in desire for all this to end. He stopped, opened the flaps to the entrance, looked back at the man he would always consider to be his father, and walked out into the moonlight.

He strode to the road leading up into the pass, turned and gazed out over the encampment. He could see the horse corrals just to the north, full of the proud and magnificent animals nurtured by the desert. He felt his passion renewed as he scanned the tents, the practice grounds, the might of the Wasteland, as the southerners called it, spread out before him.

I will do this. I'll lead my people to victory; it has always been my dream.

He raised his sword hand and shook it at the stars. He looked again at the pass, snow still shining in the moonlight and walked quickly to his tent.

"I will do this," he said, pushing his way into the tent. "This time I will not fail."

The next day promised no reprieve from the heat, but Rab'k was out early to inspect the forces Rena'x had gathered. He participated in some of the war training with the foot soldiers, laughing with some, using his great strength to beat up others and generally enjoying himself.

He hadn't felt this good in a while.

He went to inspect the cavalry, watched their rounds of deployment and inner team workings and expressed his admiration for the good work to the officers. He knew his future victories would depend a great deal on these troops. He felt comfortable assuming the southlanders had no knowledge of *horse warriors* – a separate army unto itself.

He arrived at his father's tent late that evening, excited and pleased by what he saw. He walked in, flopped down on some piled blankets to relax and smiled at Rena'x who looked up from his handwork, remained quiet and watched Rab'k closely.

"It was a good day," Rab'k opened, satisfied and happy. "You have done well."

Rena'x only smiled again, wove another layer into the whip he was plaiting. "I've done this a few times before," he said, almost winking at the young man's enthusiasm. "It's likely I've learned how to do it by now." Then he laughed when he saw Rab'k's face fall a bit.

"I've been training these men since before you arrived the first time. I missed you, my son, but I've been busy." Rena'x added.

"But where? There's no place in the desert. Where were all these men?" Rab'k asked, astonished.

"Well, if you remember you didn't stay long before you chased the Guardian up this very valley. I was afraid then he might take this way and find these troops hidden in the valley just to the west of here, tucked into a small valley. Apparently, in his haste, he didn't," Rena'x explained. "But, part of the reason for calling in all these tribes was to bring all the warriors from the outer reaches into one place. So, I had runners go to all the villages and had them send runners even further. To the sea borders of Aerolan, if necessary, to call in more.

Baalsa'n's plan to establish a new religion was part of that same plan; he felt a stronger reason than war would draw more recruits than a summons to fight. We, as a people, haven't been so successful in the south. There's always been a problem with being in that land; a problem we never quite understood. Maybe the Al-Esfer'n have been there all this time, but we're not certain of that.

So the people gathered, the mountain worships began and entire villages came with their young men. I trained you personally for this day," Rena'x paused. "You, for me, were so special and so strong I knew one day you would be called. Tomorrow, you lead our people to revenge our losses, to defeat and destroy the south-landers and their gods, the Al-Esfer'n."

Rab'k stood; he shook with excitement. He burned with hatred.

Tomorrow it will be done.

VARSPREE

Anisah found herself in the stable behind the Farlen's hotel in Varspree. She wasn't surprised she had unconsciously chosen this spot. She felt safe when she was here before.

Considering the infamy of Varspree, it seems strange to think that it's safer here than other places.

That visit seemed so long ago now. She wondered how she might be received if she went inside.

Or should I stay somewhere else. These people were so kind to me. I would hate to bring anything disruptive into their lives.

"Well, hello there. I thought you'd be in Tariny now," Col'n said, startling Anisah. She jumped and turned, feeling her new powers rising inside. But she held back, regained her composure and smiled.

"Col'n! I'm so happy to see you. I've missed talking to you. Here in the stable," she answered, waved her arm around the enclosure and laughed. "You're looking good. Is anything happening around here?"

She was trying to avoid talking about her life since she left.

"Well, not much. Was Esme gone when you were here? Wait, I remember you took her place until those guys came. Anyway, she's still not back. Why? Need your job back?" he asked.

She noticed he seemed very nonchalant about their conversation. When she didn't answer right away, Col'n added, "Guess I better get back to work." He strolled toward the stalls at the end.

Strange, wonder what's wrong. Col'n should be talking my ears off by now. Something is very wrong.

She decided to visit inside mainly because of Col'n's odd behavior.

"I'll see you later then," she yelled after him as he walked away.

She turned and walked to the familiar back door to the kitchen.

How often did I run through this door in those days.

She smiled and looked in through the screen. The hustle and bustle was evident. She didn't see Mercy but she assumed she was out in the dining hall. She pushed the door opened and stepped in.

"Who are you?" a woman grunted, disheveled blond hair stacked on top of her head. She was perspiring heavily. She turned back to the stove to flip some meat over. "What are you doing back here, Ma'm? The entry to the dining area is out front, you'll have to go around there to get in."

"No. No. I'm looking for Mistress Farlen. Is she back here today?

"Humph. I bet you are. Well, she's too busy for the likes of you. She doesn't mix with you hussies more than she has to. You still need to go around to the front," the woman shot back, obviously irritated with dealing with her.

She must think I'm one of the ladies of the evening. Wonder why? Though I'm probably dressed better than before, I wouldn't have thought I looked like that.

Anisah stood stunned for a moment, not knowing what to do next. Mercy suddenly burst into the room, carrying a huge load of trays and dishes. She walked to the sink area and dropped the lot into the water.

"Where's Col'n?" she asked the blond woman.

"He's out in the stable, said he had something to do," the cook answered.

"No, he doesn't. He's just hidin'. Again," Mercy answered and turned toward the back exit. She saw Anisah standing there.

"Excuse me, lady. May I ask what you're doing here?" Mercy frowned at her, raked her hair out of her face, and then stared. "Anisah?"

"Yes, thought I'd come by and see how things are going," Anisah answered, laughing. "Seems the same."

Mercy stunned, looked at her a moment longer. Then she burst out laughing, walked across the room and gave Anisah a big hug, raising her off the floor in her exuberance.

"Oh, Anisah. It's so good to see you," Mercy held Anisah at arm's length. "It's so good. Please sit over here and we'll talk a minute. That's about all I've got. Where've you been? What's happened all these days you've been gone?"

She stopped, looking stern. "Did them boys treat you okay? Are they here too? Look at you, all pretty and dressed up. Not like that first time, Eh? Where're you going? Surely you didn't plan to come to Varspree this time."

Anisah held up her hand. "Mercy, you've got to slow down a little. The boys were more than gentlemen. A lot of things have happened, but we can talk about that later. If you need to get back out there," she nodded her head toward that familiar swinging door, "go ahead. I'm not going anywhere. If I can stay here."

"Are you in trouble?" Mercy looked straight into her eyes.

"Not exactly. But the story is too long for right now. We can talk later," Anisah answered. "Is Mistress Farlen around?"

"Well, yes. But she's terribly heartbroken," Mercy answered. "She's not the same. She's so sad., right now."

"Why?" Anisah sat up, wanting to know what happened.

"There was two men came in about three, or four, weeks after you left. Came asking for you. Mr. Farlen, he denied you were ever here. They grabbed him, even while there were still customers in the hall, pulled him over the bar, beat him and broke his leg. But he told them nothing," Mercy gasped out her tale.

"They also told him – 'Tell that girl Sumt'r will get her yet' – as they left. Mary heard 'em say that. She's the new girl." Mercy turned and pointed at the cook. "She was helping me clean up and witnessed the whole thing. Mr. Farlen hurting real bad. He's upstairs in the room you stayed in. Ms. Farlen's with him."

Anisah couldn't believe what she was hearing.

Sumt'r? After all this time? I guess he tracked me down by asking every-where — and finally thought I was here. But I wasn't. Can there be any more trouble in my life. I've got to go up and see about Mr. Farlen. Then I should make a call on my old friend Sumt'r.

"Oh Mercy. I didn't know. I'm so sorry to hear this. I'll run right up and see him now. He's such a wonderful man to protect me like that. I'll come down and talk to you later," she said, as she ran toward and up the stairs. Mercy, her mouth open to tell more, just waved, turned and took more food into the dining hall.

As Anisah walked through the halls, she paused briefly and looked up at the opening to the loft where Pet'r and Geth'n had lived when they arrived ages ago. Or, at least, it seemed long ago. She wiped tears from her eyes. Tears for memories of their sim-pler beginnings, stood quietly only a moment longer, then contin-ued on to her old room.

"Oh, Mr. Farlen. I'm so sorry this happened to you," she entered the room and ran to his side, smiled at Mistress Farlen, bent over and hugged the badly injured man laying in the bed.

All she could see were bandages wrapping almost his entire body. He lay on his right side and his left leg was raised slightly on a pillow, his toes protruding from the wrappings. His arms were both covered and there were heavy bands of cloth around his abdomen. He seemed to be asleep, but then she noticed his eyes moving as he watched her talk.

"So. Anisah, where have you been?" Mistress Farlen, looking around at her, the pain and misery obvious in her eyes. "We have worried about you since you ran off with those boys."

"Well, my life certainly hasn't been dull. Those boys are work-ing hard to get a big project started. By the way, I did not run off with them," she pouted, then laughed. "They're out trying to get some help for some big problems we've discovered. Not certain what we can do, and we've had a rocky start."

That needs to be kept somewhat private for a while.

105

"But more importantly, I'm so sorry for Mr. Farlen's injuries. What can I do now. Is there anything I can do to help?" she asked, not wanting to dwell on what her plans were.

"I don't know. I'm so tired now I can hardly stay awake," Ms Farlen answered sluggishly, eyes red and drooping.

"I think I could help by giving you time to sleep then," Anisah offered. "Why don't you go lay down in Mercy's bed and see if you can take a short nap."

"That would be wonderful," Ms. Farlen's eyes drifted up to look into Anisah's. "I don't think I can go any further without rest. Erlen, I means Mr. Farlen, needs to be turned about every 2 hours. The time is almost up, needs about 15 more minutes. You have to place him on his back for the next turn. When I asked him earlier if the turning hurt him any, he nodded his head – so maybe you could be real easy on him. That'd be nice of you."

Anisah noticed that Ms Farlen hadn't mentioned what happened, so she didn't. She could talk to Mercy this evening. She decided she should probably stay here for several days, especially since she had now decided Sumt'r needed to be stopped.

I would've never thought Sumt'r could find me. He's a stupid, wicked man and needs to be punished for all he's done to Mr. Farlen. And I will deal with that later.

"You go get some rest. I'll wake you when I turn Mr. Farlen later. You obviously need the sleep." Anisah suggested. "I'll be very careful when I help him."

"Thank you, my dear. This was so strange. Erlen has no enemies, but a lot of friends. Many of them have helped a great deal, but, when all is said and done, we have to take care of our own," Ms Farlen added, as she rose slowly and walked over to Mercy's bed and almost fell into it. She was asleep in an instant.

Anisah sat, looking out the window she so often gazed out of before when she wished she could be something else and wished she could help more people have a comfortable life. Now she thought about the Healing College and wondered if she had any talents to actually perform the tasks to be a healer.

As she pondered these things, her vision began to blur as though she was about to go to sleep, but she wasn't that tired. Slowly an image rose in the mist clouding her view of the room.

She is watching the children. The same children she dreamed about before. The dream where she used the Ahar'n. She wants to reach out, hold them and cure their diseases. She can sense she is reaching toward them; her hands out before her. She can feel the energy flow from her slowly; sees it touching the bodies of the young, sees them improve so quickly it has to be magic.

As the images floated away, she realized she was staring at the man lying on the bed

"Are you gonna turn Mr. Farlen pretty soon," Mercy walked through the door, talking. "I've come to help you do that then I gotta get back downstairs to clean up that mess."

Then she looked over at Mr. Farlen. He was moving on his own, trying to wriggle out of some of the bandaging and mumbling something about the bother of having them wrapped around him.

"My lord, he seems a lot better. What happened to him, he can move around some," Mercy exclaimed.

Anisah's eyes leaped open when Mercy spoke. She jumped out of her seat and stared even harder at Mr. Farlen to see what Mercy was talking about and couldn't believe what was happening.

Mr. Farlen was leaning up on one elbow, trying to tear the bandages from his head with his other hand, mumbling and grunting through the bandages. Mercy ran to him to calm him.

Anisah was quickly beside her, trying to help.

"Wait. Wait. You must be careful, sir," Mercy was talking to Mr. Farlen to calm him.

He managed to pull some of the bandaging away from his mouth.

"I'm not hurting anymore. Don't you understand! I'm fine. I feel okay. Would you please get these bandages off me!" Mr. Farlen blurted out as he uncovered his mouth. "The only thing that hurts is my leg. I think it is still broken. But, and I don't know why, nothing else hurts!"

"All right, sir. Just a moment and we'll get you out of these bandages," Anisah told him as she held his arms, trying to keep him from fighting her. "Mercy, why don't you go get Mr. Farlen some clothes so we can get him dressed. Wake Ms. Farlen. She will want to be here, too."

Mercy ran out of the room.

Anisah was holding Mr. Farlen tightly, but he was impatient to clear away the rest of his bindings. She looked him in the eyes. They were a little wild but nothing seemed to indicate there was any madness with this sudden change.

What could have happened? Why is he seemingly healed? Where did this miracle come from? There were no noises, no evident change from when I first came in, no unusual happening here, or anywhere, that I recall.

But wait, I had my vision of healing again. Just before he woke, fighting. Could it have been me? The Ahar'n isn't here, so there must be something else. But what?

Mercy and Ms Farlen burst into the room. Ms Farlen was frantic and rushed to her husband's side.

"Erlen. Are you all right? Do you hurt? Where do you hurt? What happened? Can I help you? Talk to me?" Ms Farlen's questions came rapid-fire, not actually giving Mr. Farlen a chance to answer any of them.

Anisah moved back away from the Farlens and Mercy. They were excited and happy about this sudden change of events, but she was apprehensive.

She didn't understand what, or how, this happened. Though she was glad to see Mr. Farlen was so much better so quickly, she was worried. It frightened her.

If I am the reason for these changes, I have no idea how I did it. If these powers I'm discovering happen without my thinking, then I may have a problem controlling them. What am I to do?

Meanwhile, Mr. Farlen sat up awkwardly; the bandages were still wrapped around him from waist to toe. He held himself up with one of his arms and grinned.

"Honey," he told his wife, "I feel much better. I'd say I'm fine. But I think my leg is still not so good. There's lots of pain there, but everything else seems fine. The bruises in my upper body seemed to be healed. I don't know why. I don't know how. But I'm much better than I was just an hour ago," he spoke slowly, catching his breath after fighting to get the bandages from around his face. "This does seem to be a miracle."

"Anisah! You're here. When did you get here? Where have you been?" Mr. Farlen shouted at here, waving his arms for her to come near him. She walked over smiling and, hesitantly, hugged him. She and Mr. Farlen hadn't really been friendly when she had worked here before, but he had always been fair. He seemed glad to see her, despite being injured trying to protect her and, curiously, apparently not remembering her arrival just a moment earlier.

"I'm so sorry what happened to you, sir. Those men were part of the gang who, if you remember, kidnapped me before I came before. They must be searching for me. I know I made them pretty angry with me back then. But I never expected them to find out where I was hiding," she began to apologize.

He pushed her back with his free hand just a bit and answered, "You have no reason to apologize to me. I've had trouble here before, and been injured by some other japes like them. But, I believe I never admitted you were here, so hopefully, they won't come back. I actually don't need to get beat up again," He laughed, then grabbed his side where there was still pain. "I think I need to lay down. But, I'm hungry. Who is tending the restaurant? Not Mary, by herself?"

He lay down, chuckling. "Get busy! Get back to work – all of you!" He even pointed at Anisah, then laughed again.

He looked quickly at Mercy and his wife, both were stunned by these changes. But they jumped up and started for the door, stopped and looked back at him and left the room laughing and giggling they were so happy.

"Well, girl. You need to help if you will. Hell, good helps still hard to find," he spoke softly, but she could tell he did need her to help.

"Yes, sir. But are you sure you'll be all right? I can stay if you need me to." she asked, still wondering if she had anything to do with all that happened in the last few minutes.

"I'm fine. Really. We can talk about what happened later. I think I'll take a nap, still feel weak," he was already nodding into sleep, but he smiled at her. "It's really good to see you back."

Anisah didn't want to mention she was running from capture again. It didn't seem to be the right time for that. She ran downstairs and out into the restaurant. There was mayhem; so many people had completed their meals and dishes were stacked everywhere on the tables and the floor. There was almost no room to sit new customers.

She ran to the first table, grabbed a couple of stacks of dishes, hoisted them onto her arms, turned, ran to the kitchen entrance, turned just enough, bumped the doors open with her bottom, and delivered them to one of the sinks.

Col'n had returned and, when he saw her blast her way into the room, a big smile stretched across his face.

"Welcome back," he shouted and turned back to his chore of washing all these new dishes. Mary was throwing things onto the grill and stripping the cooked items off into plates and bowls as fast as she could.

Mercy bounced the door open and rushed to pick some of the prepared dishes off the washboard, turned and pushed her way back out. As she passed Anisah with her load, she only nodded and smiled at her. It had been a while since she had seen food dribbled down Anisah's pretty dress and she chuckled at that.

Anisah smiled too as she drop her dishes into the sink with a great clatter, turned and ran back out into the dining area. She again grabbed more of the dirty items from the closest table, turned and ripped back through the kitchen doors.

She did this for about an hour. She was exhausted from the rushing about, but all the while thinking about what happened upstairs. She now was convinced she was responsible – but still didn't know how. While she worked, she considered all that had been revealed and all that had happened.

How did I do that? Is there danger in using my powers? Can my father trace me with these quick and surprising outbursts? Oh, I hope not, I hope not.

And what am I going to do about Sumt'r. I have to do something. He and his men will certainly continue to come here looking for me.

When the last customers left, she cleaned the table, took the dishes back into the kitchen and plopped down at the side table where Mary was already sitting. Mary's hair was soaking wet from her exertion and she looked exhausted, too.

"By the way, my name's Mary. Sorry about my first greeting. But we get a lot of those tramps parading through the back door just to get upstairs and do their business. I don't know why the Farlens put up with that. But it ain't none of my business. I'm just glad I got this job," Mary introduced herself. "I can tell by the way you were working, you've done this before. A good job. Sure helped out today."

"Well, I actually worked here not long ago. That's the reason Mercy knew me. I left to go to Tariny but had to come back here because of some problems I've been having. Nothing serious ac-

111

tually, just something to avoid," Anisah explained, she didn't really know this woman and wasn't about to say too much.

"I can understand that. We all have our little secrets we need to keep. I stay away from alcohol because I talk too much when I get drunk. I try hard not to screw things up here," Mary responded. "These seem like good people – the Farlens."

"They are. The best. In fact, I can't believe Mr. Farlen had to defend me. That's a very long story I might be able to tell you in the future. But at this moment, I know I'm tired and need some rest. I imagine you and Mercy are probably in the same shape. So I suggest we all have a short evening and just go to bed. What do you think, Mercy?" Anisah answered, watching as Mercy and Ms. Farlen dragged themselves over to another table nearer the door and falling into the nearest chair available. "Time for bed?"

"Amen to that," Mercy wore a long face, but she tried to smile. Ms. Farlen who had been up long nights watching over her husband lay her head on the table and fell asleep without saying a word.

"We need to take this lady upstairs and tuck her in, I believe. Can you help, Anisah? I'll get you into a room upstairs when we're done.

Thanks again, Mary. You did a great job keeping up with the craziness tonight. We just got too far behind while we attended Mr. Farlen, but it's so good he's better," Mercy said, listing all the things needing completion.

She looked at Anisah as she said the last, a certain look Anisah didn't quite understand. A very quizzical look.

"Yes. Of course, I'll help. Is there anything else needing attention down here?" Anisah asked, looking around. Everything seemed clean and straight. "Ms. Farlen will certainly notice if there's something not right."

"I suspect Ms. Farlen doesn't really care right now. Mr. Farlen's sudden recovery probably made her day," Mercy answered, obviously tired and needing to rest. "I've already locked everything and I'm ready to end this day myself."

She shook Ms. Farlen who raised her head slowly, sleep covering her face.

"Let's go to bed now, Ms Farlen. Everything's all right," Mercy talked slowly and softly. "Anisah and I are going to take you upstairs and check on Mr. Farlen for you. But, he's probably just fine. You can look in on him in the morning, bright and early."

She and Anisah helped Ms. Farlen stand. Mary and Col'n plodded up the steps, they followed. They took Ms Farlen to her room, removed her outer clothing and laid her softly in her bed. She actually never really woke during the entire trip.

They went down the hallway to Mr. Farlen's room. He looked so much better without all the bandaging. He was asleep and seemed to be doing well, so they crept out of the room, closing the door behind.

"Do you and I need to talk? I mean, about Mr. Farlen's miracle," Mercy asked Anisah as they walked toward their rooms. "I'll put you in the room just beyond our old room, but I needed to ask you that question."

"Maybe we do. But not tonight because I have to think about it myself. I have a major task to attend to tomorrow. I'm going to deal with Sumt'r and his gang," Anisah said, indicating she was attending several issues herself. "But, you and I will sit down tomorrow and I'll tell you what I know. If you're interested, where I've been and what I've done since I left."

"Fair enough. Thanks again for your help today and, I believe, for what you did for the Farlens," Mercy said, laughing and holding her hand up when Anisah turned to say something else. "Tomorrow is soon enough. If I didn't say it before, it's good to see you again. Maybe you are good for something"

She laughed, turned and walked away to her room.

Anisah watched Mercy leave. She was tired and saw no reason to sit and worry about the details of the odd circumstances surrounding Mr. Farlen's recovery tonight. Besides she probably didn't have any answers.

She prepared for bed, lay down, fell asleep immediately, and dreamed.

Anisah, you are doing well. You did help Mr. Farlen today. You have an inner strength we never anticipated, you have power beyond our imagining.

We hope you will learn to use it wisely. There is not much we can do to help you in this. We have no one who holds this kind of power with us. Kalbra'n may be able to, but he is watching Baalsa'n too closely and can't leave that duty.

It may be you are able to modify anything simply by thinking you should. Be very careful, you need to use good judgment.

But we believe every time you activate your power, you send signals out. Be cautious for there are others looking for you. Others who have the power to follow these signals. Mano'n is following you.

Be prepared for him to show himself at any time.

Below in the dark, two small beings worked their way to the edge of the main street from behind a building across from the hotel.

"Is shes there?" Kesk asked. He peered into the night, looking at every window in the hotel to try and discover the one they were searching for. He warily looked back and forth from the windows to his companion.

"Maybe wes can kills her."

"But hows do yous knows shes be there, Mord? I donts understand how yous know." came the obvious question from the other.

"I dos not knows, but we has to finds this red-haired girls soon. Lady Voravia wils not bes happy, if wes fails. We wils kill this evils girl."

114

The morning sun peeked through Anisah's window the next morning., waking her when the first light touched her face. She felt rested, rose to the side of the bed, sat and thought about her dream.

So. That confirms my fears. I must be more careful. But Mr. Farlen needed my help and I'm glad I was able to provide it. But I have to be a bit cautious about Mercy's inquiries. I wouldn't want to expose her by giving her too much information that might put her in danger. And I need to deal with Sumt'r. Soon. Today is a day to start.

She rose, dressed, went downstairs and offered to help. Mercy insisted everything was under control and, though she appreciated Anisah's help, she thought Anisah needed to deal with a few other things. She winked at Anisah when she mentioned the last.

"So. Tell me, Mercy. Where would lowlifes be found in Varspree. I assume I have to start at the bottom of the barrel," Anisah asked, looking as innocent as possible.

Mercy laughed at Anisah's expression.

"Well, I'd try the Queen's Ransom. Down on Margin Street, about three, or four, streets off the road toward the Tariny. I've always tried to avoid those places down there, but I hear stories. Some not so nice, not even good. There is nothing of any value to talk about in reference to those who reside there," Mercy added, feeling she was now part of an intrigue that might provide something more interesting than gossip. "What do you plan to do?"

"That's where I'm going to start my search for my good friend, Sumt'r. Maybe I can make his day a bit better," Anisah answered. Her face now set with a look of determination. "I should have attended to this problem before, but I've been a little busy."

She shook her head when Mercy opened her mouth to ask her

115

what she had been busy doing. Mercy relented. Anisah knew Mercy was being driven mad with curiosity.

"You'll probably know – through word-of-mouth – how this goes. I may have to leave again afterward, but I'll try to come back and talk to you about all of this. Can't promise that, but I'll try," Anisah added.

She turned and walked out the back way to the stables. Col'n was forking hay to the horses. She stopped and waited for him to finish one of the stalls.

"Col'n, do you know anything about the Queen's Ransom?" she asked him, recognizing men have an entirely different view of places where men usually lingered.

He stopped his work, turned slowly, looking at her sideways for a moment.

"Why do you need to know?" he asked, now looking at her with a frown wrinkling his brow. "Kind of a dangerous place. I don't go down there, but I've a few friends who have. They came away a little worse off than when they went in. Lot of really bad people there, some all the time. They'd just as soon kill you as not, especially if they believe they can take something of value from you," Col'n answered her, but with hesitation. "Why?"

She knew he was being cautious, being protective. He was a bit older now than when they first met. He still had the boyish grin, but there were some hard lines around his face now. She assumed he'd been in a few rough places himself since before.

"Well, I've got an enemy. The same man who kidnapped me before is the same man who sent his gang members here to harm Mr. Farlen while looking for me. They didn't even try to hide what they were doing. But, I need to do something to stop them before they repeat that," she told him, watching his reaction.

"Anisah, I understand what you think you are doing, but this idea is dangerous, very dangerous. Men of that part of town will not hesitate to harm you – in too many ways. You shouldn't go down there alone. Let me gather some friends and I'll go with

116

you. Let me tell Mercy I'm going," Col'n dropped his pitchfork, brushed his hands on his trousers, turned and started for the door.

"Col'n. No," she reached for his arm, stopping him. "I can handle this. Much more easily than you know. But I can only thank you now for your offer. I'll let you know I'm all right later."

Col'n seemed disappointed, but Anisah didn't want to endanger him, or his friends, when the stakes were this high.

She gave him a strong hug and walked around the hotel to the street. The street brought back memories of that first time she came into town. She and her horse both were upset about being around so many people and she had fortunately stumbled, literally, into the Farlen's hotel where she found safety with good people.

She stepped out a few steps, looking down the street toward the west. She, Geth'n and Pet'r had traveled that road on their journey toward Tariny. She didn't remember anything about the start of that trip now, looking back in time. The three were only interested in their destinations; only interested in becoming what they had dreamed of and only mildly intrigued with getting there.

But, she did remember Pet'r left them to go northward when they got to the Tariny wide-way. She still felt some pain in that parting though she saw him briefly later when he rescued her and Geth'n from Voravia.

All that seemed to be so long ago. What she was, and knew now, came suddenly back to her. She turned onto the street and walked with special intent toward Margin Street and her date with Sumt'r.

He's probably going to be surprised to see me. Oh, Pet'r, I wish you could be here to help me.

MANO'N

He couldn't believe what just happened. Anisah had, using her own power, stopped both Voravia and him from capturing her. She disposed of Voravia without effort.

He had no idea where Voravia went. His concern now was Baalsa'n who was not going to be pleased with the events today.

Mano'n, thinking he needed to follow Anisah, concentrated and sensed the direction Anisah took when she vanished.

Tariny? Curious. Why?

He too disappeared, his destination – Tariny. He reappeared in the city, a few blocks from the education centers.

The Healing College? Probably. But why here? I doubt she's had time to begin any studies since she left Caliste. She's only been gone a few months. After she reached Varspree, I know she worked in that inn. But then she disappeared and I've wondered where she went?

Mano'n walked to the front of the college and observed the archway.

Why here? Why does she need to be here. She obviously has gained enough power to have no further need for scholarship – even her healing ambitions have been more than satisfied, based on what I've witnessed recently.

He shook his head, looked up and down the street.

"I might as well try something else. I can't go in here anyway. I'm certain there are safeguards to prevent me from entering. The building is probably protected by a spell," he mumbled, pausing only a moment. "But I'll need to start watching these three young people more closely."

He waved his hand in a broad sweep over the front of the building. "I'll just set an alarm of my own, so I'll know when she is leaving."

He turned and walked toward the inner city. He had toned his costume to match that of a businessman in the city, his simple robe flowing out behind him as he pondered the reason the girl had chosen to come back to Tariny.

Why would she come here? Voravia mentioned Anisah was captured with someone – a young man of no great power – and was rescued by another with overwhelming strength. The two young men rescued her from that idiot Rab'k, as well as all Voravia's own odd men she could muster.

Where did they get this power?

He turned down another street and headed away for the western gate, thinking he may need to go to the center of the city and start there.

Voravia believed the physical one was the Guardian of the Ahar'n. Why would the Al-Esfer'n have chosen an adolescent as their champion? I believe I remember the Ahar'n is hidden somewhere on this planet, but why? But she did say he had the amulet with him-so is it possible it has been retrieved by this boy?

What are the Al-Esfer'n doing? Are they actually intending to protect this planet? Actually preparing to defend and win the salvation of this lot of their monstrous creations? I remember they ran us away centuries ago, but it is inevitable we will win this simple fight and crush these people and their puny planet?

But my problem is not these fools; my problem is Anisah. Where did she meet these hooligans? What is their game? The girl escaping is bad enough. I have to worry about Baalsa'n's concerns about her too. He's going to learn she has developed some of her powers on her own, and it'll occur to him I have failed to both teach her properly and have her in tow by now.

He walked into the library area and suddenly sensed the girl had been there. Not that she had performed any magic but that she visited seemed unusual.

What could she have been looking for? I have to go in here and ask around about her.

He halted, looked around and modified his attire to make him-

119

self seem more scholarly. In fact, he made himself appear to be one of the ministers at the Transunion University. He walked into the halls with all the pomp of one who believes he knows a great deal.

He approached the entry desk to make his inquiry. The young lady was busy but did look up. He noticed her eyes widened a bit as though in alarm, but he avoided letting her know his awareness. She broadcast a small amount of power, but then many citizens of the city did. He wasn't certain why, but undoubtedly with so many from Aerolan coming to this, their largest city, it was likely there were those with inherent power who were unaware of it, walking in and out of public buildings. He ignored it.

"Excuse me. I'm looking for a young lady, about so tall," he held his hand about shoulder high, "she was supposed to meet me in front of the library, but I've been waiting for a while. So I thought maybe she might have come into the building since it's quite warm out," Mano'n said, smiling at the young woman. "Maybe you've seen her passing by."

"No, sir. I must admit I don't talk to everyone coming in, but I've noticed no ladies, young or old, coming in today. Maybe it's too early. The ladies often have meetings in the smaller conference rooms, but generally during the latter part of the day. Perhaps you could describe her a little more," the girl suggested, still looking at him with a certain suspicion obvious in her eyes.

"As I said, she's about that tall, wears dark colored clothing most of the time, very long dark hair and, if I may say so, is quite a pretty young lady," Mano'n answered. "By the way, I've been interested in acquiring a bit of data on the early years of Tariny. Could you suggest an area that might give me a broad view about the city? I can check on that while I wait."

"Will the young lady know you're in the library, sir?" the receptionist asked.

"Of course, we were to meet here for the research I just mentioned," Mano'n answered. He was trying to avoid too much discussion; he had no need to be readily identified.

"Well, sir. If you want you might leave her name with me and I'll let her know in which part of the building you'll be," the young lady said. She pulled forth a small note pad to write upon and looked up at him expectantly.

"I suppose so. Her name is Anisah," Mano'n said. The girl instantly glanced down at the pad, as though surprised, then wrote the name quickly, and looked back at Mano'n with an exaggerated smile.

This girl knows the name, or she knows someone who has mentioned it before. She's definitely startled by that recognition.

"Your name, my dear. What is your name. I shall commend you to your supervisor for your helpfulness," Mano'n needed to know whom this girl was. He felt she might provide a clue to Anisah's whereabouts.

"Thank you, sir. My name is Siarra. The area you are asking about is down that hallway," she stood and pointed to her left, "and you should find your information in the third reference room on your right. If the young lady comes, I'll direct her to where you are.

Things are in turmoil in another area with some more information about Tariny and Aerolan. Someone visited the area recently and attempted to destroy quite a few documents. The staff is working on restoration so that area is unavailable at this time. Possibly you could revisit later; the cleanup was promised to be completed in a few more days, next week would be a better time to visit," Siarra added.

"That's terrible. Why would anyone do such a thing? What were the general classifications for the manuscripts in that area?" Mano'n felt he needed to know that answer; he was uncertain why, but he followed his intuition.

"Legends, myths and mystical histories," Siarra answered. "The strangest part is the area only held ancient documents. The recovery is taking quite a while."

121

"That's interesting. Why would anyone want to bother with those subjects?" Mano'n asked, realizing this was an unusual occurrence.

Why would anyone want the information in those books? Why would anyone go to the trouble to expose him or herself? Who could it have been? I can think of only one person who might find that information useful and who would be familiar with these tomes existence – Rab'k. That idiot would reveal our intentions chasing after information that probably isn't available in this place. Damn him. That may be the reason for this girl's reactions; he probably dressed as I am.

"I'm sure I don't know, sir. But it was a tragic and malicious act," the girl agreed.

"Well, I think I'll check the area you mentioned to try to find my information and, again, I appreciate your helpfulness," Mano'n said, nodded his head to her. He slowed before entering the hall she recommended. As he reached it, he glanced back at the girl. She ducked her head to avoid eye contact.

So there is recognition. I've asked about something unusual. Rab'k is becoming a serious nuisance.

He stepped through the door to the conference room, observed there was no one there and disappeared.

He reappeared a moment later outside the Healer's College. Wary of discovery if he ventured to close to the building, he decided to walk around it casually. He could sense the sensory protection emanating from it.

He covered almost the entire block of streets surrounding the building and decided he would walk as close to the front entry as possible. As he rounded the last corner, he walked across the street from the main entrance. He noticed the archway and, on the front door, a large clapper – apparently to be used by guest to give signal of their arrival.

The clapper! I sense Anisah touched that not so long ago. So she did arrive. I thought my suggestions to her of the existence of the place would lead her here. I wonder if she has been here recently. But, I dare not approach it.

I'll be exposed and maybe harmed by the spell, I can feel it repelling me. A gift of the Al-Esfer'n, I imagine. They would protect places where care is given to strangers and certainly are interested in protecting their new protégé.

But, she isn't here now. There is no evidence she has been for a while.

So my next best possibility is Varspree, I think I'll have to go and discover if she has returned.

He looked in all directions, validated the streets were clear, changed his clothing back to what he was most comfortable with and disappeared.

From a window overlooking the street in front of the College, young eyes noticed the strange man's actions. She was amazed when he modified his clothing and shocked when he disappeared.

She decided she might not inform Ms. Sanderol about what she saw. It might be important to save that for a later day. Alesan decided she wouldn't tell her friend Mira either.

It was none of their business she knew the man. Intimately.

She turned away from the window and walked slowly down the hallway to her next class.

RESCUE

Geth'n proceeded cautiously. He had no need to meet Voravia's minions; his purpose today was to try to discover the whereabouts of the Ahar'n.

As he strode along, he noticed the land was barren to the west of the road, more desolate than he remembered from his earlier trip with Anisah. The terrain reminded him of his fearful dream from ages ago.

That was a forlorn experience. The place of those dreams was too ridiculous to believe, but this area seems eerily familiar.

He shook his head and stopped staring into the wasteland and walked ahead looking only to his right – into the wooded area to the east of the road.

Suddenly he heard a disturbance ahead of him. He trotted forward cautiously, looking over the embankment occasionally to determine the source. Then he saw a man, clothed in rags fighting with some beings that looked very much like Voravia's odd men, but seemed more orderly and alert. The man was covered in the soot and ashes from the west side of the road. Geth'n decided the man had run across the road to have more cover in the woods, but was caught by these beings, who were obviously professional soldiers, before he could reached the safety of the trees.

That's strange. Where did they come from? Who are they? Possibly the man fighting them has that answer. I need to help him, if I can.

He held his arms out toward the group and was about to send a surge of power toward them when he noticed someone else rushing down from the road section just north of him. This new person seemed intent on attacking the creature group, he was smashing through the forest, knocking things aside with urgency. It was a man, a young man, who was not hesitating in his ap-

124

proach.

Oh no, it's Pet'r! What does he think he's doing? He's going to get himself killed! I have to stop him!

Before Geth'n could react, Pet'r leaped into the air and fell among the fighters. He swatted the attackers right and left, trying desperately to reach the man being victimized. He grabbed the last being and threw it away. The rest of the attackers paused, looked at each other and then ran, not wanting to engage this powerful man.

They disappeared into the trees. As they ran away, Pet'r noticed there was something different about them. He recalled fighting with Voravia's odd men on several occasions and noted this group seemed more muscular, more alert and more ferocious than her people They seemed to be stronger than before as though trained for fighting.

What's different? This can't be good; this is not a good omen.

Pet'r turned, wanting to help the stranger and make certain he wasn't hurt, when the man attacked him with his staff, smashing it across Pet'r's shoulders.

Pet'r grabbed the man's hand extended to apply the blow, lifted and twirled him around in the air, and clasped his arms around him.

"Hold, my friend, I mean you no harm," Pet'r spoke, from behind the struggling man, in a mild voice. "I think you're safe now, so you need to stop fighting."

The other stopped, calmed and relaxed. Pet'r lowered him to his feet and released him, though prepared to grab the man again if he fought. Pet'r recognized the other was a military man who knew how to fight, if needed, or he wouldn't have been able to hold off those creatures attacking him, for as long as he did.

The man lowered his staff, placing the end on the ground and turned slowly to look at his rescuer. Pet'r began to smile.

"Acron'n! What are you doing here?" Pet'r asked, grabbing and shaking the man's hand. "Why are you on this road?. I thought

125

you were going to Tariny to warn Garv'n about the desert people?"

"Well, Pet'r . . . It is Pet'r, right?" Acron'n began. He was injured, blood flowed down his cheek from a head wound and he moved his right arm gingerly, winced and reached over with the other hand and pushed his shoulder back and forth slowly.

He grunted on one push and lowered his hand. He shrugged his shoulders, winced again, but seem to be able to move it freely.

"Well, that'll take a few days to heal," he muttered.

"Yes. It will. What are you doing on this road so near Voravia's lands? It's dangerous here and getting worse," Pet'r asked. He assumed Acron'n was not injured too severely or he wouldn't be moving his arms.

"I might ask you the same," Acron'n looked over at Pet'r. "The last time I saw you, you were '*just searching for answers*' but I thought at the time, going the wrong way and probably going to discover those answer would be bad ones."

"Well, I've had some interesting experiences, but, more importantly, what happened to you? As I remember you were trying to reach Lord Garv'n to warn him about a battle to come." Pet'r said, not revealing too much information for the moment.

"'Tis true. But, I was waylaid after I left the river valley up there," He pointed north back along the road leading from the Vranilla River valley. "Got caught by a bunch of these vermin." He motioned toward the departing soldiers.

"I was taken to an encampment of these things and they were different. They were orderly and organized, even had a leader. He was smart and, I thought, treacherous and strong."

"That doesn't sound like Voravia's group. Most of her people are a bit addled. Mostly bumpkins with little ability to think for themselves," Pet'r was thinking aloud now. He pointed his left hand in the direction the odd men had run. "I'll have to track them to determine where they're going and what they are planning."

"Well, I can tell you where they are. I just don't know why. They're hiding in that valley there," Acron'n said, pointing toward the northeast.

Then he reached up and rubbed the side of his head. "One of those boys cracked my head hard enough to make me dizzy, not feeling very well right now," he said, frowning.

"We probably need to see to that," Pet'r cautioned. "I don't think you're injured too badly, but you probably do need some rest. Besides, we need to talk about my *answers.*"

"Something I might be interested in, you think?" Acron'n asked. He stretched his shoulder again and motioned for Pet'r to lead the way.

"No doubt. I suspect Lord Garv'n may be in trouble," Pet'r answered. "Come, let's go down to that stream I see below. We can camp there for the night."

"Aren't you concerned those friendly fellows might return?" Acron'n looked around, still suspicious of his surroundings.

"They don't like the dark," Pet'r answered, without hesitation. Apparently something familiar to him.

Acron'n looked at the man and noticed there was significant difference in his composure and attitude from when they last met. Pet'r was not the same man as before. There were obvious differences, very significant. He wondered about the cause.

This new man, this Pet'r, is a warrior of supreme skills and one no one should have for an enemy.

Meanwhile, Geth'n had jumped from the edge of the road, himself heading toward the fighting. He was afraid to send any force into the middle of the melee for fear of hurting Pet'r, but he couldn't let Pet'r try to rescue the man alone.

Just as he broke through the undergrowth, he saw Pet'r launch himself into the middle of the conflict.

Oh no! What is he doing? Pet'r, get away. Stop!

He ran faster. He had to look at the ground often to avoid falling so he didn't see what was happening, but he kept pushing

127

through the growth, working toward the fight.

Finally he felt it safe to look up, thinking he was going to see Pet'r lying on the ground. But, then he slowed and stopped, amazed.

Pet'r single-handedly fought all of the soldiers at once, throwing them about like loose lumber. They were helpless against his onslaught.

Geth'n couldn't believe it. He hadn't seen Pet'r in a while. He was too busy to notice what Pet'r was doing at the first battle, but this display of strength reminded Geth'n of that long ago fight with the outlaws who tried to kidnap them on the road from Larilla.

The man who was in flight and fighting for his life, stopped his feeble attempts and watched as Pet'r drove away his attackers. He only stood and watched in awe.

Geth'n approached with caution, looking all about for the odd men Pet'r had manhandled with such ease. They all had disappeared into the forest. When he got close enough, he spoke.

"Pet'r. Pet'r, it's me. Geth'n," he spoke in a normal voice. He held up his hands to ward off any attack, remembering how tense Pet'r had been with fighting the outlaws and didn't really need to defend himself against his friend.

Pet'r whirled, fists cocked. But then he broke out in laughter. The other man jumped back, raising his staff again.

"Geth'n! Thank the gods you're not injured. I've worried about both of you and Anisah since the battle. What happened to us? Why did we go to other places?" Pet'r was obviously excited by this reunion. He grabbed his friend and hugged him with a little more vigor than Geth'n could handle.

"Pet'r, please put me down. I'm doing fine," Geth'n grunted from the pressure on his ribs. Pet'r suddenly realized he might be hurting his friend and placed him back on the ground.

"Acron'n. This is my friend Geth'n. He's a searcher just like myself, but just a bit more bookish. But my best friend," Pet'r ran over and introduced him to the beaten man.

"Pet'r, I think we need to tend to Acron'n's wounds. He seems a little wobbly," Geth'n responded, looking at Acron'n with a side-glance.

Acron'n heard what he said, but was so weak he began to topple over. Pet'r caught him as he fell and kept him upright.

"We were going down to a creek at the bottom of this valley. We should probably go and rest for tonight," Pet'r said, pointing through the trees.

Geth'n couldn't see anything but trees in the direction Pet'r was pointing, but trusted his friend. He knew Acron'n couldn't walk too far. When Acron'n tried to go down hill, he was simply too weak and almost fell again. Pet'r picked the man up and carried him.

"Let's go," Pet'r said as he walked toward his destination.

They arrived in short order, sat up a campsite with no fire. They were in a sheltered valley, heavy with trees and undergrowth. Using some of that foliage, Pet'r built a small covering, a lean-to, using the saplings and limbs he gathered. He left the leaves on most of them so visibility and exposure were limited. It didn't appear it was going to rain so no preparation was made for that possibility.

Geth'n decided he would take the first watch and Pet'r went to rest. Acron'n had mostly collapsed and fallen asleep instantly. They assumed he wouldn't wake again and covered him with a light blanket from Geth'n's pack. The night passed without incident.

Morning found Pet'r, on the last watch, as he wandered the perimeter of their small camp and noticed nothing unusual. He even walked to the top of the ridges just north of them without incident. When he returned, Geth'n was sitting, leaning against a tree with his eyes toward the north.

"They are coming again. Apparently, their leader was a bit upset with those men from yesterday's encounter with you. He allowed the men, without the original officer who the leader killed, to rest but didn't allow them to forget their responsibility," Geth'n spoke softly, looking at Pet'r in a way that suggested they should leave. They had known each other almost all their lives; talking sometimes was unnecessary. "Not certain what game he was playing with Acron'n, but he's not pleased with the results. Seems this group is some sort of elite unit from another country brought here by Baalsa'n. Not accustomed to defeat apparently."

Pet'r listened, looked around, concentrated on his surroundings and said, "Yes, you're right. We need to leave." He walked over to Acron'n still asleep in their small lean-to, reached his foot over and nudged the sleeping man. Acron'n spun away and was on his feet instantly, his staff raised.

Pet'r was surprised with the quickness of the man but only backed away raising his hand. He motioned for silence with his index finger over his mouth. Acron'n looked around quickly and though he couldn't see anything, he stayed silent and nodded his head.

Pet'r reached into the temporary shelter, retrieved his belongings and pushed the lean-to over. He spread the debris over a wider area and stepped back. It would be difficult to notice they had been there.

"Down this valley," he said quietly, pointing down the stream. "There's probably a lake below."

"There is and that's the way we need to go," Geth'n mumbled. "Borny'a's cabin is not so far from here."

He knew this area and knew the stream wound westwardly around the small mountain they could see to the south and back again to the east and emptied into the lake near Borny'a's cabin.

So they traveled as swiftly as Acron'n's injuries would allow. They wound their way through the forest for some distance without incident when Pet'r heard the dogs. He halted the other two and they stood for a moment.

"They are close. We need to hurry, or hide, quickly," he whispered.

Geth'n recognized the urgent need, looked to the side of the mountain, reached his hands toward a bluff and blasted the facing to expose a cave. There were no explosive sounds, just flying debris scattering into the forest not far from where they stood.

Pet'r instantly grabbed Acron'n and urged him up the hill toward the cave. Geth'n stood a while longer before ascending and watched for their new enemy as he followed. Pet'r reached the cave quickly, entered and helped Acron'n get as comfortable as possible and was going to return to help his friend. When Geth'n arrived, more quietly than Pet'r expected.

How does he do that? But wait, this has happened before. What did Kalbra'n mean when he said, ". . . you have the power to go where you will . . ." I don't know, I don't understand. Just watch and listen, idiot

"Where are they? Where are Voravia's odd men?" Pet'r asked, blinked, surprised by Geth'n's quick movements.

"I think these aren't Voravia's. They're the same troops that pursued Acron'n and are very close already. We'll have to decide how to escape and do it fairly quickly. A number of the troops are in the valley below trying to track us. It's a small lead group at this moment, but a larger group is close behind," Geth'n answered, he brow knitted in concern. "Look up that hill and see if you can see them."

Pet'r peered over the boulder, shielding himself in the shadows cast from the trees and bushes above them. Arrows flew all about him, clicking off rocks, plunking into the dirt below the mouth of the cave. He quickly dropped from view and turned to his companions.

"If this is any indication, I believe we're going to meet resistance trying to reach this cabin. Who is this Borny'a, anyway?" he said.

Geth'n turned to Pet'r. "Borny'a's a man of this forest who helped Anisah and myself when we were looking for you."

131

Arcon'n was sitting slumped over, lying on his side, further back from the mouth of the cave, sweat pouring from his brow. His face was wrapped in pain. But he was awake.

"Monsh'a. He'll be determined. I was going to be his training monkey," he groaned, slid down the wall and slumped into unconsciousness.

"These are Baalsa'n's people, not Voravia's. They are too strong for hers. Do you know who Monsh'a is? Have you heard anything about him?" Geth'n asked. He looked around at Acron'n a moment, then back at Pet'r.

"I've not heard of him," Pet'r answered, taking another quick look over his boulder.

"Well, it seems Baalsa'n's people are on the move and have invaded this area. That can't be good for more than one reason. But we have to get past them and get to Jond'r before they discover he and Borny'a are in that next valley," Geth'n added quietly, pointing toward the ridge just southeast of them.

"Actually, I don't know the name, nor Jond'r; other than knowing he's Acron'n's brother. I've not been involved in the area since the plateau. Could these be troops from somewhere else? What do you mean by *more than one reason?*" Pet'r asked, things were happening faster than he wanted. He was puzzled by the implication there was more than just their immediate problem. It didn't seem a trifling thing to him, having these strange looking beings firing arrows in their direction.

"What other reason, besides dying here?" he asked.

"Baalsa'n is becoming bolder. He hasn't been this far south before. What reason might there be to give him this renewed confidence, especially after what Anisah did to them? What has happened we aren't aware of?" Geth'n sat pondering for a moment.

An arrow skipped off a tree not more than six inches above Geth'n's head, but he didn't flinch. He was obviously unconcerned about this attack. Pet'r scooted over to sit by him.

132

"Do you mind if we proceed. We need to get Arcon'n to where we can attend his wound and talk to him. We're not even certain his injuries are superficial," Pet'r said, his face close to Geth'n.

Geth'n glanced at him and then at Arcon'n. "No, he isn't dying, just severely injured."

Pet'r frowned and drew back from his friend.

How does he know that? Geth'n is beginning to act more strangely every time he speaks.

"How do you know that?" he asked, repeating his thoughts aloud in his frustration.

"I don't know how. I just know he's in no danger from his wounds. However, these weapons can kill us all. So it's time to do something and we can get on with what we were about." Geth'n commented, almost casually and stood up.

Pet'r couldn't believe his eyes. He reached for Geth'n, but wasn't quick enough. Geth'n stepped away from him and out into the open. Arrows hummed through the air, but to Pet'r's disbelief none were striking his friend. The missiles seemed to veer away just as they arrived some few feet from Geth'n and glanced sideways into the forest harmlessly.

Geth'n looked back at Pet'r and motioned him to follow. Pet'r looked at him as though he was mad. But Geth'n and he had been friends since they were children, and Geth'n had almost always been right.

Almost always.

More recently, Geth'n seems to be correct about everything he does.

So Pet'r saw no reason to wait and stood up beside his friend. Nothing happened. As thick as the arrows were flying, all of them veered away from them.

"I believe it is time for you to protect the Ahar'n, my friend," Geth'n said and stepped to Pet'r's right as he spoke.

Pet'r's reaction was instant; he strode forward, his head held high and advanced toward the source of their problem as though

133

the projectiles didn't exist. None hit him as he leaped over the shelter where the attackers hid. As he landed, he caught several of the arrows out of the air, plunging them into the throats of the nearest enemy. The rest couldn't believe Pet'r was inside their shelter. They stood and stared at him as though he was a god.

Pet'r grabbed the next, raised the body over his head and smashed the man against another small group attempting to leap on him. The other soldiers were in shock. They stood and stared at those on the ground and seemed transfixed.

Pet'r growled, "Be gone! Leave this place!"

All eyes snapped back to look at Pet'r. They began to walk backwards, then began to slip and clatter against one another as they clambered out of his reach and began to run. If they fell, they crawled across the forest floor and through the trees, rose from the ground and, scrambling into full flight, disappeared in only a moment into the forest, running toward the northeast.

Pet'r stood, looking about fiercely for other enemies, but all were gone.

Geth'n walked up beside him. Pet'r looked down at him and Geth'n was smiling back.

"Well done, Pet'r. You know, you really know how to do that very well now. I don't remember you being so ferocious when we were young," he laughed out loud and placed his hand on Pet'r's shoulder.

"What did you do to frighten them so badly?" Pet'r asked, walking around into the cave where Arcon'n still lay slumped over.

"I simply made them believe you were invincible. They could only see a gigantic version of you. They felt intimidated, I think?" Geth'n answered, laughed again and looked over at Arcon'n.

"Why don't you pick him up. We'll need to make better time getting to Borny'a's now. He seems to be bleeding internally," Geth'n suggested.

Pet'r raised Arcon'n from the floor of the cave and cradled

him in his arms. Geth'n trotted away, moving swiftly through the forest, toward Borny'a's cabin.

Pet'r followed closely, carrying the wounded soldier with ease. He watched Geth'n running ahead of him.

He's not touching the ground. How does he do that? I need to ask him. He couldn't do it a fortnight ago. Maybe this magic thing is out of hand.

They disappeared into the forest.

INADEQUATE

Rab'k rose early the next morning. He wandered the perimeter of the camp to determine whether the watch was set properly and noted where it wasn't. He scouted beyond the encampment to determine if there were spies no one noticed. He was driven and more resourceful, preparing for this – his greatest day. He knew his time had finally arrived. He would fulfill the dreams that sustained him through all those years in the south.

He returned to Rena'x's tent, turned before entering and looked out toward the mountain pass where he was to take the troops; the same pass he had followed when the one he knew as the new Guardian of the Ahar'n had escaped him.

He recalled the conflict when he battled the Guardian on the plateau. He felt it was an even fight. He was pleased but he was fairly certain Baalsa'n was not.

Shouldn't be too much longer before I will settle that score. We can move on to conquer, not only Aerolan, but also the entire world of Narthrae in short order. Just a matter of time.

But I do wonder about this Monsh'a. Why did Baalsa'n call him to bring additional troops? What was his tie to Baalsa'n? Are these Maah'e really as good as Rena'x claims?

Tomorrow, or the next day, I should know the answers to these questions. It is time to take over the leadership of the entire army assembled here.

He smiled. He felt certain this fight would soon be over and he could receive his just awards for having done well.

"Captain. It's time to gather the troops. I advise we be prepared to have the men able to reduce to four abreast in the more narrow parts of the pass. If you haven't been up there, the passage reduces rapidly about a quarter of a mile from the summit. We should be ready for that. The other side expands rapidly. We should be near the Forest of Galyd'n by afternoon tomorrow," Rab'k advised.

The commander listened intently to Rab'k's advice. But, as he turned to go, he looked back at Rab'k and shook his head. He had his own doubts about Rab'k, but wasn't in a position to question the man's orders. But he found himself wondering about Rab'k worthiness. He walked slowly to his mount.

Rab'k excited by the moment, mounted his horse and continued his investigation.

We should make excellent time today.

The troops were well trained and seemed disciplined. They reported rapidly after the trumpets calling for assembly were sounded, gathering what they needed for their march into the south.

They had received an inordinate amount of indoctrination. These men had little prior knowledge of the southern regions, having wandered the deserts most of their lives. Rab'k actually was one of the few men they knew who lived on the other side.

Rena'x had encouraged him. He instructed his officers that Rab'k's instructions and training be diligently followed. There were some of the other men who, as spies, traveled extensively on the far side, but only Rab'k had lived there. Rab'k and those older spies, took the men in small squads and educated them, as best they could.

In short order, the troops were gathered and the march began.

Rab'k and a few of the officers rode ahead of the troops. The dust rose high above the assembly as they tramped onto the barren road and began their walk into the pass.

Some of the men looked upward toward the peaks of the mountains, but they weren't able to see the summit of the passes because they were too close. But they knew they were going to have a difficult trip up because they had always been able to see these mountains from almost every location in the desert they were leaving.

So, for hours, they trudged along jostling against one another. The movement of this new army suddenly was ragged and un-kempt.

None of the men, moving in the crowd, were experienced with forced marches, nor considered enemies other than the next tribe on the prairies. Their forays occurred occasionally when there were attempts to intrude into other territories. Generally, tribal battles were boring, with few casualties, and the combatants quickly lost interest.

Nothing of importance happened that first day. The pace was so much slower than the officers anticipated and they pushed the leaders to move faster. The squad leaders walked back and forth, giving orders to those who lost the pace, or weren't concerned enough to maintain it. The order to drink water more frequently was often passed along the lines.

More than forty thousand soldiers trekked into places they had never seen before. They were sweating within the first hundred yards or so and began wrapping kerchiefs over their nose and mouths to protect themselves from the dust. The heat from so many clustered together was much worse than riding beneath the desert sun. Everyone carried his or her own environment with him or her.

All were miserable.

The time passed. They took breaks more and more often as they pushed upward. After a while, they achieved enough altitude to reduce the intensity of the heat and, with the ground harden-ing to stone, the dust was lessened and they could uncover their faces.

But now they were having problems breathing. The altitude was impacting these desert natives dramatically.

They marched most of the day but had to halt sooner than ex-pected when it began to rain. Unaccustomed to rain, the men broke ranks, despite the officers shouting at them to hold their lines, and either sought shelter under the overhanging bluffs or stood in the cool falling rain to relieve their suffering from the heat and the work.

Then the wind speed increased where there was hardly a breeze before. This last caused the temperature to drop and the cold soon became an enemy.

The company was halted because its integrity completely failed. The men were uncomfortable, weary and couldn't recognize the importance of their efforts. They were wretched and most were beginning to doubt this idea to go fight the enemy was worth it. There were some desertions while they were marching, but more now the rain was falling.

Rab'k talked to his officers and they decided to send small squads back down the mountain to capture those men escaping and bring them back. One additional problem occurred. Some of the men sent in the squads also escaped. None of these men had experience with the mountains but necessity taught them how to hide from their pursuers.

Rab'k finally decided to call a halt for the day much sooner than he had hoped. They were less than halfway up this side of the pass and now he knew he needed to stand guards to protect against mass desertions. There were no enemy about, but he was losing to the surroundings and, now, the cold.

The men gathered themselves, some without protection from the rain because their tents, if they carried them at all, were made for the desert, and the rain sprayed through the fabric and made the inside of the tents only slightly less wet than the ground outside. So it was a miserable night for Baalsa'n's desert warriors.

The next morning the clouds were still thick, gray and billowing, but the air was clean, blowing lightly down the mountain and fortunately, it wasn't raining. Though the clouds provided shelter from the heat, they still posed a threat of more rain.

Rab'k, early the next morning, decided to send his officers out to rouse the men while they were more comfortable, get them on their feet and start the march up to the pass. They could at least march to the original plateau planned, then have the men sit, eat and rest without being drenched by rain.

Of course, there were loud complaints about being awakened too early and not being allowed to have the morning meals. The grumbling persisted until the march stopped later in the morning. Fortunately, the clouds remained to cover the sun and the journey was, if not enjoyable, less troublesome.

But then the snow began to fall. The snow was only dusting the ground, but Rab'k was aware this was only a foretelling of things to come with the weather in these mountains. There was danger of a heavier snowfall at any time.

"Have the officers join me in my tent, captain," Rab'k told his first officer. "We need to discuss how to get these men over this mountain. Tell them to get here quickly."

Looking down through the driving snow from above, three nebulous images stood watching the struggles of the young commander. Though nothing was spoken, they gave each other knowing smiles and nodded in agreement.

"We've probably succeeded in delaying Rab'k for a short while, but our young people need to do more in their preparations. We cannot hold these soldiers indefinitely," Guit'l's thoughts were first.

Andr'a was still watching the men below struggling to get up the mountainside, but he offered a retort. *"You can say what you wish about our young people, but the decisions of the council and the declarations, particularly those of Kalbr'an, have always stated we are to allow them free will and not interfere."*

"Certainly you're correct, but I believe we've already interfered. Why should we not? We too are at risk if Baalsa'n is able to gather a force this time. We barely escaped him the last time we were here," Guit'l replied.

Rang'x added another idea. He most often thought situation

140

through before contributing his concerns.

"I think the danger in our being involved is worse if we are discovered by Baalsa'n or Mano'n. We may be exposing ourselves. I personally am uncomfortable. We should leave immediately, or we may have created more problems than solutions."

They each nodded to the other, looked around them as though they were able to perceive something sensing their presence, nodded their singular agreement and disappeared from the scene.

Almost immediately, Mano'n appeared on the ledge where they were standing. This was Baalsa'n's territory and it was closely watched. Mano'n, who was still attempting to locate Anisah in the southern portion of Aerolan, was alerted by the immense band of censors he had placed throughout the mountain range and on both sides of them for miles into the flatland

He responded instantly, but the delay from the system and the action of those standing on the ledge was enough to thwart his plan for them if those three had remained a moment longer.

He wasn't pleased and the interruption in his search for Anisah made him even angrier. But he was satisfied his ring of censors had done its job.

"I'll get some of these aggressors soon, especially if they persists in these small attacks," he looked down at the desert troops working up the trail and noted the snow now falling on them was creating a problem. These people were not trained for such weather, or altitude, and he decided he should intercede since he was already there.

He raised his hand toward the dark, damp clouds racing across the mountains above him, stared at the movement only a moment longer and the snowfall ceased, at least where he was. It would take a bit more time for the air to clear. The sun broke through while he waited. He was able to see the crowd below looking up toward the clouds and hear their cheers as they experienced the first warmth in several days.

141

He noticed some of the men, obviously officers, raced toward the small pavilion near the pass and decided there were be a little less concern for the meeting to come. He thought he remembered Rab'k was to be in command of these troops.

"Might as well help, little brother. You, unfortunately, may need more. We'll see," He looked down and around himself a moment longer.

And I need to return to Varspree and determine where that girl and her friends have disappeared.

With that, he left

Rab'k waited for the officers with some concern. The snow was making it almost impossible to move his men. He knew they weren't far from the summit of the pass. He passed this way not long before when chasing the Guardian. He also knew the snow must stop or he would need to call a halt of the troops until it did.

The path, or road, down the far side was not going to be pleasant if frozen and slick. He ran the risk of losing many more of his troops. Already he had problems because of so many defections.

He felt Rena'x would probably have spies, would apprehend the men trying to sneak back into the desert and would have much to say, and do, to these men to force them to follow later. So he wasn't so worried about them. But he did worry the men still pushing up the mountain would simply stop, unwilling to go any further. He couldn't determine what he could do to prevent that.

Then he heard the cheer rise from the outside just as his officers ducked into the tent. There were smiles on their faces. They came to the table in the center of the tent, stopped and saluted. Rab'k could tell they were excited.

"What happened?" Rab'k asked.

"The snow stopped and the sun is shining through. It seemed

miraculous," Nart'e answered. He could hardly contain himself. He kept looking over his shoulder, eager to get outside and start preparing what to do with this change in fortunes.

"I have to admit the change was sudden," Macr'a added, though he gave Nart'e a look of disdain.

Macr'a was the oldest, and maybe the wisest, of Rab'k's generals. He came highly recommended by Rena'x. He offered experience with troop movement and use because of his many years controlling the skirmishes common between city-camps throughout the desert. Rab'k, more often than with the others, listened to Macr'a's advice.

Oldr'e only smiled and watched the other two.

Rab'k glanced at him but recognized Oldr'e was going to hold his council until after he had an opportunity to determine what miracle happened. He seemed pleased things had changed, but he wasn't going to make any promises about what could be done with the new circumstance. Rab'k relied on Oldr'e's hesitancy to balance the advice of the other two.

"Well, gentlemen, I thought you were coming to inform me of our dire straits. I am aware of those concerns, but possibly we now need to reassess our position and discuss what may have transpired. We must decide what we may, or may not, be able to do with this new situation," Rab'k spoke slowly and deliberately though he was seething inside.

He worried about his showing in Baalsa'n's eyes and, if these assumed changes had improved his options, he was excited by the prospects of completing this part of his mission successfully. But, he wasn't going to show this increased confidence to these men.

"If the weather has changed in our favor, we should make plans to depart within an hour, or so. But make your determinations and report back to me within that hour. Then we'll decide what we can do. Hopefully, we'll rid ourselves of some of this anxiety about this mission. Dismissed," Rab'k was calm as he instructed them. He looked down at the information on the center table, as though studying it. But, in fact, he was avoiding looking into the others' eyes. They all left without speaking.

Rab'k most feared his personal inclination for breaking down and losing his temper under the pressured circumstances he experienced to this point. He struggled to control this; he wanted to lash out at someone, or something, in a rage and destroy the things hindering his progress.

But, he also recognized he wasn't alone in this fight. He was going to need to control this overpowering desire to do this alone and he knew he couldn't. He had to accommodate the inconsistency he saw in others and attempt to hold command of himself, and these others, while getting through this difficulty.

He knew he still had to get off this mountain and, perhaps worse, handle the situation with this Monsh'a once he arrived on the other side. He now wasn't so concerned about the present, but that future encounter bothered him a great deal.

Are there problems there I've not been made aware of? What do I need to know about this man I've not been told? The Ravelan are, by legend, ferocious people. Is this commander going to be someone I can control easily, or will there be disagreement?

He walked to the tent flap and raised it, watched, for a moment, the bustle of the camp now preparing to depart and noticed the sun was indeed beaming down strongly, causing mist to rise from the melting snow. He smiled and let the flap fall.

I must be able to do this thing. I will be in command.

The preparations were going to take some time and Rab'k called his officers together again, to let them know what he expected. They decided the next morning would be better for leaving than this late in the day. There were a great number of things to repair, unfortunately including the men themselves.

The soldiers suffered more than anyone expected with the severe weather. To assume they would be totally prepared for any further tramping through snow and mush seemed an unreasonable expectation. It seemed wiser to allow the environment to become friendlier. The best situation would be the snow melting before they reached the lower levels of the mountains, but the contingency response would be to be prepared if it wasn't. The officers learned a great deal about the suddenness of mountain weather and now felt more prepared to deal with them.

Rab'k stood before them and began his instructions.

"The first thing tomorrow, Nart'e, I want you to assign one of your officers the task of taking a small lead group to determine if there are any trouble spots ahead. I have a feeling there are still going to be large ice patches. This path is, at best, not a good means to travel through these mountains. It was never intended to support a large body of people moving from the desert to Aerolan. But it's the path we've taken and we will complete it.

You, Oldre'a, provide me a report on how many men have deserted?

These have probably attempted to return to the desert. Some may have died in that attempt, but most were able to accomplish what they wanted. Rena'x commands, at my request, patrols watching the bottom of the passage for those men returning, with preparations to capture and send them over the mountain to our encampment after this weather problem runs its course."

Rab'k noticed Oldr'e frown about his assignment and made a mental note to be cautious of the man. He had to have these men cooperate, if there were any problems he needed to eradicate them. He thought of Jond'r at that moment.

I don't have time, or the patience, for another Jond'r. I will deal with this Oldr'e quickly if I need to.

"Macr'a, I want you to command the entire group while Nart'e and Oldr'e are involved in resolving those problems. There may be more difficulties going down the other side of these mountains than there were coming up. There will be an additional strain on the men physically. My own experience has shown me we are not able to maintain the downward inclinations as easily as

145

we might assume. The legs and back muscles rebel against the pressure of the constant impacts of stepping downward. You need to plan on having frequent stops, so unfortunately we must provide for rest periods in between marches. We need to have these men battle ready when we reach the valley below.

Also, we are going to be joining a small force from Ravelan. As I understand, they are already in position and engaged in acquiring recruits for the area while they wait for our arrival. I'm not certain about their skill level, but I do know they have some prior experiences in the area we are going into. So, I think we have to assume they are highly trained. I don't want to leave impressions with them that we are less than what they provide.

Any questions?" he asked.

Waiting a moment, he watched the officers' faces for reaction. Two of them, Nart'e and Oldr'e eyebrows rose at the mention of the Ravelan, but Macr'a face was placid. Rab'k decided the older officer was probably going to be his chief asset.

He dismissed them and returned to studying the maps he possessed showing the Aerolan forests and prairies. He was familiar with most of the southern coastal regions but he had some trouble with the area near the mountains. There were few reasons for going to those regions during his stay in the south.

In fact, the only time he'd really been involved with activity in that region was when he had attacked Garv'n and stolen the small book of text that supposedly revealed the whereabouts of the Ahar'n. But, back then he left most of the deployment plans to Jond'r, who was a native of the region, and so was basically ignorant of possible offensive attack points.

Above, in an intersecting valley, the three Al-Esfer'n were surveying the pathway taken by Rab'k's troops. They were intentionally looking for some way they could disrupt the progress of the army and make it seem a natural occurrence.

They knew Mano'n had responded to their prior weather disruptions, but also knew he left almost immediately. They were surprised because they expected pursuit and there was none.

"We should create at least one more problem," Guit'l suggested, as they searched the valleys along the route down the mountain road.

"We could, but what is gained by doing anything more," Andra'a interjected. *"We've delayed Rab'k and it will take a effort for him to recover."*

"Actually, I think Guit'l has it right," Rang'x added. *"If we can create a circumstance where a great deal of energy is expended by this desert army, it would certainly add to the time our young leaders need to gather forces.*

I suggest this instance should be a large one. We, I think, should cause an avalanche in that narrow valley at that point," he added and pointed toward a specific location along the trail where the cliffs on each side closed in toward the road.

"By closing that gap, we can delay this group for a day or two. They have come this far and now must continue. The group will expend the extra effort to clear the pass with no equipment to assist them. The effort will be all manual and these are soldiers, not laborers."

They talked a bit longer about the suggestion and agreed to activate a small earthquake along one ridge and have the boulders and debris fall from that side into the canyon. They also decided this should be their last effort on this project.

One of the problems was obvious. Mano'n who could reappear at any moment. Another was the discovery by the council, and particularly Kalbra'n, of their covert activity. They suspected the recoil of that discovery could be severe and should be avoided for their sake.

So, Guit'l stepped forward a bit, concentrated on the ridge they had decided would create the most debris and triggered the small earthquake. The ground shook along the pathway, but the effect wasn't severe enough to notice if one was standing along the way. The outcome was correct for what the three wanted to accomplish.

Along the top of the ridge, cracks formed, segments of the bluffs begin to shift and slide toward to edge and pieces, breaking away, began to plummet into the valley. The momentum increased and the rubble plunged into the small ravine careening and crashing noisily down into the valley, filling it quickly.

The three on the bluff above were already gone before the valley closed. Dust and small clumps of stones, trees and dirt fell the distance to the blockade.

When all settled, the roadway was covered with debris four times as tall as a large man and as wide as three wagons. The small stream flowing next to the road was partially dammed and the water began to collect and fill the valley. There was some run-off but the stream was going to form a small lake.

On the road above, Rab'k thought he felt a tremor beneath them. He stopped walking his horse, dismounted and waited for any sign there might be problems, but the movement stopped and he dismissed it as unimportant.

Probably just a minor movement somewhere along these upper ridges. Shouldn't be a problem.

As planned, the army began the slow process of moving again. The journey down through the valley below them was going to be difficult, in part, because of the narrow trail, but also the ice and snow remaining made footing difficult. The steepness of the trail varied and would cause discomfort, the cold from the storms still held in the higher and thinner mountain air. The sense of being cold was enhanced.

Rab'k knew the cold would dissipate as the troops marched, but he still worried about the general passage.

Things should begin to improve soon. We do need to have a few things go right with this march. I may be a novice at this but I have to believe we are over the worst.

148

Below, in the valley of ruin, the dust still fell occasionally and the water collected behind the new dam. The passage would be covered with water soon.

WARRIORS

Above all things, freedom is the most desired. There are those who thrive on achieving complete freedom so a choice for their live path can be made without hindrance.

There are others who demand freedom for themselves, but who would control others intent on leading free lives.

When the hope for all except those who wish power is crushed, the life flows from a culture, a society, and the survivors remaining ache for the days when they can know freedom again.

But those who seek power will enslave, ofttimes just to extend their power, being unsatisfied with what they have. There are many reasons given, but there is never a legitimate one. To enslave another is to belittle the essence of life.

Our young heroes will discover the agony of believing all wishes can be and that they are allowed the freedom of choice. They will make mistakes in judgment because of this belief.

But first, let us look at what is happening since our last visit.

These three are to be involved in a war to retain their freedom and that of all the others on

their world - Narhtrae. . .

Geth'n led the way to the top of the ridge. Pet'r followed closely.

They looked down over the valley and the lake, but both peered intently at the cabin to determine if any danger lurked anywhere.

"There's no one about except those in the cabin, but strangely, there's someone there I don't know. We should be cautious," Geth'n spoke softly to Pet'r who was still carrying Acron'n.

"Should I go ahead to scout closer?" Pet'r asked, turning to set

Acron'n to the ground.

"No, I'm comfortable no one unusual is down there. We have certainly left Monsh'a's forces behind. You scared those creatures and they probably lost all desire to follow us. Since we covered our trail very effectively, it would seem they have no way to know where we are. Borny'a has been considered a peaceful unpleasant nuisance for Voravia – her people refuse to bother him. Don't know why, but they keep away. Because of that, they are unaware he has injured staying with him."

"But his brother is down there," he nodding his head at Acron'n, "and he probably is feeling much better than when Anisah and I found him along one of those roads on the other side of the valley. We should walk down with some caution. Borny'a might be our biggest problem, since he doesn't expect us. In fact, he may already know we're here."

Pet'r looked around at his friend and nodded silently. They moved over the ridge and back into the forest. There was little undergrowth this high in the central mountains and the path was fairly straight as they moved to the lower levels.

They were approaching the lake's edge when they were suddenly surprised by a voice from the underbrush.

"That's probably far enough," a voice came from just behind them, "you'll be smart to stand a moment."

Pet'r whirled around, still holding Acron'n's, but he saw no one, nor sensed anyone.

"Areb'l?"

"No. Borny'a. It's me, Geth'n. Come to visit with a friend or two," Geth'n spoke without moving.

"Are you now? Whose your friend?" the questions came from nowhere, as far as Pet'r could tell.

"His name's Pet'r. He's a friend of Anisah's too," Geth'n answered and turned toward his left and looked up into a nearby tree.

Borny'a was sitting on a blind stand, with bow drawn, looking

151

down at them over the top of an arrow pointed at Pet'r.

The man released the tension on the bow. Geth'n smiled and Pet'r relaxed a bit.

"It's been a while, young fellow. Is this the friend you and Anisah were looking for before?" Borny'a smoothly moved the bow into position onto his back to protect it, swung down effortlessly from his perch and landed quietly in front of them.

"Yes, it is. Pet'r, I'd like to introduce you to Borny'a. He helped, and gave sanctuary to Jond'r, the soldier we found in the hills when we were searching for you. A good man to know," Geth'n said to Pet'r, noticing he was not quite at ease. Geth'n didn't want any tension between these two.

"Hello, sir. I've heard quite a bit about you. Glad to finally meet you," Pet'r tried to offer his hand but wasn't able to, holding Acron'n.

"That certainly was a surprise. Where did you learn that trick?" Pet'r nodded his head at the tree stand.

Borny'a looked up at the stand.

"During a war, many years ago. I was a sniper, doing what I could. Often worked behind the lines, but that's not important. Glad to see you back, Geth'n," Borny'a said, turning to Geth'n and giving a warm handshake.

Geth'n noticed the difference and wondered if Pet'r did. Quickly checking Pet'r, he noticed he was looking around for other danger, still holding Acron'n without effort and not concerned about Borny'a any longer.

"Who's the fellow Pet'r's carrying? He looks a little familiar. In fact, both of your friends here look familiar," Borny'a asked, nodding his head toward Acron'n.

"Jond'r's brother. Pet'r helped rescue him from a band of soldiers and I, of course, had to rescue both of them," Geth'n grinned and looked around at Pet'r who grinned back, shaking his head.

"Well, let's get down to the cabin," Borny'a said, nodding his

152

head toward the building below. "I'm sure Jond'r will be glad to see him, but it looks like this brother needs some medical attention. We've another visitor – compliments of some of Voravia's crew."

"Who?" Geth'n and Pet'r asked, at the same time. Then chuckled about that.

"A rich fellow, according to Jond'r, from Tariny. Voravia's little men brought him down to trade for food. Seems a little odd they'd be asking for food, but I parleyed with them and rescued this fellow," Borny'a added.

"So Jond'r's up and about?" Geth'n asked, motioning with his hand for Borny'a to lead. They began their walk down the hill.

Pet'r took another cautious look behind them, turned and followed them down the hill, looking around occasionally until they cleared the tree line near the banks of the lake.

As the other two walked away, he stood for another moment, intensely listening and surveying the surrounding hills. Finally he was satisfied and caught Geth'n and Borny'a just as they reached the cabin.

"I've set a number of traps for signals around the perimeter of the lake and further up into the hills. That's how I knew you were headed this way. Had a little experience with preventing trouble," he spoke to Pet'r, recognizing the boy's tension. "You can probably relax some, young fellow. You can bring this fellow into the cabin then we can have a talk."

Pet'r looked at Borny'a, brow knitted with a frown. Then he relaxed, noted Borny'a's explanation with a nod and carried Acron'n into the darkness of the cabin. Borny'a moved quietly around him and indicated he should lay Acron'n on a pallet in one corner of the room.

"Guess I lose my bed again," Borny'a said, chuckling. "This little place has become a regular hospital. " He motioned toward Jond'r and Garv'n lying on the cots. "Do you boys expect any more visitors?

153

Geth'n looked over at Pet'r, turned back, and answered, "No, we are all that's left of our group of friends and allies, except Anisah. But she has proven she's able to take care of herself and we can get in touch with her any time we want."

"But there is a larger problem, we believe this area is soon going to be overrun with a new band of soldiers. We've not seen this group before, but we now know they are extremely dangerous. It might be advisable for all of us to leave as soon as possible."

"What'd these new troops look like?" Borny'a asked.

"They resemble Voravia's little people, but are larger, stronger and smarter. They show intelligence. Acron'n, before he lost consciousness, mentioned someone named Monsh'a. Apparently, the new group's leader. We don't know whether Voravia is involved, but we are fairly certain a leader named Baalsa'n is."

"Baalsa'n? Monsh'a? Well, your estimate of the danger they present is valid," Borny'a said, he paused a moment, looked toward the ceiling as though pondering something, took out his pipe, tamped it, struck a match and puffed until a small amount of smoke rose above his head. "You can add them to the extremely dangerous."

Geth'n and Pet'r looked at each other, then back at Borny'a.

Baalsa'n was, and I guess is the leader, of the Om-Esfer'n, a rival group intent on obliterating Kalbra'n and his people.

Another time, another war. These creatures invaded years ago. How we managed to drive them back I don't know, but something, or someone, helped us and we survived. Monsh'a and his people are the Ravelan, ruthless, vicious troops from Mavelan'g. The Andreus Wall was built years ago to slow them down if they decided to attack again.

They must now be able to come by water down the Magin'n Gulf if they are back so secretly. We, and everyone in this region, are in more danger than any of us needs to be" Borny'a said, his face showing his concern even if he wasn't expressing it.

154

"What war? How long ago was this?" Pet'r asked, looking to Geth'n who shrugged his shoulders. He had never heard of, nor read about, any war being fought in Aerolan.

"Too long ago. I fought alongside some brave warriors back then. We actually were involved in more than one war for those years. I had hoped we drove all these away, but things change," Borny'a answered. He again looked around his cabin, out the window at the distant hills and looked melancholy. "Sure hate this change. You're sure that little girl is safe?"

"Well, safe may be stretching it, but she has more power than she, or we, ever knew," Geth'n said, and Pet'r nodded.

"Power? What power are you speaking of?" Borny'a turned to face the boys. "What is happening?"

Pet'r turned to look at Geth'n again with a bit of frown on his face then he nodded.

"Well, sir. We are on a mission for a group who wants to drive Baalsa'n out of Aerolan, and off of Narthrae. We've been, sort of, commissioned to organize this inevitable war. We didn't ask for these jobs, but, I think, we have accepted," Pet'r answered.

"This group? Does it have a name? Wouldn't be the Al-Es-fer'n, would it?" Borny'a asked, looking out the window at the lake laying calmly against the forest in the distance. "Would it?"

Geth'n walked over to stand next to Pet'r. If there was to be trouble here, they needed to be together.

"Yes, sir. That is the name we know. How did you know about them and why do you ask?" Pet'r answered, bracing his body for possible attack.

"Worked for them. Worked for them back then. That war I mentioned," he answered, took a draw on his pipe and slowly expelled the blue smoke into the air. It had a pleasant odor, a soothing aroma. "They were the ones. They gave all of us some sort of strength we knew nothing about – and with that we drove that Baalsa'n fellow and all his from Aerolan, we thought. Maybe they just went somewhere else to recuperate. But that was ages ago, I

155

wonder why it took so long. Why, it's probably a hundred and sixty or seventy years ago."

"Sir? You were in that fight?" Pet'r asked, astounded.

Geth'n had walked to the fireplace, no longer feeling any danger. He released the surge he felt when he sensed certain danger.

"Yes. I was the only person, living here back then, who had prior training, besides Areb'l. He and I gathered a small army. He mostly worked the small squads using silent attacks to harass those ugly troops. I had a stronger and larger force I led to flank and destroyed the exposed troops. It was a slow process but we succeeded, eventually, in driving them away," Borny'a seated himself while he talked, looked at the ceiling and released more smoke, crossed his legs, and set with his brow wrinkled as though he was remembering those days.

"But, that means you have been here for centuries. My ancestor was Areb'l, according to Kalbra'n," Pet'r suddenly spoke. He was staring at Borny'a with a shocked look. Geth'n didn't understand.

Borny'a looked around at Pet'r quizzically

"Thought you looked a bit familiar. You have his eyes, and obviously his strength. Yes, I've been around awhile. Areb'l decided to go to the seacoast, moved to a little town there. Peetle, I believe was its name. I loved the mountains. So here I am," Borny'a looked out the window again, gazing at the hills.

Geth'n and Pet'r both looked at each other at the mention of Peetle.

"We are from Peetle, Geth'n and me. We know no one named Areb'l, nor have I ever heard of him. How long ago was this?" Pet'r asked.

"I don't keep track of the passing years, but I'd have to guess a couple of hundred years, at least. Areb'l was always crafty and quiet, a smart fellow, maybe he changed his name," Borny'a answered. He was nonchalant about revealing his information.

156

"But you. How can that be? How can you have lived that long?" Pet'r asked.

"I just did. You mentioned Kalbra'n and I wonder where you met him. He felt he needed to have more than one person here to watch for Baalsa'n. There actually was another, Asin'a, who lived across the Magin'n Gulf from Mavelan'g many years ago. But I think he died somehow; haven't heard from him in ages. About Areb'l, I don't know what happened to him. Maybe your town history would tell you.

"I suppose that makes me the last of those from Varkan still living here, as a human. But, from what you two are telling me, I suspect Kalbra'n and the other Al-Esfer'n must be trying to organize another defense. Good idea, choosing you young folks."

Geth'n had been silent through this whole discussion, thinking through this new information.

Pet'r's been talking to the Al-Esfer'n? To one of them named Kalbra'n? Now we learn Borny'a is one of the ancients? Why haven't I heard about these people before? Why haven't we been told the stories of our land?

"I'm sorry, but I find this difficult to believe," Geth'n interrupted. "I don't understand any of the things that have been happening to us – to Pet'r, Anisah and myself. How can you have lived so long? Who are the Al-Esfer'n? None of this makes sense and I've been studying the Ahar'n most of my life."

Pet'r looked quickly around at his friend at the mention of the amulet. He was wearing it during the battle on the plateau and had failed to use it to win. He was still wearing it. He realized now he was more aware of why the three of them were chosen than either of the other two.

"We were chosen, Geth'n. Chosen by the Al-Esfer'n to fight the enemy of our land - the Om-Esfer'n," Pet'r said. Kalbra'n and the information he gave him surprised Pet'r. He had assumed Geth'n and Anisah had also been told the reasons behind their inclusion in the plans of these immortals. But, he had no idea that one of the ancients still lived.

157

"You know about all this? So how are we to help? We only guessed we were being led toward some sort of destiny, but why weren't we informed before now so we could be prepared?" Geth'n asked Pet'r.

"Well, young fellow, if Kalbra'n had come to you sooner, would you have accepted the truth?" Borny'a asked Geth'n.

"You're right. I suspect not. I never assumed I would have the strength to follow such a path as you and Pet'r are talking about. So what is there we need to know? What are we supposed to do?" Geth'n asked the other two.

"I was told, by Kalbra'n, that Areb'l was my ancestor. He told me you were one of his descendants," Pet'r answered. "Areb'l was a Varkanian who helped the Al-Esfer'n escape from that disaster and later they brought him here to help with the fighting. I didn't know there were others, like Borny'a. Nor that there was a previous war between the Esfer'n ages ago. - here on Narhtrae."

"I have another surprise for you," Pet'r reached inside his jacket and pulled forth the amulet. "I have the Ahar'n here."

He held it out toward Geth'n who sat staring at it. He reached for it to hold it, but Pet'r withdrew it.

"You can't, Geth'n. It will bring you harm if you try to hold it. I'm apparently the only one who can," He looked around at Borny'a for validation.

"Yep, the boy's right. Only Areb'l could carry the orb. Never knew exactly why, but apparently the magic used to create this was intended only for one person, one human. That person was always called the Guardian. Areb'l was the first. Maybe Pet'r here, is another," Borny'a added. "I do know its power extends to the person wearing it and the purpose of the person wearing it is to protect the amulet and to follow the purpose of protecting the Al-Esfer'n."

"So we three are the *chosen ones*?" Geth'n seemed disappointed. "That's the reason I was having all those dreams. Maybe they weren't dreams at all, but foretelling future events. Now I can un-

158

derstand why I have more confidence and always have a sense of being in control."

"You have been kind of pushy lately," Pet'r spoke up, then he laughed. "But somebody's got to do it, I suppose."

"How does Anisah fit into this? How is she connected to the Al-Esfer'n?" Geth'n asked the other two. "Have either of you any information about how she's involved?"

Borny'a shrugged his shoulders. But Pet'r turned and looked out the window toward those mountains and the dark clouds hovering there for weeks now.

"I know something. Kalbra'n told me Anisah's heritage is more that of an Om-Esfer'n than otherwise. She has powers I don't know the strength of. But it seems, because of her mother, she has no knowledge of that either, nor does she seem to have an evil intent we've discovered to be part of the Om-Esfer'n nature," Pet'r answered. "Anisah is a blessing in disguise. It may be she has more power than you and I both."

Borny'a listened to the last with increased interest; he glowered at the boys.

"An Om-Esfer'n is involved with you two. One of you. That little girl?. Why? They long have been the enemy. These people have destroyed civilizations. Mine was – and my home planet destroyed.

I'm troubled by the news about Anisah. I admit I'm certainly going to be more cautious around her though she was nothing but kind to me before," Borny'a said. He stood, walked to the fireplace hearth and knocked the ashes from his pipe. "Maybe that information is mistaken, or maybe there are other reasons she has the same objective the Al-Esfer'n have, but, I'll admit, young fellows. That bothers me. I will be watching her carefully when she's around."

He turned, shrugged his shoulders, picked up his bow and walked to the door.

"I need to take a look around," he said, opened the door and closed it behind as he left without speaking again.

Geth'n and Pet'r were uncertain what they could say. They too had only met Anisah at the beginning of this journey. They had no knowledge of who, or what, she was, nor about her part in fulfilling the goals to expel the Om-Esfer'n from their planet, nor why she was appointed by the Al-Esfer'n as an important person to contact.

They did know, or believed, she was their friend. They believed their dreams; those stressing her importance to this cause. But that she was an Om-Esfer'n, at least by birth, surprised Geth'n.

Pet'r had been particularly upset when Kalbra'n told him. He realized he felt real and strong disappointment. He'd felt uneasiness; a real sense of loss somehow though he didn't understand why. It bothered him so strongly, it affected him emotionally. For now, he kept that feeling to himself.

"So, does it make a difference?" Geth'n asked Pet'r. "Do we stop trusting her? I, for one, think we need to ask her a few questions when we are able to get back together. But, right now, we have a greater problem. You, me and our future decisions and these three." He motioned toward those injured laying about the room.

"So, Geth'n. What do you think we should do about us?" Pet'r asked, uncomfortable about discussing Anisah. "Should we continue, or inform the Al-Esfer'n we aren't interested? Now we know Borny'a's real identity. Are there problems if we continue?"

"This is what I think. About Anisah, I have no reason to not trust her. Secondly, I, for one, want to continue. Our country and, maybe, our planet, are in danger of annihilation. That seems important and, if I can help in some way, I want to continue. Lastly, Borny'a has proven his loyalty. He really doesn't require our decision on that. He undoubtedly will be the strongest ally we can obtain," Geth'n rattled off his statements quickly. It seemed obvious he believed these ideas to be solid and binding, certainly for himself.

160

"Good, I am a part of this then. So, as you said, let's get Borny'a back in here and talk through what we need to do next. One of the obvious first things we should decide is where do we go to fully work out our objectives?" Pet'r answered, ready to continue and end this war.

Borny'a stepped back into the cabin, gently pushing the door closed. He looked at the boys momentarily, then walked to the fireplace, reached in to catch a wick splinter on fire and puffed on his pipe as he held the splinter over the bowl.

"So, gentlemen, what are our options. I'll hold further judgment on trusting Anisah. She's not given me any reason to doubt her sincerity, but she hasn't faced our opponents directly, as far as we know. I'll need to witness such an occurrence to satisfy me. Now what do you think we need to do?" Borny'a asked, as he drew on his pipe, the smoke curling softly to the ceiling.

"We've been talking while you were out," Geth'n answered, pointing at Pet'r. "We have decided to become more active. We have felt, within us, some of the powers the Al-Esfer'n have given us. But we are not educated in the ways of these powers, nor the ways of war.

We are friends and have been together since childhood and we recognize we're young and accept that as a limitation, but do not accept we can't learn. We believe we can help. But, we ask you to provide leadership as we all bring these things together."

"I know, from talking to Acron'n, both he and his brother, Jond'r have military experience," Pet'r related some of the information he knew about the injured. "Though limited in the battle experience probably, they do have the discipline to take orders and fulfill them. Me. I don't have any, but Kalbra'n told me I am now the Guardian of this amulet and both provide and receive strength and protection from it. I don't know the older gentleman."

"The amulet you're wearing is definitely the Ahar'n," Borny'a revealed. "You are honored, as Areb'l was, to be wearing it for it

161

holds a great many of the mysteries, the lifeline and the wealth of both Esfer'n groups. It was also the device the Al-Esfer'n used to escape from Varkan originally and I imagine for transport from planet to planet as Baalsa'n pursued them. You are right about your personal use; in the right circumstance, you will have unnatural strength and should be able to protect the Ahar'n and yourself from harm – though, as I remember, there are some limitations. You were chosen to bear this as a trust; a belief by the Al-Esfer'n you would uphold the rules of its use.

What you are telling me about the two younger men is also good news. It's rather rare to meet military people now after all these years of peace. But, I also am not aware of who the older gentleman is. But, I do know he is extremely wealthy, according to Jond'r. That alone would put him into the leader class in this country, maybe the world. I do believe Jond'r, once when he was conscious, called him Garv'n but that name meant nothing to me."

"Well, maybe we have a team to start with," Geth'n said. "Even as banged up as we are, we have a small force to contend with the evil we perceive is too near now."

"Yes. We'll need this and more. A lot more," Borny'a added, looking around the room, shaking his head. "Another thing, we all need to be somewhere we can plan what we must do."

The three of them talked long into the night.

The next morning, they resumed their discussions and trying to determine some next steps when Pet'r suddenly became alert. He raised his head and looked around the room.

"What is it?" Geth'n asked, noticing his friend attention had changed.

"Anisah," Pet'r answered. "She has called for me. Can't explain it but she seems to be wishing I was with her for protection."

"Where is she?"

"I can't believe it but I think she's in Varspree. Anyway, I need to go and help her before she gets into too much trouble," he chuckled a bit at that thought. "Wouldn't want that to happen. I'll be back shortly and I might as well bring her here with me so we can put ourselves into a better position to have all our resources in one place – at least, for this planning stage."

Pet'r stood and disappeared.

"You young folks certainly have learned some of the Al-Es-fer'n tricks quickly," Borny'a broke the silence. "Gonna make it handy when we really get into the mess we are headed for. I suppose now I'll have to see how I feel about Anisah."

Geth'n nodded his head, turned to look out the small window and wondered what the world was going to be like in only a few days, or weeks.

There is more to all this than any of us could have ever imagined. Thank the gods for Borny'a. He should be able to help us survive.

SUMT'R

Anisah had no trouble finding the Queens' Ransom. As she arrived, a body came flying out of the door, slammed into the street and slid against the wall of a building on the other side. As best she could tell, it was a man.

Maybe I've bitten off more than I can chew. If reputation is any indication, this can be a dangerous place. Should I not do this? Is it petty to wish for revenge? Should I wait to see what's going on here? After all this time, why am I hesitating now? Whatever! It's time I dealt with this.

She hesitated only a moment, took a deep breath, and casually walked into the tavern.

The place smelled and was noisy with all the drunken chatter, but became quiet immediately. The air was thick with smoke, the smells of liquor, blood, urine and sweat of dirty men. It reeked. It was so bad Anisah almost retched after standing there a moment.

She almost walked away, but then there was a problem. As soon as those men closest to the door realized what she was – a female alone – they closed that exit behind her. She turned only enough to look over her shoulder to verify that. But she also noticed another door in the rear of the room.

If needed, that door may be my only way out of here now.

"Well, Missy. Welcome to our humble tavern. Could I get you a drink?" a large man rose from the chair at the table on her left.

"Come on in, my lady," the barkeep yelled, then laughed. The whole room, so silent before, burst into laughter. "We'll make ya welcome here." Another round of laughter filtered around the room.

"Yeah, we're always friendly to sweet young things," another shouted from the dark. More laughter ran quickly around the

164

room.

Well, I'd hoped to make this a little more private. But guess not.

She could feel the power rising in her. She realized she was getting angry and needed to hold long enough to survive this ordeal.

At that moment, Col'n, with several friends, arrived. He was standing just inside the door with his group. But he wasn't able to push his way through the men who congregated at the door.

"Anisah! I'm here behind you. You should come out with us, if you can get to me," Col'n called to her.

"Ah-h. Anisah. Pretty name for a pretty girl. Want to have a little fun, Anisah? I'm sure several of us would be happy to oblige you," a large man stepped forward. His belly hung over his belt; his shirt hung out in all directions; he was greasy, filthy and the stink was overwhelming.

Anisah paused, looked past this idiot into the dark, as best she could.

"I'm looking for Sumt'r," she said, trying to not expose herself to any real danger. "Anyone here know a man named Sumt'r?"

"Girl's looking for her man!" from another area of the bar. The laughter roared and filled the room. Then just as suddenly the quiet returned.

I believe this crowd is thinking too much. Way too much for me to be here alone — despite my powers. I've made a mistake with this move, just as Col'n warned me. Oh, Pet'r. If you can hear me, I desperately need your help!

"Col'n, please wait. Don't leave. I'm going to come to you!" she yelled out, began to try and push her way through the crowd to the door. Col'n's crew began to push aside some of those standing in their way as they worked across the room toward Anisah.

But his group, young and not experienced in this sort of situation, began to suffer serious injuries from knives, clubs and other hand-held weapons, and was beaten back.

Then the crowd closed ranks on Anisah, making it impossible

165

to escape. They began grabbing at her, pulling her one way and then another, bouncing her off tables and chairs. She realized she had to stop this, or be trampled or worse.

Holding herself as steady as possible, with the arms and hands hitting her all over her upper body, she raised her hands over her head.

"All right, boys! She's ready!" one of the men shouted.

She brought her hands down. There was a humming in the closed area that grew louder. The men began to grab their ears from the raucous sound and its intensity. They began to stumble backwards and fall on their neighbors, over tables and chairs, trying to get away from it.

Everyone still in the room was affected. Everyone staggered back from her, some retching from the impact of the noise, some simply losing consciousness and falling to the floor, most just moving quickly away from Anisah.

Anisah lowered her arms and the screaming sound stopped. The room suddenly quietened.

"Come here," she said, motioning to a man standing nearby. He tentatively stepped forward, then again, but he wouldn't venture any closer.

"I asked a question. Do you know where Sumt'r is?" she insisted, holding the man within earshot by her will. She had stopped him at the distance she was willing to accept.

"Ain't no need to be too pushy, bitch!" someone yelled at her from her right side. She whirled to look into the smoke and dark and recognized Garr'k, one of Sumt'r's gang, standing and pointing his finger at her. "What do you think you're doing here anyway. You want to have a little fun. My buddies and I can certainly assist you with that."

The crowd, still stunned, laughed again but tentatively. They didn't take their eyes from Anisah – this time in fear and not with intent for mischief, as before.

"Garr'k! Have you gotten potty trained yet?" she asked, delib-

166

erately baiting Garr'k. "I remember you had a little trouble with that."

Everyone in the room turned to look back at Garr'k, slowly some began to grin, then they began to laugh, finally they guffawed so loudly they could hardly stand. When they settled, they all looked back at Anisah.

Suddenly, and no one remembered how he got into the room, a tall, young man pushed through the edge of the crowd with no effort and walked to Anisah's side.

"Need some help?" he asked her, leaning over a bit to whisper in her ear. "I believe you called me."

"Pet'r! Oh, thank the gods. Am I glad to see you," she looked into his face and instantly knew she was safe. Then she slowly turned her attention back to her task with a certain satanic look in her eyes. "Where's your boss?" she asked Garr'k again.

Garr'k only stared at her for a moment. He now recognized her.

"Why do I care what you want?" Garr'k yelled back at her. By now, the whole crowd was turning their heads in unison to look at each of the two speakers.

She began to walk toward Garr'k.

"It's only me, idiot. Remember the girl you boys kidnapped and who created a big intestinal problem for you? Do you remember? Well, I do. I'm here to teach you and your friends lessons in manners!" Anisah's anger was breaking out. She was having a difficult time holding it.

Behind her, one of the men at the bar started toward her. As he left the bar, he broke a bottle on the edge and began to run toward her back. Suddenly, he was lying on his back with the broken bottle jammed into his shoulder, his hand and arm broken.

Pet'r had his knee in the man's chest.

"I don't think that was a wise thing for you to do," Pet'r looked down at him, then stood, leaving the man writhing on the

167

floor, screaming in pain.

Anisah looked around at the commotion, then to Pet'r. He just smiled at her, folded his arms across his chest and nodded at her.

She turned back to her task and began to walk toward Garr'k. She wasn't aware of it, but Pet'r walked just behind her. The crowd, seeing her anger and having just witnessed what Pet'r could do, flowed away from her. She advanced quickly to confront Garr'k.

As she approached, the rest of the gang gathered in front of one particular table. She assumed Sumt'r was probably sitting there.

When she was only a few feet away, she raised her right hand toward the men standing guard, motioned only slightly, and they all flew to the sides, flailing as they sailed across the room, ramming into other men in the saloon as well as furniture and whatever else was in their path. They crashed, yelling and moaning.

One of them, having sailed into a bunch of men standing together, wasn't injured. He rose to attack Anisah without thinking about Pet'r and that turned out to be a serious mistake. Pet'r propelled him through the air, out the front door and into the street where he lay. The crowds outside simply walked around him.

"Sumt'r. So glad to see you again," Anisah turned back to the man sitting at the table. He was sitting straight in his chair, looking about the room for help.

"It's been too long, I think. I've decided to repay your kindness. First, I wish to thank you for your hospitality to me and secondly, for your recent visit to a close friend of mine. If you haven't noticed, I do have friends now," Anisah informed him, motioning to the small unit behind her.

Col'n's group, those who remained, had pushed their way through the crowd finally and stood behind Pet'r. He challenged them as they approached, looked at Anisah for assurance, which she gave with a nod, and relaxed. Most of them were in awe of

Pet'r, but recognized he had no ill intent toward them.

"I don't know what you're talking about, girl. I ain't done nothing to you," Sumt'r defended himself without shame. "You deserved whatever you think I did to you. I don't even know who you are."

"Really, I suppose your two boys didn't visit Mr. Farlen asking about me a couple of weeks ago either? Are you going to deny that when I have a witness with me who saw Red and Kar'n come calling and seriously injured Mr. Farlen. Is that correct, Col'n? Do you recognize that man?" she asked pointing to Kar'n, lying against the bar motionless. "Where is Red?" Anisah asked. "Wouldn't want Red to miss this. Ah yes, there he is."

She pointed at Red who was lying still next to the back door where he had landed and had been quiet since. Kar'n had scooted across the floor and slammed against the bar itself, several people in the crowd had to quickly leap over him as he went by, and the spittoon, usually sitting at the corner, had flipped over and spilled its contents across his face.

"Yes, those are the two who beat up Mr. Farlen," Col'n responded after looking at the two men. There was a low murmur, and not a few growls, in the crowd.

These men had no problem fighting with each other and any other ruffian who strolled into town, or maltreating any new visitor they wanted – male, or female – but they didn't care for one of the older, and well respected, men of the town being mistreated.

Anisah turned back to Sumt'r," she smiled at him, "and for trying to bring me harm in another time, I believe I have decided to punish you."

"Yeah, what do ya think you can do without your boyfriend here helping you, ya little slut," Sumt'r was not concerned with Anisah, but he had some concern about Pet'r. He had noticed the man, though not talking much, was glaring at him.

"I don't need my *boyfriend*, Sumt'r. In fact, now that two of your gang have called me a name I'm not pleased with, I think I'll let you visit someone who might fit the billing those names imply, and she can put you to good use, I imagine," Anisah smiled again, raised both hands in front of her for just a moment.

Every one in the room felt the air tingling, like an itch that couldn't be scratched. Every one in the room, able to watch, saw Sumt'r disappear and then all his men. Every one in the room, except Pet'r jumped back a step or two, even Col'n and his small group, and started backing toward any exit they could find.

There was a stunned silence for just a moment, then with great exodus from the Queen's Ransom, all went running as fast as they could to get out of Anisah's sight, even the bartender decided he had no need to still be there.

"You sure know how to excite a crowd. That was certainly effective. Where'd you send them?" Pet'r asked. grinning.

She looked up at him and smiled, "I thought Voravia would love to have the boys come visit. I remember you being quite the hero there before," Anisah laughed aloud. Pet'r joined her.

Anisah turned to leave and walked over to Col'n who as amazed at Pet'r, standing tall and peaceful beside her.

"Pet'r, I'd like for you to meet Col'n. He's a good friend and helped me today. He came when I told him he shouldn't and I'm grateful," Anisah introduced Col'n. He and Pet'r shook hands.

"Nice to meet you. I believe I remember you from the hotel when we visited before," Pet'r told him.

"That's right. I was just a working slave then," Col'n added, then they both laughed.

"I appreciate what you've done to help Anisah, both now and in the past. You take care and be a bit more careful about who you chose to attack, or how, when the culprits are this sort. Just some friendly advice. I, too, feel I can count you as a friend," Pet'r told Col'n. "But we have to leave now. Good luck to you. Until later.

Anisah, I'm glad I could help. I'm sorry I have to rush you, but we need to go now. We need to get back with Geth'n and the others. A lot has happened since we last were together and we should get you back as soon as we can," Pet'r urged Anisah.

"Pet'r, what's the hurry. We can talk in just a bit," she said to Pet'r., placing her hand on his arm. "I need to be with these friends for just a little longer."

"But, Anisah, things are so much worse than before. We really do need to leave," Pet'r implored. But he recognized Anisah was going to take the time to talk to these new friends and, though he was anxious, relented, relaxed and waited for her.

She turned away from him and began talking to Col'n and his group.

"Col'n, I want to thank you and your team again for being here today. You helped me get through some difficult moments and I can't express enough my gratitude for all of you. Thank you very much."

Anisah's small group weren't the only ones outside the bar now. But there were only a few stragglers returning. Many of those there before who had wandered back to the bar saw Anisah was still there, turned and walked away. Anisah, Col'n and his group strolled away from the building while chatting among themselves. They all would have quite the tale to tell about this day.

"Your world has certainly changed a lot since I last saw you. You obviously have become someone I believe even you would not have thought you'd be," Col'n said to Anisah, still recovering from witnessing Sumt'r and his group disappear. "Did you know these things before?"

"No, I didn't. Everything is so much more complicated than I would have ever thought they would become. But I will tell you this now; there is a need for the people to band together, to create an army of citizens to help fight what Pet'r, myself and Geth'n, the other man who left with me the last time, believe to be a horrible and destruction future if we do nothing. But you can help; you can tell the people what is coming and help us save our world," Anisah spoke solemnly. "Let's walk back to the hotel and I'll reveal what I know as we go."

They strolled toward the hotel. The other young men who had volunteered offered their good-byes and went their separate ways. Soon only Anisah, Col'n and Pet'r were left as they approached the hotel and entered, still talking earnestly.

After they got to the hotel, Anisah told all her friends she had to leave again, but warned them about the coming war.

"Col'n, would you please reveal what you saw today to Mercy. I promised we'd talk when I got back, but I believe Pet'r needs for me to return with him fairly soon," Anisah told her friend. "And tell others what Pet'r and I have been explaining. The more messages sent out to warn everyone, the better." She and Pet'r were hopeful spreading the story about their experiences would help the community began to plan for their own defense.

Then Anisah took Pet'r aside.

"What is happening? What is the urgency?" she asked him. "Where are Geth'n and the others?"

"We, at the moment, are all at Borny'a's cabin, but we have to get back there very soon. There are armies marching to capture that whole area and it isn't safe. For any of us," Pet'r explained. "We really do need to leave as soon as you have gathered your things. You've tried to warn those here you needed to, but there is no time to lose. Besides, I sense someone close by who, I suspect, does not have our best interest in mind."

"I thought I felt something, too. Could be Ole Bas. I mean, Mano'n. I believe he's following me." She added. "His pursuit of me is another story. We probably need to wait until later for me to tell it. Let me get my clothes from upstairs and we can go."

She turned and ran up the stairs. She was back within minutes. She and Pet'r stood together in the hallway. They could see no one about, glanced at each other, then they were gone.

Just down the street from the Queen's Ransom, one of those in the crowd, watched the young lady and her escort leave. He followed them and now stood across the street from the hotel wondering what he should do next. He realized suddenly his daughter had just departed again and he had no idea where. This time, the signals were scrambled somehow.

She's much more powerful, at this time in her life, than I would have ever thought possible. She has a force beyond what I would've ever expected, and she apparently has strong friends now. If she doesn't change her views about what Baalsa'n needs her to do, we are lost. We are lost, if we cannot stop her. I need to talk to Voravia.

Mano'n walked outside, looked up and down the street, walked a short distant, turned into an alley and disappeared.

Across the way, two small creatures, strange in appearance, looked out from the shadows of the same alley.

"Whos dat, Mord?" Kesk asked, shrinking from Mord who wasn't very happy.

They had tried to get close enough to Anisah to inflict some harm, but now the girl seemed to have gained too much power. They weren't certain what to do.

"Ifs mans in blacks cannot dos this things, how can wes?" Kesk wondered. This time Mord did smack him behind the head, but Kesk was prepared for the pain and only whimpered for a moment.

"I donts know, Kesk? I donts know," Mord answered truthfully.

They slinked away into the darker regions of the alley and waited for nightfall. But when they came out again, the girl was gone.

"Where'd shes go, Mord?" Kesk asked and stepped away from his companion.

But Mord didn't strike his partner this time.

"Ims afraid I not knows. I donts," he answered, looking

173

around at the dark that engulfed them.

A WAR TO BE WON

It was morning when Pet'r and Anisah arrived. She ran to Borny'a and gave him a great hug. Borny'a let her do so, but didn't return it. Anisah was so excited she didn't notice.

"So how are my patients? I hear you have a few more now," she chattered, excited to be back with Geth'n and Borny'a.

Borny'a seemed reserved. He stood back while Geth'n and Anisah were responding to being together again. Pet'r noticed Borny'a's withdrawal and moved closer to him.

In a lowered voice, Pet'r asked Borny'a to go outside with him. They walked away from the cabin a short distance.

"You must build your trust on what you believe about Geth'n and me," Pet'r spoke softly to the other man as they strolled quietly. "If you truly believe I'm a descendant of Areb'l, I hope there is enough strength in that trust to allow Anisah to prove herself to you again. I know you did trust her before and the discovery her family may be of Baalsa'n's, though disturbing, has not proven she is untrustworthy. She has to explain that to us. So I say we should hear her out."

Borny'a slowed and stopped.

"What you ask is difficult. I saw so many of my loved ones and so many of my friends destroyed by the Om-Esfer'n under Baalsa'n's leadership. It is difficult for me to accept this is not a deception," Borny'a answered. "But, though I'll be watching closely, I will give the young lady some time to prove herself. I must admit she never once gave me a reason to doubt her before. She truly has Jond'r welfare as her principal concern, she treated him with compassion. So, I can wait, but I will be watching for anything suspicious. I can promise I'll have patience, but I'll be watching."

175

"I wouldn't expect you to be any different. You are, as best I can tell, sincere and certainly honest about this. I have to respect that," Pet'r added. "I'll talk to Geth'n. He and I will also be watchful. And I do know this. When I reached her, she only needed my help briefly, but there was, at least, one problem. Someone — and she named him as Mano'n — was following her. I don't know that name, but I assume you would"

Borny'a snapped a look at Pet'r with the mention of Mano'n. He frowned and looked about the area cautiously as though expecting something dangerous to happen.

"Being chased. Wonder why? I think Anisah has a great deal to explain, if she knows Mano'n. We could all be in great danger," Borny'a answered. "She'd better have a good story."

Borny'a turned quickly and walked back toward the cabin. Pet'r, not entirely surprised, followed closely. They burst into the cabin.

Anisah and Geth'n were sitting at the table, having a general conversation. Each mildly involved in revealing their recent adventures to the other. They looked around with Pet'r and Borny'a entered and both noticed the anxious look on Borny'a's face.

"What's wrong?" Geth'n asked. Pet'r, standing behind Borny'a, shook his head at Geth'n. "Or shouldn't I ask?"

"Now that all of us are here, we need to talk. We need to talk seriously and with haste," Borny'a blurted out, turned and stood near the door; his arms crossed over his chest.

"What is the problem?" Geth'n glared at Borny'a.

"I cannot abide any deceit; I will not be able to work with this group unless something is resolved to my satisfaction," Borny'a answered. The look on his face was evident, he was filled with hatred.

"What explanations do you need?" Geth'n asked. Pet'r stepped quietly between Anisah and Borny'a. Anisah wasn't aware of the change in the room. Jond'r, Acron'n and Garv'n were all still unconscious and she was attending each of them.

176

"I need to know what Anisah's allegiances are!" Borny'a was getting more angry by the moment. Pet'r wasn't certain he could control the older man if he became wrathful.

"What? What's wrong? What did he say?" she stood, turned and was looking directly at Borny'a. "What is it about me you don't know? I consider us friends. You saw how I cared for these men, how I have supported our efforts. What's wrong with you?"

"I have been told you are part of the Om-Esfer'n family!" Borny'a was shouting now. Pet'r moved closer to Anisah and took a defensive stance. Geth'n had risen and walked across the room to where Anisah stood. "I'll not abide being near you unless you can explain to me what you are doing here?"

"Oh, so you've been told what Voravia said," Anisah said, looking askance at her two friends. "Well, I'll tell you whatever you want to know, but I must first tell you. I'm not certain of all the details.

I've only recently been told what you say is true. I grew up in Caliste, not far from here, as a farm girl. Almost totally unaware of what the world was about, just wanting to find some happiness. I was being mistreated, or thought I was, by my family and I wanted to go to Tariny to learn to be a healer because the man who cared for me all my younger years died and I wasn't able to save him.

So I ran away and, during my trip to Tariny, I met Geth'n and Pet'r. It seemed our destiny to be together. None of us knew why, but we knew we needed to be together.

"When we ran into trouble, it was the worst kind. Voravia captured Pet'r, and Rab'k had captured Geth'n and me when we were in the caverns below her castle.

"I don't know how but Pet'r was able to escape and rescue Geth'n and me, but before he did I discovered, and was told by Voravia, I was the daughter of Mano'n. I had no idea who that was. I refused to accept what she said. But she and I have such strong resemblance it's almost impossible to disbelieve what she

177

said. Still I resisted it."

We three then were involved in a battle with Voravia and Rab'k. We were able to escape with our lives. But, once again, Voravia insisted we were related. More importantly, I discovered I had some magical powers. Very limited, but still there and I was surprised.

But we all disappeared at the end of the battle and I re-appeared in Caliste. I saw my mother again. But an older member of the community, Ole Bas, stepped forward while I was there. Suddenly and magically, he began to change form and became a much younger man, dressed all in black.

He made some statements about my being his daughter and, I guessed correctly, he was Mano'n. I denied I was his daughter and asked my mother for the truth. She, with grief, admitted I was and that this amulet I wear had come from him."

She pulled the black crystal from around her neck into view. It began to glow with a deep, dark light reflecting from the walls about them. She quickly pushed it under a cloth on one of the beds.

"During our conversation, Voravia suddenly arrived and ridiculed my disbelief. I had, when I was younger, discovered the amulet was a magic talisman. I had inadvertently used it in anger and, in that way, discovered some of the truth about myself.

But, they attempted to capture me and take me to Baalsa'n. I refused to do that and, I think now, surprised them with the magic I've learned on my own.

"I was able to send Voravia back to her castle – against her wishes. Mano'n was unable to use his magic against me. I also discovered what each of us is able to do now – and I transported myself to Tariny and into the Healers' College. But, realizing Mano'n probably wasn't going to give up so easily, I immediately lifted myself to a safer place, strangely Varspree.

But, even there, I had trouble. I discovered another man was following me. Sumt'r, a thief and scoundrel, who kidnapped me

178

when I first began my journey to Tariny. I was able to escape him with some tricks I learned when younger. But he tracked me somehow to Varspree and had his men torment one of my benefactors there. He was going to continue placing those people in danger because of me.

I decided I needed to remedy that problem. I did so, but I asked Pet'r to help and he did.

I can't deny what you are saying. I assume now it's true. But, that family did not raise me, nor have I ever been involved with them. I was totally unaware of the connection because my mother hid those facts from me.

I'm telling you, and Geth'n and Pet'r, I have never, nor will I ever, act toward you, nor anyone else in our group, as those people would. My first true desire is to help those in pain and suffering in any form. My whole being is tuned to spare those I can from evil and suffering. It is beyond my nature to believe I could ever do harm to anyone unless that person creates pain, or proves to be evil.

You have seen my desperation over other people's pain; my overwhelming, and almost crazed, desire to cure them. I have dreamed of the Ahar'n, which I know Pet'r now carries, and I know I will use it to bring health to others, particularly to children.

I believe I cannot have contempt for the world as the Om-Esfer'n do. The actions of Mano'n and Voravia have shown me the despicable attitude they have toward our people. I do consider the inhabitants of Aerolan, and of Narhtrae, to be my people. My mother is and I am my mother's daughter.

I have no way to prove I am loyal to Aerolan and I understand your apprehension. I can only promise you, and my two friends here, my heart and love for the Al-Esfer'n and the people here is real. I believe my actions have shown that to be true."

Pet'r had edge closer to Anisah as she talked. He now touched her shoulder with his and looked defiantly at Borny'a. He had only recently met the man, a man who acted distrustful of him when they first met.

An immortal, or not, the man hadn't proven to him his worth, and, as far as Pet'r was concerned, Anisah had. Pet'r was going to protect her, if it was necessary, against anyone declaring to be her enemy.

Tension filled the room. Geth'n moved nearer to Anisah.

Borny'a looked at Geth'n and Pet'r. They were coming to her defense and he began to calm himself. He remembered how she acted when they first met. How she seemed to suffer when they found Jond'r – as though Jond'r's pain was her own. He remembered her spending long nights caring for the injured man; and today he witnessed how she asked for and ran to attend Jond'r, Acron'n and Garv'n, the latter two whom she had never met, as soon as she entered the cabin.

He shook his head, turned his back and started to leave the cabin.

"Wait, Borny'a. Please," Anisah spoke to him. She placed her hand on Pet'r's arm and pulled him back a step. "There is only this I can do. Please take this amulet." She reached and pulled the black glass stone from under the covers of the bed where she placed it earlier and held it out to him.

"This, I believe, is an unholy relic and piece of the larger amulet we saw at our first battle. I have no need of it. I believe my powers come from another source. I believe that stone does not bind me. But I want you to keep it, or destroy it, so you can be certain it isn't to be part of what we are and must continue to be.

We have to trust each other. We are in danger – more than you three know – and I'll not be able to help if you can't accept me for what I am. I'm a friend and want to be. I'm certain, as certain as I can be with the limited resources I've used, I will not be influenced by this stone, nor the Om-Esfer'n, for any reason.

Please trust me. My life, and love of it, is really in your hands. From what Pet'r told me about you, I will be honored to still call you my friend and call you my warrior, if you'll let me."

She took a deep breath and waited. Borny'a had stopped and waited until she finished. He stood with his back to her during her supplications.

There was just a moment of silence. Then he turned to her, smiled and held his arms toward her. She cried with delight, ran, jumped into his arms and held him tightly. They embraced for several minutes, released and stepped back from each other.

"Let's go back to what we knew before. I will cast your black stone into the lake here and we should be able to forget it exists," Borny'a extended his arms, reached and held her shoulders. "I am sorry about this. But, so much suffering has been imposed by the Om-Esfer'n. I couldn't bear to live with that again. But maybe, I can call one of them my friend. If the day arrives I'm wrong, I'll know only grief. But I think, at this moment, I should not be concerned."

"Thank you, Borny'a. I love you for that," Anisah said to him and smiled so completely he knew she wasn't lying.

Pet'r relaxed during the embrace. Geth'n stood composed near the fireplace, watching this reconciliation.

Borny'a turned and quietly left the cabin and walked away toward the south end of the lake. He disappeared into the edge of the woods and out of anyone's sight. After a moment, he walked to the edge of the water, looked out over the lake at the beauty of the place; a place soon to be lost to him after all those years.

He stood for a moment, head bowed, remembering the peace he felt here after his own losses ages before. He looked down at the amulet in his hand, his rage rose and he threw the stone as far as he could out over the water. He watched until he saw it splash, turned and walked back to the cabin. His thoughts and grief were his alone.

The others had been chatting about the various things that happened to them since the battle on the plateau when he entered. Borny'a looked at each one then nodded his head. It was

181

finished.

There was a very quiet moment then. They all felt their world come back together again.

"So what have you gentlemen decided we must do?" Anisah spoke first. "I think I have a lot to learn."

"Wait, before we start I have something to tell everyone that might lighten our thoughts at this moment," Pet'r interjected. "I think this should be mentioned. Though Anisah may not want it to be. Yesterday, Anisah call me to help her with a little problem. It was significant, but not critical in terms of any danger to her. But you should have seen it. It was amazing."

In fact, when Pet'r gave them a brief segment of the small conflict in Varspree. Geth'n and Borny'a laughed with their friend. Anisah stared at Pet'r but she too laughed with the others.

"I'll not forget this Pet'r – you'll pay someday," Anisah said, a false frown on her face.

After a moment of light conversation, some still teasing Anisah. Geth'n interrupted after a moment.

"I think we have to become serious about our situation now," he said, his face showing his concern. "The one thing of immediate importance we know, we desperately need to leave here as soon as possible. There is imminent danger; an army surges toward us as we stand here.

They are the enemy. They've been casting about in villages, kidnapping men who they modify, somehow, into creatures, more aggressive and more brutal, than those Voravia has. Not certain where these soldiers are from exactly, although Borny'a believes they came from Ravelan and were part of a group Baalsa'n used in the previous war." He was simplifying but felt Anisah and the others were aware of what the issues were.

"We've decided to transport all the wounded here to Rab'k's old castle on the southern coast," Pet'r added, pointing toward the older man. "Jond'r was an officer there and is a familiar face to the people. We know Rab'k isn't likely to return. So, it's our de-

182

cision to move everyone there unless you think that unwise."

"That plan sounds good to me," Anisah added. "And, at this moment, we need to determine how to get these injured from here to either this castle, or to Tariny and the hospital there. The soldiers are a bit tougher and should do well at the castle. I think the older gentleman should go to the hospital."

"His name is Garv'n," a voice came from one of the cots.

They all jerked around. Pet'r and Borny'a jumped apart and into a battle stance. Geth'n stood and moved quickly between them with his hands exposed, pointed toward the speaker.

Jond'r held up his right hand.

"Wait! Wait. It's only me," he grinned as he reached out, hand up. "You gentlemen seem a bit jumpy."

He was sitting on the side of the cot. They didn't hear him rise and hadn't expected it at all. His left arm and shoulder were bound tightly with the bandages Anisah had applaud, and those Borny'a had replaced, so his arm was held tightly to his body.

"Do I know any of you? Who are you and what are you talking about?" Jond'r tried to stand, but wasn't able. Borny'a relaxed and walked to him, helping him rise.

"You I remember from outside this place," he nodded at Borny'a. "I remember him – Geth'n, wasn't it?" he looked at Geth'n and smiled.

"But who are you?" He looked at Pet'r and then around the room. He spotted Garv'n still lying quietly on the other cot. Then he looked at the person lying on the floor. "Who's that?"

"It's your brother," Pet'r answered. He had relaxed after all the tension subsided.

"What's he doing here?" Jond'r staggered a bit. "What happened to him?"

"He's had a bad couple of days himself. But we got him back here and Borny'a has patched him enough to believe he'll be fine in the next couple of days," Pet'r rose to help Jond'r who looked at him suspiciously.

183

"Who are you again?" Jond'r, though weak, was alert.

"Me. I'm Pet'r, a friend of Acron'n. We're here because Geth'n knew he needed to return – we've come to rescue you and the others."

Jond'r smiled at the news about his brother, then looked around. "There was a girl. Where's An. . . Anisah. . . . Where's she?"

"I'm here," Anisah had stepped back to ease her own tension. Too many confrontations, one with Borny'a and now this sudden one. She was, in her own way, still shocked by the admissions she made about her family. Her life was changing more quickly than she was comfortable with.

"That's great. I'm very glad, for many reasons, to see you again and meet some new faces," Jond'r added, moving his left shoulder a bit, wincing as he did. "Looks like you did a good job wrappin' me up. But, it sure is sore."

"Probably will be for a while," Borny'a said, making certain he didn't harm the young man while holding him. Jond'r leaned a bit and Borny'a helped him sit down again. "You need something to eat. Let me get that while we try to answer your questions."

"Where Rab'k?" Jond'r asked. "Since Garv'n is here, I assume Rab'k continued his attack and obtained whatever it was he wanted from Garv'n."

"He may have destroyed everyone who was in that group, except Garv'n, who was barely alive when Voravia's men delivered him here," Borny'a answered.

Geth'n spoke up, "After we left here, Anisah and I discovered the place where the attack occurred. We found no one alive though there were body parts scattered about. It was a total massacre as best we could tell. Garv'n wasn't there when we arrived. I can now only surmise Voravia's people took him away before we got there".

"They brought him to trade for food," Borny'a interjected while he fumbled around in his stores. "They weren't hostile par-

184

ticularly, so I traded."

"Rab'k is alive and well. Geth'n, Anisah and I were recently involved in a confrontation with Voravia. He was there with her. I remember hearing one of them mention he was a brother. I was a little busy rescuing this guy and Anisah," Pet'r pointed toward Geth'n, "to notice which. But, I do remember thinking how odd that sounded."

"It could be. It could be. Baalsa'n never liked the creations of the Al-Esfer'n, but he didn't mind mating with some of the women to acquire progeny. In fact, if those two are brother and sister, then there was, or is, another. Mano'n. We already know who he is. Older than the other two. He came from Parsenan, another world destroyed by the Om-Esfer'n," Borny'a added, nodding his head toward Anisah.

"Who's Baalsa'n?" Jond'r asked.

"He is our nemesis. He is the leader of the Om-Esfer'n – a division of the Esfer'n – trying to destroy every world settlement he can find. He is here now – with the same intent," Borny'a answered. "There is no mercy for the inhabitants of any of the planets, nor the planets. Everything is destroyed. Centuries ago, he was here but failed because the Ahar'n was held here. Through its magic, this planet was spared. He passed on to another world, farther away. But, in his rage, I assume he never quit wanting to destroy this place, so he's returned."

"So, if we choose to fight back, we'll have our hands full," Jond'r replied, nodding toward the two younger men, but talking to Borny'a.

"Yes. I'm from another planet also. I was brought here to fight against this monster. But, the peace here has held for all these years. It's been a blessing. These two were born here, just as you were. So, they have a strong allegiance to their home and have, as it turns out, been given some special powers they are not yet familiar with.

It'll be one of their purposes to learn more about our

strengths when we can organize and begin to call in others to form our troops," Borny'a added. "We need them, and we need Anisah, who saved your life, to be with us. Or we are certainly lost."

Jond'r was nodding his head during Borny'a explanation. He watched the two boys react to some of the presentation; he noticed a resolute expression on the face of both.

"Is this place safe for us?" Jond'r asked Geth'n.

"No. Pet'r and I have already run across stiff opposition just north of here. We know there are other troops in Voravia's territory from Ravelan. And we know they are gathering random men from the villages up there to apparently change them to either one of Voravia's odd creatures, or to something even worse," Geth'n explained.

Pet'r was nodding his head as Geth'n talked. He looked to watch Borny'a and Jond'r's expressions as the story unfolded. They, the old hands, the military stalwarts, became more and more worried as the discussions continued.

"Are we going to find a safe place?" Pet'r interjected. "We can talk a great deal about what we can do, but the fact is we are going to be overrun here in a few days. If we intend to deal with all these problems, we need to leave."

Jond'r looked around at his brother and at Garv'n lying, injured and sick.

"I have an idea. I agree we should go first to the castle where Rab'k lived on the southern coast, near Roahan. I believe I've mentioned it before and it actually belongs to Garv'n. I assume Rab'k won't be returning. I was assigned by Garv'n to help Rab'k, in his support role. I believe I can get access to it very easily. In fact, I'm probably expected."

"That's fairly close to Peetle where we're from," Geth'n mentioned.

Borny'a watched the others nodding in agreement and, though he hated leaving his home even knowing it was to be lost to the enemy, agreed the move there would be the best possible plan at this time. "I think we need to do this."

Geth'n stood and walked over to the fire hearth and turned back slowly to the others.

"I have a suggestion. Pet'r, Anisah and I have a rather handy power we've only recently discovered. It seems the Al-Esfer'n have given us the means to teleport at will," he said. "We have used it individually on separate occasions though, at times, we weren't aware we could. It's proven useful. I would imagine Anisah also is able to do this though we haven't seen, nor heard from her, recently. But, I'm not certain – and Pet'r may know – I'm able to transport someone else with me."

"I do," Anisah was listening mostly while attending Acron'n and Garv'n. "I'm able to teleport myself to places I'm familiar with. But I'm not certain I can *blind shoot* a place." She turned back to her work.

"I'm not even certain whether, or not, I can do this," Pet'r spoke up. "It has only happened for me when I was in danger."

"You boys need to test this and quickly," Borny'a said, perking up on the mention of such skills. It had been a long time since he struggled alongside the Al-Esfer'n, but he remembered that ability came in handy on more than one occasion. "I remember the Al-Esfer'n could move others. Why don't one of you chose a place you're familiar with and let's determine if you can willing go to the place by yourself."

Geth'n stepped up.

"I'll test this. I'll go to Larilla where Pet'r and I spent many hours in the library. I should be able to return quickly," he volunteered.

Pet'r looked askance, but said nothing; he also noticed Anisah looked up from her work and raised an eyebrow. He nodded at her understanding her concerns. He knew Geth'n and knew he wasn't foolish enough to try something he wasn't comfortable

187

with. He nodded at his friend.

"Leave something on the last table in the library. Say one of those arrows," he pointed to Borny'a's quiver hanging by the door.

"I'll try to retrieve it," Pet'r said, watching the other two men for their reactions. Borny'a seemed calm about it, but he noticed Jond'r was a bit nervous.

Geth'n agreed, retrieved one of the arrows, stood in thought a moment and disappeared.

"Well, I guess we wait," Jond'r said, moving around on the bed, trying to get to his feet.

Pet'r walked to him and helped him stand, "There you are, sir. If I can do anything else, just let me know."

Borny'a noticed this respect toward Jond'r, nodded to himself and smiled at Jond'r. Jond'r nodded in return.

"Thank you, Pet'r. Pet'r is correct, isn't it?" Jond'r responded. "I'll probably need to try a little harder on my own, but I accept your offer."

"Yes sir. Pet'r is correct," Pet'r answered.

At that same moment, Geth'n reappeared. He seemed a little troubled.

"Did you have trouble with your trip," Pet'r asked him quickly, noticing Geth'n's anguish look.

"No, but something has changed there. Not certain what. Maybe you and I, when we get done with this move, should go and investigate. Anyway, I put the arrow where you suggested," Geth'n answered, but looked away and out the window toward the lake. He saw something in Larilla he was upset about.

"Well, I'll be back shortly," Pet'r said. He bowed his head just a bit in concentration and he too disappeared.

It was only a short moment before he returned. He looked around anxiously to make certain where he was. He was more nervous than when he left.

"Any problems, Pet'r?" Borny'a asked. Pet'r looked around at him with a drawn and frantic look in his eyes.

"No, sir. No problems with the trip and here's the arrow," Pet'r responded guardedly, handing the arrow to Borny'a. "Just strange. Too much was changed and too many things I saw were almost alien. Could it be the Om-Esfer'n have already been there? Geth'n and I need to visit Peetle as quickly as we can."

Borny'a stepped forward now.

"I understand your concerns. Let's finish this test as quickly as we're able, gentlemen. No need to wait. I volunteer for the next transportation," he walked to Pet'r's side. "You and me, son. I'll take my bow and arrows with me this time. Maybe we can scout around and determine what happened on that peninsula."

"Geth'n, I suggest you take Jond'r to the castle and see if we can access it because we definitely need to get there quickly. We should meet back here no more than two hours from now. The sun is directly centered, so be cautious and be alert; the danger is all about us," Borny'a said.

"Even recognizing Anisah has the ability to take at least one of these men to safety, I think, if she is willing, she would best be used if she can stay with Garv'n and Acron'n until one of us returns. Acknowledging the danger of trying to move these men without awareness of either location, could endanger Anisah and the two injured. There is the potential for the three to fall into a dangerous situation staying here, but, I suspect, she'll be able to handle what comes to her. I base that on what has just been explained about her new-found skills," Borny'a was more comfortable in command than being a follower.

Anisah completed her inspection of the wounds and bandages of her new patients and was listening to the conversation and plan for departure while continuing her work. She looked up when her name was mentioned and nodded her agreement to his plan.

Borny'a gathered his things, "All right, son. Let's do this." He walked over and stood next to Pet'r and they disappeared.

189

"I'm not exactly certain where the castle is, but I've been to Roahan a number of times when our fleet from Peetle visited the immense seafood market there. Is that fairly close to the castle and will that be too far for you to walk?" Geth'n asked Jond'r.

"You're right. Roahan is the closest village. I think I'll be fine, at least until we can see the castle. Then you can gauge the distance and transport us the rest of the way. I'm a little edgy about doing this at all, so bear with me a moment. I need to make certain I have my shoulder drawn closer to me to prevent jarring and, I'm not ashamed to say, this scares me," Jond'r admitted, but he laughed.

Geth'n smiled at him.

"My first time was a huge surprise. Right in the middle of a big fight, I popped out. Ended up in Tariny in the basement of the library there. It was so dusty and smelled like a thousand trapped books. Which was true. But, now I've traveled a good deal, so I consider myself an old hand. Shouldn't be too bumpy," he laughed and walked over to Jond'r to make sure the bindings were snug. "Comfortable?"

"Yes, do you mind if I close my eyes?" Jond'r implored.

"Go ahead. I'll let you know when we are there," Geth'n chuckled. "We'll see you later, Anisah. Take care and, if any trouble arrives, let us know as soon as you can. We'll come if you call." He looked around the room to make certain they weren't forgetting something, then looked out the window to sense if anyone was nearby. Satisfied, he walked next to Jond'r and nodded his head.

They were gone.

Later, Anisah, tired from her ordeal in Varspree and wondering how this terrible war was going to end, was sitting in a chair near the fireplace enjoying the warmth and relaxing for a moment when she heard noises outside.

She rose and walked to the window with the view of the lake

190

and the distant mountain and saw movement of foliage along the pass beyond and along the ridge just above the cabin.

She turned and looked at her two patients and realized she had to do something to keep them safe. She went to the door, cracked it a bit to see if there was anything between her and the lake edge and, more importantly, on the south side of the cabin away from those coming through the forest.

Making a quick determination about what she had to do, she stepped through the door closing it softly behind her and, holding her skirts high so she wouldn't trip, ran quickly behind some larger trees next to the cabin. She looked out from her hiding place and was stunned by the number of beings, creatures that fit the descriptions Pet'r and Geth'n gave earlier, shuffling down through the trees and undergrowth.

"I've got to stall these monsters until Pet'r, or Geth'n, returns," she mumbled. "But how?"

ANGUISH AND REVENGE

Pet'r and Borny'a appeared just outside the library on the campus of the college in Larilla. They decided to quickly go to Peetle and headed in that direction, but, it was difficult for Pet'r. A number of the buildings had been ransacked at the college and that trend was evident as they left the outskirts of the town.

Along the road toward Peetle, homes had been ravaged, fields burned, most of the people were gone. Only stragglers here and there clinging to their belongings were evident as they trudged along the road toward Varspree.

Pet'r became more and more angry as they pushed down the road. Borny'a was cautious with the boy, not wanting to disturb him while the scenes they came across became more and more difficult for Pet'r to bear. He had never been involved with war, nor the horror of one-sided battles when citizens and their families were murdered and the land ravaged by the offending army.

"Who could have done this? Why is this happening?" Pet'r stopped , looked around at all the destruction, and yelled at the top of his voice, which boomed across the countryside.

"I can only believe Monsh'a's people swept through this area on a random and singular attack. My thinking is Baalsa'n is the culprit; he decided you two boys interfered too often in his plans. I think this is a lesson for you and Geth'n to show his power, his strength," Borny'a answered.

He didn't like his answer anymore than Pet'r did, but his long history provided a quicker insight into cause and effect of this powerful enemy.

"We have to stop this maniac. There's no justification for these offenses against innocent people. They have done nothing to him, or his. Why does he feel justified in doing this?" Pet'r could

192

hardly hold his desire to become violent. He wanted to rage and destroy whoever had treated his homeland this way. He wanted that to happen now.

But his enemy was far away, hidden in the mountains to the north. The only possibility for Pet'r to relieve his anguish would have to be local for now.

"Baalsa'n doesn't require justification except his own. He hates all of the people of Aerolan and of Narhtrae. He will destroy everyone eventually. Purge every living thing from this planet, scorch and burn all things this planet represents, make it devoid of life, in his hatred of the Al-Esfer'n," Borny'a explained.

"He has no qualms about doing this. He has decided he will not allow the Al-Esfer'n to advance their plans to settle this universe with intelligent beings on livable planets. He believes all of us, though not the Om-Esfer'n, are evil and a scourge of the living. He's passionate about acting on this concept quickly. He's a hard man to stop."

They walked in silence for a while.

"I know this because they completely destroyed my home all those years ago. Your ancestor, Areb'l, found me beneath the rubble of my home. My family were thrown about in the house and in the yard, slaughtered. He saved me and brought me here when we were able to escape.

Baalsa'n followed others and us to this place many years later, but he came with a small force and we were able to drive him away. I believe there was another, more irritating place, for him to attend to, so he went to finish that. But we survived that first attack and we must build our strength to battle against him now he has returned. But we must know he has not come undermanned this time," Borny'a talked softly as they pushed onward toward Peetle. Neither of them looked away from the road; neither could abide inspecting the ruin and devastation.

When they finally arrived at the top of the low hill that overlooked the plain reaching out to the sea and saw Peetle, it over-

193

whelmed Pet'r. He stopped, dropped to his knee and wept. The town did not exist anymore. Almost all the boats of the fishing community were destroyed, or gone; almost all the homes were burned and damaged beyond repair. Smoke rose from most of them, even now. There was no way to tell how long, prior to this destruction, the force had attacked except by this ominous sign. The smoke rose only in certain spots. They could see no one about.

"There must be someone left, someone who survived this," Pet'r cried out his pain. "There must be someone we can save."

Pet'r began running down the hill toward the town. He searched across the small prairie and the part of the town he could see from the road.

Suddenly, he stopped. He dropped to a crouch. Borny'a who was following him closely slid to a stop and dropped down next to Pet'r.

"There is an encampment, just north of the town. I saw the tops of the tent through the smoke," Pet'r almost whispered though he wasn't out of breath. "There are troops still in the area. Why?"

"There must be some resistance. That means there are some alive and holding back these troops. I don't know how but it seems evident the force wants to destroy everything and hasn't done that yet. So they're still here," Borny'a answered. "That's the only logical reason for the delayed departure."

"Let's see what we can do about that," Pet'r almost spit the words. He rose to look in the direction of camp and motioned Borny'a to follow him. He diverted toward the south of the town and accelerated his pace. Soon he was skimming across the open area, fast enough he seemed to fly. He made no attempt to conceal himself because he assumed the smoke from the town hid him. Borny'a trailed just behind him.

They reached a place familiar to Pet'r. The old meeting hall where the announcements for the town had been read to the people. The tales of good fishing, the weather signs, new marriages, new births and the hopes for the future of Peetle were shared among the town folks. It had been a good place to live.

He stopped and stooped behind the back wall of what was left of the building. He began to claw at the rubble laying on the ground near the foundation. Borny'a wondered what he intended.

Then, Borny'a saw why the boy was digging. Soon there was a door to a cellar exposed. Borny'a bent to help clear it.

When Pet'r finally uncovered the door, he bent next to it, bowed his head in fear of what was below, knocked on the wood a few times and yanked the door away from the opening,. Then he ripped it completely away and threw it beyond the edge of the yard surrounding the building. Borny'a was barely able to step aside and avoided being hit by the missile.

Pet'r jumped down the short stairs and stood at the bottom. There were screams from inside, people yelling, trying to hide in a place already full. There was nowhere else to hide. All those hidden could only see Pet'r's shadow against the light. They had no way to know who it was, nor had anything to hope for if this was yet another soldier.

Pet'r called out his father's name.

"Vandr'e! Are you here? Is mother here? Who's here?" Tears ran down his face, now covered with the soot and ash from the fires. The old building creaked with the change in the air sweeping into the cellar area.

"Please, don't hurt us anymore. Please leave us. Please don't kill us." The moans and cries came from the dark.

"Please anyone. It's Pet'r. I've come back. Please, someone identify yourself," he stepped sideways into the dark and away from the backlight. His features became more visible.

Borny'a stood outside the cellar, scanning the area to avoid any watch patrols wandering the area. All was clear at the moment, but he knew he had to stay alert until these people were rescued.

"Oh, Pet'r. Oh, no. Oh, no. We're dying. We're so frightened.

195

Please help us. Please," someone begged for help. Someone who knew Pet'r well. But he didn't hear his father answer, or his mother.

He raged, stood upward under the low ceiling and ripped the floor above him and cast it as far as he could. The piece flew through the air, hit the ground near the docks and skidded across them and into the sea beyond.

Those inside screamed again and huddled together. Pet'r strength was not something they expected. But they could see him more clearly.

"Pet'r, please help. We have several who are near death. We need water and we need food. We lost hope. You've returned. Thank the gods," someone spoke from the near darkness.

Borny'a cleared his throat.

"Pet'r, I'm afraid your launch of the floor into the water has alerted the troops. They seem to be gathering a few squads to come investigate the noise," he informed the boy. He thought Pet'r was being incautious, but he remembered his own anguish from many years before and held no blame for the boy's anger.

"Let them come!" Pet'r's eyes flashed as looked up into the light at Borny'a. "I welcome them."

"I think these folks should stay here until we deal with this problem," Borny'a added. "We need to clear these troops away."

"Agreed," Pet'r answered and looked back at the people still cowering in the semi-dark of the exposed cellar. "I promise we will be back to see to your needs in just a moment, or two. We need to rid ourselves of soldiers who are nearby."

"How are you going to do that?" one of the men, a friend of Pet'r's father, asked.

"We should have no trouble," Pet'r answered, calm now he knew he could save someone. "But you must stay hidden, as best you can. We will be back."

With that, he rose, walked up the cellar stairs and stood with Borny'a. They looked across the town's center courtyard and saw

196

there were a number of soldiers running toward them, weapons ready. Some sort of odd creature, Pet'r saw only recently, was with them.

"Sort of big, aren't they?" Borny'a suggested.

"Yep, but too slow. All of them seem to work toward their right side. Don't know why. But it was an obvious movement, so I suggest we both work toward the left to avoid unnecessary confusion. When we reach the middle of the pack, we probably should stand and fight, rotating to the left. I doubt if they're going to give up since we are obviously outnumbered." Pet'r said, smiling at Borny'a who nodded and chuckled.

They turned together and advanced toward the troops at a slow trot. As they got near the first squad, they separated slightly to allow room to maneuver. Then plowed into the group without slowing.

The Ahar'n glowed, its surging light surrounded the two men and the grounds were lit by the outburst.

Grunts, yells and screams rose in the air. The two swept aside the weapons of the first few men. Some of these punctured the soldiers to each side, they fell instantly. Those in the second rank tried to stop and turn.

Borny'a and Pet'r attacked viciously. Using the weapons taken from the first rank, they skewered the second and threw them aside. Each following group suffered the same fate.

The two continued to trot in the direction of the main camp, bodies of the soldiers flying away from them and littering the grounds as they moved steadily toward their objective. The soldiers, skilled though they were, couldn't contain the two men.

The officers in the camp noticed the squads were not doing well. In fact, the second squad was struck as though by a maelstrom. Bodies of dead, or dying, flew away from the center, lifeless. The two men advanced without hesitation.

One of the officers sent his personal guard out to attack, an especially strong and well-trained group. The two men advancing

197

waded through them, even to the extent they were beginning to throw the bodies of the dead toward the encampment in high arcs. The bodies were falling from the sky and crashing into tents, scattering the troops inside.

The squads were still assembling, but began to circle the two men more cautiously. So, Pet'r and Borny'a noticing this and modified their stance.

"Center!" Borny'a yelled. They closed the small distance between themselves and stood back to back, never ceasing to break the attacks of the men nearest them. Now the bodies of the soldiers almost filled the air. They were crashing to the ground all around. The officers began to gather their papers and weapons and were backing away. But, they weren't fast enough.

The two attacked the lead tents, tables flew apart, horses posted near the officers began to jump about and pull their leads from the hitching stations. Tents began to tumble from the bodies striking them. The air seemed filled with bodies.

Yet the two men kept coming. They were unharmed, and untouched, despite the efforts of the odd creatures attacking. More of the troops were called forward as the officers continue to tread backwards away from the melee.

Soon the officers ran beyond their encampment, still ordering the remaining soldiers into the fray, realizing too late they had no chance to win this battle. Hundreds were lying about dying, or dead. The soldiers though persistently aggressive couldn't get close enough to the two to even attempt to strike them.

Yet, the two had no weapons.

A few of the monstrous beings, still standing, began to back away from the brawling. They were obviously not interested in attacking these indestructible men. They didn't understand how these two could be fighting the way they were. They didn't even know why these men were there.

One of the Ravelan officers wondered as he tried to mount his horse.

198

"Who are these men? Were did they come from? Where they not here when we arrived. Monsh'a told us this would be simple; there would be no repercussions. What is this?"

Pet'r reached and yanked him back to the ground and stood over him.

"You! You get to live another day. Go tell Baalsa'n we aren't going away. We are going to fight and he is on my personal list to extinguish," Pet'r snarled into the man's face. He picked the soldier up and slammed him into his saddle, turned the horse northward and smacked his rump. The horse bolted with the officer hanging on, relieved he escaped the madness.

Borny'a, still fighting, rid them of more of the Maah'e. Pet'r stepped in beside him and, with more ferocity then before, ripped the lives out of a dozen more.

Then there were no more. The bodies lay behind them from the center of town, along a path some 20 meters wide and up to and into the encampment. All the tents were lying on the ground. Any Ravelan soldiers, or Maah'e, trapped inside were dead. All about there was nothing but death. None of the enemy even moaned.

Borny'a and Pet'r looked around. It was done. Pet'r turned back to look at his old home, sat on the ground and wept some more.

"My family may be dead. My friends, old and new, gone. Our village is no more," Pet'r held his head in his hands for a while. "But we have to save those who live. We have to get them to safety. I propose we take them to the castle. It's just beyond that point of land to the west," he added, pointing toward the water west of them. "But first we need to find them all."

Borny'a nodded and headed back toward the meeting hall cellar. Pet'r rose from the ground and followed. They found twenty or so hiding in the cellar. But Pet'r knew of other homes with cellars and hoped there were others hiding in them that hadn't been discovered.

199

The first one they reached was unforgiving. The door had been broken in and there were a number of people, young and old, slaughtered and laying about in the semi-dark of the exposed cellar.

Pet'r couldn't believe the carnage. He was beginning to despair and worried about his own family. Finally, in the last place possible, he ripped the door away and met his father's eyes. They had taken shelter in one of the older homes near the water. The cellar they were in was half filled with seawater and the odor of the still salt water was strong, but they were alive though all of them sustained an injury of some sort.

Geth'n's family was there too, except for his sister who had perished trying to help others find shelter. She was caught in the open grounds and quickly decapitated. Pet'r knew they should find her body and give her a proper burial.

The survivors began to gather in the south and west of town, near the piers.

"I think we should load the boats with everyone and get them away from here to safety," Borny'a suggested. "I see no better way to handle this many people at one time. You may be able to transport one or two, but this many may be beyond your skills."

"You're right. That's a good idea. All the men here are skilled sailors and though injured, should be able to get to the other coast. There are a few young men who can handle the navigation and setting of the sails, so the journey should be safe enough. Certainly safer than traveling on the road," Pet'r agreed. "We should begin to tie the boats into a large raft for containment and help the wounded and helpless into the boats as quickly as possible."

So for a while, they worked to build the composite raft of boats. Finally, they began to place the wounded in various boats and tried to make them comfortable. The remainder of the people gathered evenly with a few men, women and children, some of the aged working their way into the boats.

Suddenly one of the women screamed and pointed back toward the road. A cavalry group of the Ravelan was roaring down the hill toward them.

"Everyone settle into place. You must shove off now. Please sit where you can and hold on because we are going to push with quite a force to get you away from the coastline. Sail to Roahan, or go to Ralff'r Castle! Please sit and find something to hold onto," Pet'r yelled out to everyone.

The people worked their way into position fairly quickly. grabbed lines, each other and any stable element on the boat to brace themselves. Pet'r and Borny'a stood in the water and pushed the large raft with all their strength. It moved away rapidly, creating a large wake, and didn't slow until it was several meters from the shore.

Pet'r and Borny'a waded back to shore and onto solid ground. The cavalry group was almost upon them when they braced to meet the onslaught.

"I'll get the archers!" Pet'r shouted at Borny'a who nodded he understood. Borny'a was knocking horses and riders to the side. Some riders rode too hard toward the shoreline, so he stepped into the animals and pushed them into the water, using their momentum, taking the men with them.

Others were sliding to a halt with swords slashing at the two men and often, since everything was jammed tightly, striking one another in their own group.

But, some of the cavalry group were archers and firing their arrows toward the people in the boats. The boats weren't far enough out to be out of range. Pet'r blasted through the first line of horses and began to knock the archers off their horses. In some cases, he leaped onto the rump of the horse, grabbed the archer and flung him into some of the other.

But, some arrows were launched and flew out. Some of the villagers cried out and many of the men protected the children and women from the flight. There were some strikes and the people hit screamed out their pain.

This intensified Pet'r's attack. He moved with speed beyond the enemies imagining, slashing throats with a sword he had snatched for one officer just before he killed him, snapping his neck with his violence. He couldn't be stopped and was killing everyone around him. But, there were a few in the rear of the squad who were still mounted and, instead of aiming for the boats, fired directly at Pet'r.

He was hit, but reached down, yanking the arrows from his body. He screamed his rage, leaping from horse to horse, decapitating each archer as he flew through the air. Some lowered their bows and tried to escape, but he was too quick for them and soon all but a few were dead. Those raced their horses over the road toward Larilla and he wasn't able to give chase.

He fell to the ground, some of the arrows still protruding from his back and side. Borny'a ran to him, but didn't know what to do to help.

"Just push them through and break them off," Pet'r told him, grimacing with pain. The Ahar'n glowed intensely.

"I don't think that's wise. I believe the Ahar'n will take care of you," Borny'a answered. "I'll snap some of them off but leave them where they are in a vital spot. I fear, young fellow, you're not quite immortal, despite the Ahar'n. So I need to get you to safety, too. There's one more boat. We'll take it. We can do nothing more here. Come, let's get you out of here."

Borny'a broke a number of the arrows, tossing them aside. Pet'r just grunted at each tug on his body. When the task was done, Borny'a picked Pet'r up and walked him to the empty boat and laid him among the lines as carefully as possible. Pet'r was quiet and didn't complain.

"I guess I shouldn't have let that officer go. An ego thing for me. I'll not be so full of myself the next time," Pet'r mentioned, his brow knitted from the pain. "I can't believe we don't have the opportunity to find Geth'n sister and bury her. But I'm probably

202

going to pass out soon. Are you comfortable taking the boat out to sea?"

"Don't worry, young fellow. I'm fairly well qualified, I imagine. I was a sailor for a hundred years way back, traveled all the seas on our world. Learned a few things in that time. You just relax so you don't tear your insides anymore than necessary. Maybe I can get us to Roahan and get you some help," Borny'a told him.

They pulled away from shore. Pet'r looked sadly back at his home. His life as a young man, and young fisherman, had been spent there. All his hopes, his dreams and his plans seem to have been lost.

I think Geth'n's going to be very unhappy. That is probably a given. He'll want us to return to see our loss. He'll want to return to see what has been done to our home. He'll want to return to bury his sister. We will. I can't imagine what happened to all we didn't save. Where are they? Are they alive? Geth'n and I will need to discover those answers.

Pet'r's eyes began to close. He was losing a great deal of blood and weakening. The Ahar'n had dimmed and was allowing him to relax, but it was still a dangerous situation. He looked over at Borny'a raising the sail and smiled.

We will return.

RETREAT

Anisah ran behind a small building, some sort of storehouse she thought, and pushed her way into the undergrowth. She needed to determine, if she could, who these soldiers might be. She could vaguely see them across the lake, but those coming down the near ridge quickly came into her view. She realized, when one of them stepped into a clearing to signal the others to move faster, she had never seen anything like them before. These soldiers were a powerful force. They were large, muscular, and well trained in concealment and organization.

This must be the foreign army Geth'n and Pet'r had to avoid to get here. This is not good. I have to do something. I can't leave Garv'n and Acron'n to the mercy of these men.

She watched, trying to decide what she could, or should, do. There had to be a way to either lead them away from the cabin, or divert them in some way. She also decided she might be the reason the isolated place had been discovered.

She wasn't certain if the amulet Borny'a had thrown into the lake retained its power, or not. It might be transmitting some sort of signal Mano'n could detect. Since he always seemed to eventually appear whenever she teleported herself, there must be some way he could detect her uniquely.

Therefore her best option would be to expose herself to these troops and then flee from them on foot. She needed to move quickly but keep her pursuers in sight because they would need to see her. This was a case where she couldn't just disappear to Varspree, or Tariny, again. She would have to keep these men following her but not get caught.

She considered her plan for a moment and decided all her skirts would have to go. She removed all her clothes but her short

204

shift and hid them behind the small storehouse. She chose a small cape from the pile to cover her hair when she was certain these men following her were far enough away and she could return to the cabin. She loosened her hair, which flared bright red and hung down below her shoulders.

They should be able to see that.

Nervous and shaking, she prepared herself to walk out along the lakeside, in sight of the group just reaching the northern edges of the lake, to reveal her whereabouts.

As she dashed out and began to run along the southern shore, shouting rose along the line of soldiers. When she looked over at the first group, there were a few of the men who separated from the larger group and began running toward her.

She ran along the lakeside, hair flying, until she reached the southernmost point of the lake. Ahead of her a ridge climbed steeply up the mountain, there was little shoreline left. She also noticed a number of soldiers running toward her from that side of the lake.

So, the way is south from here. I wonder how deep the forest is in that direction. Makes no difference now. Got to run.

She took one look back at the cabin and was comforted by not being able to see it. The cabin had been built just under the shelter of the trees on the western shore, far enough into the trees to blend into the scene and was practically hidden from view from any angle.

She turned into the forest and ran as fast as she could. She could hear the reaction of the beings and knew there were some of them in pursuit.

I'll need to run as far as I can in this direction, just enough to be hidden from view of those around the lake. Have to keep some distance between myself and the ones following. If I can. I should be able to do something about them when we get far enough from the lake. I'm not certain what, but I can decide when I need to stop and attack.

She ran for a short distance further. Then she stopped quickly, listening for her pursuers who were quieter now, looked around and decided on a new route. She took the cape she was carrying and covered her hair, turned right, down through a small ditch, ran across several streams she came to, and generally began to work her way back toward the cabin.

Later she stopped, hid behind a large tree for a moment, waiting for the squad following her. She could hear them closing on her position. When she thought the time right, she stepped out and hoping things went as expected, dispatched the closest group, making them disappear. She started running again.

She noticed, looking back, there were fewer chasing her. She wasn't certain she had actually rid herself of the others, or whether some decided the chase needed only a few and returned to the lake. She stopped again, turned where she stood. The group following tried to stop, sliding in the damp undergrowth, but they were too late and they disappeared. She began to run northward now.

I'm too far from the lake, that's not so good. I've got to get back quickly now.

Soon, she came to the open lake area again and stopped just inside the line of trees. She could see just to her right she had circled far enough around the cabin she was now on the other side of it.

She'd like to have her clothing back, but, if she had to, she would wait for that. Staying hidden behind the tree line, she crept toward the cabin. She still had her hair covered and crouched as low as she could as she dashed from tree to tree.

The troops were busy near the lakeshore where most of them had gathered after returning. Apparently, her escape plan had worked fairly well. She looked back toward her original approach the lake on the west and saw the few who thought they were still chasing her pop out of the forest, surprised they were back and that near the water. She couldn't determine whether they saw the cabin, or not.

It seems I've confused them. Mano'n must not be here, or he would discover the amulet wasn't around my neck anymore. Got to get into, or near, the cabin. Wouldn't want either of the two there to come stumbling out of the door now. I've got to do something more drastic to get rid of these invaders. But what? Do I have any real powers without the black stone? I have no idea where those soldiers I made disappear went and wasn't certain I could even do that at the time.

She moved slowly behind the cabin and returned to the small storehouse where she retrieved her clothes and redressed. Looking at the troops still around, she realized her efforts to draw the troops away from the area had not been so successful. There were too many to eliminate easily.

She needed a better plan. She sneaked closer to the cabin and, when she thought no one was looking, ran along the edge of the trees, around the front of and into the cabin. She quietly shut the door and leaned against it for a moment. Only then did she realize she held her breath the entire time she was trying to be secretive.

"What is going on outside?" a voice asked quietly. "What's happening?"

Anisah jumped and spun around to ward off an attack, then she stopped and slumped against the door again.

It was Acron'n. He had gained consciousness, rubbing his head through his hands and now sitting on the cot where Jond'r had been

"Who are you?" he asked. "Where am I?"

"My name is Anisah. I'm a friend of Pet'r and Geth'n's. You are now where they brought you after you were wounded. There's a large group of soldiers out near the lake looking for me, I think. I've tried to eliminate some but there are too many for me to get rid of all of them. So, I came back here to try and decide what to do next," Anisah answered, between breaths. "I've been running around in the forest trying to draw them away from here, but I think they are responding to the black stone Borny'a threw into the lake."

"Black stone? What black stone?" he still was trying to gain a clear head, but having some difficulty.

"Please. That's not important right now. It is something magical that has drawn these troops here," Anisah answered, irritated with what she considered an unnecessary conversation. "The troops are the problem. The others, including your brother, have gone to establish a place for us to hide and plan what we must do to combat others, like the ones outside, when the time comes."

"I understand now. What can I do?" Acron'n stood, struggled to stand, walked to the window and looked out cautiously. "They don't seem to be looking this way at all. Maybe they think the cabin is empty."

"Maybe you're right. But, I think we have only a short time before they discover us," she said, her brow wrinkled from trying to think of what she could do. The only other person awake, besides her, was still weak and probably unable to fight, the other one was still unconscious.

At that moment, arrows began to strike the outside of the cabin. The attack was vicious. The soldiers were now becoming aggressive and probably about to attack, since there was no response to their volleys.

"Well, I think the time has passed for escaping, if that was part of your plan. We could fight, I suppose, but all I see is one bow and a few arrows to do so. Seems we need a better plan," Acron'n spoke very casually. It was obvious he had experienced battle before.

"This is ridiculous! We must use whatever resource we have, and I only know of one. That's me," Anisah growled.

Acorn'n surprised, looked around at her. She was standing in the middle of the cabin, her brilliant red hair flaring around her, her eyes seemed to look beyond the cabin as though she could see through the walls.

"Please come and stand behind me," she asked. "Quickly!"

Acron'n hobbled as quickly as he could to do what she asked. Anisah, building her power from within, stood facing the front wall. The air inside the small room began to swirl around her. Acron'n took shelter by staying directly behind her. He was uncertain what was happening and didn't want to interfere, nor get caught by her attack. But, it was obvious all this activity was highly magical and, from his previously limited experience, he knew this was beyond his control. It was best to take shelter if there was any.

Suddenly, the air paused then blasted toward the front of the cabin. The walls shattered. The other walls began to drop without the support. Part of the roof exploded outward. The logs flew apart and sailed just above the ground. The soldiers directly in front of the cabin never knew what happened and flew, along with the timber, out over the lake and beyond. Most of the troops had gathered on the cabin side of the lake, looking into the water for a sign of the black stone; most would not see another day.

Other squads began to rush toward the cabin. Then the trees and boulders behind the cabin began to rise out of the ground. Both rose high enough to clear the top of the cabin remaining.

The soldiers who were attacking, seeing this, tried to stop but many in the rear rushed toward the front and the whole pushed its way forward.

Suddenly, those objects in the air became missiles. The trees began to spin lengthwise, making high brushing sounds as they circled. Then all were released, spread outward above the ground as the mass rushed past the cabin and rushed toward those in the general area on the west side of the lake. The soldiers there, though knowing it was going to happen, never had a chance to take cover, nor was there much they could have done. The onslaught, with these huge objects involved, wasn't easily avoided.

Then Anisah marched out of the cabin and stood looking for anyone else within her sight. She saw most of the soldiers still

209

alive north of the lake were trying to escape through forest, trying to get over the ridge and away from her.

She created a wind vortex, a cyclone over the lake. It began to suck water from the lake, wobbled a bit from the added weight, and headed north, ripping through the trees, drowning everything in its path. Soldiers, dirt, boulders, small trees and other refuse were swept up in the flood, some carried higher into the air, some running down the side of the mountain toward the lake. The mountainside north of the lake, and the one on the east, were almost stripped bare of anything living. The storm lifted its lower part slowly and disappeared all together, much of the water falling into the hills and running back into the lake. Anisah turned, walked back into the cabin and looked at her two wards.

"I think that should get rid of any trouble for the moment, but I fear we shall have unwanted company soon," she told Acron'n. He was still standing near the fireplace unharmed and Garv'n lying on the cot was not affected at all. Anisah had apparently placed a ward of some sort to keep them safe from the holocaust she created. Acron'n didn't bother to go outside and look. He just watched the girl and waited for her decisions.

"Do you know anything at all about Rab'k's old castle. Where it is or any other information that might help me locate it?" Anisah turned to Acron'n again as she walked to Garv'n's cot.

"I was there a few times working with Jond'r and Rab'k on some crucial disturbances Garv'n wanted investigated. I probably can describe where it is and, certainly, can tell you what towns are near by, if you've ever been to them," he answered.

"I've not been any further south in Aerolan than Varspree, so the towns wouldn't help me. If I have an inkling of the castle's position, and that has to be visual, I can probably take us all to somewhere near. But, it is almost critical I not take us where a building, or shack I'm not aware of, exists. That could be dangerous for us," she explained. "I suspect Geth'n will be here soon also. He probably is in no danger, but I will leave a coded message telling him where we've gone."

She walked quickly to the mantle over the fireplace and pressed her hand to the wood. Light smoke rose from where hand lay. She lifted her hand away, turned and walked back to the cot.

"I think we have to leave soon. I've decided. I'm going to take you two to Tariny, to the Healers' College. They have the facility and ways to help Garv'n and you, if you think you need it. But we can't stay here. I already sense the arrival of people more powerful than myself. We have to go now," she spoke emphatically. "You simply have to place your hand on my shoulder. I'll attend to Garv'n."

Acron'n walked to her, placed his hand on her shoulder, took a look out toward the lake and the destruction the girl had produced, and shook his head in disbelief. Never had he seen such a display of violence in all his years of being a soldier. Never.

Anisah leaned forward and touched Garv'n gently on his chest.

They vanished.

VORAVIA'S PLOY

Voravia was sitting in one of her chosen places, with a view of the mountains to the north, to rest. She liked to come to this site to ponder thinks. Today she was thinking about what occurred over the previous few weeks. One of the things she was realizing was she was becoming more and more disinterested in Baalsa'n's plans. She was certain she had no problems with this world – her home world – continuing to exist.

But, she knew she was at a disadvantage. She had no bargaining power, no influence in the games these boys were playing, and she wanted to change that.

I need to have Monsh'a and Baalsa'n believe I'm striving for the end they have in mind. Actually, I don't care for their plans, or those of Mano'n or Rab'k. I've found a certain peacefulness here and I don't have a reason to change that.

Monsh'a seems to be in favor with Baalsa'n. These beings he's brought with him are remarkable specimens. Just large enough to be real warriors, not intelligent enough to question orders. Tomorrow I'll learn about the process for converting men into these warrior creatures and produce some of my own.

Thinking of my own, I wonder whatever happened to Mord and Sesk and their quest to kill my niece. If they were successful, I get a feather in my cap from Baalsa'n. But they seem to have disappeared, and I never heard from them.

Suddenly, the quiet in the castle was broken when a crashing sound punctuated by a human shout came from her tower room. She hastened up the steps and opened the door.

A blubbering, fat, filthy man lay on the table in the center, losing the contents of his stomach on her floor. He looked at her briefly, then trying to scramble off the table, he fell backward

212

into a chair, knocking himself unconscious.

She walked around the table and stared at the man. His face was distorted because he apparently landed on it. He was bleeding from his nose and mouth.

Suddenly, she sensed a disruption in the air above the castle. She ran back to stand in the doorway. Just as she reached it, two more men slammed against the table with the results being the same as the beast's.

She stayed at the door for a while after several more fell. When she could no longer feel the impulse of teleportation, she walked near the pile of ruffians, her new possessions apparently. She decided these men would make marvelous entries into her special guard. But, first, she had to question the fat one. She suspected she knew where these men came from and, if she was guessing correctly, she would have them be her very special guards.

She called down into her chambers for her Hundr'a to come and clean the room. When they arrived, she went to her study to ponder how she might benefit from what she assumed would be a great deal of anger these men probably held for Anisah.

My niece is learning faster than I would have expected. She's actually being rather creative in her anger. Wonder how that will develop? Now I don't care where Mord and Kesk are.

When she checked on the process of imprisoning her niece's gifts, her people, gathering the bodies, were grumbling about the difficulty of moving humans about but efficiently doing their job. Some of the men were too heavy for the small creatures so they simply dragged them down the stairs, the men's heads bouncing against the hard stone as they went.

After all were taken to her dungeon and safely locked away, she paid them a visit. The fat one was awake though still groggy.

"What do you think you're doing, witch?" he shouted at her as she approached. "When I get out of here, I'll help you die a very slow and painful death and, believe me, Sumt'r keeps his word. You can't treat me and my boys like this!"

213

She looked at him a moment, then turned to walk back upstairs. Then she stopped and faced this obnoxious human.

"You've obviously mistaken me for someone else. I don't know you, nor will I. We will talk again. Later," she turned and answered his threats over her shoulder. As she walked into the dark she added, "But, be forewarned, I have less sympathy for you than Anisah did. You are truly in danger now."

She stopped on the first landing and called another creature. One she had place in command of the household since Mord left.

"Take a message to Monsh'a, directly to only him, that I'd like to meet with him here within a few days to discuss plans for the war to come. Ask him to please inform me before he arrives and I'll have a special event for him," she instructed, "and be quick about it."

The little creature, actually showing shock at her softened tone, jumped backwards and went running down the stairs to use one of the tunnels she had developed so her troops could move in secret. He was gone in a moment, racing along underground.

Voravia looked forward to this talk. She felt certain the exchange would help rid her of a number of problems.

Later that day, Monsh'a came riding down the road from his camp with a small entourage of cavalrymen. When he was near her gate, he had his men move off to the right of the road and set a small camp there. The men stepped down from their horses and began to groom and care for their animals.

Monsh'a had one of them accompanying him.

Voravia hadn't seen these new soldiers until now and she was very impressed by their size and manner. She'd never been able to get her little beings to behave in a human fashion though they too were originally from a group she had *practiced* on. The results weren't to her liking, but they obeyed her.

Monsh'a, and his man, were to be shown to the tower room.

Voravia was more comfortable there than in any other part of the castle and the view out to the ocean was outstanding. She often sat in the tower looking out over the water wondering what lay beyond.

Unlike Mano'n, she was born and grew to adulthood in a small coastal village; she never roamed very far from it. The Magin'n Gulf coast seemed less dangerous than the desert though unappealing in its simplicity and barrenness At least, there were light breezes in Ranome.

She was happier here, by the sea, because there was a hint of green to everything and she could walk down to the seaside whenever she wished. The Beyhon'd Sea was far more interesting with its crashing waves and great storms rolling into the coast than the meager lapping of the gulf where she lived as a girl.

Monsh'a came to the door and, politely, asked permission to enter. He motioned for his man to stand by the door without a command. The new soldier was huge, a bit smaller than Monsh'a, and stood immobile staring only at the darkness of the hallway, stretching out toward the front of the castle.

Monsh'a walked to the area where there were several chairs, of extreme comfort, formed in a small circle. All the chairs, but the one Voravia sat in were empty, and, for the most part, seemed to be largely unused.

"Please have a seat, Monsh'a. Or should I call you General," Voravia motioned to one of the chairs directly across from her. Monsh'a only nodded at her, noted she didn't invite him to sit next to her.

His frame was so large he had difficulty sitting in the chair. He thought once he'd just stand because that made him more comfortable, but decided against it.

He needed to learn who this woman was. Baalsa'n had placed Monsh'a under her command and he wondered what her skills were, or what special appeal she had for Baalsa'n.

Voravia watched him look around the room as he entered. He

actually smirked about the austere decor and shook his head.

Perhaps I have certain leverage here. He's not aware I'm Baalsa'n's daughter.

Voravia took some pleasure in knowing her secret. She assumed he was being wary.

He, undoubtedly, could care less about me but he would never think, or say, that to Baalsa'n. So for the first part of this small trip, he is attempting to discern what power I have, or think I have.

"If you wondering what I can, or cannot, do, I should warn you my skills are fairly numerous, and dangerous if I'm provoked," she looked at him over the top of her wine glass. She originally was going to offer him some of the wine, which she considered possessed an excellent quality, but, while watching him, assumed he wouldn't accept anyway.

So why bother?

"Are your people comfortable at your site?" she asked with no intimation of excitement. It was a conversational inquiry.

"Yess, my ladys. Thish is certainly a fines setting for this wars, for the strengths of your people I've seen," Monsh'a answered. "Wes has no difficult recruiting and modifying thems. Much in the same manner as yourselfs, I see," he answered, without blinking, or smiling.

What is this strange inflection of speech? It is so familiar. Is there something in common with my own spells to recreate my people and his?

"Well, that's excellent. I guess you're having a good hunt then?" she asked.

"Wes are doings well enoughs," he mumbled. Looking around, he noticed the sombre appearance of the room, the open view of the land to the north and beyond, rich with forest. He also noticed, as he approached her castle, the land along the way was not so healthy. Death pervaded the landscape. He wondered why.

"I'd like to request a favor then," Voravia wasn't interested in wasting any more time than necessary with this buffoon.

"I have, for some time now, been able to create my own slaves,

216

but my methods seem raw and uninviting next the example such as the one you have in the hallway. I need to know how to improve my methods for conversion. I have regarded your men and I'd like to be able to duplicate your methods to make my own group stronger. But, first a question. Are these creatures loyal to you?"

Monsh'a was taken back by Voravia's quick entry into this discussion. He deduced from looking at her people she didn't have the knowledge of the purer method for these transitions. With what seemed to be a strong personality and, obviously some magical power, the revelation she lacked an ability to accelerate her program seemed strange. He was wondering even more than before, why Baalsa'n wished him to be under this woman's command.

"Yes, my ladys. There's no questions from my mens," Monsh'a answered. He had no intention of giving her a stronger sense of command than he could afford.

He stood when he finished, quite ready to turn and leave. He would ask Baalsa'n why he had to deal with this woman.

"Are you intending to leave without my permission? Without giving me what I need from you?" Voravia sat up straight in her chair. Her eyes steeled, looking at him with contempt.

"Yess, I sees no value in our discussions," Monsh'a said and started to turn to leave.

But, he couldn't turn. Something held him in place. As strong as he was, something had locked him in place and time. He could see beyond the window, birds were flying easily. But he couldn't move his head. He peered sideways toward Voravia and realized the woman was standing, one arm extended toward him.

She was a great deal more powerful than he thought. She walked around to face him.

"You will not be released until I want to do so. In case, you are unaware, I am Baalsa'n's daughter. My power is considerable. I do not like to be ignored, or disobeyed. I asked you for something I

217

want and you will give it to me, or suffer unusual consequences," she spit the words at him.

He could only move his eyes, but then she moved her hand slightly and his head became his again. He turned toward her, seething inside.

"Yous will haves what yous want, but you too shoulds be awares I wills remembers this," he spoke haltingly, but with strength that surprised her.

"Then you are free," she back away from this monster several feet and released her hold on him.

He punched outward with his fists, though not trying to strike her, and stretched the muscles in his upper body to relax them.

"I did not says I woulds not give you the secrets. But I musts asks of Baalsa'n's permissions to do so. Hes is the one whos gives the powers to do these things. I wills do so immediately and sends the methods back to yous," he rubbed the muscles of his upper arms, huge in comparison to hers, but made no aggressive motion toward her. He just looked at her as though he could see through her.

"I will send one of my men to your camp. Please be certain he will bring me what I need. Baalsa'n should be pleased with me for my desire to improve my army for the war to come," she stood, unafraid of him, with hands on her hips. "I'd like this as soon as possible. I have much work to do."

"Mark'a, come to me. I need you here now," she shouted.

One of her small beings came quickly around the corner into the room, bowing and creeping along in fear. "You will go with this person," she said, pointing at Monsh'a, "and bring back the information he provides. Do not delay in returning, or you shall not be happy with the results."

Monsh'a stood looking at the little creature, annoyed by its actions and compliance, in fear of Anisah's commands.

A miserable useless little creature. It would be better dead. Maybe her too.

He looked up to see Voravia was watching him, waiting for him to leave.

"I shall dos as you says," he bowed his head slightly but did not take his eyes from her. "I wills sends this as soon as I cans."

He turned, quickly went through the door grunting at his soldier in passing, and they left the castle.

She watched Monsh'a, from her tower room, as he left her. Watched him cross the courtyard, gather his men from the roadside and saw him look back the castle and snarl some oath in her direction.

"Men. Or one who was. They think they can rule me. Sad. Too sad," she mumbled, turned and went to prepare her new men – Anisah's gift.

Voravia puttered away most of the afternoon before she remembered Mark'a. She wondered if he returned as yet.

"Gern'a!" she shouted.

Another little head peeked around the corner of her study.

"Is Mark'a back?" she asked, without looking up.

"Yesh . . . Yesh, hes is," the servant mumbled, looking down at the floor. He didn't want to look at her. But she didn't notice.

"Where is he?" she looked up then and noticed Gern'a withdrawal. He was trying to avoid looking at her.

"What's wrong?" she rose from the table. "Where is he now?"

"Hes in entrys hall," was the answer.

"Tell him to come to me!" Voravia snapped. Gern'a backed away; his eyes growing large with each step.

"I afraid, missy," he fell to his knees, crawling backwards to get out of her sight.

"Stop!" she yelled. He still was crawling as quickly as he could, down on all fours.

"Take me to him!" she stood up and began to walk toward the door.

"I afraid, missy," Gern'a repeated, but he stood, but in a crouched position, cowering.

219

"Come. Now!" Voravia blasted past him in a flurry of gowns. She would not have this sort of behavior from her Hundr'a. She stomped down the steps.

Gern'a followed but fell further behind as they neared the entry hall.

Voravia turned the corner and stopped suddenly. Had Gern'a been closer he would have run into her. She stood and stared at the presence standing at attention just inside her entry door.

It was one of Monsh'a Maah'e.

"What is he doing here? I thought they all left with the big man?" she turned on Gern'a. He cowered even more.

"Theys did, missy. Theys did," he was shaking in fear now. He didn't want to be in the room, but not because he feared Voravia. It was the sight of the soldier. He wanted to hide from it.

"Then what is this?" she insisted. She walked around the being. There was no response from it. She didn't feel endangered but there was something almost familiar about it. She just couldn't decide what it was.

"Who is this? What is it?" she asked.

"Its . . . Mark'a, Mistress," Gern'a muttered, slinking backward toward the door leading down the hall. She turned to find him. She could hardly hear what he said.

Then she realized why Gern'a was so frightened. She whipped her head back to look at Mark'a. She backed away several feet.

"What happened to him?" she was astounded. Then she realized what and was shocked. The changes made in the little creature were now amplified almost beyond her belief.

She walked around it, looking at all the differences she could identify. The most astounding change was the huge structural increase. This beast was powerful, destructive, silent and dangerous.

So, Monsh'a thought my request a little too flippant. So he sends me a message. How quaint. So, we have a game now. I'll remember this, too.

She walked around to the front of the beast and looked up into its brutish face.

"You will report to me now!" she commanded.

"Yes, my lady. I am at your command," it answered, saluted and dropped to one knee, then, just as quickly, stood again.

She jumped back when it moved. But was astounded once again at the horrible beauty of the thing.

"Mark'a?" she asked.

"Yes, my lady. At your command," Mark'a, the new Mark'a, answered. It remained at attention.

She pondered a moment on what she should do with it. One thing was certain, Monsh'a had delivered a sample of his new creatures. In a rather surprising way, but he delivered.

"Do you have instruction from Monsh'a?"

"Yes, my lady. I have this written document," he produced the vellum from beneath his vest, quickly handing it to her. His uniform was not the garb he was wearing when he left. This creature was in full battle paraphernalia, it was prepared to fight in an instant.

On the paper were written instructions on how to produce this creature from whatever volunteer was available. It explained that, in Ravelan, it was an honor to be selected and to become a member of this elite military group, the Maah'e.

The formulation for the transition wasn't too complicated but it did require some skill with magic. That surprised Voravia.

Who in the Ravelan camp possessed the ability to use magic? I doubt Monsh'a has that. There must be a wizard that accompanies him. That person could be a possible ally, or an enemy, when the time comes for war. Regardless, I now have the ability to modify any being, apparently, to one similar to Mark'a. Let's see.

This should be fun.

"Mark'a, follow me!" she commanded her new protégé'. He immediately step forward and followed. She turned and almost danced down the hallway to the steps leading to her dungeon.

She waited for Mark'a at the entrance, then let him precede her. She wasn't interested in him being behind her in the darkness

221

of the caves. When they reached the bottom, he stepped aside to let her pass. She was apprehensive but walked by him and headed toward the cells where she had placed Sumt'r and his gang.

When she arrived, Sumt'r, who heard her coming down the steps, started ranting about her placing him below ground.

"You witch, if I could get my hands on you, I'd strangle you slowly. Then feed you to my men just before you croaked," he spat at her as she turned the corner.

"Well then, it's a good thing those bars are in your way. By the way, I'd like to introduce you to Mark'a. Mark'a. please step close to these bars, reach through and grab the man talking," she pointed at Sumt'r.

There was a quick movement as the soldier stepped forward and did as she commanded, snatching Sumt'r off his feet and slamming him into the bars.

Sumt'r wasn't prepared for this attack, even had he been there was nothing he could do to avoid it. The impact broke his nose, which began to bleed, cut his forehead over his right eye socket, broke his left arm when he tried to stop the action, and was crushed against the bars so tightly he could barely breathe. His eyes began to bulge.

"Meet my new friend Mark'a. He actually doesn't care whether you die, or not. Of course, I do. But he will keep pulling you into the bar as long as I let him," she grinned, raising one eyebrow in appreciation of the utility of her new toy.

"Really a marvelous creature, don't you think?" she thrilled at her power.

Sumt'r could move his head a bit, he nodded his agreement then fainted.

"Drop him!" Voravia commanded Mark'a. "Follow me!" Sumt'r clumped to the cell floor and didn't move.

She looked toward the other members of the gang in the next cell. They weren't able to decide whether she was going to let them go, or they were going to receive the same treatment as

Sumt'r. The men inside were in shock. They cowered at the back of the cell, packed together as closely as they could get. They were correctly assuming her attitude was not good.

She walked to door and unlocked it, then she pointed at Red.

"Ah, the red-haired one. I've a certain fondness for the color," she smirked, flipping her own hair to make it fly about. "Take him out of the cell and bring him with us," she told the giant.

Red jumped back trying to hide behind the rest. The creature grabbed him just below his shoulders, lifted him, turned and marched out of the cell. Voravia waited until he was through, pushed the cell door back and locked it, then turned and walked down another passageway in the cave. Her monster, carrying Red in front of himself, followed.

"If the fat one awakens before I get back, tell him I've a surprise for him," she shouted back over her shoulder, walking away. Then she laughed as she disappeared.

The other men watched her. The monster, walking along behind, carried Red who was screaming with his fear.

When Voravia and Red were beyond their hearing, they began to chatter to each other. All were trying to talk at the same time. Their fear was evident.

"What's she doing? What's she gonna do to Red?" Garr'k blurted out.

Legg't moaned and asked, "Who's this witch anyways? Is this the witch, Voravia, we've all heard about?"

"What are we gonna do? I wish Sumt'r would wake up," Kar'n paced the cell now, looking over at his boss lying on the floor, moaning.

The others started walking around. Occasionally, one of them would stop and look toward the cave entrance through which Red disappeared.

"What's she doing to Red?" asked Rar's. "What's she doing?"

Then they heard the scream. It pierced the caverns with its intensity. It lasted only a moment, but all of them turned to look in

223

the direction it came from. The cavern openings looked more ominous than before. The men could only stare and wait for the next thing to happen.

Another scream ripped through the air. They all ran and huddled together at the back of their cell.

At that moment, Sumt'r began to regain consciousness. He moaned, rolled over onto his stomach and tried to push himself up, but his arm was seriously damaged and he fell on his face, smashing his nose again. He yelled and groaned in pain, rolling onto his back, his left arm limp on the floor, his nose bleeding more from the impact with the floor.

His men all ran to the side of their cell nearest to Sumt'r, grabbed the bars and pressed their faces through them as far as they could.

"Sumt'r. Sumt'r! We got troubles, boss. What are we going to do?" Rar's spit his question between the bars.

"Yeah, boss. What're we gonna do?" Garr'k asked.

Sumt'r still lying on his back, turned his head toward the men peering into his cell. His vision wasn't too clear. His left forehead was bleeding into that eye and he couldn't bring himself to raise his right arm and wipe it away. His chest ached and he still found it hard to get a breath

"What?" he mumbled through bruised lips.

"Boss. She's taken Red. We think something terrible is happening to him," Legg't was almost shouting. "What're we gonna do?"

Sumt'r rolled his head to look the other way. He could just make out the entrance to the other cave area.

Suddenly, stepping out of the darkness was the creature Voravia had used to assault him. Except something was a little different. The creature seemed to have red hair, not dark. It wasn't in uniform as the other had been; it's clothing hung in shreds from his body.

Red's clothes were too small, it appeared. It looked at him as if it knew Sumt'r as it thumped toward him. It stopped in front of

224

his cell.

"Afternoon, Boss," it spoke directly to him. "Are you having a good day? My lady thinks you might not be enjoying your stay."

Sumt'r rolled his head away; he tried to pick himself up, but he couldn't. He tried to crawl to the back of the cell, crying to himself as he pulled himself across the floor.

The new creature, Red, turned away and clumped to the cell of the other men. Voravia arrived followed by the original monster.

Again Sumt'r's gang all ran and grouped together in the back of the cell, but this time they didn't watch Voravia. Their eyes darted back and forth between the two creatures. They knew who the red-haired one was.

Voravia stopped in front of the cell of Sumt'r's cell again.

"Red!" she commanded. "Choose someone and bring him along."

All eyes inside the cage turned toward the new creature. It stepped into the cage, bending to avoid striking its head, reached and grabbed the closest one.

"Not me, Red. Please not me!" Kar'n, who couldn't move in the grasp of the beast. He screamed into its face and was ignored.

"Come along Red," Voravia ordered, commanding the beast to follow her.

They again left the cave of cells and marched into the darkness. Both beast followed Voravia, one carrying Kar'n. He was begging for mercy, begging to be let go, begging for his life.

Voravia, disappeared into the darkness, laughing as she went.

Sumt'r watched from his position against the back wall of his cell. He knew she'd be back; he knew this was to be the last day of his life.

Sumt'r screamed his panic into the darkness; his men remaining took up the chorus.

In the distance, Kar'n too joined in, but only for a moment.

225

The men stopped in that moment, paused to listen, then began to scream even louder.

CONFLICT OF INTEREST

Rab'k stood on the summit of the pass, looking down at his soldiers. They dragged themselves past where he watched, paused, slid over the top and stumbled down the meager road. Rab'k was reminded of a caterpillar, inching its way along.

They had suffered greatly, many men had simply fallen by the wayside, some dying from the extremes they were not accustomed to, some weary, some sick of trying and some just wanting to return home. The cold weather was unbelievably damaging.

Rab'k wasn't certain why this was such a disaster, but he knew these men were never prepared to endure such an arduous task. They never really wanted to go into the southland. All of them, like him, hated it. There was no way to change that feeling.

As the last of the men shuffled over the pass and down the other side, Rab'k mounted his horse and trailed behind. He was looking at the canyon they were pushing through, and knowing the weather they suffered though could have left weak places in the formation above them, worried there might be yet another delay further down the canyon.

A small stream cascaded down its course on his left, splashing spray and tumbling over boulders as the water surged down the mountain. He knew, having passed through this area, the stream might overflow as it neared the bottom of the canyon and that might present yet another delay.

I'll worry about that when I need to.

He was tired of dealing with moving a large body of men. He, in the past, always worked with small squads. That allowed decisions to be made quickly and the responses were completed with minimal delay. The hazards seem to mount with a group the size of this desert army, especially since he had to take them through a different environment than they were accustomed.

He hated this trip. He felt he could have assembled a force of handpicked volunteers who would have been much more effective than this motley group. He wasn't angry at the troops so much as with Baalsa'n for deciding this was the way to accomplish this mission. Rab'k felt left out somehow; he felt like a fool manipulated and out of control.

Voravia reached Monsh'a tent, stopping briefly to observe the preparations for war. She gazed out at the forest, the encampment and the troops milling around. The Ravelan troops impressed her. They were quick, intelligent, and certainly efficient in their execution of duty. She noticed, near the southern point of the assembly, the Maah'e held their own war games. From where she stood, these looked extremely violent and deadly.

She was developing her own creature men as duplicates of those she noticed standing in the training area. She was enhancing the strength of her own small group by adding the qualities she observed. Monsh'a had advised her on the possibilities and arranged for her to obtain the magical formula to make these transformations. Not too far away, a small squad of her new creations was practicing war games with a similar sized squad of Ravelan trainers. They seemed to be doing well and she was pleased with her success.

Monsh'a entered the tent and sat down at the center table used for discussions on the progress of the new war. He was enjoying himself. She turned from watching her men, noting the weather had cleared nicely after the rainstorms the past few days, and sat down across from him.

"Where's this Mano'n?" he asked, almost growling. "I understood he would be here this morning."

"I'm not certain, but I do know he's having some problems with his daughter and is trying to capture her. I assume he's still having difficulty. It's rare for him to be late, as I understand," she offered. She had only been around Mano'n on two, or three, occasions and really wasn't aware of his habits nor cared one way or another.

"His daughter?" Monsh'a growled. "Does he not have control of his own? Why is he wasting time with this girl?"

He stood and almost stomped to the front of the tent, looked out, surveyed the area beyond quickly, turned and walked back to the table and slumped into his rather large chair. Voravia watched him without comment but looked out onto the training fields to divert her attention from the monster.

Not a patient creature.

Voravia had her own reasons she thought Mano'n might be late. One was Rab'k's delay. But certainly, that wasn't the only problem Mano'n had. She felt there was some private problem between Baalsa'n and Mano'n, but she wasn't certain of that.

But the girl was becoming a huge problem.

Baalsa'n was never going to be pleased as long as the girl was allowed to roam freely. That she had powers had been confirmed on more than one occasion now. Voravia was still a bit sore from her own experience with Anisah. But since that time, she had received a few donations from an unknown source as candidates for her own creatures, which she incorporated without concern. She assumed the provider was Anisah, disposing of her own trash.

"This girl, as it turns out, is exhibiting quite a bit of rebellion and, unfortunately for us, is disrupting a number of our plans with her recently discovered magical powers. She is, after all, Baalsa'n's granddaughter," Voravia mentioned. Though she gave the girl high marks for her pluck she felt certain Anisah would probably be captured soon.

"Well, while we wait for Rab'k and his troops," Monsh'a turned to her with a raised brow showing his frustration with another child of Baalsa'n.

"I've initiated and deployed some of my men to try and cap-

229

ture some of these young people you have spoken about. Particularly the two young men from Peetle who seemed to have gained some sort of powers of their own. You, as I understand, had a personal encounter."

"Yes, there were two who professed to be friends of the girl. But didn't you tell me you also ran into difficulty when these two young men passed through this region? Wasn't there someone else involved too? A south-land soldier?" Voravia, ignoring his rude question, asked.

"Yes, I captured a soldier several weeks ago. He was quite intelligent and I hoped to use his skills to train some of my specialty squads. He refused to become one of my officers so I used him as a decoy for a squad of Maah'e I wished to observe. They were supposed to track him through this forest and capture him. Strangely, he headed toward your territory at first where my squad was able to capture him near the border. I thought it strange he would choose that direction because I assume he would have known your lands were there.

But, the squad claimed two men, one who were extremely powerful, able to defeat them and take the prisoner back, surprised them. Difficult to believe but I saw my squad members when they returned and there were severe injuries.

Then the three men escaped, but the squad leader felt the soldier was wounded during the fight.

The three disappeared entirely for a while. Then were discovered heading toward the southeast and my men tried to capture them but again they escaped, so my men followed their trail. They went to a secluded area where the three apparently stopped at a cabin. My squad reported to me by messenger and waited.

So, I sent the messenger back instructing them to break from their pursuit. I also instructed them to push further into the southern peninsula to create as much destruction as possible and to capture any seaports they came to. I thought a seaport captured there would accommodate any movement Baalsa'n might

230

want to make from the eastern coast. I haven't heard from the squads recently and just a while ago sent a messenger to determine their status," Monsh'a answered.

"Interesting. The sequence of events is similar to my encounter with these young men. The strong one, I know, is the Guardian and possesses the Ahar'n; the other I believe is a fledgling wizard of some sort. Interestingly, they both are from that southern peninsula you just referenced. Maybe your men can kill two birds with one stone," Voravia noted. She recalled her own troubles with the young men, in question, and would be glad to see them out of the way.

"Well, I also sent a rather large force, of several hundred men, to surround the cabin to capture the two and the soldier who escaped me and have all of them brought back here to deal with as I please," Monsh'a added.

He returned to surveying the maps on the table, making a note near the cabin and one in the southern peninsula indicating those areas were captured. He showed no concern for his troops; he assumed they would be successful.

Voravia had no reason to doubt him either, so she was thinking about her next steps and looking forward to the capture of Anisah.

But where is Mano'n?. We have some important decisions to make about Rab'k's troops and about how we are going to sweep through the small villages and lay siege to Varspree and Tariny. This war should be completed within a few weeks.

Rab'k was watching from behind the troops when he saw a rider returning from his scouting squad. He also noticed the troops were halting involuntarily and beginning to sit along the trail.

He pushed his horse though the soldiers, not interrupting their action because he knew they were exhausted, and rode to the forward point where his officers were talking to the scout.

"There's a flood? How far down? Is there a lot of water?" Or-dre'a was interrogating the man. "Can you tell me why the water is rising this high in the mountains?"

Rab'k reined in his horse, dismounted and walked to where the men were standing. He heard some of the last few questions, but couldn't hear the answer because the scout was turned away from him.

"Well, gentlemen, what seems to be the problem?" he asked, as the other men turned to him.

"It seems . . . ," Nart'e began to answer. Rab'k raised his hand for silence and glared at him.

"You, young man, tell me what you saw," Rab'k asked the scout, ignoring his officers. He hated news transferred from source to source. Besides, he could as well receive the informa-tion as have one of his officers repeat it. He had a problem with too many hands in this affair anyway. The only reason he allowed for these officers was Rena'x had asked him to use them. It wasn't his first choice.

"Yes, sir. There was an avalanche on the east side of the canyon. It has tumbled debris across the canyon, covering our road," the young man answering Rab'k, demonstrating with his arms, trying to build a picture of how the rocks and debris had moved down into the canyon. Then he pointed to the water flow-ing by the road.

"There was enough dirt, rocks and trees to also fill this stream. The water has backed up the canyon for several meters. The wa-ter behind the dam may be some 15 meters or more, but is not getting any deeper because the water is now flowing over the top. The water might clear the way with time, but it will take a while."

"Take me to where I can see this," Rab'k told the scout and headed for his horse.

"What about us?" Macr'a asked, "Should we follow?"

Rab'k hesitated a bit before mounting, then hoisted himself into the saddle.

"I'll take care of this myself," Rab'k told the officers. "I think you should probably attend to your men, keep them busy, or do whatever you officers do in a situation like this. I really don't need you to be tagging along after me. There are other things to do. You'll know things are clear when you see the men moving, or I'll send another scout back to let you know to start the march again."

He nodded to the officers, turned his horse, waved his hand to the scout who had been waiting, and they rode to the front of the troops.

The scout's description was accurate. Rab'k sat and looked at the scene and the irritation built inside him. He dismounted and walked to the edge of the debris on the road, turned and looked across at the other side of the canyon.

He determined there would be no way his men could navigate the water because the stream was flowing too swiftly over the top of the impromptu dam. He would lose too many of them while he tried to clear the path.

But, as his looked at the slope of the canyon on each side, he decided he might be able to move the debris on the road more to the center of the dam, which would allow his men to wade through the shallows. The slope on the side with the road made it lower than the dam, so the water naturally was flowing that way.

He might be able to clear the road enough for his troops to pass through by further damming the stream. His thinking was to let the flowing water help him clear the road. But the debris on the road had to be loosened in order for his plan to work.

He turned toward the troops sitting along the roadside and motioned for them to stand.

"I want the first fifty men to rid themselves of their weapons and come with me," he shouted over the noise of the stream. "Be ready within the next few minutes."

He turned back to the small lake and waded in up to his knees. He made certain he was far enough from the original bed to

233

avoid falling into the vortex that swirled just behind the dam.

When he reached the point where he could determine the level of the water, he motioned for the men to follow him. They came, with hesitation. These were desert men with almost no experience with bodies of water, certainly no experience with wading through them, not knowing what lay below the surface.

Rab'k directed them by using hand signals so he could stay nearer the eastern wall as they came to where he stood.

"I want you men to form a line from here to the bottom of the debris along this wall," he pointed toward the western side as he shouted instructions.

"I want you the pull some of this debris – any rocks you can move, trees that will pull loose and other items you can lift and move back toward this spot. It doesn't have to be distributed in any special way, just moved it away from, or further up this way, onto the road. I'm going to try to get the water to flow toward the road. You'll be trying to lower the height of the blockage and lessen the drag, assuming I can get the water to flow that way. But don't get the height of this blockage below the water line we have here."

The troops waded to the barrier and began to pull away the items they could. They worked at this for some time. Finally, Rab'k yelled to them to come back and get out of the water. Most started back up the road quickly, some stopping long enough to wash away the dirt sticking to them.

"I want everyone to go up the road another 30 meters and stay there. I have something I need to do and maybe we'll be able to get by this problem shortly."

He waited for them to move from the area then walked through the water to the remaining debris over the road. He paused, looked at his problem again, pulled the black stone amulet from beneath his armor and clasped it tightly, bowed his head for a moment, then placed the amulet back in his pouch.

Then, he did something none of his men expected and something they would talk about for weeks.

He grabbed a very large boulder, one the men were not able to move, raised it above his head and tossed it into the canyon wall just above the dam across the stream. The jolt of the boulder striking the other side of the canyon thundered through the hills. Some of the small rocks, some slate broken from the cliff face and other debris was shaken loose and slid down over the dam. The water crossing the dam flowed a little more toward the west.

The men just stared at where the boulder had landed.

When they looked back at Rab'k, their eyes large with shock and surprise, he had another boulder, even larger than the first, above his head. He threw it against the opposing canyon wall with an even greater impact than the first. The ground below them trembled. The debris rush down onto the dam making it even taller.

The water from the lake formed by the dam, began to flow through the breech in the lower part across the road. The stream seemed to be changing its course somewhat.

Rab'k stepped away from the original dam formation, raised another boulder, turned and tossed it at the cliff wall. It struck with another resounding crash and large amounts of debris began to slide from high above the bluff, tearing away more as it flowed down the face of the canyon wall, and out and over the old dam. More water began to flow toward the west side of the dam.

The men began to be concerned Rab'k might be trapped by the new flow and not be able to escape. But Rab'k turned and walked toward the dam, picking up another boulder and slamming it into the east wall. Then he stepped to the next boulder and threw it eastward. As he walked over and onto the original dam, the water flowed faster and faster on the roadside of the canyon. He finally stopped tossing the boulders and stood, near the center of the original dam, while the water gushed toward and through the new opening, letting the stream drop in depth as

235

the new direction freed the stream to flow, at least at the level of the road. Most of the debris on the road and on the west canyon wall was soon washed down into the lower canyon.

The stream now was only as deep as the roadbed and only barely trickled along the road as a low, fast moving stream.

Rab'k then turned to the task of clearing the original stream bed. He took a number of the larger boulders from the dam and tossed them down the canyon where they bounced along, gouging out wider places in the bed and allowing the water to begin to flow in, or nearer the original stream. When the water no longer flowed onto the road, Rab'k stopped his task, looked down the stream satisfied he accomplished what he intended, walked across the tamed stream and onto the road.

The men who had been standing watching this spectacle in awe, spontaneously cheered for Rab'k, his strength and their new-found admiration and allegiance for their leader.

Up until that moment, most of these men, who had never heard of Rab'k because he lived in the south-land for so many years, realized their leader was a god-like man, a man who - they now believed - could not be defeated, a new hero to proclaim in their legends, and he won their devotion and loyalty.

Rab'k, scruffy with dirt and water, walked to his horse and mounted. As another cheer rang out, the shouting could be heard further up the road. When the celebration reached the officers who were not able to view the obstructed area, they only looked to each other and wondered what miracle could have occurred.

Rab'k rode back up the hill and dismounted when he reached them.

"I need to clean this mess off me, but I want you three to go to the front of the column, find the four squads I sent to clear the rubble and lead them safely through the debris there so we can finish this disaster. Hopefully, our war against the infidels will go much smoother," he barked out at them.

As he turned to go into the water to clear the mud from his

clothing, he shouted at them.

"I said Go! Get the men moving. I'll catch you shortly. Don't worry about me. Go!"

They quickly jumped onto their horses and began to work their way down the road, now almost filled by the men standing and talking about Rab'k.

Rab'k stood in the stream, his head bowed. He was somewhat tired from his ordeal at the dam, but felt energized. He felt he had accomplished something besides clearing a road. He gained personal confidence and was, he believed, something of a magician to the others.

I still can't believe the wreckage of this trip. There surely will be some relieve when I get beyond these damnable mountains. At least, I'm familiar with the people there. I find it strange I'm not familiar with these desert people any longer; there is a strangeness about them I don't understand. I always thought my people were aggressors, but they aren't. Why not? Are things so different than they were centuries ago when Rena'x helped Baalsa'n fight these people? Or am I different?

Mano'n stood alone by the lake, looking around at the damage to the land and his men.

Too late again. Anisah, why are you running from me?

He could sense the black stone chip, he had given Anisah, laying below the surface of the lake.

Why would the girl give that up? Is she without the powers I know she had when she was younger?

He reached his arm out and, without concentrating too hard, drew the stone from the bottom of the lake into his hand, pushed it under the water's surface at the edge, washed away the mud covering it and placed it in the pouch at his hip.

He turned to look up toward the cabin, or what was left of it. He turned further around to look at the near mountainside. It was almost devoid of trees and boulders, only a mudslide down and into the lake showed evidence of what the landscape was be-

237

fore.

The question. Before what? What, or more likely who, had decimated this whole area? Which one of these three young people has this kind of power? Some ingenuous methods were used here.

He could see that a number of the Ravelan were killed either by drowning, or they were submerged in the mud along the hillsides. The lake had been despoiled by trees, rocks and tons of mud and dirt. The water had been pushed over the south end of the lake and into the forest beyond where fallen trees marked the extent of the flood created. There were no troops around. He decided that some may have escaped and were probably moving back to Monsh'a's encampment near Voravia's castle.

It seems someone used Baalsa'n-like cyclonic storm to empty the lake and destroyed almost all the troops with one fatal instrument of destruction.

Even Baalsa'n would admire this.

He chuckled at that thought, looked up the slope at the cabin and walked to it to determine what may have happened. The one room was not remarkable; just a forest cabin.

Its size revealed only one person, someone skilled in the techniques of living in the wilderness, had lived here before. He found a couple of arrows jammed into the wall on the inside, a couple of cots and, strangely, some bed pallets on the floor. One cot had coverings, but the others were devoid of any.

That's a bit strange. Why would only one have covers?

He walked to the fireplace, looked into the hearth and across the mantle. Then he stopped, place his hand along an area that seemed burned into the wood of the mantle. It appeared to be a hand print.

It is a hand print burned into the wood — a small hand print. Who would have left this? It seems to imply a message? How could anyone of these ordinary people have left such a mark . . .?

But wait. Anisah may have been the only one who might be able to do this? If so, did she burn this mark before she lost the stone, or after? Why

238

was she here anyway? How is she involved with these other two? Most im-
portantly, where did she go and how did she become so adept at using tele-
portation? I've got to find my daughter before she gets both of us in trouble.

But, now I've got to go to Monsh'a's camp area and meet with him along
with Rab'k and Voravia. We have to decide how and what we need to do
now to end this little war quickly.

Mano'n walked from the cabin, took a last look all around and
determined no one had walked away from it. Though he was uncertain how many were in the cabin at any one time, he assumed
there could have been others besides Anisah. He only knew she
had been there.

That would mean she made the hand print on the mantle. But why? If
there were more than her, how many have magical powers? Did it take all of
them to produce the wreckage and the attack on the forces around the cabin,
or did only one of them? There are no ready answers here. But one thing is
clear, these young people somehow are seriously dangerous when they turn
their attention to fighting back.

He scanned the lake and forest in front of the cabin again,
shook his head at the implications and disappeared.

After a very slow process of getting through the debris left by
the washout below the dam, the march down from the mountains
was largely uneventful. Rab'k gave a sigh of relay as he watched
the ground become more level near the front of the marching
army. The open fields and scattered trees of the foothills were a
welcome sight.

He called a halt to rest his troops on a lower slope of the
mountains. They camped on a small plateau only a half days
march away from where they were the day before.

The eventual escape from the torturous hills was inevitable by
then. Rab'k enjoyed his first good night's sleep in almost two
weeks. He felt his men probably relished the rest as much he did.

When they reached the flatter terrain and came to the crossroad that ran parallel to the mountains, Rab'k called a halt and

gave the troops another break.

One thing he considered a benefit from having traversed the mountains was the discipline of the men; it definitely improved. The men acted as though they accomplished something, seemed to be more involved in what was happening and some showed certain pride in being a part of this new army.

He, thinking about the deserters, hoped Rena'x was able to catch most of them and reward them with an exacting punishment. To him, taking each one to the center of the desert and letting him wander, with no water, seemed just.

Within the next couple of days, his troops finally reached the valley where Monsh'a had chosen to establish himself.

Rab'k found and reserved an area within a highly forested area just south of Monsh'a's zone. Monsh'a's alien guards wandered just beyond his group, but he established his own guards to protect the edge of his encampment and, in part, to present a show of strength.

Then, when his men were settled, he rode to Monsh'a's tent. The guards, apparently forewarned and having seen the desert troops move into the area, made no attempt to stop him from crossing into the central area.

A bit too confident, I think. There are a number of reasons to take this seriously, especially for the desert kin. This Monsh'a seems to find respecting any others concerned a problem. He sent no one to bring us into the area and now he allows a stranger to wander into his camp unhindered. Rena'x told me Monsh'a is highly respected by Baalsa'n. I wonder why?

He rode to the center of the complex and walked his horse to the largest tent. It was obviously the command tent,. He paused to look about then dismounted.

The ugly guard at the entrance was huge and Rab'k, though a large and powerful man, felt dwarfed. But, again his presence wasn't contested. He was allowed to enter the tent, without question and with only a nod of the guard's head. No salute was offered.

That guard was rude! I am after all a child of Baalsa'n's. Is there no respect for that?

Rab'k wasn't in a good mood when the darkness of the tent closed around him.

Voravia was sitting on a mass of cushions on his left, mostly, dressed this time. She seemed to enjoy the shock value of exposing her body.

Another man, in all black, sat on the right, tall like him and a bit older, he thought. The man turned and watched him closely, rose and walked toward him with his right hand out and his other one on his belt knife.

"Rab'k, I assume?" he asked. He held the hand out a bit longer then let it fall when Rab'k gave no indication he was going to accept a handshake.

"Yes, and you must be Mano'n?" Rab'k responded. He could now remember when he first saw Mano'n, at the initial gathering of the children of Baalsa'n. Those moments when Rab'k was ordered to live among the southlanders. He lost most of his youth fulfilling that command.

The man in black nodded his head, turned and walked back to his few cushions.

Rab'k nodded toward Voravia, walked slowly to the table, spread with maps, stopped and stood while the creature, which had his back to Rab'k, studied something he was holding.

The creature spoke before he turned, "I assume you had some difficulty since you and your group are late."

Rab'k reached for his sword at the insult. Out of the corner of his eye, he noticed Mano'n shaking his head slightly and, when he looked, was persistent in the movement.

"Yes, we did," Rab'k answered, still holding the hilt of his sword.

The creature turned and looked at Rab'k from under his thick eyebrows. The thing was unbelievably huge. His bulk wasn't the only thing that made him unique.

241

In human terms, he was hideous. He was taller than Rab'k by a head. His ears were extended as large attachments on each side of his head; the top of the head seemed to be horned with no covering of hair to hide it. His eyes were deep set, solidly dark with no color variation and they had no eyelids. His eyes nictated, instead of blinking.

His arms, of course, were massive and his hands elongated and heavily knuckled. His body frame was extended from his shoulder area and down his back. The legs were bowed but like tree trunks. His feet were bare with toes long with mangled nails extended. He wore no boots.

"Then you won't be surprised if I tell you we three," Monsh'a waved his hand toward Voravia and Mano'n, " have already begun to pursue our victory without you and your desert men."

"I'm not surprised," Rab'k answered. He steeled himself, despite his rising anger. He knew the stone was trying to arouse him, but he thought it unwise to act without considering the consequences. "I believe my men are ready to contribute. I have a rather large force; larger than yours, I believe. We should be able to push into the field immediately."

"What do you really know about your men. I understand Rena'x, a most capable commander, trained these men in the desert and they have no real experience. Are they actually prepared to face an enemy?" Monsh'a added to his insults. He obviously was attempting to antagonize Rab'k.

"Yes, they are untried in battle. But our journey here was extremely hazardous but fortunately educational as well. With the men I have left, I vouch for their ardor and enthusiasm for our cause," Rab'k answered, without pause. He fully believed his answer was validated by his men's current attitude.

But, they haven't seen these monsters yet.

"Then you should know I have already sent a battalion of men toward the east coast who are instructed to move from here to the peninsula near where you lived before. I'm expecting reports

242

of their advances at any moment," Monsh'a was continuing to be brusque.

Rab'k wasn't certain why but he assumed Monsh'a had a problem with him. Rab'k was a true son of Baalsa'n and a military man; maybe this monster considered him a challenger for the admiration of Baalsa'n.

He should reconsider. I feel no allegiance to Baalsa'n. He's wasting his time with that.

"Excuse me, Monsh'a," Mano'n interrupted. "Did you say you had a force headed toward the east coast?"

Monsh'a turned and glared at Mano'n.

"Yes. Why do you ask?" he rumbled. Mano'n paid no heed to the giant's insulting demeanor. He knew he had the advantage and had no doubts about his strengths in relation to this creature's.

"I happened to be investigating an incident in the low mountain to the southeast of here just before I arrived. If I'm correct, your battalion ran into some difficulty. Actually, they didn't get too far along on their journey, as I recall. I suspect what remains of your men will be returning a bit worse for wear," Mano'n was accustomed to speaking in a belittling manner to others; he had no hesitation to use that talent with anyone, certainly not this creature of war.

"What do you mean? What are you talking about?" Monsh'a walked toward Mano'n, a threatening glare on his face. Mano'n held up his hand and Monsh'a progress stopped. Rab'k couldn't help but grin and he noticed Voravia had a bit of a smirk on her face as well.

"Just what I said. Your battalion, unless they sent others on a lesser mission, was, for all practical purposes, destroyed. Now that I've arrived, I can see where the victims came from. It wasn't a pretty sight. Something, or someone, used a bit of magic on your troops. I would expect some of the survivors are fairly near, struggling to get back, as we talk," Mano'n answered, not concerned with the creature's anger.

"You seem to be having trouble with these peasants. If Voravia hasn't explained it to you, there are a few who seem to have the gift of magic. They appear to not like us," he added.

His tone changed to nonchalance, demeaning in a polite manner. He released his magical hold on Monsh'a, stood and started toward the exit.

"I suspect you are going to have a great deal more trouble. Rab'k has lived among these people; those were his instructions from Baalsa'n. He understands them, certainly better than I, or Voravia. And most certainly better than you. You were here before; you were part of our escape from here in the last effort. We need to be smarter, not more ruthless. Those tactics from long ago will not work now.

The Al-Esfer'n have decided to fight back, and they are not stupid. I'm going to my quarters, if you have anything further to discuss with us," he pointed toward Voravia and Rab'k. "I would ask you be more civil toward us in the future; we may be the only real weapons you have."

He walked toward the opening and waited. Voravia rose from her seat, walked by Rab'k who was still standing in review before Monsh'a, openly smiling at him. Rab'k nodded his head, turned to walk out, too. He almost laughed aloud as he approached the entrance.

"What are you grinning about?" Monsh'a growled at him.

"Just amused. That's all. I'll be going back to my camp now. If you need me, you know where I am," Rab'k spoke curtly, keeping his back to Monsh'a, bowed slightly toward Mano'n though keeping his eyes on the other as he did, backed away a bit, turned, walked out and headed toward his own encampment.

Mano'n followed him until out of sight of the others. Voravia returned quickly to her castle.

"Please come to my tent at your earliest convenience. We need to talk. Voravia's been invited also. Be prepared to discuss what

244

you believe needs to be done," Mano'n asked Rab'k and walked away toward his tent.

Rab'k nodded. As he walked further out of the main encampment, he spotted some of Monsh'a's men walking through the forest toward the main camp. These soldiers weren't attempting to follow military protocol as they approached. They kept looking over their shoulders at the valley to the south as though overwhelmed by fear of something only they had seen. They straggled along, carrying some of the wounded, a rag-tag group who obviously had barely survived their ordeal.

Rab'k watched them as they passed, then smiling to himself, walked on into the forest.

It appears the Guardian and his friends have come to fight.

Meanwhile, Monsh'a stomped about his tent in a rage. He wasn't vocal about his anger, but he could hardly contain himself.

These whelps of Baalsa'n's can't insult me like this. I will avenge this insolence. They will need my ruthlessness when the time comes. We'll see then what makes war what it is.

As he returned to his seat behind the table of maps, one of his young officers came to his tent and requested an audience.

"Come in. Come in," he waved his hand impatiently.

"Sir, I must report we have lost a battalion. For the most part, almost everyone was killed. It happened over the last few days, but the results are not good. There are some survivors coming in, but we're not certain if there going to be more," the young officer seemed to cower during his report. He was obviously frightened. He knew it wasn't going to be a good day for anyone in the camp.

Monsh'a rose from his seat. He seemed to swell as he rose. He stood for a moment then roared his anger. He roared so loudly, the men in Rab'k's camp heard him. Rab'k looked up from studying his own maps, realized who was angry, shook his head and laughed aloud.

245

Voravia was pondering what might come next. She sensed the Guardian was more active than when she met him. She wondered too about Mano'n's daughter who exhibited a great deal more power than she would have expected. Power used hesitantly, power used with no emotion, but obliquely as though she was unaware of it. The realization of the power the girl held was disturbing.

This girl will be our ruination.

Mano'n, sitting deep in thought about what he had seen in those hills, wondering about his daughter, raised his head slightly, amused.

This fool has no knowledge of what is to come; he has no inkling of the trouble we are about to meet. He will not be able to withstand the onslaught and the power. Baalsa'n will not save him from the fallout.

This creature will be sacrificed. We three, and Baalsa'n, may not be safe either.

REFUGE

Geth'n and Jond'r arrived at the docks in Roahan without being seen.

Jond'r stumbled a bit trying to orient himself. His shoulder and left arm were still heavily bound but occasionally pain was evident from the look on his face. This trip didn't bother him too much.

"Where to from here? Can you walk through the town?" Geth'n asked. He wanted to allow a few moments for Jond'r to recover from the teleportation queasiness. But Jond'r nodded. He felt some sense of vertigo from traveling, but wasn't overwhelmed by it. So they began to walk slowly through the village.

Roahan wasn't very large. It was about the same size as Peetle, just as quiet, just as dependent on the fishing harvests. On the distant shore, across Grac'a Inlet and the Noend peninsula, Peetle lay on the coast. Geth'n glanced in that direction but he knew it was too far to see anything.

Geth'n actually felt at home walking through these streets though he only visited with his father a few times in the past. The way the boats were tied at the docks, gently rocking with the waves, the masts waving in the air, the smell of the salt water and fish and the seabirds screeching for food made him feel more comfortable than he had in a while.

Pet'r and I could probably enjoy this area and, maybe, get to go home for a short visit. I wonder how he and Borny'a are doing.

They decided not to have too much conversation with the people of the town in case they were being pursued. They arrived late enough, no one was about anyway. A small tavern in the center of town, where the men went to relax after a long day, still had candles burning late.

247

The walked a steady pace in order to not tire Jond'r too much. When they reached the western edge of the town, Jond'r pointed toward the southwest.

"The castle is more, or less, in that direction. I assume this road branching in that direction will take us there, though I never traveled on this one. I usually came on the road from Varspree which probably could be reached by taking the other branch," he informed Geth'n.

Geth'n nodded and scrutinized the rather flat coastal plain in the direction Jond'r pointed.

"I can see in the distance a low rise. I can get us there, then we will look further. We'll need to take this in jumps because I'm not certain I can control a landing if I'm not aware of the landscape," Geth'n said, looking again at that small rise. "Let's try it."

Geth'n looked back toward Roahan, paused a moment to make certain no one was interested in the two strangers walking through town. Satisfied, he reached out and held Jond'r by his right arm as a precaution, in case their landing wasn't as good as it should be. There was no need to cause more injury to the Jond'r's left one. He nodded his head slightly and they were standing on top of the rise he had chosen.

Jond'r shook his head. He still wasn't accustomed to this kind of traveling. He felt dizzy each time they arrived at their destination.

Geth'n looked further along the road and couldn't see the castle. So he selected another rise further along.

"Let's maintain this general direction until we can see the castle. Then we probably should only go to the gates and ask permission. You, obviously, will be best candidate for that," Geth'n mentioned, looked to see if Jond'r was ready, held his arm and launched again.

From this point, they could see the castle just a little further on. It was near the coast but far enough away from the water there was no danger from major storms.

248

"I'm going to take us to that last rise just before the castle. No need to shock anyone on watch. We should be able to walk the distance without too much trouble. Are you ready for that?" Geth'n looked at Jond'r who was becoming more disoriented with each jump.

"I think so but we probably need to rest a bit before the walk," Jond'r mentioned. "Just as a precaution. Wouldn't want the folks there to think I'm drunk."

They both laughed. Geth'n, once again, took them forward. They were hidden from the castle where he stopped. So, Jond'r and he sat down beside the road, rested and talked about what was happening with the world.

"As far as I know, we are in trouble. We have no armed force. Pet'r, Anisah and I have very little knowledge of warfare – we mostly are fishermen, or country folk. We, undoubtedly, will be going to war. So we three are heavily dependent on the skills of yourself, your brother and Borny'a who appears to have done this before and on more than one world," Geth'n revealed all he could and as simply as he was able.

"War isn't so complicated. It's all a function of preparation and surprise. My brother and I have actually limited experience. We both worked for Garv'n in our youth and Acron'n still does. Garv'n assigned me to Rab'k. I was part of the deal as a gift to Rab'k, with the castle we are going to.

Fortunately, my brother and I have skills we learned by living near the mountains when we were young. We roamed those hills hunting and camping – so we know the land. We know Aerolan very well, having traveled extensively in our youth and later," Jond'r talked on, more relaxed now. His recovery went slowly just after he was attacked, but he was doing better now because he was up and moving more. Also, he was regaining his strength and could handle small difficulties more easily.

"Borny'a is a god-send. He should be our true leader. It's good he and Pet'r went together to determine the problems in Larilla,

249

and maybe Peetle. Those two will be our strength for needed leadership. Anisah and I may be able to add a bit with our ability to use magic except we aren't very accomplished. Anisah would rather be healing people than fighting a war. But she, like me, will do what she must, I expect.

When you get settled, I need to return to the cabin and help her come here with your brother and Garv'n. That should get all of us together so we can plan what we must do," Geth'n explained his feelings openly. He trusted all the new combatants, and certainly Pet'r and Anisah, but he was still worried by the power of their opponents.

"I think I'm ready to walk now, if you are," Jond'r mentioned. He stood up and walked a short distance toward the castle and looked over the top of the ridge.

"About a half a mile, not too difficult. Wonder what reception we're going to have?" he added.

Geth'n walked to stand beside him, looked at the castle and agreed their arrival was going to be interesting. So they walked, rose over the rise and started down the road toward the castle, the activity along the wall increased dramatically.

"How many do you think are still there?" Geth'n asked.

"Probably a decent number, mostly servants I would think, but there also may be some of the soldiers Rab'k left behind for general safety in our absence. We left in a hurry. Rab'k was intensely motivated to pursue Garv'n. Of course, I know why now," Jond'r answered. He still found it hard to believe Rab'k was a desert native and now an enemy. Jond'r had to admit he never trusted the man, but he never expected what came to pass.

They walked to the gate and Jond'r hailed one of the soldiers on watch.

"No one allowed into the castle now. Go away and leave us alone," a soldier yelled down at them.

"But it's me, Jond'r. Open the gates. I need to get into the castle," Jond'r yelled back at the man.

250

"Jond'r is dead," came the answer in return.

"That isn't true. I *am* Jond'r," Jond'r frustrated, wanted to add more to insult the idiot refusing this permission, but instead held his temper.

"How can you prove it?" came the reply.

Jond'r had to remember who was with him that day Rab'k attacked him. He assumed some of those men had returned.

"Is Aran'a there?" Jond'r called up. "He can vouch for me."

"Aran'a? Did you say Aran'a?" the soldier shouted down.

"Yes! If Aran'a is there, he can identify me," Jond'r shouted back.

"Let me check on that," The soldier ducked his head back and was gone.

Jond'r began pacing, but his arm hurt too much to continue for long. Geth'n watched him and also checked the direction from which they had arrived for any activity. An attack from any unknown would be something they didn't need.

"Who asks for Aran'a?" a new face looked over at them. Jond'r recognized him.

"Aran'a! It's me, Jond'r!" he backed away from the gate and raised his right arm in salute.

"Jond'r! It is you. I thought you were dead!" Aran'a shouted back. "Wait! Wait, just a moment and I'll be down!"

Movement behind the gate became obvious, the great bar holding the gate closed could be heard being raised from its rests. Then the gate began to open a small amount, enough to allow the two men to enter.

"Jond'r. Rab'k never returned," Aran'a ran up to him and almost grabbed Jond'r in an embrace, but held back when he realized it would breach protocol. He stopped and saluted instead.

Jond'r had begun to draw back in expectation of being crushed by the soldier's arms and he didn't need that to happen. But Aran'a resisted his first impulse. Jond'r was thankful the young soldier had changed his mind.

251

"Aran'a, I'm very glad to see you. Are you in charge here?" Jond'r asked, he had promoted Aran'a to the level of sergeant when on their journey with Rab'k. "I don't know where the others are, but I can tell you Rab'k won't be back."

"Come, you have to tell me what happened," Aran'a said, turned and walked toward the castle. Geth'n and Jond'r followed

Once inside, Aran'a led them toward one of the larger rooms, a dining hall, walked to a table, and invited the two men to sit.

Men and women were shuffling in and out of other rooms, going about their daily activities. Nothing had changed, those who only knew what they were to do next, if given no different orders, were running the castle.

Aran'a began talking as soon as the doors were closed.

"We assumed you and the others were not going to return. We waited for a week then decided we needed to return. We were hopeful someone would.

How do you know Rab'k won't be back? What happened after you left the general camp we set up last?" Aran'a asked, surprised to hear Jond'r being critical. It was unusual for Jond'r. "And what happened to your shoulder?".

"When we left here, it was Rab'k's intent to track down and attack Garv'n's company. Just after we found Garv'n's group, Rab'k attacked me when he realized I wouldn't be a part of attacking Garv'n and his men. They were apparently on some sort of mission from Tariny and had traveled so far north they were almost to the mountains," Jond'r revealed.

"Garv'n possessed something Rab'k wanted. Rab'k was willing to kill him and all his men to possess it. He revolted against Garv'n and tried to kill me because of my resistance."

"How do you know that?" Aran'a asked, having a difficult time accepting this strange story.

"Because this man," Jond'r pointed toward Geth'n. "He and his friend found me lying near death and were able to rescue me. I have been a while healing. But, we were just with Garv'n', he isn't dead, but is seriously injured and we need to bring him here."

"Where is he?" Aran'a looked out toward the gate, which was closed and barricaded again.

"Some place safe for the time being, but we need to move him as soon as we can. Geth'n will see to that when the time comes. But, we need to establish a planning room to discuss the war that is to come. And provide living quarters for about nine people. I'll give you a list and you'll need to take charge. I don't have enough strength to do these things and I know I can trust you.

Are there any other officers here?" Jond'r asked.

"No sir, you are the ranking officer now," Aran'a answered, standing immediately.

Jond'r motioned for the young man to relax, "No. No, I wasn't trying to establish anything for myself. Please sit down. We expect others to arrive shortly. In fact, I'm a bit surprised they aren't here." Jond'r looked at Geth'n who shrugged his shoulders, "maybe we need to give you a description of those coming, probably traveling from Roahan as we did. You should inform the men on the walls, so they don't have to go through the problems we did."

"Yes, sir. I can see to that immediately," Aran'a jumped up again, anxious to please.

Jond'r grinned, "Wait. I have more to tell you. Among the people arriving, will be Garv'n and, my brother, Acron'n; a young lady who helped save my life, Anisah; an old soldier, Borny'a, who will probably become our commanding officer and a friend of Geth'n's, Pet'r. They all are welcome and are needed for what we have to do."

"But what war are you speaking of? We've not heard of any war," Aran'a spoke, trying to determine what was afoot.

Jond'r looked at Geth'n and then back to Aran'a.

"We know, and have witnessed, very aggressive moves coming from the mountain regions in the north. Some of us have been attacked by large groups of soldiers, some of them with appearances similar to but larger than Voravia's man-beast. Acron'n recently witnessed the kidnapping of a group of men just north of Caliste when he returned from the wasteland.

Geth'n, Pet'r and Anisah have firsthand exposure to some of the attacks from some strong wizards. We definitely think a war has been declared on us. In fact, Pet'r and Borny'a went to the Peetle peninsula during our attempts to discover how best to get here because Geth'n witnessed some sort of unusual destruction over there.

So it appears we are in grave danger.," Jond'r explained to the young man.

"Then we have to prepare the castle for possible attack," Aran'a answered quickly. "We have to be ready."

"Correct. Now, maybe we need to send some scouts out toward Roahan to determine where Borny'a and Pet'r are. Would you see to that, please," Jond'r was tiring. The trip and this discussion had worn him down. "Maybe, you could find Geth'n and myself some rooms. We're tired from our long day."

"Certainly, sir. If you'll follow me, I'll take you to your rooms immediately. We, if you remember, always keep a few rooms open for visitors in the wing near the stables. You two certainly can choose which ones you want." the young soldier helped Jond'r to his feet, turned and walked slowly in front of the other two.

I'll send out men to look for the others as soon as I have you comfortable. In fact, there's someone who could start that search walking toward us now.

Why don't you go to your rooms while I arrange for that? You, sir, know the wing for guests. Why don't you and Geth'n go there. I'll be along in a moment to help if there's a problem with bedding, or whatever." He turned toward another soldier walking toward them.

"Corporal Grat'a, I need you to do something for me." Aran'a

254

called out, to get the other soldier's attention.

Jond'r motioned Geth'n to follow him as he moved toward the wing Aran'a had mentioned. They were both quiet as they covered the short distance. Jond'r was almost staggering he was so exhausted. Geth'n came to his side at the last and holding his right arm, helped him finish the passage through the open hallways.

"This'll be mine, I think," Jond'r motioned to the room in front. "Your room could be this next one, or any down this hallway you want. I'm certain I'll be asleep quickly. As you saw, Aran'a's a good man. If you need help, he'll be the best source."

"I have to go help Anisah, so I'll choose one of the rooms near the end of the hall and probably disappear for a while. No need to be alarmed. We may be longer than I plan. Also, there's another family I might bring back with me – not certain they'll be willing but I need to try." Geth'n spoke softly, but intensely. He knew Jond'r's attention level was low and he had to be specific for him to retain the information.

"I'm going to bolt my door for privacy's sake. Tell Aran'a not to worry, I'll be safe. Have him lodge Borny'a and Pet'r in this wing also. We'll all need to talk this evening after we've rested.

The beginning is today," Jond'r mumbled.

Borny'a docked his small boat on the south end of the docks in Roahan. He deliberately planned his arrival for the middle of the night. He really didn't see any need in exposing Pet'r anymore than he had to.

"Pet'r. Pet'r wake, boy," Borny'a gently shook Pet'r's shoulder to wake him. Pet'r opened his eyes slightly.

"I'm going to find a cart, or a horse, to take you across country. We still have a way to go to get to the castle," Borny'a raised the man closer to him, held his mouth close to Pet'r's ear and whispered as loudly as thought he could.

Pet'r's eyes, bleary with pain, opened and looked around until

255

he found Borny'a. He nodded he understood.

Borny'a lay the young man down gently and sneaked into the village. He was soon able to find a small hand-pulled cart he thought would work. He looked up and down the street, wheeled the cart out onto the road and pulled it back to where he had hidden Pet'r.

"Well, a gift for a gift. Someone gets a boat, someone loses a cart," Borny'a mumbled as he tied the boat tightly to the dock, dropped into the boat and lifted Pet'r. "Don't want to lose my balance here."

Fortunately the tide was in and the top of the boat was just a bit higher then the dock. He stepped gingerly onto the dock, walked to the cart and placed Pet'r into some straw he had also taken in passing.

"Sorry for the ride, lad. But we should be there soon," Borny'a spoke quietly to Pet'r, not expecting a response.

He pulled the cart around the outskirts of the town. The terrain was fairly even and smooth, but there were still some bouncing and a bit of moaning behind him. He tried to concentrate on finding a smoother path until he could get to the road he remembered would lead them to the castle. He, many years before, had been here and remembered the path.

Just as he found the road, several men jumped from the high grass and surrounded him.

"Give us your name now," one of them commanded. The others tightened their circle.

"Name's Borny'a and I've a fellow, Pet'r, in the cart. He's severely wounded and needs medical attention soon," Borny'a responded.

"Well, sir. I'm Corporal Grat'a and we're here to help. Jond'r sent us. I think we probably should move away for this area as quickly as we can. Do you wish to handle the cart by yourself, or do you need help? What can we do?" Grat'a asked. He looked at the man on the cart, assuming he was one of the people Jond'r mentioned.

"If it's not too much trouble, I could use help to pull the cart and watch the road. My eyes are a little older and I'm not good with this dark. We need to follow a smooth route and avoid jostling him. "

They tracked through the night for hours until they saw the fort walls ahead. The late hour helped. No one bothered them. A few times, the bouncing cart caused Jond'r to moan, but the journey was uneventful otherwise. They drew to a stop outside the gates.

"Who goes there?" one of the guards yelled down.

"It's me – Grat'a. Let us in. We have an injured man here," Grat'a yelled, his voice loud enough for the guard to hear.

"Will do. Give us a minute," the guard answered then he disappeared from view.

Borny'a heard noise behind the gate and it swung open enough to allow the cart to be pulled through before closing quickly behind.

"We need to find a healer quickly for this man," Borny'a told one of the guards who was peering into the cart at Pet'r.

"Sorry, sir. But we have no healer here. But two others arrived yesterday and we could get one of them, if you wish.

"Yes, I assume you mean Jond'r and Geth'n. Arouse Geth'n and bring him here immediately. I'll not move this cart any further without help for this boy," Borny'a ordered the guard. None of the guards reacted, one turned to go, but paused.

"Do it *now*!" Borny'a commanded.

The guard, who paused at first, jumped and ran into the entry. The time passed too slowly for Borny'a's satisfaction. Then Geth'n appeared, stopped suddenly and stared at Pet'r lying in the cart.

"What happened? Is he alive? What do we need?" Geth'n asked. It was obvious Pet'r was in trouble and he needed more information to determine what to do.

257

"He's shot through in several places, but the amulet's keeping him alive. I didn't pull any arrows out, nor allowed him to. So the wounds, though dried and closed now, still have the arrows in them. We need to get those out, as quickly as possible, to avoid infection," Borny'a answered calmly though he didn't feel comfortable about the boy's chances.

"Geth'n. Peetle's destroyed. How those forces could be down here so quickly I don't know. But Monsh'a isn't hesitating. He's going to sweep across the land, if we can't stop him."

Pet'r, Oh, Pet'r. Hold on we're going to take care of you now," Geth'n looked down at his friend and tears ran down his cheeks. He didn't intend to ignore Borny'a but, for this moment, his only thought was for his friend. "Let's move him inside."

Geth'n and Borny'a lifted Pet'r from the cart as carefully as possible. They took him into the castle, to the wing where Jond'r and Geth'n were staying, entered another room, laying him on the bed. Borny'a went to another room adjacent to Pet'r's to bring Jond'r out if he wasn't asleep, then returned quickly.

Jond'r was awake. He arrived and began ordering the soldiers to bring water, get clean bed coverings, a clean gown for Pet'r and any surgical instruments that might be available.

Geth'n, Borny'a and Jond'r waited, watching the labored breathing of their friend while those things were gathered.

"Can you do anything?" Jond'r asked Geth'n. Borny'a turned to the young wizard, too. "Anything at all?"

"Maybe, but I'm not certain. I'm afraid to try the one thing I believe I know. It's certain we can't push the arrows through without further damage. I think we have to get Anisah here and quickly.

I'll go get her. You two can cut the shaft of the arrows shorter so he can, at least, lay on his side," Geth'n answered, "I'll be back, with her, as soon as I'm able."

He backed away from the rest and disappeared.

ANXIETY

Geth'n arrived at Borny'a's cabin. He immediately scurried and tries to hide because of the destruction around him.

"The gods, what happened here?" he muttered, wondering why the roof was partially gone. Then he turned further and saw that the front of the cabin had been blown completely away.

Where are Anisah and the two injured?

He ran outside looking for them and saw the devastation along the lake and up into the hills on the northern side. Bodies lay all about. He recognized them as Ravelan, the soldiers he and Pet'r saw when they rescued Acron'n.

He ran behind the cabin and looked through the forest on both sides and found no one alive. He went back into the shell of the destroyed cabin and could find no sign of any of the three. He had no idea whether they had been taken away, murdered and thrown aside somewhere, or whether Anisah did something.

He chuckled to himself.

I suspect Anisah did something. Something astounding, I expect. That girl has more power than all of us and maybe a number of others who would rather she didn't. If she did take the men somewhere, surely she left a sign somewhere to tell us where she went.

He looked around near the cots, particularly the one without coverings.

Curious?

He examined the floor. He looked just outside at the trees, or the side of the cabin with the wall still standing. He could see nothing revealing where she went. He was becoming discouraged and concerned his first guess about what happened here was going to be true. He went to the fireplace and stirred the ashes to try to find some clue that might have been destroyed and found

260

nothing.

He stood and leaned on the mantle.

Wait, I don't remember this mark. What is this? It's a hand print. It's Anisah's hand. How could she do that? He stared at the burned portion of the mantle, disbelieving.

Whatever, it's hers. She's telling us she and the others are still alive. But, what does it tell me?

I know that, we, at the least, must have visited a place before we can teleport to it. Where has she been she would take two wounded men? Of course, she's taken them to the Healers College in Tariny.

He turned to look out through the empty place where the front wall was before and chuckled again, "Borny'a is going to be real unhappy about this mess."

Once again, he vanished.

Anisah was attending her patients in a room, which allowed sunshine in the morning. Acron'n was healing quickly and no longer needed his sling. Garv'n was not quite ready to get out of bed as yet, but he was able to sit.

One of the bigger problems for him was his inability to speak. The knife thrust through his neck had damaged his throat severely and he might never be able to talk again. But he was in good spirits and very surprised to be alive.

Mira came to the door and interrupted Anisah's reverie, "There's someone here to see you. I think he's a little anxious about you and these two."

At that moment, Geth'n stepped through the door from behind the girl. Anisah jumped out of her chair and ran to him, giving him a hug, which he returned. She clung to him for a while then relaxed, stood back, tears running down her face.

"Seems you had an adventure back at the cabin," Geth'n said, holding her away and smiling, "I'm very glad to see you and your patients in good health. I was beginning to wonder, then I realized only you could have made such a mess."

261

He laughed. Anisah huffed at bit when he began to laugh, but soon she was giggling and then laughing herself.

"What are you two laughing about? That was the most frightening thing I've ever witnessed. There's no doubt I was glad to be on the right side in that maelstrom." Acron'n said from across the room, his face showing his amusement.

"Ah yes, Anisah's little episode back at the cabin," Geth'n said, went and shook Acron'n's good hand. "Well your brother is safe at the castle, along with Borny'a and Pet'r. But Pet'r isn't doing well."

.Anisah's who had been studying the bandages on Garv'n jerked her head around at the mention of Pet'r.

"What is wrong with him? What's happened? I thought the Ahar'n protected him. What went wrong?" the questions flew out of her. She flopped down into the nearest chair and began to cry anxiously. Geth'n walked to her side and placed his arm around her shoulders.

"That's the reason I pursued you so ardently. I need you to go back with me to the castle. Pet'r desperately needs you. His wounds are grave though the Ahar'n is keeping him alive. I felt anything I did might be fatal, so I tracked you and came as quickly as I could."

"We need to go now!" Anisah jumped up and ran to the door, "Mira, Mira." She called down the hallway. The girl arrived fairly quickly.

"I must go and help someone else. Someone very dear to us. I haven't time to explain, but I believe the College will see a great deal of me over the next few months. I should be back soon," Anisah explained. She hugged the girl briefly and turned to Geth'n and Acron'n.

"Let's go. Now," she told them and touched both of them on the arm. They vanished.

The girl, who never saw anyone disappear before, stood gazing at the spot where the three were standing only a moment before, unbelieving. She stared out the window.

What is happening to our world?

The three travelers arrived in the castle hall quickly and looked around for help for Acron'n.

"Where is he? Where's Pet'r!" she yelled at a soldier passing on his way outside. She almost grabbed him.

"I'm sorry, my lady. I can't tell you that information," he answered her, backing away all the while from this crazed woman.

She was with Geth'n and another man. The soldier recognized Geth'n as one of the new visitors, and he understood he needed to reveal something to this woman quickly. Geth'n felt Anisah's energy level rising rapidly.

When the young man looked to him, Geth'n nodded.

"That . .that way, my lady," he quickly pointed toward the hallway where Pet'r was being watched for signs of difficulty.

She turned and ran toward the hall, leaving Geth'n standing. He followed and caught her just as she ran by the room where he remembered Pet'r being placed.

"Wait, Anisah. Here," he stopped and pointed to the room. She stopped, pivoted and rushed into the room, throwing the door open. The room was empty.

"Oh, the gods have betrayed me. Where is he?" Anisah screamed. Her eyes were now frantic, glazed with fear. "Where is he?"

Borny'a stepped through the door behind, "We had to move him to the small hall near the kitchen. We felt we needed the water hot enough to wrap warm cloth around him to avoid the shivers. He's struggling, but alive."

"Where is this room!?" she demanded. Borny'a stepped back, but motioned and led them to the other kitchen area, not too far away.

She broke by the men and ran to Pet'r. She was going to hold him close and comfort him. But when she saw him, she broke down weeping.

Acron'n walked to Jond'r. His eyes were wide with astonishment. Jond'r grinned at him.

"Is she always like this? Are these three always able to fly about?" Acron'n asked his brother.

"I think so, but there's no doubt they have control," Jond'r mumbled. "and surprises are probably going to happen more often now."

"It's amazing. Garv'n's back in Tariny; they'll probably bring him in, too. So, I guess the disappearing thing will become commonplace with these two. And, Pet'r seems to have the knack also. It's really beyond belief. They have the power of the gods," Acron'n mentioned. Jond'r grinned and nodded assent at his brother.

Anisah couldn't stop crying,

"What can we do? He is so badly damaged. What can I do? I've not had any real training. What can I do?" she stood, tears rolling down her cheeks.

Then she stood straight for a moment, her face twisted with fear and fainted. Fortunately Geth'n was there to catch her.

She awoke a few moments later, looked at Geth'n. Then she gathered her courage to stand by Pet'r and withstand the possibility he was going to die. He was lying on his side to avoid the arrows pushing against the table. He hadn't bled a great deal, probably because of the amulet. But he was unconscious and nearing death despite its help.

Anisah reached and held one of the arrows. She closed her eyes, moaned slightly and the arrow evaporated. Those around, except for Geth'n, gasped in amazement. Then she did it again.

She continued through all the shafts and all went wherever she was sending them.

As soon as the last shaft was eliminated, she stood and gazed at Pet'r and held one of her hands over his heart. There were several moments when no one in the room breathed.

The wait seemed endless. Suddenly, Pet'r gasped and tried to sit up, but Anisah wrapped her arms around him and held tightly until he stilled. Then he opened his eyes briefly, saw her near, smiled, and fell asleep again.

"The Ahar'n should heal him now," she said. "He should begin to recover quickly."

She staggered a bit, tried to walk to a chair and almost fell. Borny'a caught her, raised her into his arms, took her to the seat and placed her there gently

She sat with her head held in her hands, eyes closed and exhausted by her efforts.

Geth'n sat beside her and they talked quietly. He was trying to calm her and she knew she needed to get her energy levels down.

"Are you in control now?" he asked her.

"I think so," she replied.

Geth'n asked her where she sent the arrows.

"To the cabin. Into the floor, I imagine," she answered quietly, "at least, we have almost everyone here now. Just Garv'n's left in Tariny."

Geth'n's brow wrinkled. He was troubled not knowing what was happening to Siarra.

"Now that you've helped Pet'r, I must go help another," he said, looking around at the others watching them.

"Who?" Anisah asked. She wasn't aware of any other they needed to bring here.

"Someone I've met. Someone I want to bring here, maybe with her family," he answered quickly.

"Her?" she asked, looking at him sideways, "is this someone we know?"

"No, but this is important. This shouldn't take long and we'll be back shortly."

"If you think you need to go," Anisah replied, "you should go. But stop by at the Healers College and check on Garv'n for me, if you will."

Yes, I'll be able to do that. I was going to Tariny anyway," he told her. You take care of Pet'r. Maybe we need to plan on some conversation with the others, before I go, about any plans they have to stop, or end, this stupid war."

"I'll not be much help now. I've got to watch Pet'r closely. But, maybe, we can talk with the others, though war isn't something I know a lot about." Anisah looked fragile, sitting and talking to him. He knew he too was probably unprepared for anything concerned with war.

He was thinking he was only an historian and she was just a farm girl.

Sort of.

"Let me make some inquiries and organize a meeting with everyone before I go," Geth'n said. She looked at him and nodded. He touched her hand, rose and walked out of the dining hall.

Anisah looked at Pet'r lying on the table where they left him, waiting for him to wake again. She looked toward the door when Geth'n left and wondered about the things they brought together.

Will we be able to win this war? Will we survive it? We all are so young, except for Borny'a, and know nothing about what we are doing.

She looked across and noticed Jond'r watching her, waved and turned away to hide the tears moving down her cheeks.

We just wanted to follow our dreams.

CONSEQUENCES OF WAR

After a few days to acclimate themselves to the area and the castle, the leaders gathered around a large oval table in one of the dining halls.

Not the one where Pet'r had barely survived his wounds. Neither Anisah nor he could stand to go into that one. But a much larger setting where all could gather around the table while they determined what they needed to do; how they were going to do whatever they came up with and finally, try to determine how much time they had to do to stop the advances of Baalsa'n's forces already roaming the country.

The entire concept of this small group attempting to establish themselves and plan for an impending war, seemed an over-whelming tasks for the three younger members of the group, the new leaders, the ones chosen by the Al-Esfer'n.

Their lives had been so much simpler before. Yet they had wanted to achieve more and now held in their hands the means to protect the world they lived on. Now, they had more, maybe too much more. A daunting set of events they were not even fa-miliar with lay before them. The three, in a random and coincid-ental manner, discovered the others gathered. There was no plan, but all were of like mind.

Anisah looked around the table and felt a chill. The immensity of the task was overwhelming.

Are we really the ones? Can we do what we must do? We have no choice but to try. We must save Aerolan and the world.

That was the whole of what had to be done. Everyone gathered was intensely concerned about what they could do to accomplish this one task.

"Gentlemen, and lady," Geth'n spoke first, bowing toward An-

267

isah in deference. "We all know what we have to consider, so there's no need to recap all the details we have so far. However, the principal problem we have at the moment, I fear, is that Baalsa'n's armies are already moving along the eastern seaboard and are as close as the Arvat'x peninsula.

Larilla and Peetle have already been overrun. I suspect the actions of Borny'a and Pet'r have come to the attention of those in charge of that force by now. We need to devise a way to stop that flow or, at least, slow it.

Other than that immediate problem, what are we to do about increasing our own forces. We obviously and desperately need troops. We're not able to fight this war with just the few of us here. Any suggestions?"

"This was long ago, but what we did at that time," Borny'a spoke solemnly, " was send out runners to all the other countries. There were strong countries in those days on Narhtrae though now I don't know how many there might be. Most of them were very war-like and were constantly at odds with each other. Aero-lan, back then, was an exception, and that may still be true.

But there was a treaty made with them all, a pact to stand together against the Om-Esfer'n. All of the lands and the people felt a certain bond, a certain kinship with each other and that proved to be Baalsa'n's undoing."

"Was there a name for this pact?" Anisah asked.

"Yes, it was called Granoblistia Fealty and all the nations swore to uphold it," Borny'a answered.

"Do you think it possible that some of these nations know, or remember, their allegiance to this pact?" Geth'n asked.

"I don't know. It's been a long time. Most of the natural leaders have died, I'm certain. I know of no other who might be considered immortal. I never met any. Areb'l may have but I'm not aware he did."

"So how were these other countries contacted?" Jond'r asked. He was learning a great deal but he, and his brother, had decided to listen mostly. They assume Borny'a was to be their commander and they only waited for that to become true. They trusted him explicitly.

"The Al-Esfer'n were not as involved then as they seem to be now. But, they did provide critical information about the location of the leaders of each country. Mostly, Areb'l and myself traveled to these places to contact the separate rulers to make our requests. These, mostly men though there were a few women who ruled at that time, were willing to listen and we all came to an agreement to work together. Honestly, Areb'l, nor I, could believe our high rate of success. We later, in discussing this willingness, decided the Al-Esfer'n had something to do with influencing them."

"How did you and Areb'l get to these other lands?" Acron'n asked and grimaced some because of his wounds. He was only up and about a few days now and he still wasn't feeling so well.

"That's the strange part. Neither of us had the ability to transfer ourselves the way Geth'n, Pet'r nor Anisah can. But the Al-Esfer'n pointed out another, and rather odd, way for us to get to the other lands.

They were able to discover several gateways, some sort of guidance apparatus, the Om-Esfer'n set around the globe early in our conflict; many of these were destroyed to limit the range of the Om-Esfer'n but some were kept and moved to new locations by the Al-Esfer'n. They were very effective and required only the awareness of the location and, of course, the ability to teleport.

The Al-Esfer'n, and Areb'l, were very familiar somehow with the operation of these gateways and taught me how to handle my limited use sufficiently. I was given some of the power for transference and, at least ,was able to move about from one of the sites to another with no difficulty. I never knew the power source; the *ransect'r* simply worked.

They were relatively small, generally intended for only one person, though the ones I used seemed to have a capability to carry

269

more than one. They were probably constructed for people the size of the Ravelan, or Maah'e. They were quite effective primarily for the ease, and quickness, of travel. Also these gateways were impressive examples of power for those having never seen them before, they were in awe on our arrival. That made negotiations much easier."

"Where are these gateways now?" Pet'r asked. He was still recuperating too and, since his wounds were very nearly death dealing, his body, even with the help of the Ahar'n, was taking a longer time to heal. But he was alert and listening intently to this conversation. Anisah watched him while he talked; she was pleased with his progress.

"I have no idea. Areb'l and I returned from one of our expeditions and landed at one of the sites not far from here, near Farsea, in fact. The Al-Esfer'n took all those they could locate and hid them, after the Om-Esfer'n left, but I don't know where. It might be they're still workable, but I'm not certain we have the time to search for them. And we definitely don't know whether they still perform," Borny'a answered.

"Do you think you'd remember how to control transferring with one of the *ransect'r*, if we could find one?" Geth'n asked. He thought this idea more than interesting and felt it a possibility worth investigating; his line of thought was insistent on that point. But he said nothing.

"Again, I'm uncertain. It was a very long time ago I moved between these portals and I might be able to control them, but I really can't say I can" Borny'a shook his head, expressing some doubts.

"Geth'n, you told me you needed to return to Tariny to find your friend," Anisah interrupted the general discussion with some suggestions. "Could you try to research the Fealty to determine whether there were stipulations prohibiting our approach when meeting with these other countries?

We need to learn a great deal more about available countries and their current attitudes concerning a return to those days of the old Granoblistia Fealty compact, if at all possible.

These *ransect'r*, even if we're to have only one, could be one of our most valuable assets. They certainly would be a means to investigate the movement of Baalsa'n's armies and might provide a way to, at the least, make first contact with the other countries. Also, a gateway could transport Geth'n, Pet'r or myself to these lands as a primary location matrix.

But, we have discovered there is a limitation in our magical means to move about. It is necessary we visit, or be able to view, a location before we can send ourselves to that place. So, I suggest one, or more, of us go to a country, attain a sense of its location and, because we are from here, teleport ourselves back. We need only a small memory of having been where we wish to travel."

"That's been my experience. We could go by sea to a distant place and be able to return but it would obviously happen more quickly with teleportation. Either method would provide a two-way connection. For instance, I can't go into the Wasteland because I have no reference using teleportation. But Pet'r could since he most recently visited there. So, we have to resolve that difficulty and, maybe, this gateway could help us with that."

Others at the table were nodding their heads in agreement.

"Pet'r, you seem to have the closest, and more personal, contact with the Al-Esfer'n. Do you think you could inquire about these?" Geth'n asked his friend. He, the more he thought about it, felt this avenue of inquiry was going to prove the most realistic way they would have to combat Baalsa'n and his horde.

"I'll certainly try. My contact, Kalbra'n, the leader of the Al-Esfer'n, must be contacted first to ask for his information. I'm fairly certain he would be able to answer our question. But he has to understand a problem to resolve before he talks to me. I suspect this crisis falls into the category of the unresolved. I'll have to work on the problem," Pet'r replied, thinking he could do this

271

soon. He brightened when he realized he could possibly contribute to their cause quickly.

"Hopefully, these portals will allow us to try and renegotiate the pact with the other nations, but I have another question about Baalsa'n's forces," Anisah started, after waiting for Pet'r's comments.

"When I encountered the soldiers at Borny'a's cabin I was astonished at the size, strength and discipline of some of the special troops that attacked us there. The cabin, I fear, is no longer liveable. There were some extraordinary circumstances to deal with and had to be a bit creative. Sorry Borny'a , but we can put things back together, when all this is over."

Borny'a laughed, "Not a problem, Missy. Besides I was thinking about moving anyway. To a quieter place."

Everyone chuckled.

"Can you tell us a bit more about them. I was mostly surprised at their resemblance to Voravia's small people. They didn't display the same timidity hers did when Geth'n and I encountered them in the caves beneath the mountains. What about these strange soldiers?" she asked.

"They are the Maah'e; they live and train in Ravelan, or did. Monsh'a proved to be one of the stronger and more intelligent ones so Baalsa'n placed him in command. But these creatures were created by a wizard named Drang'm who is from Ravelan, an avowed disciple of Baalsa'n" Borny'a began to explain.

"He used the model given him from an earlier formulation for such an army by another wizard from Barnelias, another world destroyed by the Om-Esfer'n. That is the model Voravia has used to produce her group. Her smaller version are tenacious and can be effective in numbers, but Drang'm's creation is a skilled, intelligent and powerful modification of the human form. The resemblance of them to Voravia's is minimal.

The Maah'e accounted for themselves very well in the past war. Had there been a larger force of them, we might not have been able to drive the Om-Esfer'n away."

"Are they aggressive?" Geth'n asked. "They seemed to only act on command."

"They are deliberately created to take orders and to act only on those orders. However, the only thing that stops their obedience to those orders is death – either theirs, or their victims. At that point, those still living will desist from further action and can simply stand in one spot for an indefinite length of time. They are very dangerous and are machines of destruction.

"They are very difficult to fight and resilient. But they can be killed though it is difficult. I ran off more than I killed. Despite their strengths, I found they will not die needlessly if in a situation where a victory is not possible for them."

"That's possibly a small weakness we can exploit," Pet'r mumbled. He still wasn't quite up to contributing too much to this meeting. His healing rate was greatly accelerated because of the Ahar'n, but it was going to be a few days before all was back in order. Anisah watched him struggle through his statement and wished he would go and rest some more. But he was stubborn and she wouldn't be able to convince him. He had to decide.

"Are there any other questions about what we need to do?" Geth'n asked, looking around the table.

Everyone looked around the table, waiting for other ideas about what lay ahead. No one wanted to deal with this horrendous future. But all knew there was to be no reprieve.

Borny'a spoke up, "I have one request. In the morning early, I'd like to meet here with Jond'r, Acron'n and Pet'r, if he's able. We have some serious war planning to do and, as everyone knows, so little time."

Jond'r and Acron'n nodded. Pet'r looked at Anisah, then to Borny'a. "I'll be there."

Anisah's face showed concern, but she said nothing. All of them knew the days to come would reveal the consequences of war and no one was relieved of that concern.

"I'll probably return to Tariny and check on Garv'n soon. I will accompany Geth'n. That way he can attend to his research about the Fealty, his personal business and provide me with a little protection. I would like to get Garv'n and return here with him as soon as possible," Anisah informed everyone. "So, Geth'n, when you are prepared to leave, please let me know."

Geth'n nodded.

Anisah looked at each of the faces at the table. She wanted to remember them as they were. She wanted to hold to that vision, the vision they all were working so hard to make work, with a hope for a different reality for the people.

We can only hope now we are making the best decisions. We must believe in what we are about to do, but we too must depend on the assistance impaled from our brief association with the Al-Esfer'n.

Can we win this war, as those did before us, and can we finally destroy Baalsa'n and rid our universe of his terrible evil, or are we only going to die as so many before us have.

I wish I knew now what our future holds.

NEXT OF KIN

The need to have allies, particularly within a family unit, has always been a way for men of war to have about themselves co-conspirators who could be trusted. Or, at least, that was the assumption.

But, of course, there are exceptions, and will always be, and the wise are best to keep a vigilant observation of those they believe can be trusted. In other words, who can be?

For those who think they must war against their fellow man, there is almost always an inner sense that no one can be.

So, we find the three siblings of Baalsa'n, knowing they must prove themselves to him and to also gain some ground in this war against the civilization of Narhtrae and Aerolan, contemplating each their own strategy and evaluating the aspects of trust of each other. There are no easy answers and, most often, such considerations given are often tainted with misgivings and, ultimately, mistrust.

So now let us observe the children of evil . . .

Mano'n paced in his tent waiting for the others. He had no great love for either of these two, or for Baalsa'n, but he needed to gain control to establish himself as the leader, for his own purposes.

Before it's too late.

Rab'k was the first to arrive. Frowning and growling under his breath, he entered in a great rush and with no formal greeting, walked to the backside of the tent, turned, stepped forward about two steps and almost stood at attention. He sullenly watched the front of the tent, apparently noticing Voravia wasn't there and assuming the meeting, though called by Mano'n, wouldn't start until she arrived.

"Welcome, little brother??" Mano'n was deliberately chiding

the other man.

Rab'k turned slightly, stared at Mano'n a moment, raised his chin in recognition and turned back to watching the tent flaps. It was as though he expected an attack of some sort. He was very restless.

Curious. Wonder why he's so restive?

Mano'n looked askance at the man for a moment then grinned and busied himself with the papers he had on his planning table at the end of the tent. Rab'k actually amused him though he also recognized the man was powerful in his own way. He also noticed Rab'k wore a piece of the black stone, maybe even the original which he probably obtained from Rena'x.

It really made no difference to Mano'n. He wasn't interested in building power, just in having his way about specific things. He wouldn't allow others to stand in his way about those.

He considered Rab'k again then sat and waited. There was no reason to attempt conversation. This meeting wasn't a social event. He remembered briefly the one other time they had all been called together.

This isn't much different than when we last were all together, except Baalsa'n is absent.

Voravia plowed into the tent. She threw the entry flaps back defiantly. They were then caught and held by one of the Maah'e accompanying her.

Mano'n jumped to his feet and growled at her. "None of Monsh'a's people are welcome here." he almost shouted, but held his voice in order to maintain a certain reserve. He needed this meeting to go well.

Voravia stopped instantly, looked at Mano'n, sneered her reply, "He's not a Maah'e. He's mine. I created him and his kind are called the Akab'r. His name is Mark'a. He's my bodyguard and will stay with me, or I'll not attend this little gathering."

Mano'n raised himself to his full height he was so angry at her impertinence. He could've completely destroyed her and her new

276

pet, as well as Rab'k, at that moment had he chosen to do so. He actually considered it briefly. He noticed Rab'k drawing himself up as though preparing for a fight.

But then Mano'n stopped himself. He actually needed both of these idiots to help him accomplish his agenda. They would be key contributors in his major endeavor, if he could persuade them to go along with his plan. An endeavor he didn't want to bring to Baalsa'n's attention, nor did he want to deal with Baalsa'n until he had all the elements in place.

"Very well," he turned and forced himself to be calm. "I see no harm. These beings are largely worthless unless given a direct command. They'll not help you make decisions except as you use force to change things."

"Exactly," Voravia snapped back at him. She looked around the tent, noticed Rab'k standing alone, said nothing and moved to a small chair facing the table. Mark'a followed her and stood, at attention, directly behind her. Mano'n was told the being could stand without moving until given another command. And they could do so without tiring apparently.

A powerful force for destruction, if needed. Something to keep in mind.

"Did you hear about Monsh'a's forces he sent to the east," Voravia casually mentioned as she gathered her robes about her, making certain everything was in order. "It seems they ran into considerable resistance."

"What sort of resistance?" Mano'n, despite his wish to begin the meeting, asked. "Who, or what, could resist beings like yours in a battle?"

"Someone, or more than one person, with magical powers, I believe," she answered quickly, trying to surprise him. "There were two distinct confrontations. Both disastrous for our host, as I understand." She looked over at Rab'k when she mentioned the last and noticed, with amusement, his reaction.

Mano'n raised an eyebrow. He was surprised and suddenly more concerned than he was before she mentioned this.

"What were the costs to Monsh'a?" he asked, trying to be casual himself. "What was lost?"

"An entire battalion in one case, and a large cavalry contingent in another," she was pleased she was the first to mention this. She knew Rab'k was aware of this news, but she knew she was quicker than him intellectually.

"Were there any witnesses?" Mano'n asked, moving the papers into an order he wished to use to pursue what he called the meeting to talk about. He was irritated with the discussion, but there might be something in this he needed to know.

"Only one, in each case," she answered, amused at Mano'n for attempting to be casual when she deduced he had, at least, one concern related. "Seems those who created the disaster wanted the message to be brought back to Monsh'a. The culprits were familiar with who he is and what he's doing. They were not kind to the forces involved."

"Monsh'a didn't send his wizard with them?" he asked, lightly inquiring about the situations and trying to avoid direct questions.

"Actually, no. He was here. Monsh'a is on a modest campaign to convert every moving being in this area into more troops, more Maah'e. So Drang'm was busily employed in that task," she answered. She was getting tired of this discussion now. She wanted to say one thing and finally decided to be blunt.

"I suspect your daughter had something to do with the battalion incident, and probably one of her little friends, maybe the Guardian, with the other," she said. "Don't you think they are the only ones with that sort of ability? At least, in this country?"

Mano'n's head snapped up and he glared at her from across the room.

Rab'k turned toward Voravia when she mentioned the daughter. He wasn't aware Mano'n had a daughter, much less that she might be roaming Aerolan. He'd never heard of anyone with powers before, but he had witnessed some unusual demonstrations of strength, especially by the Guardian.

Rab'k took a quick glance at Voravia but turned away when she looked up. Now he was acutely interested in Mano'n's reaction to this news. He wondered why this daughter was a problem.

Is it possible Mano'n has lost his grip on this girl? Who might it be? Wait, the girl I captured at Voravia'a castle. Her resemblance to Voravia was obvious. Voravia and the girl argued about being related. Could that little girl somehow have magical powers? How dangerous can she be? A very interesting twist.

"You have no proof of that," Mano'n barked at Voravia. The being behind her started to step forward and she held up her hand. It stopped and returned to his military stance.

"Really?" she retorted. "Who else do you think might be out there who could do something like this? Surely you haven't forgotten our little foray in Calliste. A bit awkward for both of us, as I remember. By the way, since I left there suddenly, just how did that work out for you?"

Mano'n was bursting with anger. He was holding himself from attacking, destroying this whole area and leaving for other places. But, he struggled. He fought these urges because he knew there was no place he could hide if Baalsa'n knew he'd killed these other offspring. Nowhere.

He turned to stare at the ground behind the table. Then he walked back and forth a couple of times, stopped, placed his hand on each side of his papers, leaned on the table heavily, with eyes down, trying to remain calm. He stood there a moment staring at his hands then slowly raised his face to look icily at Voravia.

He laughed.

Voravia wasn't prepared for that response. She sat shocked. She was hopeful Mano'n would lose control. She had some ambitions of her own to pursue and she hoped this attack on her older brother might make him succumb to his anger. But she could tell she wasn't going to win using that tack. He wasn't going to break.

Too much at stake for him. It will take a direct attack from me, or someone, to unseat him emotionally. But the girl is a trigger, as I suspected. I now have proof Mano'n has plans of his own, no doubt related to Anisah's welfare. Strange, I wouldn't have believed that possible.

"Well, to answer your question," Mano'n forced a grin. "She put me in my place, I think. It was a new and an interesting experience for me. You should have stayed to watch."

He was deliberate in making the last statement. He was, after that incident, aware Voravia wasn't powerful enough to fight Anisah. He wanted Voravia to understand he knew.

I've got to take control of this meeting and now. We have wandered away from what I intended.

"So, now we've had your bit of news and discussed it, let's try to conduct an exchange of ideas about how the three of us should proceed," Mano'n started. "We have nothing to gain by being at each other's throats. We need to join forces and determine a plan we can use with our strengths to gain an advantage for ourselves.

Our first problem? How do we gain power over Monsh'a and disrupt his influence with Baalsa'n? Secondly, how do we combat the obvious?

We have to admit that these three young people have extraordinary powers. Rab'k, your incidences of contact with the Guardian have shown us he is extremely dangerous. He isn't Areb'l, but he's learning , quickly. Areb'l, by the way, was another human who served the Al-Esfer'n as the Guardian centuries ago. It was believed he remained here after our last attempt to destroy this planet failed.

The Al-Esfer'n are different than they were. In the past they refuse to engage us directly, especially since Varkan, Areb'l's original home, was destroyed. It was the planet where the Al-Esfer'n first tried to assemble a group and fight back. That was their undoing, but not all the leaders were found and put to death. There were some who escaped somehow and fled.

280

At the time, we were unaware of the Ahar'n. It seems the Al-Esfer'n have transferred their living essence into the amulet and someone, and we suspect Areb'l, carried it through all those years until this planet came into existence.

Once we discovered their whereabouts, we pursued and attacked. But the changes they made in their methods caught us by surprise. We took too long to determine where they were and there were many more of their progeny here than on any other planet we attacked. They were able to assemble. And, we still don't know how, all these new inhabitants of Narhtrae built a strong force and simply overpowered us.

They drove us away. We left here and continued along a path of least resistance, destroying other planets and lives in other areas, with a return to Narhtrae always in mind.

But we returned.

I also know, so far, neither Monsh'a nor Baalsa'n seem to be aware of what is causing our delays. Are we three up to diminishing these problems, or are we at a loss for dealing with them? Without a resolution for the first, I think we can assume the latter is true."

Voravia was amazed when she realized how old Mano'n must be. Rab'k only raised his eyebrows and continued to pretend his disinterest in the meeting.

"Which of the three is the weakest?" Voravia asked, feeling certain the answer would agree with her observations.

"That's actually difficult to decide, but I do think, as you do, Anisah is the strongest," Mano'n answered.

He had been trying to decide the relative strengths of the three for several days. His path, while fruitlessly pursuing Anisah, had crossed each of the other two on more than one occasion.

"I think one of the boys, probably the Guardian. I don't know what his real name is, but I'm afraid we'll soon know. He seems tenacious in his limited abilities. I say limited because I think he has no magical powers other than his ability to move with teleportation, but his strength frightens everyone.

One of the things, I believe I've observed, is the three of them seem closely tied psychically.

The last incident I saw with the Guardian was when Anisah inserted herself, for some reason, into a barroom incident. She was alone initially, then the Guardian appeared as though summoned. Not certain of the validity of my assumption on this, but there is a tie between the three that seems to hold over distances. Some sort of extrasensory perception," Mano'n added.

"That incident provided me with a few of my new creatures, I believe," Voravia said. "The individuals she sent me were men who attempted to harm her in some way before she discovered herself. I suspect this action, on her part, was a vengeful one.

But, as far as the Guardian is concerned, he has unlimited physical strength and is very crafty. I think you're correct. But he seems to have no magical skills, or, at least, I had no perception of any in our two encounters, though he can teleport."

"He definitely has the strength of more than a few men. I don't know about the magical inclinations. He didn't use any when we fought," Rab'k spoke for the first time. He was lounging near the rear of the tent and seemed uninterested in joining the conversation. But he did have his own grudges to settle with the Guardian.

"Then what about this other one. How is he involved?" Mano'n asked. He looked toward each of them and it seemed they knew nothing about the boy.

"When we fought on Black Stone Ridge after their escape from my castle, the other boy seemed an afterthought and I cast him away when the fight began. My interest was directed toward capturing the girl," Voravia added, becoming interested in identifying their problems.

"But, strangely, he returned and interfered with my attempts. His interference was effective. He was able to thwart several of my personal attacks, so I never was able to fully measure Anisah's

282

strength. I suspect he thought he was protecting her.

At the time, I had no idea who these young people were, except for the Guardian. So I was surprised. I do believe Anisah called him, Geth'n. But I have no idea how he's involved with the other two."

"He's a scholar," Rab'k said. "He and the Guardian are from the east peninsula, near Peetle or Larilla, where Monsh'a sent his troops. I saw the Guardian during, I suspect, one of his first battles. The scholar wasn't too involved in the fighting, but he was able to control the rage of the Guardian. I think they were, or are, personal friends.

The Guardian's name, by the way, is Pet'r. Or that is what the scholar, Geth'n called him at the time. When I fought with the Guardian on the ridge, I really didn't have time to become acquainted," he chuckled.

There was a moment of silence when each of them looked at the others.

Then Voravia burst out laughing, Rab'k sputtered and too began to laugh and Mano'n surprised the others with a smile.

"I'd suspect your correct," Mano'n said, chuckling. "But we do have to determine how we can separate them, both psychically and physically. Together they appear to be formidable. Individually, there is some hope for some weaknesses, particularly the two boys.

We must destroy the boys. But, and this is important, I do not want Anisah destroyed. I insist we attempt to capture her and capture her alive. She is, after all, my daughter and beyond that could be of value to us, and possibly Baalsa'n, in the future. She is too valuable within herself to lose her."

He's trying to avoid this knowledge reaching Baalsa'n. Particularly any information about his daughter's strengths.

Voravia thought about that discovery and decided this preliminary plan would be a good beginning and not draw attention to them unnecessarily.

She looked at Rab'k who, in return, glanced around at her. She shrugged, he then nodded and turned back to Mano'n.

"You're probably right," Rab'k admitted. "I'll continue to track the Guardian when I can, but first I have to deal with Monsh'a. Do either of you have a suggestion?"

"Play along," Voravia spoke up, to Rab'k's surprise. "He believes himself to be in favor with Baalsa'n and probably is. But I have my own scheme I'm working on and I believe it will eventually be the means to displace Monsh'a from his present seat of leadership. Don't worry about him, but my advice would be to avoid fighting against him at this time."

"Probably good advice, for a while. Monsh'a didn't succeed the last time he, years ago, was in command. If anything limits his thrust for power, it will be the deterrence of that defeat hanging over him. We should be able to take advantage of that," added Mano'n. "More importantly, we must proceed cautiously. I want to make certain we each understand we have to work together on this small conspiracy, or we will all lose. At least, for the duration of this war, we have to trust each other."

"Agreed," Voravia spoke first and stood preparing to leave.

"Yes, it would be wiser. Rather than continue without awareness of each other's plans. I too agree," Rab'k said, as he started to go.

"Before you leave I should add, let's meet at least once a week for a while. We shouldn't be away from this camp for long and must limit the absence of all three of us at the same time. So, one week and I propose we meet at Voravia's for our next gathering," Mano'n said. The other two nodded their head in agreement and left.

Mano'n looked down at the papers on his worktable.

"We have much to learn in such a short time. We can't afford any mistakes. And for now, I have to trust these two," he mumbled.

Outside the darkness was still and, in the shadows, a figure standing near the tent smiled, turned, and walked away, slowly fading into the night.

GARV'N

Geth'n and Anisah arrived just outside the west gate of Tariny. The streets of the city would definitely be too crowded to make such an appearance inside the city walls. The crowd as bewitched would stone them.

Making certain they hadn't been seen, they walked into the city. As they passed the gateway, there was one observer, an old beggar, lounging there, collecting alms, who smiled and nodded his approval.

The college wasn't too far from the gate so they passed quickly into the public area where the college, the hospital, the library, and another institution of learning were established.

All ancient reservoirs of knowledge were here and near enough to each other to be of help to those who wished to become more than they were. Tariny was famous worldwide for this knowledge center.

They approached the Healer's college, watching everyone who noticed them for signs of recognition. All they saw ignored them.

They walked quickly to the alcove of building and used the great doorknocker to announce their presence.

Mira opened the door slightly, glanced out and recognizing Geth'n stepped back, pulling the door open for them. They stepped inside, closing the door quietly behind them.

Mano'n stepped from the darkness of an alley a block away and watched them disappear inside.

"We've come to check on your special guest," Anisah whispered. She wasn't certain who else might be in the building and she didn't want their arrival to be announced.

"He's much better, but still can't talk. We can go see him now; he just woke. Is there a reason you've come to visit and in such a secretive way?"

"Yes, there is. We need to speak with Mistress Sanderol about some of the problems we are aware of. It's for the good of the College. If you wouldn't mind bringing her to Garv'n's room, we do need to talk to her," Geth'n said. He was trying to alarm no one prematurely.

Mira nodded her head and left them in the hall outside Garv'n's room. Anisah opened the door quietly and looked in. Garv'n was gazing out the window overlooking the streets below. He seemed to be better. He heard them and turned to observe his new visitors. He gave no expression of surprise, or fear. But he seemed to still be in a haze.

"What's wrong?" Geth'n asked her quietly.

"Probably shock," Anisah answered.

She walked to the bedside. Garv'n looked up at her. He smiled at her for a moment then reached for a small stone tablet with marking chalk lying on it.

Are you my rescuers? He wrote on the slate.

Anisah nodded her head. Geth'n walked up behind her. Garv'n, showing no fear, smiled and nodded at him.

He looked down at the slate and wrote again.

Sorry, can't talk. Injured my throat.

Anisah realized Garv'n didn't remember how he was attacked, or any details of who stabbed him. Geth'n and she were certain they knew, but only Jond'r could confirm that.

"We've come to take you to your castle near Farsea," Anisah told him, leaning down to straighten his covers.

He looked puzzled and scrawled on the slate. *I have a castle?*

Anisah and Geth'n glanced at each other. They knew the damage extended beyond the wounds Garv'n experienced. He was troubled but remembered very little. Anisah knew she was going to need to work with the gentleman a while before he would return to the present.

She and Geth'n walked to the window overlooking the street

287

below.

"Do you think it's wise to transport him to the castle?" Anisah turned and asked Geth'n quietly.

"I don't know about his family. I suspect he's from here somewhere and we might be able to find them. But, we have so little time. I think you should take him there because he might be exposed to the dangers of being alone, if we don't," Geth'n answered.

"Well, I should be able to help him regain his memory. I'm not certain about his voice though I can try. If they haven't figured a way to resolve the last here, I probably can't do any better," she suggested.

"Who was that?" Geth'n suddenly grabbed her and ducked away from the window.

"What . . . ? Who?" Anisah, yanked aside so quickly, gasped. Geth'n motioned for her to stand back while he peered around the curtains for another look at the street below. A young lady from the college was walking back from a building about three buildings from the hospital. Geth'n was fairly certain she had been talking to someone who stepped back into the alley between the buildings when he looked out. Someone broadcasting toward the college with immense power.

He pulled back from the window.

"Is there someone following you?" he asked her.

She looked at him a moment and looked around the room, thinking.

"Possibly. I thought I felt something just as we entered the square outside, before we were allowed entry. But, I wasn't sure. Could there be someone looking for you?" she asked.

"I doubt it. If anyone was looking for me, they would probably do so near Borny'a's cabin. I haven't exposed any magical flow since then, except for you and I coming here," he answered, thinking through his past few weeks.

"Then someone was waiting for us. But who?" she pondered a

moment, then she looked up at him with a look of realization on her face. "Actually I think I do know."

"Who?" Geth'n asked.

"Possibly my father," she answered. "I suspect there's a reason he and Voravia approached me in Caliste just after our battle at the black stone plateau. I was trying to get back to you and Pet'r. They intercepted me there. I don't know how they are able to track my whereabouts, nor why, but I think they are trying. Could you tell if it was male, or female?"

"It was male. The odd thing is that a young woman from this building was talking to him just as I caught a glimpse of them. He ducked back behind the building at the end of the second street and she returned here," Geth'n responded.

"Could you identify her?" she asked.

"No. I've not noticed her before, but then we've never been here for very long," Geth'n said. "Maybe we should ask Mira if there are any new girls. I can go do that. You stay here and, if you can, take a look out where I indicated. Maybe he'll show himself again."

"I'll do that and start trying to help Garv'n too When we leave, as obviously we need to, I'll go to the castle and take Garv'n with me. Are you coming too?" she nodded. She knew how to get back to the castle now, but she also knew she had to try to re-solve this problem of Mano'n following her. She was almost cer-tain he was the person that persisted in these attempt. She needed to rid herself of the problem, or deceive him into believing she might go with him until his attention was diverted.

"No. I need to attend to a personal matter and go to the lib-rary to investigate the Fealty," Geth'n looked out the window to-ward the east.

He had some details he desperately needed to resolve. He now felt confident Anisah could take care of herself, if nothing else what she did at Borny'a's cabin was proof enough of her strength. If this person following her had some powers, he

289

thought Anisah could probably take care of that without difficulty.

"I've got to help someone else get to a safe place," he added.

"I understand. I too concern myself for someone and would
never allow anyone to harm him. So you go and do what you
have to. You know where I am and how to find me. I'll leave
signs if I have to go quickly," she confided.

He looked at her with concern on his face, but he also knew
she did understand. She knew somehow there was another he
had to save from this evil rising over their world and she wanted
him to resolve that so he could concentrate on what lay ahead.

Geth'n turned to look out the window again, looked back at
Anisah, nodded his head and disappeared.

Anisah wandered to the window and looked at the street for
her stalker. Mano'n, without hesitation, stepped out and returned
her gaze. He nodded his head, turned and walked away down the
street, hidden from her view.

"So, I have a problem. But, first I need to determine how this
girl from here is involved," she mumbled, headed for the door,
looked over at Garv'n just to assure herself he was quiet and left
the room.

She walked down the hallway to the stairway. Mira was waiting
for her there.

"Is there something wrong?" Mira asked, joining Anisah to
walk down the stairs together.

"Maybe. Is there a new girl here? One I probably don't know,"
Anisah asked.

"Hmmm. Maybe Alesan. She arrived recently from the east
coast, somewhere near Tayrun. Rianne, I mean Ms. Sanderol,
talked to her when she first came and seemed to think she had
some talents. The girl made the request and asked to attend the
college. We know little about her, but she had some credentials
and was allowed to enter, though I'm uncertain what the credentials were," Mira answered, wondering why Anisah was asking

290

about the girl.

"Could you find the girl and have her go to the library. I'll ask Rianne if I may use it for a while and meet her there. Her name was Alesan, is that correct?" Anisah asked. Mira nodded her head, so Anisah walked away toward the main offices, looking for Rianne.

Fortunately, Rianne was in her office when Anisah knocked.

"Oh, Anisah. Welcome back, by the way. I apologize for not coming to see you, but, for some strange reason, we are being overwhelmed with new patients. Most of them seemed to have been involved in some sort of fighting not far from here. Do you know anything about that?" Rianne said.

"There is fighting north of here. It isn't a well-known as yet, but I believe we are being invaded and I suspect your patient numbers will soon began to rise even more rapidly than now. But, I need to request the use of your library and I'm going to need to speak to one of your apprentices. I've already requested Mira find her and ask her to come and see me," Anisah was in a hurry to resolve any suspicion of the girl so she could take Garv'n to safety.

"Certainly, I have no objection. Why do you need to talk to a novice?" Rianne asked her.

"Just to discover if she knows someone from our mutual past," Anisah answered, recognizing she was evading full answers to Rianne's question. "I shouldn't take more than a few moments to make my inquiries about that."

"Well, if there are any problems, please let me know," Rianne answered. "Are you going to be staying for longer? What about the last patient you brought us?"

Anisah thought a moment.

"I'm fairly certain I will be leaving by midday and probably will be taking him with me," Anisah answered. "I think he is well enough to travel and I know a place where he can relax and re-cover quickly. The college is a great place for beginning treatment, but I would be remiss in leaving him here to take a bed you are probably going to need soon. I'll let you know when I decide to leave."

"Thank you and I hope the young lady has the information you seek," Rianne said. "If I don't see you again, have a safe trip and come back to see us whenever you wish, or can begin your studies."

She glanced down at the papers on her desk then looked back at Anisah and smiled. Anisah knew it was time to leave Rianne alone, but she did notice the open invitation to *return to study*. She nodded and left.

She went directly to the library and entered. She was surprised when she entered because the girl, Alesan, was sitting calmly at the table waiting.

Anisah went to the opposite side of the table, across from the girl, and took a seat.

"Are you learning a great deal here? I've tried to come for the training myself, but I've been so busy I haven't been able to begin," she mentioned, watching the girl. "But I understand you've traveled quite a long distance to come here to learn. Are you comfortable?" Anisah was deliberately casual. She wanted to hear what the girl had to say and, more specifically, how she could interject she was aware Alesan knew Mano'n.

"I am. It's quite nice here and I traveled further than I thought it would be to get here," Alesan answered. "Why are you here?"

Anisah was surprised by the quick question from the girl, but she noticed something else about the inflection in the girl's statement.

This girl has lived in Varspree at some time in the past. She has that slurring of "r's in her speech I noticed when I was there.

"I'm from Caliste, north of Varspree. Have you ever spent any time in that region?" Anisah asked.

"No. Not really. I've always lived on the eastern seaboard," Alesan answered and took just an instance to glance around the

292

room, specifically at the window at the far end.

"I wondered. I thought you might know Ms. Farlen from there. A really nice person who runs one of the hotels," Anisah answered casually but was watching Alesan closely. What she noticed didn't surprise her. The girl deliberately straightened herself in her seat and looked down at the table; she wanted to avoid looking directly at Anisah.

This must be Esme', the girl Col'n said ran away with a sailor just before I arrived in Varspree.

"Well, I just wondered. I noticed earlier you were talking to a gentleman, dressed in black, on the street. I think I know him and wondered how you did," Anisah asked, pushing her point while the girl was uncomfortable.

"We met several months ago in Tayrun. He was kind to me when I was having some difficulties straightening my life and we became friends," Alesan answered. "How do you know him?"

"He's my father," Anisah answered abruptly.

Alesan almost jumped from her chair, but Anisah was prepared for that and magically held her in place.

"It seems you are a little more aware of who I am than you are admitting," Anisah pointedly accused the girl. "Esme."

The girl, despite the restraints, stood.

"I don't want to talk to you any further!" Alesan gasped, as she stood. "I don't have to stay here."

Alesan tried to turn and walk away, but Anisah forced her to sit.

"Actually, you do. But I have no intent to harm you. I must warn you that despite his seeming kindness, you are in danger associating with him. He is not what he seems," Anisah explained. "But I need you to tell him something. I want you to tell him I'll meet with him in about two hours. At the library steps. If he doesn't follow me here at any time before that, I will come in peace."

Alesan's eyes grew more and more round as she listened. Anisah could tell the girl's courage was near its limit. But she needed the girl to make the arrangement.

"Do you understand," Anisah finished and waited.

Alesan looked all about the room, expecting a trap of some sort, then looked back at Anisah.

"You have no reason to destroy me. I am the Esme' you mentioned but I needed to go on with my life . . ." the girl started.

Anisah held up her hand.

"I don't care about you, or your past life. I just wanted you to know I'm aware you are lying. I won't report this. I have no reason to unless you failed to do as I request.

Just deliver the message and I'll not bother you again. Though I think I should inform you, I visit this place often and will continue to do so. Be aware that I will expose you if you do not behave yourself while you are here. And finally, once you have delivered my message, you should return here immediately and probably remain sequestered here for a long time. You are safe from Mano'n while inside these walls, but you would be unwise to venture out, even with others," Anisah finished and started to rise. She released the ward on the girl who immediately rose and started to leave.

"Wait," Anisah said. Alesan stopped and looked back at her.

Anisah admired the girl for her strength, thinking the girl would probably make changes that would benefit her and, maybe, others in the future, if she freed herself from the trap where Mano'n had placed her.

"Learn to be calm and avoid lying," Anisah advised the girl. "You will gain so much more by doing that. You may go now."

Alesan nodded, turned and left the room, ran down the hall and out the front door. Anisah was sure she would run to Mano'n and deliver her message.

Anisah waited only a moment, left the library and moved upstairs to Garv'n's room. She looked out the window, caught site of Alesan talking to Mano'n. He looked up at the window where she stood and bowed his head.

Alesan backed away slowly and began to run toward the college. Mano'n made a gesture to destroy the girl as she ran, but when he looked up at Anisah, she was shaking her head. He did nothing, turned into the street and walked out of sight. He would be waiting.

SIARRA

Geth'n took a moment to go by the library after he left Anisah, looked for Siarra as he entered and but knew she wasn't
there. He wasn't too disturbed since she hadn't been there the last
time he visited. He assumed she had gone home and decided he'd
try to find her there.

He needed to do that bit of research about political agreements with other countries while he was at the library though. So
he went to the proper area and looked for the data about the
Granoblistia Fealty. What he found pleased him. It was evident
the countries who signed the Fealty had pledge to honor it into
perpetuity. He was satisfied the team they would send could use
that, at least, as a stepping-stone to an introduction for their supplications for assistance. He restored the documents to the correct location, looked around to make certain no one was about
and vanished.

Geth'n arrived at a point just north of Crosspoint, near the
shoreline of the Norts'a Reach. He was away from the normal
roadways, but walked quickly to the nearest one. He knew the
area fairly well so decided to explore it some before he entered
the city. He needed to determine whether any enemy was nearby.
He walked to the top of the tallest rise along the road but saw no
sign there were invaders, but he did notice something wrong with
the area.

This, as he remembered, was an area rising from the water of a
fairly gentle cove. There were evergreens of various sizes and
open grassland on the leeward side of the wind currents rising
from the water's surface. He assumed it was generally very quiet
in the area, but today he noticed there were a number of people
on all the roads headed toward Tariny. He noticed smoke rising

296

to the west of him.

He became concerned, turned westward, and started walking steadily toward the buildings and the smoke, he could see in the distance. He decided he shouldn't use his teleportation skills because there were too many travelers around him and he didn't know his exact target in the city. He didn't talk to any of those passing by, thinking it unnecessary.

He had no idea where Siarra's parents lived in Crosspoint, but he assumed he could inquire when he got nearer and would find her quickly.

When he topped a small rise and could see the city beyond, there was smoke rising in various places. He stepped up his pace as he drew nearer and entered the city on the main street, which ran almost north and south through the central portion and ended at the bay he saw beyond.

There, obviously, were attacks on the city recently and he wondered where the troops were. He decided it would be wiser to move to one of the lesser streets that ran parallel and ask individuals, still there, for directions.

He turned right, stopped to look up and down the main avenue again, then entered a crossing street to reach the back street. There were fewer people on this avenue, but still most were trying to leave. He arrived at the back street and turned southward again, walking around people packing their belongings, readying them to leave as quickly as they could.

People were clustered everywhere but all heading toward the roads leading to Tariny. Some carried bundles on their backs, others were pulling small carts laden with their belongings, and some just rode their horse or were leading one or more. There was an exodus from the city.

"Excuse me, sir," he stopped one man, traveling with his family. "May I ask you a question?"

"Ya can ask all you want but don't expect any long answer. Me and my family, we're leaving before those vandals return," the

297

man answered, still busy placing a pack of personal goods on a cart. "Got to be moving soon and soon may not be quick enough."

"What happened. I just got here," Geth'n tried to ask his questions quickly. He began helping the family load their belongings.

"Humph. Them savages attacked us without warning. They swept through here, killing some but mostly just stealing and taking food. Seemed awful interested in getting food. Then they just raced back through town and headed north toward Varspree," the man told him, grunting from the effort of lifting some items to the top of the stack, pointed his thumb in the direction from which Geth'n had just arrived. "Weren't you here when they came through?"

"No, I was coming from Pull'r and didn't see them over there. They must have gone to Varspree, like you suggested," Geth'n answered, trying to avoid suspicion. "I'm from Peetle. We're having similar problems there and other areas were having trouble all along the way. Was kind of rough to travel at times, but I managed to get here.

I have a question though. I'm looking for a young woman. Her name is Siarra. I worked with her some time ago in Tariny and, since I was close, thought I would come by to see her. Now I'm worried about her and her family," he asked. "Would you happen to know any young woman by that name or know where her family might live?"

"I don't think so. Maybe my wife. Willa, do you know a young woman named Siarra?" the man turned and asked his wife carrying another item from their house. She stopped before she tried to raise the item onto the pile on the cart. Geth'n stepped forward, took the bundle and raised it to the top for her.

"Let me think. I don't know for sure, but I think there might be family who lives about three streets down with a daughter by that name. Sad though, someone got killed during the raid down there. I don't know who, but that's what I heard," she answered.

298

"But you might try down there." She pointed to a street Geth'n could see. "You should turn right, I believe, to get to their house," she shouted to Geth'n who was already walking away.

"Sure am sorry for that boy. There was a lot of fighting down there." She shook her head, looked at her husband, turned and walked back into her lost home for more of their belongings. "Yep," The husband looked up and watched Geth'n walk away, said nothing more, then continued to load the cart, tying off one area hanging too loosely on the side.

Geth'n didn't run, but he hurried toward the street Willa pointed out. He got to the corner and looked around a building to determine if there was any dangerous activity within his view. He saw no sign of trouble.

The street, actually, was almost deserted. Only a few wandered along, some even walking into the prairie land west of the city. Some dogs were wandering along, digging into pile of trash for food and moving on. He began walking from house to house looking in through many of the hallways, or doors, left open by the departing residents. He knows no other way to look for some sign of Siarra.

He was becoming discouraged and concerned as he approached the end of the street.

"Geth'n! Geth'n! Here!" someone shouted behind him. He turned just as Siarra ran up to him, hugged him and held on for a moment. Then she blushed and stepped back.

"Oh, I'm so glad to see you. Please come back to my house. I just happened to see you walk by. Why are you here?" He could tell she had been crying. He pulled her to him and held her.

"Because I want to be here. I was looking for you and need to help, if I can. "

"Oh, Geth'n. You won't believe what has happened. Those vile soldiers came and attacked people along almost all the streets. My father and oldest brother went outside to try to chase them away from our home and some of the neighbors joined them.

299

But . . ." she broke down crying, holding her hands to her face.

Geth'n held her closer, trying to comfort her. "My father was killed. They hacked him down so easily," she started crying again. "I can't bear to think about that. But then they grabbed my brother and dragged him away. He fought back but they knocked him unconscious, bound him and took him. I don't know where. But my mother is having such a hard time and I can't believe all this has happened and so suddenly."

"Let's get off the street and back to your house," Geth'n pushed her away gently, "and we can talk. Maybe I can help. I will try to the extent I'm able."

She looked up into his eyes and nodded. They turned back, walked to her home and entered. Her family was sitting in the front room, wide-eyed with fear, waiting to leave.

"Mother, this is Geth'n. The friend I met at the library. He's come looking for me and wants to help if he can," Siarra explained to her mother.

Siarra's mother's face was tear stained. She sat looking out the window, rocking back and forth, moaning in her sorrow. Her look was wild, she was confused and frightened. She stared at Geth'n for a moment.

"You're not one of them, are you?" she asked Geth'n, holding his eyes with her own. Staring with hatred at everything about her, even her daughter. "You one of them?"

"I'm not," Geth'n answered. He wanted to hold the woman whose mental strain was obvious but was concerned she would think his actions some sort of attack. She didn't need anymore fear.

I need for Anisah to help this woman. She shouldn't have to suffer anymore than she already has.

"Siarra, are you all right?" Geth'n backed away from the mother and turned to his friend.

"I'm not sure. I seem to be, but I can't seem to blank my father's death from my mind. I can't believe this happened. My

300

poor brother, why did he have to die. I don't know, what I'm doing to do," she answered, tears flowing down her face again. "What is happening, Geth'n? What has happened?"

"The country is at war, Siarra. It's only just begun, not just here in Aerolan, but the whole world is involved. We are in serious trouble. I don't understand why Crosspoint wasn't damaged more than it is. The people here are fortunate, if you can understand that. It seems these soldiers were just trying to get supplys. The capture of your brother is another thing entirely and he may be still alive. We can only hope.

What we need to do now is get you and your family to safety. How many other family members are here?" he asked her, not wanting get too detailed about the war. He realized she needed some time to understand this tragedy for herself.

"I have a younger brother and sister. We hid them upstairs when the fighting started," she was trembling. Geth'n just wanted to stand and hold her some more until she calmed herself. But he knew he didn't have time.

"We need to bring them down here. What about your father's body, where is it?" he asked bluntly. Nothing was going to make Siarra's father's death any easier, so he might as well do what the man would not be able to. Get his family out of harm's way.

"I don't know. They dragged it along behind some horses and disappeared into the prairie at the end of the street," she stood looking at him, sadness digging its way into her. If he didn't act soon, she too would become as vacant as her mother had become.

"Go get the young ones. I'll prepare your mother," he told her and pointed up the stairs. She stood looking at him as though he spoken in some strange language. "Siarra. Now!"

She blinked, turned and rushed up the stairs.

Geth'n turned back to the mother and squatted in front of her.

"I'm going to make your hurting go away and let you sleep

301

now," he told the woman who needed only kindness for the moment. "Please relax and go to sleep." He held his hand just over her head. She looked up at his hand, vaguely staring and questioning with her eyes, then she closed them, slumping into her chair. He helped her lay back so she wouldn't fall.

Siarra came running down the stairs, stopped and stared at her mother, shock visible on her face.

"What did you do? What is wrong with Mother?" she ran to her mother's side and tried to hold her up into a sitting position. Her mother was limp and unconscious. "What did you do?"

She rose accusing Geth'n by implications with her demands to know what he did.

"Siarra, I did nothing to harm her. I needed her to be calm and comfortable for our trip," Geth'n answered. He could understand her alarm. "It's all right. She'll be safe from her fears until I can get her real help. But we do need to leave here. Now."

"Where are you taking us? How are we going to travel there without help? What about our belongings? What about our home?" she demanded, her face reddening with anger.

"I cannot save any of those things. Where I am going to take you will provide all these things, except your personal belongings and your family losses. But I can save you and this part of your family. But you must be willing to come with me. I can't do what I have to do if you don't want me to or you fight against it," he answered. "You have to be willing."

"Willing to do what?" she seemed to be angrier with him every time he explained, as though his statements made no sense to her. "What do you want?"

Well delaying the answers to her questions only makes this worse. I have to do what I can. I need for this woman, and her family, to be safe.

"For you to trust me. I am going to ask you to just trust me. We haven't known each other very long, but I care for you and want you, and yours, to be safe," he told her. She looked up at him, tears still glistening in her eyes, and bowed her head in sorrow.

"What can you do?" she mumbled. "All is lost. We are doomed."

"Not yet," he answered. "Please. Everyone hold hands in a circle. Siarra, you hold one of your mother's hands and your sister can hold the other. It is important everyone hold tightly to each other."

Siarra and the others, at first, just looked at him with puzzlement, but then they followed his instructions.

"Now I want everyone to close your eyes. We'll all feel a wind blowing over us, but don't be afraid. We'll not be harmed. Just hold tightly until that feeling is over," he instructed them.

They did as he asked. He held Siarra's and her little brother's hand and concentrated. The sensation of rushing air came and went.

"You can open your eyes now," he told them.

They opened them slowly and looked around them. They were obviously not in their home.

"Wow! How did you do that?" Siarra's brother asked. He and the younger sister began to stare around at the interior of the castle amazed, knowing magic brought them to the new place. Siarra's mother stood and stared at the Geth'n without comprehension.

Geth'n motioned to one of the guards who came running to help.

"Please take these youngsters and their mother to my general quarters area and arrange for rooms for them. Also, for this young lady. She may want a private room," Geth'n instructed, not looking at Siarra directly.

He could tell she was fuming from anger. He really wanted to have the talk he expected, but in private not in the main hallway of the castle.

The soldier indicated to Siarra and her family they should follow him. She refused just as Geth'n expected.

Geth'n turned and looked at her then pointed toward a meeting room across the great hall. She huffed, turned and headed toward the room, not looking back at him. After they entered the room and Geth'n shut the door quietly, she turned and glared at him.

"How did you do this?" Siarra indignant. He had never had an opportunity to explain his new skills to her. "Are you some sort of wizard?"

"I guess so," he answered, uncertain of her reaction. "But it's not something I knew about just a few months ago. I'll admit when I met you, I knew. There's a lot at stake now. I have two friends who live here too. We apparently were chosen to be involved in what is now becoming one of the most important things that's happened in our country in hundreds of years.

We three were instructed to gather good people and to bring together a force to combat a powerful person who wants to not only destroy our country and its civilization, but wants to eliminate all living things on this planet. You've personally witnessed the results of the initial attacks. A war has begun.

We feel obligated now to try to help those we can. I wanted to bring you and your family to safety. I'm so sorry I didn't arrive in time to save everyone but I wanted to help. Mostly, I want you here for your safety. We all need to work to save what we can."

"But why you? Why your friends?" she asked him. She seemed to have passed being angry, but she wanted to understand why he was what he seemed to be.

"We don't know. Though one of us, as it turns out, is related to a person who long ago, and on another world, fought against this menace and lost everything. Now he, a friend of mine since our childhood, has been attacked and almost died. That makes this a personal thing. He was to investigate our home, the village of Peetle, and discovered it had been attacked by troops of soldiers in much the same manner as Crosspoint. He came away injured following a confrontation with the troops still stationed

304

close by.

So he and I must continue.

Our friend, Anisah, we met when taking a trip to Tariny. She, we have discovered, is the granddaughter of the tyrant who wants to destroy us. But, her mother is one of us and Anisah was taught right from wrong. She is heavily supportive of what we must do and is the other person who can manipulate time and space to move about the way you, your family and I just did. We don't know how we can do it, but we have used it for a number of incidences and are getting better each time. She will probably be back here soon and you can meet her."

"What's your interest in her?" Siarra asked, raising an eyebrow. "How close a friend is she?"

"Well, not as close as you're thinking. In fact, I think she and my friend, Pet'r, have a fondness for each other. I haven't asked but she felt a great deal of grief when he was wounded and was instrumental in his survival," he answered, inwardly chuckling at her question.

"So, what can I do?" she asked. "I need to be involved. I also need to go and make certain my mother is comfortable. The kids will want to wander around and discover things for themselves after they have calmed themselves. We all loved my father, a good man, and his loss and that of my brother, is tearing at us right now.

I wasn't trying to be as hateful as I may have seemed. But all these things have happened so suddenly. I don't know what I'm to believe. I don't know what I think about you. Though I want to thank you for this kindness. Can you have someone take me to my room?"

They left the room and were walking toward the left wing of the castle when the soldier who had taken her family to their rooms returned and reported to Geth'n.

"I'm sorry, I failed to ask your name before," Geth'n asked the soldier.

"Halr'a, sir," the soldier answered, drawing to attention.

"Well, Halr'a, if you will, please show the lady Siarra to her rooms."

"Yes, sir," Halr'a started to turn and guide Siarra back to the rooms.

"Wait. Siarra, don't worry about anything but your family. You and I can talk when things are calmer. I need to go check on Pet'r and we probably will have another meeting with everyone in the next few days. You're invited to come, if you wish," Geth'n told her. "All right, soldier, you may help her now."

Geth'n smiled at Siarra, turned and proceeded across the great hall to a door leading toward the rear of the castle.

She watched him stride away, wrinkled her brow, turned back to look at the soldier and nodded her head. As they walked toward her rooms, she looked back to see Geth'n but he was already gone.

She frowned, turned and followed Halr'a to her room and family.

GREATER PERIL

Voravia ordered all her house staff to report to the tower room. There were about 20 of them. Mark'a, Sumt'r and all his men stood, at attention, near the great window. Their presence made the room seem small.

Today she was observing the older group of her household servants, her Hundr'a. She looked over the group, trying to decide which to keep as small and mild and which to modify for her new purpose.

She had not resigned herself to being only a helpmate to Monsh'a, even if she technically was suppose to be in command of him. The writing on the wall seemed clear to her. There were other ways to influence outcomes and, having been a person on her own for all her years, she was directing her activity toward establishing herself as a principal, not just a participant, in the war to come.

But she needed to have her own army to do so. She had accumulated, in the years of attending the castle near Grafnid, some twenty thousand servants. Some had aggressive skills because of their history; others no more than those of a servant. Those with the sense of combat were her vanguard within her underground network of caves and tunnels throughout the southern part of the mountain range. Her reach extended as far east as Doom's Woods and as far south as Ran sea in the central part of Aerolan. She had never attempted to extend this into the Wasteland, largely because she had no desire to return there.

Her power was hidden but she had resources. Now she wanted her reach to exhibit power recognized by everyone. Even Baalsa'n. But she knew, from her early days in her home, Baalsa'n had some means to read thoughts of others if the effort was extended to thoughtful planning. She remembered that from her earlier days. She had no desire for Baalsa'n to know what she was thinking now. So, she avoided thinking about her own plans; she slowly put one piece with another over a long period.

Of course, her long periods were getting shorter since Monsh'a arrived. But, she managed to manipulate one of Monsh'a people, giving her an advantage of sorts, by beguiling and gaining the confidence of the wizard who produced the Maah'e. Drang'm was a relatively easy problem to solve with her talents for persuasion. He gave her a written account of how he modified living creatures into the Maah'e and he sent her a sample - Mark'a.

She already had Mord and Sesk out in the country looking for Anisah. So they would have to be included in the odd men she kept for the servant group. There were about twelve, or thirteen, candidates here in the tower room; almost all were simple servants. She, on looking them over as a group, decided that none of them would be good candidates for modification to Maah'e.

She would need to have all the others, the aggressive ones, come to the castle, preferably undetected, from the caves and tunnels.

This is going to be such great fun. My own army hidden away from the sight of most, particularly those who would try to interfere. I believe I've now taken the advantage from these men who wish to control what I do and me. I think my plan will alter that attitude.

But I must find a way to deal with these three young wizards, especially my niece. Anisah will be the strongest force against changing anything in this world. It's not important what her birthright is; it's what she believes is important for her. I need to keep that in mind. In fact, I should send out and have Mord and Sesk return. They're wasting time I could use for other tasks.

"I have no further use for any of you today. Mark'a, please take Sumt'r and his men to the new lodging in the caves just east of here and wait for my command. The rest of you should return to your current tasks. I will not be needing your assistance. I do need for Arla'n and Timr'e to stay," she added, noticing the two she named stiffen with fear. She could see the relay on the faces of the servants she dismissed. The word had spread they were to be changed. When she didn't, the in-house group quietly expressed obvious relay.

She needed to send out messages to her underground commanders and have them report. She needed the two servants to deliver the messages. They, of course, thought immediately they were to be included in a Maah'e modification. She waited for the rest to leave the room then turned to them, smiling.

"Don't be afraid. I need you to be messengers. I want each of you to go where I assign you, but do not reveal anything you have seen in the castle, nothing about the Maah'e, to those with whom you speak. If you do and I become aware of it, I will eliminate, or change, you.

My message is simple. Tell each commander to report with his full unit to the castle. Give each group a day after they depart their areas as you proceed through the caves. You will go to the units closest to here first and travel out to all the tunnels in a slow process. When you have completed the delivery to the last group, you should follow them back. If you find any other units on the way back, you should follow the same procedure with them. Do you understand?" Voravia glared at the two servants.

They nodded their heads but continued to stare at the floor in front of them. She could tell they were eager to leave and were only barely able to stand because of their fear.

Sometimes it's good to have a captive audience.

"I expect you to be on your way today. I also expect the first unit to arrive within two days after you depart. You will assure these commanders I have given this message personally. I have here a medallion identifiable as mine. You will take it as proof I am giving the commands. Take it and be into the caves within the next couple of hours," she continued with her instructions.

She held a medallion, taken from some forgotten landowner

she had eliminated ages before, in her hand for a moment, infusing it with spell that would shock each recipient when touched, and handed it to Arla'n. His hand shook with the vibration of the spell, but he placed it in a pouch tied to his belt and continued to stand with head bowed, waiting for this audience to be over.

These Hundr'a of mine are like children. Properly disciplined children. At least my discipline. Good. They, as always, will perform well.

"Now, Go! You have little time to prepare. Don't delay," she added. The two backed away slowly, always with their eyes down, until they reached the door. Then she could hear them bolt down the steps and heard the sound of their footsteps fade.

Now I should be able to continue my plan. In a few days, the first unit should arrive. I have the Stone of Krels'a that Drang'm gave me, the spell he devised to make the changes and should soon have my own small army.

I need to keep the newer converts close at hand until some of the nearby caves are empty. Then I'll have more room to house them. These Akab'r have no great needs other than obeying my commands. A factor that makes it easier and very convenient to hide them.

Days later, the first of her Hundr'a began reporting. There were about twenty-five of them and, of that group, she chose fifteen of them she felt would best qualify for her needs. The rest she chose to leave unharmed to be used either as her personal servants, or to maintain surveillance over her small underground empire. She would no longer have this group try to protect her interest beyond her castle grounds. She now had a group to do that with greater skills and stronger presence.

The conversion of the ones chosen went smoothly and now she had a truly strong escort group for her personal use. She wanted to use this group as the base for her plan to expand her secret army. She placed them, along with Mark'a, Sumt'r and his group, into the map room chambers discovered by the troublesome rebels, Mano'n's brat and the scholar, when she captured them. Her intention was to continue to build her Akab'r group and place them strategically across the central part of Aerolan, just south of the mountain range.

She was particularly interested in keeping them out of everyone's sight – including those in her family. Especially those in her family.

They don't need to know of my activities, or my plans. They might think them a measure of subterfuge contrary to Baalsa'n's general plans. Possibly they're correct. Possibly.

Voravia felt her private intentions were her business. She lived, suffered and survived a long time alone. She felt no allegiance, nor familial relations, with the other members of her genetic family. She, in fact, had a certain disdain for all of them.

This invasion of her lands by Monsh'a and his forces was contemptible. She despised the trespassing vermin. The only good to come from it was this new gift from the Ravelan – this gift of her hidden army. She had paid so little for it.

Drang'm wasn't exactly a man to trust, but neither was he demanding. He too has his own agenda. He too had survived through his guile and perceptive observations of the Om-Esfer'n and seemed to have no fear of them.

Certainly a plus if one was looking for an ally under adverse circumstances. And he had a certain appeal as a man, she felt a kinship and a bit more for him. Strangely, she enjoyed his company. His rewards were pleasing to her.

But she had other matters needing her attention. There should be another group of the Hundr'a arriving soon. She looked forward to their arrival, to enhance her power. Both were certainly worthy of the time spent accomplishing her goal.

A very special goal, I think. Outcomes are results of plans, patiently conceived plans. The validation of those plans will come about when they accomplish what I want. Not what others might want.

I will have the power I need.

MANO'N REBUFFED

"So we meet again, daughter. I thank you for giving me this opportunity," Mano'n said, as soon as she appeared. Her arrival wasn't as spectacular as Mano'n expected. Based on their prior meeting, he thought she would be shielded and wary.

But she wasn't. She walked around the corner of the street where the library and hospital stood. He waited on the long steps used by both buildings and looked down at her from the top step. She approached him unguarded and he was tempted to use that foolhardiness to his advantage. But her look changed his mind. She wasn't so naive as to not be prepared for a meeting she had no desire for.

"Yes, here I am to talk about the future. But I probably should add that your attempts to persuade me, in any way, to follow your example are a waste time," she said, her voice was calm.

His daughter was much older than before, not in her physical presence, but in the look of confidence in her eyes, by the way she held herself. It was a marvel to him her development had been self-attained. She now was a young woman of beauty, allure and, yes, power. He recognized she had the latter beyond anything he ever imagined for her. He could sense it.

"I assumed that would be true when I received your note," he admitted, "but I would add that I too can be persuasive."

"I should likely hear a better summary of that quality from my mother than you," she added, a snap in her eyes revealed her irritation with this direction for their conversation.

"But I wanted to tell you to desist in your effort to control, or engulf, me. You will stop stalking me. It serves no purpose other than to irritate me. I can always tell when you're close. It is a senseless effort and I'm tired of dealing with it.

If we are going to have this war, then we should proceed. I'm not going to be so patient with the patterns in this game as I was in the past. Part of my problem then was my ignorance and being naive. Now I'm prepared and ready to engage in my effort to drive you and my grandfather from this world. That is my intent and I'm unconcerned for myself. But I will not rest until that has been accomplished, whether there is a future for me or not."

Mano'n felt a certain pride in her forthrightness and courage, but he scoffed at her intent.

"Of course. And exactly how are you going to do that, daughter?" he asked, grinning.

Anisah tensed, noticing his smirk, looked to watch the birds flying into the eaves of the old buildings above them for a moment to regain control of her emotions, turned back to him and said, "Simple. We, and yes there is now a *we,* are going to invoke the Granoblistia Fealty. We're going to gather a force that will overwhelm your minions. We will fight for every inch of ground across Aerolan and beyond.

It is my intent to not only drive Baalsa'n from this world but also to destroy him. If you choose to maintain your allegiance to him, your life could be in jeopardy. You, Voravia and Rab'k are of no importance one way or the other, but, if you persist, you, and they, may die. I will not hesitate to be the dealer of that death.

Fear of you, or them, is no longer part of what I feel," she walked toward him as she spoke.

He almost relented to a sense of fear for himself by taking steps away from her, but he held his ground as she approached. He couldn't get over her innate self-confidence and the quiet beauty of her as a woman. He was astonished at those changes, recognizing he was pleased as her father, though not as her enemy. Realizing he couldn't allow himself to follow the fatherly view, he looked over her head at the building beyond while he collected his thoughts.

"So, are you threatening me? Do you propose we attempt to

313

destroy one another today, on this spot?" he asked her. He didn't blink; he simply stared back at her. But he could only do so for a moment. He looked away again.

Anisah shrugged and looked directly into eyes, "How many have already been killed? How many have been captured and exposed to the magical powers of the Ravelan? How many will be killed? All of us? Every living human on this planet – as has happened before in other times and places? Don't plead you are blameless because you're not. You're a servant of Baalsa'n carrying out his orders.

From what I've been told, you've been very active in taking innocent lives for centuries and on many worlds. Why? To appease my grandfather, a truly despicable person, if he is a person. By what right and for what reason?

I have talked to the Al-Esfer'n through dreams and visions. I know what this is about. I have received ,from my birth through you, certain innate talents. Some of which you've seen demonstrated. I've learned other tricks from those who wish to help. I've been a bit creative on my own with no help from anyone, or any group.

You, and the others like you, are in trouble if I have my way. It is odd it occurs to me you may want to reconsider what is being threatened. It really depends on whether you wish to survive this charade or not.

If the time comes for me to destroy you. No, when it comes time to do so, I will not hesitate.

Will you, if that table is turned?" she said, with severity and bluntness. There was no hesitation, no withdrawing in fear, no misunderstanding about what she said.

He stepped back.

Does this woman, my daughter, have these powers? Can she fulfill these threats and do so without dread or concern? Can she be cold-blooded toward us, her family?

As though reading his thoughts, a talent he thought he alone

314

could manage, she answered all his questions.

"Do you wish to test those possibilities? I am willing to begin with you, if you wish. I will not allow these things to happen and I will, if necessary, lead an army to the destruction of Baalsa'n. You and Rab'k are plotting something against one another and for yourselves. Voravia, I know is plotting a different world, and I suspect you know this already, and has her own agenda.

I will not hesitate to use my powers to their greatest extent. Do you wish to start today?" she walked up a few more steps.

Mano'n backed away though knowing he shouldn't. He stopped and stepped toward her. She stood waiting resolute, only a slight movement of her hands revealed she indeed was ready. The air crackled about them. The sky began to gather clouds overhead. A breeze swirled the dust around in the street.

Some of the attendants briefly opened the great door of the library and were about to leave but they could feel the changes about them and quickly retreated back into the building.

Mano'n, noting the distraction, took another step.

Lightning streaked from one of Anisah's hands and crashed into a lightning rod atop the hospital. She turned both hands toward him.

"Is this the day this will end?" she asked him, very casually. "Do you want to test this now? For I'm telling you, and have already warned you, I am willing."

She glared at him now. He started to raise his hands to show some strength but she held his arms to his side with only her mental strength. He was unable to move them.

"What do you think you're doing?" he yelled at her. "You can't do these things without consequences."

"The only consequences I perceived will be inflicted on you if you wish it. Do you?" she snapped back at him.

Mano'n stopped struggling and the force around him subsided. He relaxed and the air quieted. He stepped back from where he was and Anisah's hands fell to her side.

315

"I think not. Not today. There will be great pressure inflicted upon you personally for this action of yours. There will be consequences. There will be times when you will not want to endure these things that are to happen to you. You have not known, nor ever heard of, the kind of power that exists within our family," he said, backing further away.

"We are the base for the Om-Esfer'n and our strength alone has conquered a multitude of other cultures and people. The Al-Esfer'n have never attempted to resist us with any strength and we do not expect they can this time, whether with, or without, you.

The effort here in the past was not fulfilled simply because we did not have the time to pursue a victory. There was another place where the people had developed their own protection and we had to attend to that little problem. Which we did without fear of failure.

So don't assume because I have not forced you into coming into our group you are able to avoid it. We can, if necessary, deal with this little problem without you. Then I will force you to come with us.

We will destroy this world," Mano'n said, his eyes ablaze with anger. He was indeed threatening her now.

She stood and listened without any signs of the distress he was expecting. She turned her head to the side occasionally as though giving additional thought to something he said. But she did not retreat He knew she was containing the situation and that worried him more than any physical threat she may have impaled.

She isn't afraid. She disbelieves me. She thinks she is stronger than we are. Oh, Anisah. Your sadness will overwhelm you in the end. My sorrow at your plight will be profound.

"I am already sad. You have forsaken sensibility in your fogged image of your right to be cruel to others. You have given your soul to a self loathing and cowardly being. Baalsa'n sinks beneath the bedevilment of his own senses in his hatred of the Al-Es-

316

fer'n. For what reason? Why can he not accept there can be others in our universe? If everyone, except his admirers are slain, will he be happier? Or will he begin to enslave those who followed him to that destination?

I foresee dissolution, fear and possible destruction for this demon. Why? Because he's your father? What of the others? Why do they? Because they seek power. But, if everyone else is dead, who becomes the most powerful then? It is, as I mentioned earlier, a game for fools. I, for one, have no need for this. I will protect these people and, if successful, may do so for others.

But my first concern is you and yours. Don't pretend any melancholy exists about my welfare. You are blinded by your abject slavery to a maniac. You shall end as his victim. So, in that, I pity you. But, if the time comes when we are still enemies and facing each other on a battlefield. I will have no mercy," Anisah spoke with a constant beat.

The pulse filled the air around them. Mano'n could feel his heart pounding to the same rhythm and it disturbed him. His uncertainty welled up inside him. He became afraid of what he knew.

She is beyond my control. We will not have it so easy here. I've waited too long. I have contributed to this probable failure. My daughter will be my undoing.

"You are likely to learn more about me and what I am capable of. For the time being, I would like for you to go and tell my mother I am well. You owe her an apology and I would have you plead that case with her, now.

Good-bye, my false parent. We will be enemies unfortunately, when we next meet. The circumstances will be different," Anisah finished.

He next expected her to disappear, but instead, he found himself back in Caliste, in the same spot they had last confronted each other. When the trees and stones Anisah had suspended crashed to the ground around him. On that occasion, he sank to

317

his knees, feeling the rumbling of the earth and found himself alone.

Looking around when all became quiet, he stood and walked toward the town to find Callex. He was going to oblige Anisah's request. He did need to do that.

Anisah stood for a moment after Mano'n left. She looked at the sky, the clear blue, almost sparkling, sky.

Why does fate hand a person a past and a future with so many unknowns. Then pushes each person out the small door into life and reality, watching while the struggle moves him or her through a measured life until it ends. Each survives to the extent he, or she, can with nothing more than the creative urge to maintain a life and, if possible, attain some satisfaction from having tried.

She stood and tears slowly flowed down her cheeks.

Then she turned and walked back to the hospital. She knew she needed to take Garv'n to the castle of Ralff'r and she needed to return to help with the organization of a machine to fight the war to come.

I hope to attain a good life. I hope I am capable. My hope includes all who will have to live through this hell to come and who are destined to be someone different, if they survive.

Hope is the only thing we have.

She walked to the end of the street, looked back at the library, turned and disappeared around the corner.

SECRETS IN THE NIGHT

Insisting there must be deception within a group, whether one of the same mind, or those not in agreement, often leads those who would try to find comfort in their own secretiveness into moments of self-deception. The observer fails to include the ideas promoted from within. Does anyone never suspect oneself?

And do those who deceive assume that others aren't aware of what is happening? And how does the observer enhance the lays by being more devious than the other participants?

Is it true that by living in lays, one isn't aware of either continuing to deceive, or doesn't any longer realize that the ideas promoted are lays and exist on tenuous thread of inconsistency? It is difficult to build on the first lay, but most often the building only constitutes another lay being told.

A clandestine meeting of the evil siblings here reveals at least one of the three is having strong misgivings about the success of the endeavor to destroy the planet. Logically, if there is no other place to be, then destruction includes the loss of one's life in the destruction. And there are doubts about success on this path to destruction, will it actually be possible, in this unique case? The enemy is rising against the assumption they will do nothing. What are the probabilities of a successful defense?

What are those ideas in the mind of the attacker and how does that affect their outlook? . . .

Voravia watched out the window as her two brothers rode toward the castle.

How small they look. Two of the most powerful men on this planet and they look small. What is our significance?

She stood watching for a moment more then turned to look out over the sea, waves crashing into the land. Dusk was approaching, dimming the world.

319

Is war a way of nature? Is it not an invention of man? Everywhere I look there is only conflict. Even I am torn. Do I go with the power that dominates, or should I just savor the moments I have?

I'm almost immortal, but what does that gain me? Would that be different on some other world, some other place? Are we humans no more than the grains of sand tossed by the sea — just a part of the whole? Are we no less than the smallest living thing, wishing only for survival?

What are we?

"Probably less than we believe," she muttered, looked again at the two arriving at the gate. "Might as well see what these two are concerned about. I suspect, very little. One is too stupid; the other is lost in himself. They want to talk to me? What do I want? Who are we that we worry so much? "

She turned away from this view of her world and walked out of the room to attend the concerns of her siblings. Two, among the many, she cared little for them anyway.

Voravia, you are being far too philosophical this morning.

Her people let them in through the main gate and into the great meeting hall on the bottom level, as she had instructed. There weren't many embellishments in her castle, she had no need for them. Things she possessed were there mostly for utility, if there was any ornamentation at all. But the tower hall had chairs and a large table where they could sit and talk about what came next.

This should be interesting — or maybe not.

The two were waiting for her. They sat, not talking to each other. Mano'n was looking up at the windows high above the room that sent the only light available casually over the center and the seating.

As she walked across the room toward them, they both stood and waited until she sat.

What are we doing here? Aren't we curious? And chivalry? How quaint.

"So, what do you gentlemen want to talk about?" she asked,

320

pressing her gown out with her hands and settling into her chair.

"We have a great deal to discuss. We want to know what you are doing?" Rab'k blurted out. Never one to be concerned about anyone else, he was the most annoying person Voravia ever met. Many who bothered her with such arrogance, in the past, were now dead. That memory brought a smile to her face.

Mano'n looked around at the younger man and shook his head.

"What we probably need to do is determine what all of us are doing so we might plan to use our resources and determine how we can eliminate Monsh'a in the process," he said, trying to diminish the bluntness of Rab'k.

"Eliminate Monsh'a? Why would you want to do that? Baalsa'n seems to have a high regard for his skills," Rab'k shot back. He was no admirer of Monsh'a either, but felt the man could be used for his benefit. He hadn't actually thought about Mano'n, or Voravia, or what they wanted to do. In fact, he saw no need for this meeting at all.

Just stick to the plan and execute it correctly. Simple things keep trouble away. Monsh'a can be useful in achieving victory.

"If we don't, we will have him attempting to dominate us. Can't you see Baalsa'n has pushed all of us aside in deference to this warrior. I remember, from before, when we lost here, Monsh'a pushing aside any suggestions I made. We were driven from the place by a small group of people. Those same people, you hate so much, were able to gain, with guile, the unexpected and were able to drive us away.

So Monsh'a, despite his outward appearance, is a liability. I was surprised Baalsa'n called him back," Mano'n said. He wanted no part of another loss here. He was concerned about many things, but losing again was not something he wanted.

Voravia looked to each one of the men and listened politely when they spoke.

Why would Rab'k want to win, except as a victory over these rebels? The concept of destroying the planet, as well as the people, doesn't seem to have occurred to him. Is his own life is unworthy?

She turned away while the other two pushed the issue about. She looked up toward the windows.

What is wrong with this place, this time, this world? Why must it be destroyed?

"Well, I think we would be wise to not trust Baalsa'n nor his henchman," Mano'n added. "We three have limited power and we must think in terms of what we can do to achieve our end."

"What is our end?" Voravia asked him.

He looked over at her quickly, raising an eyebrow. Voravia had never known what he thought of her, but she could guess.

Surprised, are you? Surprised I actually spoke? How dare you, you weak man. A man wanting to save his small world. I'm no fool, Mano'n. You want to save your world – this one.

"We must assure ourselves of victory. We have to admit these young people you and Rab'k lost one battle to, have powers that gives them a stronger possibility than those who defeated us years ago," he answered her. "I want to make certain we understand them and are ready for them before they arrive. Baalsa'n seems to believe ignoring them is a safe thing to do. I doubt that."

And so you can save your daughter. One of the ones who could seriously damage Baalsa'n's plans. You have to remember, Brother. Rab'k and I did meet her. I personally fought with her. There is no question, in my mind, she can take care of herself and probably you, if she wants. I have no desire to face her again.

"What's to understand? They're a group of idiots and have no real power," Rab'k blurted out. "I know I'm more capable of winning a fight than that boy. He caught me off guard the last time. That won't happen again."

Voravia and Mano'n glanced at each other with that remark. Voravia smiled then raised her chin to look out the window at the darkness closing in on them.

"That may be," Mano'n added, "but they are dangerous. What

322

can we do about them? Or do we want to?"

Voravia looked back quickly at her older brother.

That's interesting. A change of heart? What motive does Mano'n have now? Has he turned from Baalsa'n?

She tried to determine, without asking, what Mano'n was trying to do here, as darkness approached, talking to them privately. She couldn't hold her question back.

"Do we want to?" she asked. "That's a strange question, brother. What do you mean by that?"

Rab'k was looking at her, then back at Mano'n, frowning. He didn't understand what was happening. Nor why the conversation had gone a direction he certainly didn't expect.

His sole goal in this endeavor was to rid the world of the southern rabble. He wasn't thinking beyond that. He was thinking this meeting was about how they could work with Monsh'a to accomplish that destruction. The overwhelming concept of the world being completely destroyed hadn't occurred to him, he wasn't associating a *dead* planet with the loss of *all* life. He wanted his people – the desert people - to have this world to themselves and gain the wealth the southerners had.

Voravia watched as the younger man repressed his anger. He jumped up from his seat and began to pace across the room. She noticed Mano'n watching Rab'k, shaking his head.

Too impatient. Was and is. A shame. He has the zeal, the desire, but lacks the patience. He'll make mistakes often and will endanger others and himself. A person to stay away from.

"Rab'k, you know these three only want us to go away. So, they have their lives to consider, as well as those they want to protect. If we attack them, there is no way to measure what they can do. Baalsa'n, nor Monsh'a, had to face such a strong foe before. Everyone who lived here then was frightened and cowed by the presence of someone like us. But, still, these people with a few who could help, held us back and forced us to leave.

All I'm proposing is that we need to determine the risks of

continuing our plans of attack until we know our enemy. What is wrong with waiting until we know how to fight these young people?" he asked.

The other two simply looked at him as though he hadn't spoken.

"Well. One important factor exists," Voravia offered. "Baalsa'n is showing signs of his own impatience. There'll not be the time you mentioned to make such a determination before he becomes angry with us for lacking impetus."

"That is true, and likely," Mano'n turned to talk to her directly. He had grown tired of the contentious Rab'k who bored him anyway. "But, can we at least come up with our plan to investigate these three?"

"I don't think so, brother," Rab'k walked closer to Mano'n and pushed his face into his brother's. "You're stalling. Why?"

Voravia turned to look at the younger man.

Now that's perceptive. Maybe he isn't as stupid as he acts.

"Look. I was here before. I saw what happened. We assumed the people here were weak. But, they still held belays about their origins. They had Areb'l and his friend, Borny'a, who was alive at that time too, to help them form a simple plan and the execution of that plan defeated us," Mano'n stood and pushed the younger man back as he did.

Voravia thought they might come to blows, but knew Mano'n had called on his personal reserves if he needed them.

Rab'k back away a bit.

"Now do you have a plan, or not?" he almost shouted at Rab'k and advanced on the man as he did. "Tell us what great plan you have, Rab'k. Tell us how you are going to defeat these young people – who, by the way, seemed to have found Borny'a on their own – without knowing how you are going to do it. You know they are powerful. You and Voravia have had opportunities to rid us of this menace on more than one occasion and have failed to either win that confrontation, or devise a means to do so. So, don't push your lame ideas at me. I do what I do because I admit the danger. No one can push aside the obvious simply because we seem to have numbers.

They have numbers. A real number – three. Three uncontrollable people with magic powers. Do we? Voravia and I have capabilities, you don't. Baalsa'n is more powerful than all of us, but his chosen people do not. But these three? They have shown themselves to be serious about what they are doing and they are extremely dangerous." He snapped away from talking, glanced at Voravia a moment, then turned and walked to look out the window toward the sea as she did earlier.

Voravia realized Mano'n presented a valid point.

He's right. We've been fools because we are afraid of Baalsa'n. We have minimal exposure to these young leaders and all of us have failed to make a dent in their armor. I wonder now if we will ever do so.

The only disadvantage these young people have is they lack experience. But it appears they have gathered good people to help. As they gain more of both they become not only dangerous but also formidable. Strangely, Baalsa'n hasn't mentioned them to anyone. Surely, he knows? Strange.

"I say we support Monsh'a, help him build his forces and march as soon as possible before they can build an army," Rab'k pressed his point. "We can defeat them now. I've heard that the girl and her bulky friend have left Aerolan for some reason. Maybe they're afraid."

"What? Where did they go?" Mano'n turned, walked back to Rab'k and pointedly asked his questions.

"We don't know. We only know there have been fewer attempts to stop the harvesting of recruits for Monsh'a and I, trying to track this Pet'r, have not had any reports of him in several days," Rab'k answered, turn and, returning to his seat, slumped down.

"They've discovered the *ransect'r*," Mano'n blurted out, smacked his fist onto the tabletop and walked away a short distance, looking up into the darkness of the ceiling above them.

"The what?" Rab'k asked, looked around at Voravia and shrugged his shoulders.

"When we were here before, we installed a system which we could use to move about this world quickly. But, since we established our troops and went to war so rapidly, we abandoned the idea of using them, but never had the opportunity to remove the system. Borny'a would have known about it, but that presents another question.

Where were they hidden? Probably the Al-Esfer'n. But I've not noticed any in my passing over this country, so possibly somewhere less accessible. And how did our young friends discover the means to use them?

This is a serious complication. In the past, the people of the different countries were more commonly communicating than they do now. Those rebels, at that time, used that ability to recruit and bring in allies from those lands and form a greater force than we anticipated. And remember, those rebels won with that help. If they are on a mission to do this again and are successful, we are certainly going to have a more difficult time," Mano'n explained

"But why were those other countries not destroyed before they could help?" Voravia asked the obvious.

"We felt Aerolan had the stronger willed people and, if we defeated them, we would have no difficulty with the others. Bringing those others here changes the entire assumption," Mano'n answered, looked about the room again and shook his head. "I'd say, at this moment, Baalsa'n's efforts are going to fail. We probably need to inform his as soon as we can.

Rab'k. Could you, or Monsh'a, send a message to Baalsa'n informing him?"

Rab'k nodded his head and then, as he turned away, he grinned at Voravia.

She marveled at Rab'k's insolence

He's not going to do it. Why not? What is Rab'k planning? Are we all

326

turning against Baalsa'n and following our own path? Mano'n isn't fooled by Rab'k willingness to forward the message, he knows he probably won't.

Mano'n looked down at some of the papers he brought with him. He was trying to conceal the amusement that probably showed in his eyes though he was still concerned about his greater problem.

Rab'k, such a fool. He has an egocentric view of this whole mess. What am I going to do to protect Anisah? If Baalsa'n does learn of these emissary missions, he will immediately react and go to war. If Anisah is gone from Aerolan. Anisah stands to lose Aerolan and this war. Who do I help now? Who?

Voravia watched the two men, both obviously trying to decide what each should do and trying to keep that a secret from each other and her as well.

But, both were open books. She had no doubts. Rab'k would be running to Monsh'a as soon as he left. Mano'n would probably try to find Anisah. He was as capable, or more so, in the use of these new devices as anyone. He probably would be looking for these *ransect'r* soon after he left.

She sat watching the other two. She had nothing to add and, realizing her own dangerous predicament, had nowhere to run. She had to gather her wits.

"Gentlemen, I believe you have wasted enough of my time. It seems apparent we have no agreement about what is best for either ourselves, or Baalsa'n. We will all probably go our own way – for better or worse," she stood as she spoke. "I think you should leave now."

She turned and walked out of the room. The two men watched her walk away and noticed one of the new guards she had acquired walking toward them through another door.

As she moved through her realm, she couldn't imagine what was to come.

How little they know, or understand. If they don't cooperate with

Baalsa'n, he will destroy them. But, if they do, they will destroy themselves. They should better plan their survival and what they can do with it at the end. Or, they too will be lost, if Baalsa'n becomes unhappy with their contribution.

She walked more slowly and climbed the steps to her chambers, pondering the future.

What are you going to do, Voravia? What are you going to do?

ANISAH AND PET'R

Anisah arrived with Garv'n, at the white zone, and there was an immediate hustle and bustle to get them to safety.

Just after the Aerolan forces took possession of the castle, there was some discussion about how to be cautious with the teleporting groups and how to accommodate that ability without hindering the general activity, especially during wartime.

There were two areas near the entrance, one a bit smaller than the other, and a third for larger groups designated as landing sites. Anisah magically installed warning alarms in each to announce the arrival of incoming traffic to those in the castle, or on the grounds intended for the third one.

A single person accompanied by one of the three would use the smaller one. It was designated the white zone.

The second area was originally the quarters of the older inhabitants of the castle during the early years of small wars between colonies and wasn't being used for that purpose any longer. It was designated the blue zone. Its purpose was to allow for small groups to arrive accompanied by one of the three.

Then the third one was available for movement of large to very large groups, to arrive in a separate zone outside the immediate castle area. This area was the red zone. Squads of soldiers, and other large groups, could be transported in and out of this without interfering with the general activity in, or around, the castle itself.

This created a precautionary area for the local inhabitants, those training in the encampments, and any other group arriving, or leaving. Its purpose was to allow for these large groups to arrive accompanied by one of the three.

Garv'n still couldn't speak, but he made adequate use of the small graphite board to give messages to his attendants. He also still could not remember who he was.

Garv'n was taken to the medical center and helped to relax after his quick journey. Anisah, who followed him to the medical unit and made certain he was comfortable, immediately began to look for Pet'r. She expected him in the recovery area, but she couldn't find him anywhere.

One of the attendants told her he took one of the rooms on the north side of the castle to rest. But they also mentioned he actually rested very little, but maintained a certain vigil watching over the building of ramparts, enhancing the moat, and building other defense battlements on that side of the castle. He also worked with those men busy building even further protection across the southern end of the peninsula.

He assisted with establishing residences for the refugees who were flooding onto the land south and east of the castle. They were arriving from as far away as Safe Inlet and down along the entire eastern coast. Huge tent cities spread from one side of the peninsula to the other. People of all ages came wandering in on a daily basis; the land was filling with the helpless, injured and dying.

Anisah burst into Pet'r's room without knocking. She was angry. It didn't occur to her, at that moment, he might not be expecting anyone and might not have been clothed.

But he was.

So much for a reasonable entry. That could have been embarrassing, but then do I care.

He was standing in front of one of the lookouts and turned quickly, dropping into a combative mode with a weapon drawn. Seeing her again, he rose, dropped his weapons on a table in the center of the room and embraced her.

He looked so pale and seemed to have difficulty moving quickly. She wanted to resist and reprimand him for overextending himself, but she couldn't push away from the embrace. There was comfort in being where she was at that moment; comfort she needed after her very long week.

She held him even tighter and listened to his heart beating. There was nothing else happening that concerned her at that moment.

Finally, he released her, reached to hold her shoulder and push her away from him for a moment.

"Yes, I know I should be resting. Yes, I know you want to scold me for not having done so. But, believe me, I am much stronger than I possibly appear. I feel stronger each day and should soon be able to go about business as usual. In fact, I need to go talk to Kalbra'n about the *ransect'r* and I need to do that soon," he started talking before she could open her mouth. So she waited for him to finish.

"Just how do you call this resting. As I understand, you are one of the busiest people in the castle, attending to almost all the activity around this area. Alone. Couldn't Borny'a, or Jond'r or Acron'n attend to some of these things?" she insisted. "And where are they?"

"They're away recruiting. We need more soldiers and, even if we have volunteers, so few of them are trained to fight. And, if we have none, we are at the mercy of Baalsa'n's new soldiers," he answered. "We can't afford to wait for me to be totally healed."

She backed away from him. Now she was really angry.

"Why do you need to go see Kalbra'n? Why can't I do that? Why can't I ask him these questions?" she huffed at him.

"Because you are our strength. We cannot afford to lose you, in more ways than one. I'm not certain Kalbra'n will, or can, accept you because of your heritage. Maybe he can, maybe he can't. But we all know he will accept me. So I'm the most likely person to make the contact," Pet'r answered. She knew he was right.

He didn't want her to think about other options she might use to instigate a meeting with Kalbra'n. He couldn't rationally believe she couldn't, but this was a time of haste. He was the most likely candidate.

"But, you know I could do this. You know I am able. So why do you insist on pursuing something you're not quite ready for?" she insisted. "Why must it be you?"

"Because I know where the cave is. I know Kalbra'n as a friend. I know what he thinks about your family. What I don't know is what he thinks of you personally. I'll not risk an error by either one of you."

"Who are you to make that decision?" she blurted out.

She could tell she stunned him with that. She suddenly realized they were much closer than either imagined. They were one now. They would be one forever, or as long as forever lasted.

"I do so because I want you safe," he said, simply. "I think I want much more. I want trust between us. I want to know you and we have to hold to each other to win this horrendous battle we are about to face. I do want you with me. Always."

Pet'r looked at her a moment then looked back at the papers and weapons on the table without saying anything. Then he abruptly turned toward the door and walked out into the busy hallway.

Servants were bustling along, trying to help some of the new arrivals – of which there were many. Soldiers pushed their way through the crowds, changing their posts for the day. In the center of the great hall, there were many people hobbling toward the hospital unit set up by Anisah.

When Pet'r burst out of the room, a great number of people stopped immediately and stared at him. His face was well known in the castle, but some of the newcomers marveled at his appearance. The white streak in his hair, now quite long, seemed to stun most of them. Each person stared after him as he passed, and each recovered quickly and continued his or her progress. Few spoke to him and seemed, most often, to want to avoid him.

Anisah was right behind him, which did cause a ripple in the bustle of the crowd.

"I forbid it," she shouted at him. "You are not well enough to make this trip. You cannot. Or I will . . . . "

"What will you do?" he stopped, turning so quickly she bumped into him and staggered back a bit. "Send me somewhere else? I've many things to do and am not going to stand here and argue with you now. When I return, we can discuss your problems!" The crowd parted as he turned and pushed his way through then it closed behind him and he was gone.

She couldn't believe he said the last. She was stunned and stopped. As people walked around her, she watched him disappear into the war room. Tears ran slowly down her face. She wiped them away with an indignant swipe.

"Well, I don't want you to go," she said, mumbling to herself. "I'm afraid for you."

But, of course, he never heard that. He had so much to worry about he couldn't take the time to talk to her and, deep inside, she knew that. So she decided to help in other ways.

She could do whatever she wanted.

I can find Jond'r and help him and the others recruit the right men for our army. If Pet'r can go out into the field, I can too. I'm as capable of selecting good people as any of them. I'll not be pushed aside. I am a strength for them and I'll prove it.

She spun about and marched across to the hospital area to inspect all the patients; helping some with small aches and pains as she went.

Then she walked to the gate entry, waved to the soldier on duty who feared interrupting her. Anisah's reputation preceded her – no one wished to upset her, or make her angry.

The guard could easily tell she was angry about something and he didn't want to be on the receiving end of any trouble with her. So he nodded as she burst out into the sunshine.

She stopped just at the end of the bridge. He wondered what she intended.

Then she was gone.

333

AND THEY CAME

Jond'r stopped and peered from behind the brush where he was hiding, waiting for movement in the area he could see. His brother, and the others of their squad, lay on the ground quietly. Jond'r was spying on an encampment just recently created they assumed was intended to create new monster soldiers – the Maah'e.

It occurred to the brothers, while talking about the mass movement of villagers across this area, there was a wealth of men and boys who probably would rather fight alongside them than be the victims of the witchery changing them into these strange creatures of Monsh'a. The Ravelan, to capture unknowing candidates from these groups for their creation process, would attack and kidnap those selected from the possibilities the travelers, in their attempts to flee the area now invaded by the Ravelan, offered.

So Acron'n, having had his own incident and near miss with the Ravelan army, suggested they attempt to rescue these separate small groups from the Ravelan for their own recruits. He knew, from his experience, that most of the captives were coming from the eastern part of the country.

They both knew that any forces on that side of Aerolan were minimal and couldn't protect the villages from the attacks, nor the kidnapping taking place.

So they decided they best could provide fighting men for their own cause by rescuing these men and boys. They were convinced these would volunteer if their rescues were successful.

Jond'r thought they should consult with Borny'a, or Pet'r, before they tried to test the idea. But Acron'n was certain this trick would be all that would be necessary to turn the tide for increas-

335

ing their own recruits.

Those kidnapped would surely want to fight back was his reasoning and, even if a few of the captives refused to join them, they would still gain by the effort and save lives in either case.

So, it was decided. The brothers, on this engagement, brought a small force with them on what was supposed to be a scouting effort. Their men were now scattered throughout the woods behind them, waiting for the command to work their way through the forest to spy on the encampment they were observing.

The Ravelan usually took guards that also included a few Maah'e, powerful soldiers in their new bodies. They were solidly entranced by the witchery that transformed them into these odd creatures. They would all have to die in this effort to release the prisoners, but killing them would be difficult despite their small numbers, especially the Maah'e. The brothers decided an archery attack would be the best against such strength and several of their men were outstanding archers.

While they were observing the activities in the camp, they heard a group of prisoners tramping through the forest nearby, entering the area being watched, trudging along, hands tied behind.

Jond'r quietly moved his group to the edge of the path just ahead of the forced march. Most had suffered wounds of some sort and none of their wounds were healing, so fairly often someone fell. The usual remedy for this problem was instant death.

A boy, young and struggling with his wounds, stumbled, caught himself, stumbled again and fell. The line stopped as one of the Maah'e clumped back, looked down at the boy and raised his weapon to crush the boy's head. Before he could swing his club, an arrow ripped through his neck.

The monster stopped, grabbed the protruding arrow and snapped it off. He turned slowly toward the direction from where the arrow came and another struck him in the face. For a moment, he stood, staring. Then slowly he lost his balance, toppled backwards and hit the ground without moving again.

Jond'r's men began to fire a volley of arrows at the other guards and soon all were down. The captives, not knowing what was happening, fell to the ground when the first guard was attacked and were still laying there when Jond'r spoke to them.

"Gentlemen, you can relax. We've rescued you. But we need to move you into that section of the woods before we are discovered," Acron'n told them, pointing toward where he wanted them to run, or walk. Some of his men moving through the prisoner group, cut their bindings as they went.

"So let's go, some of you help those having trouble. We need to disappear as fast as possible."

Everyone began to scramble to leave the area along the pathway. Jond'r troops were also helping the wounded. Soon they were hidden in the trees. The squad walked over the area making certain no sign of the group was evident, followed into the trees and stood on guard, watching the trail from behind cover of the trees.

Jond'r waited for the captives to sit on the ground as best they could and get settled.

"You people are free to go wherever you wish. But we have to ask one thing of you," Jond'r said, waiting for them to look up at him. Very few of the captives stood during this.

"This is not the first moment you've known we are at war in Aerolan. These aren't the first of these soldiers, and creatures, you have heard about, and now know about, scavenging our lands for victims like you. We don't know what is happening to our women. The enemy isn't going to stop, unless we stop them. We are going to find care for you and help you heal but we also ask you to come with us and join our efforts when you've recovered."

The group of now ex-prisoners looked around at each other. Most knew the rest of their fellow prisoners because usually one village was ransacked and, then another close by, before the march to change them to monsters began, though these people didn't know the last was to be their future.

They were still in shock, their eyes showed the pains of their ordeal, from having been captured in the first place to the march across the land while bound. Now this man was telling them they were free – but was asking them to fight for an army. Many had died along the path they just struggled along, many were dying where they sat.

One man, a leader of one of the villages, asked, "How can you ask this of us? How can we fight these things? They are too powerful. Won't we just lose our lives anyway? Why should we help you?"

"You're justified in asking these questions. I cannot promise our efforts will succeed but I do know we will become what you fear, if we do nothing. We are men who have either experienced what you have, or have barely escaped ourselves. We are not strangers to your fears. But, if you wish to see this land further victimized and lose your villages to these monsters, you cannot run away, nor hide. Not because we wish to capture you, but because you will be found and attacked again. The leaders of this terrible horde, trying to defeat and murder us, wish everyone in Aerolan only death. There is no compromise," Jond'r answered.

At that moment, there was an unusual snap in the air. Everyone turned in the direction of this new sound. Anisah stepped forward, seemingly from nowhere, and looked over Jond'r's group and at the men sitting about on the ground. She smiled at everyone but said nothing. She walked calmly to Jond'r and nodded her head.

"Thought I would see if I could help," she said to him. He and the rest of his men stood stunned. The captives sat with their mouths opened in disbelief. They had never seen a magical occurrence in their lives, but only heard tales about it. But they knew this woman appearing from nothing was magical. Some of the captives even shrank back trying to hide.

Then she turned to the captives, "Please be calm. I am from Caliste. I was born there. You have no reason to fear me."

Still the captives, even Jond'r and his team stared at her. The men from Ralff'r castle had seen her before but only in passing – except for Jond'r and Acron'n. But the impact of her sudden appearance shocked them all.

"Anisah, why are you here?" Jond'r finally asked, pulling her aside for a moment.

"I seem to be in the way at the castle, so I thought I could come and help with the recruitment. This is a good idea for many reasons but mostly because these innocent people should be saved," she answered. "May I talk to you a moment – alone."

Jond'r looked around at the captives and his men some still had their mouths open, staring at Anisah.

"Acron'n. Have the men stand down and see if you can help the captives with their wounds," he told his brother, who followed his instructions immediately.

Anisah and he walked away a short distance. He wondered what the secrecy impaled.

"You're in danger here. There are at least several more war parties following this one. I need to help you get these people to safety before they arrive.

But you have to convince these people and prepare them for a transfer to a place not far from here where I can work with their wounds and make them more comfortable. I suggest you and your men stay here for another attack. But we've only a hour to get this done," she explained. "I want to help and, right now, this is the best way for me to do that."

Jond'r listened, looked around at the captives and his men.

"Does Pet'r know you are doing this?" he turned back and asked her.

"No," she answered.

She quickly turned away, ignoring him and looked into the

forest. "You really should prepare these people for what I'm about to do. Now."

Jond'r looked at her and nodded, shook his head and walked back to talk to the captives. Anisah stood watching him and prepared herself for the effort she knew would be needed. She chose a small glade to transfer these men to and she knew she would have to return to this spot in only a short time. There was a certain sense of urgency needed and she was a little anxious herself.

Jond'r asked the captives to get closer to one another and he and his men carried the wounded inside a circle Jond'r had mentally measured for the task.

"Now, you men are going to be taken to a safe place. But when Anisah comes here to talk to you, she'll ask you to close your eyes. You will be wise to do so. There will be magic involved but all of you will be safer afterward," he explained. The captives were still casting glances at Anisah.

"My men and I will stay here. Anisah has informed me there is another group of captives, with those creatures guarding them, not too far away. We have to prepare for another attack. We want to help as many as we can, so please work with us and we will attempt to complete as many rescues as we're able."

The captives rose and walked, or scooted, and moved closer to each other. Acron'n has his men lift the severely wounded and placed them into the circle. Most of the captives were wide-eyed and alert but totally unaware of what was going to happen.

Jond'r turned to Anisah, "We have placed them the best we can, considering. Are you certain you want to try this? Is there any danger to you? Pet'r will kill me if any harm comes to you."

"Don't be afraid for me. I can handle this. You only have about 15 minutes before the next group arrives. We should be able to confront several of them today with no problem. Let me handle my part and you handle yours and everything will work out," she answered, with a bit of tension in her voice.

"Besides, Pet'r is busy with his own problems, probably will not know about this little adventure anyway, and maybe doesn't even care."

Jond'r looked at her a moment.

They've had a quarrel. She's going to prove her worth. As though she needs to. Ah well, can't stand in the way. If she wants to help, I'm not the one to try to stop her.

Anisah walked to the captives, "I want each of you to reach out and touch at least one person near you. You don't have to hold onto them, just touch them and wait."

There was some shuffling then quiet. They responded to her request without complaint. Jond'r looked at his brother and Acron'n shrugged his shoulders then turned, and with hand signals, dispersed his men back into the forest. In short order, they were prepared for what they needed to do.

Anisah walked to the nearest captive and place one of her hands on his shoulder. There was a tingling sensation all around. Jond'r felt it and knew what was about to happen.

The captives and Anisah disappeared.

Jond'r turned and giving more hand signals melted into the forest himself. It never ceased to amaze him – this disappearing thing – but he was pleased the only three people he knew who could perform it were his friends.

Anisah and her group reappeared in the glade she remembered from her childhood. Many of them opened there eyes and were shocked by what they saw. They couldn't believe this was happening to them.

Anisah waited a moment then proceeded to walk through the group, stopping over the worst of the wounded. She would pause for a moment, reach down and touch each one. It was obvious to the others she was using magic because the ones she touched would begin to heal immediately. She knew she had finally achieved the means to heal. All her girlhood dreams were coming true. All those long nights in Caliste; all those days of watching

341

Mistress Elspeth and wishing for this power had finally come true.

She worked swiftly and talked to each of the men as she passed.

"Now, gentlemen, we have one more trip to take. We'll arrive on the grounds of a castle in one of the southern peninsulas. If you will touch your nearest neighbor and close your eyes again, we've a final and safe destination," she announced. All the men, now able to move about, quickly gathered into a smaller place. Again, Anisah walked to the nearest one and placed her hand on his shoulder. "Is everyone ready?"

There was a small murmur among the group and they disappeared again. This time, as Anisah told them, they arrived in the field across from the moat bridge.

"You men, if you wish to volunteer to fight against the evil you have been exposed to, have this opportunity to join the only group creating an army to fight back. If you do not wish to do so, you are free to go. But we can certainly use your help. Go to the castle and tell them Anisah brought you," she announced. "I have to return to help others."

She vanished.

On that day alone, she and Jond'r rescued some 150 men and boys. Pet'r, though surprised and angry with Anisah, could only accept the gifts she brought to his door. He feared for her, but knew she wanted to be a part of what was happening. It certainly wasn't for him to command her to stop.

Besides she'd probably place me someplace I'd never be able to get out of, even if I tried.

He had to chuckle.

The word spread across the eastern portion south of the mountains and into the open plains about these magical incidences. Men and young boys began to leave their villages to join the fight. The women, in those villages where the men left, were quickly escorted to the west regions and some were taken to other safe places in the mountains to hide in caves.

The number of volunteers increased with this steady flow. They gathered and walked the roads toward the south of Varspree, arriving in groups. They were mostly untrained young men and there were almost no skilled soldiers. The only soldiers were actually men who had served under the several landowners, such as Garv'n, and generally had no war related experience at all.

But all were needed and, as they arrived, Pet'r tried to maintain an area across the northern part of the peninsula for campsites and field setups. Placing those men who were, at least, partially trained in crucial positions to protect the others from attacks.

Out on the prairie north of Varspree, Geth'n, embroiled in a battle with a small platoon of the Ravelan and their Maah'e, looked around and sensed the good that emanated from the passing of this magic through the air.

I should return to the castle. I can fight all these beings, but will it bring my sister back? It won't. I need to work with the others. I cannot win this war by myself.

He encouraged the men around him to be more ferocious and they soon finished the alien group. He lost a man, but there were many more of the enemy lying on the ground.

"Come on, men. Let's take ourselves to the castle and safety," he shouted. There was a brief shout of approval then the group formed a traveling configuration and began to trot down the road toward Varspree. Geth'n dropped in behind them to protect their exit, but he was comfortable with his decision. He would soon be able to see Siarra again.

343

We should be home by tomorrow late.

Some distance away, there were others who noted the disturbance this new magic made in the surrounding area.

Voravia only smiled and continued to work on her own preparations. Rab'k raised his head to look around but returned to his work, unaware. Mano'n knew who it was. He was pleased and afraid for his daughter. Somehow he needed to extract her from what was to come without her knowing he did so. A difficult proposition at best.

Baalsa'n was not so pleased. He was not informed there were others besides his offspring who could use magic. He wanted to know who was able to use the power besides himself and his. He sent runners from his own guard into the southern lands to determine the source, or sources. He wasn't happy, specifically because he suspected his children were deliberately keeping these others a secret.

He was not pleased at all.

GETH'N'S REVENGE

After he arrived at Ralff'r, Geth'n did get to be with Siarra again. He took the opportunity to sit and talk to his family, listening to their horror story about those last days in Peetle. And he enjoyed a few days with Siarra and her family and listened to their story. He seemed at peace for a few days afterward, and he wasn't talking about the coming war.

But then he became more and more angry, he wouldn't talk to Siarra about the things that troubled him. But she knew something was wrong and she knew what he was probably going to do. He was going to leave and pursue his devil, his anguish.

"I'll be back soon. I must go bury my sister. I can't leave her as Pet'r and Borny'a had to. I'll be fine. I plan to be careful," he told Siarra, that last evening.

She knew he was lying to her. She knew he went to look for the enemy and he wanted to wreak his vengeance on them.

Two days later, he left.

Geth'n walked into Peetle alone.

It had been a few weeks since Pet'r and Borny'a returned from the town after their confrontation with Baalsa'n's troops. They told a horrific story and, of course, Pet'r suffered the consequences of his rage. Borny'a had wrapped Geth'n's sister in bunting and buried her quickly before they departed the peninsula. Geth'n's family, and many others, escaped through these efforts and were now at the castle, but he wanted to give his sister a decent burial.

He missed her.

Geth'n originally intended to take some people with him but he decided, at the last moment, to not include anyone else.

345

Geth'n was no longer the smiling and cordial scholar, but a demanding and skillful tactician on matters of war. He was no longer a happy man.

His anger showed on his face. He used his increasing hatred to find better and more efficient ways to eliminate this loathsome enemy.

He often traveled across the southern regions of Aerolan trying to recruit and help towns and cities build some protection from the attacks from the north. These attacks were becoming more frequent and much more brutal than previously experienced.

But whenever Geth'n came across a group of the enemy, he showed no mercy. He slaughtered all who opposed him. Sometimes he withheld his magic and allowed his people, if he had a scouting party with him, to deal with those they encountered. As time passed, he more and more seemed to delight in the action himself.

One thing he did that actually unnerved many of his followers; often making them cringe in their disgust. His own people often turned away.

He burned all the bodies. He made his men gather all the bodies of their foe, piled them high in an open field and, with his power, ignited them. This enemy was unforgiving, but Geth'n gave no quarter either. He totally destroyed everything the Ravelan and their commanders left behind though he didn't exhibit the same wrath against the Maah'e, which surprised some.

His intention for going to Peetle dealt with that matter. He wanted none of the filth these monsters left behind to exist in Peetle; he wanted no reminders of what they did. He wanted the deaths of his people to be remembered, but not the destroyers.

So he walked the road to Peetle. Whenever he saw any trace of the enemy in the peninsula, he eradicated it. When he came to the outskirts and looked down from a small ridge, he dropped his head to his chest, stood silently and wept.

The town was still deserted.

Nothing was what it should be. His home, his world, was nothing but rubble. Some of the buildings stood defiantly though large portions of them were gone, spread about on the grounds where he played as a boy, were he lived with his parents and where he worked alongside Pet'r for their fathers.

He clenched his fist and shook with rage.

Just north of town, some of the tenting of the enemy still stood. He looked at that a moment and began to walk deliberately toward it. When he was within a few yards, he raised his right hand and stopped. Flame screamed from his fingers, enveloped the entire campsite and turned the tents, and everything that lay about, into dust.

From the sea behind a wind rose and flowed gently over the land, picked the dust from the ground and blew it high into the air.

Geth'n looked at the cloud of dust, pointed at it again and sent it northward to where he knew encampments were. He had transfixed the dust with his rage and he knew when it reached another, more lively encampment, it would destroy, in flame, that place and scorch the earth below. It would last as long as it found any Ravelan in that direction. There was no way to deviate the path it took – no magic was strong enough. Its final destination would be the sea beyond the desert in northern Aerolan. There it would be extinguished.

He turned back to look again over the devastation that was Peetle. He stood for a while, tears still running down his cheeks. With his head down, he walked toward the place Borny'a described as the crude burial place for his sister. He didn't look toward the ruins of his home but pushed toward his one goal.

Turning down a once familiar street, he stopped suddenly.

Ahead of him a small band of Ravelan, with bows across their shoulder and back, were riding on horseback, patrolling the town and peninsula. He decided these must be the same archers who attacked Pet'r and Borny'a, but he hated them whether that was true, or not.

They were turned away from him and weren't aware of his arrival. His body began to shake. He could hardly control his shivering body. His anger overflowed into a torrent of pain and anger within him. His eyes burned and glowed with an inner fire.

"You there, turn and face your deaths!" he shouted at the evil he saw. "Let it be known. You will die for the evil you bring us!"

The sound of his voice showed his hatred loudly. He knew it would ride upon the winds. He wanted all to know he was intent upon the destruction of this intrusion into his world.

He braced his body, standing taller and walked toward the squad which turned their heads to see who dared be in their town. There was a brief pause then the officer gave a command. The squad turned in unison, executing a precise military formation, drew their bows, nocked arrows and waited for the next command.

But there was no call from their officer. They looked around and saw that his body sat atop his horse, blackened and falling into cinders on the ground. As they watch the body crumbled into ashes, the wind again took the dust away.

They turned back to see where Geth'n was and found he was just beneath their stirrups. They tried to turn and fire their bows, but Geth'n raised his arms and the bows disintegrated, falling to nothing. Suddenly realizing they were facing a wizard of overpowering strength, they kicked their horses to gallop away, to escape.

But the horses ran from the death encompassing the bodies of the soldiers. Death rode the animals as they ran free of the dust lingering in the air. There were no signs these beings were ever present on Peetle's streets. He didn't concern himself with escape; he had no need.

Geth'n stood for a while longer, looking ahead toward his original goal with sadness. His sister; and his memories of who she was, would now be honored as she should be. He walked on, without noticing anything around him, and came quickly to the hastened burial spot. Borny'a was so busy trying to get Pet'r to safety he only had a moment, or two, to hide the girl from the soldiers. Geth'n carefully extracted her sheathed body from the shallow grave

But, he knew he should find a better place for her. He remembered one of her favorite places was Riles' hill near the sea just south of the town. He carefully gathered her body, took his precious burden, walked to the hill to that small place that rose higher than the lands surrounding it. The location gave a clear view of the sea so one could almost see the peninsula across the Calm'n Gulf. The house lay about in shambles over the grounds.

He held her in his arms and walked to a small cellar, used for hiding from storms when the sea roared and for storing food during winter, slammed the door open and gently laid the small body within the foodstuff, covering her in spices and other goods to hide her decay and placed the covering door back over the grave.

Geth'n hid the cover with a spell to make certain it could never be disturbed. He placed no stones to show its site. But they were the children of sailors and he only had to get his bearings to know where she was. One day, the family could return and bless this ground with their love – for her and for each other.

He stood for a moment more. He looked out over the sea, and watched its calming rhythm for an hour or more and made no attempt to do anything else. He missed her now and always would.

"We were young here, little sister. We lived here in peace, with our past as pleasant as we could make it and hoped for a future that would make our lives easier. But now this evil has overtaken us by surprise and innocents, such as you, have suffered the consequences of being here.

In this here and now I feel grief and pain. I wish another life for you and will try to stop this desecration; this overwhelming travesty. I make that promise to you and my memories," he told her and wept again.

Finally, he turned away and began to walk back toward Larilla. When he reached the rise in the road where he could still see his home, he looked back, standing for a moment longer.

Then he turned away and walked on.

His pace was calm and more peaceful than when he arrived. He expected no problems from anyone, but then he saw no reason to avoid them. Everything around him was a reminder of those who destroyed Peetle. He obliterated many of these. Not in haste, but in the belief his people would return and rebuild. The land seemed barren and he bowed his head for a moment, remembering.

As he neared his old college town, he noticed smoke rising from near the coastline of the Barn'n Gulf and couldn't resist smiling.

He entered the city and walked its dead streets. There were a few people in Larilla, trying to hold to their world. But Geth'n went to the college because he thought it might be a place of refuge for many of them. When he found where they were hiding, Geth'n informed them of refuge, helped them organize themselves for the journey and sent the group on to Roahan.

So it has begun for me. Now I have engaged the enemy personally. Today I was able to revenge a lost, loved one. I'm not certain I gained more than knowing she is buried as she should be. But maybe I know a bit more about myself and the hatred I've hidden inside. I'll need to use what I have discovered about myself in a constructive way. I must use my hatred to stop these atrocities and defeat the one who wants to destroy us all.

He returned to the road and headed in the direction of Pull'r. After he walked a while, he noticed a cloud of dust rising above the hills ahead.

Seems the enemy is going to be persistent. Maybe I'll work on my control tomorrow . . .

350

MONSH'A AND RAB'K

Rab'k pushed his way through the creatures that were freely roaming Monsh'a's campsite. He had no fear of any of these because they recognized him as *friendly*. But today he was going to be anything but that. He was tired of Monsh'a's edicts about how this war should proceed and he was going to confront this stranger, even if Baalsa'n considered Monsh'a a better leader than any of his children.

Rab'k had waited too long and struggled too hard to have this intruder push him aside whenever decisions were being made. Of late Rab'k had not been invited to the meetings Monsh'a had with Mano'n and Voravia. That was more of an insult than Rab'k could accept. It was time to do something about being ignored.

Just as he got to the tent, Monsh'a stepped out into the open. Rab'k was taken back, impressed by the man's size, but only for a moment.

"I need to talk to you," he growled.

Monsh'a turned and looked down on the shorter man, "About what?"

Rab'k knew Monsh'a thought this was a disruption he really didn't need, but Rab'k persisted.

"Why are you excluded me from your plans? I brought thousands of men to this battle and not only are you not using them, you are ignoring us. I demand an explanation," Rab'k felt justified in his irritation.

"Your contributions are noted," Monsh'a grunted and started to walk away.

"Wait, don't be insulting. You haven't answered my question," Rab'k shouted, ran forward and placed himself in Monsh'a's path.

"How can I insult you, boy. You haven't done anything. You've made no legitimate suggestions other than we have to kill them all. You've added nothing to what we are trying to do here. And you've not been making any effort to infuse your troops into the forces we have available,"

Monsh'a was annoyed and getting angry with Rab'k. He obviously considered him a nuisance and was attempting to control his own temper by allowing the man to even live. Were it not for Baalsa'n, Rab'k would have been disposed of much earlier.

Maybe the young man was a prince in the desert, but he was useless here. He certainly held a great deal of information about the people in this region, but none of it was important when the need to gather the people became an issue.

Something had changed. The capture of native men for recruits seemed to be reliable at the beginning, but was now either ineffective or stopped all together. His people were now having difficulty finding any inhabitants of the villages they were raiding. Apparently, if there were some men found, the rebels were recapturing them and taking them beyond his reach. He was losing his soldiers, and some Maah'e, in this effort. He couldn't discover why, nor how, this was happening. Particularly the complete disappearance of these captives within moments bothered him. So his efforts to find new recruits were dwindling to nothing.

The recent scouting reports also mentioned the sudden insurgent growth of the opposing forces and the increase in losses inflicted along the front. He was losing soldiers faster than he wanted or could afford. The Maah'e were proving ineffective as guards for the kidnapping of villagers and were being killed. They were too slow for the tactics being used in this guerrilla warfare.

How can the recapture of the prisoners be happening? It seems magic is at work, but the only people I know, besides Baalsa'n, able to perform any magic are in this camp. So how are these captives being rescued?

"You're an idiot!" Rab'k shouted from behind him as Monsh'a turned away. "You're being lead around by your nose!"

Monsh'a whipped around and stomped back toward Rab'k who, strangely, didn't back down, nor run away. Monsh'a stopped and reached to grab Rab'k by the neck. But Rab'k easily stepped back and avoided him.

Monsh'a reach again and missed. He stopped to ponder why he couldn't reach the man. He never tried to attack Rab'k before because he felt him insignificant, but this was annoying.

"Stand still, little man," Monsh'a shouted at Rab'k.

"Why, so you can strangle me? Is that your problem? Well, here. Try it," Rab'k said, stepping near enough Monsh'a could have grabbed him easily.

Monsh'a crushed the smaller man in his hands, or thought he had. But when he stepped back to let the man fall, Rab'k stood smiling at him.

"I'm probably not the only one who can avoid your ugly face," Rab'k snarled up at the creature. "I find this amusing, don't you? My brother and sister are leading you around. Those you have to trust are tricking you. And you don't want me to be involved?

I tell you I want these people destroyed. I've always wanted to rid the desert people the ignominious distinction of begin the only people who were defeated by these vermin.

You were there. You know what I say is true. You too were defeated and driven back to your miserable homeland. So you and I have a mutual hatred that can't be denied. We can be enemies or you can let me help you understand these people.

You push me aside. Now you've discovered you can do me no harm. I'm the bearer of the Black Stone now and you could never harm me. It might be you couldn't have done so anyway. I'm closer to being immortal than anyone except Baalsa'n."

There is a secret you are unaware of and won't be told about until it's too late. But I'm quite willing to share it, if some consideration is given me."

Monsh'a had staggered back when he realized he couldn't harm this man. No one had resisted his power before, but this display was beyond belief.

There is magic here. This man should not be able to simply ignore what I did to him. Yet he stands there, grinning at me. If he were to attempt to harm me, would he be successful?

Rab'k stepped forward. Monsh'a stepped back. He wasn't willing to test his curiosity today.

"What do you have to say to me?" Monsh'a asked, without malice.

Rab'k visibly relaxed, "Let's you and I talk peaceably. We together have a large force of warriors and should be able to end this thing quickly."

Monsh'a motioned for Rab'k to enter his tent so they would have certain privacy. Rab'k walked immediately to Monsh'a's private cabinet, opened it and withdrew a bottle of wine. He poured himself and the creature some of wine into some small glasses on Monsh'a's desk, raised his glass and saluted the other.

"We should plan how best to do that. You and I can't trust my siblings. One is undermining your efforts in secret and the other is preventing your success. Both have their own agendas and are going about those plans with impunity. I would suggest you and I could do without either. But we must be cautious about how we handle them, for they truly are powerful magically."

"What about Baalsa'n?" Monsh'a asked, holding the wine and pondering the strangeness of this meeting.

"Well, you know him better than I. But, I'm assuming he's involved in something else besides concerning himself with the destruction of this planet. He probably is already planning his next conquest. Are you going to accompany him on that mission? Has he promised you anything besides this world he wants you to destroy? Haven't you wondered what will be left? You and your people are in the same situation as mine. Neither will know any peace and may be destroyed with these southerners we're suppose to fight.

When Baalsa'n says he wants to destroy a world, he means en-

354

tirely. Remove it from the heavens, from this space. He wants complete destruction because he is an immortal and he fought against creating these new worlds in the beginning. Now he only wants to destroy them."

"How do you know these things?" Monsh'a turned away to look through the ventilation opening above him at the clear sky, still holding his glass without drinking. He was listening intently to this offspring of Baalsa'n. He might learn a few things he was unaware of.

"Because my father . . . my true father, Rena'x The dominant leader of the desert, taught me about all things. You, or some other in your position with your people, may have fought alongside him in the first effort here. He is loyal to Baalsa'n but he told me these things to allow me the opportunity to determine my own path," Rab'k answered and took a swig of the liquor in his glass.

"I want, more than my siblings do, to destroy these infidels. Whereas they only want their own imagined rewards," Rab'k added, "so possibly you are more interested in talking to me now. If not, I shall have to destroy you and use your men in the way I see fit."

"You'll do what?" Monsh'a was staggered at the audacity of the little man – son of Baalsa'n or not. "You believe you have the strength to harm me."

"Yes," Rab'k answered without hesitation.

"You're asking me to be your partner in this new tack of war you propose, or you'll destroy me?" Monsh'a asked, slowly setting his glass down. "How will you do that?" He brought himself to his full height, looking down on Rab'k with eyes now squinting with hatred.

Rab'k sat his glass on the table, reached before Monsh'a could react, grabbed the sword belt around the creature's waist, and without effort, raised him a few inches from the ground and threw him across the tent. Monsh'a bounced once but was

355

quickly on his feet, ready to charge across and attack this idiot.

"You really shouldn't," Rab'k held his hand, asking the other to pause. "I'm not here to be your enemy, but we should decide how to save our people and take back these territories lost centuries ago. But you must decide I'm the person to help you do that and trust me."

The guards came running in when they heard the noise of Monsh'a bouncing across the ground. But, as they burst in with spears ready and swords drawn, Monsh'a stopped them.

"Halt. Return to your post. This man was only demonstrating a battle point that will benefit us. Good job, soldiers." He waved them back toward their positions outside his tent.

"You have proven your point and, at least for now, I believe what you say. You are right. I have often wondered how Baalsa'n was going to end this. I will take your word about his intentions until it is proven true otherwise. But you should know, I may be able to resist your threats to destroy me," Monsh'a said as he turned back to Rab'k, brushing the dust from his uniform.

"There is no reason for your concern. You and I need each other for what lays ahead. We have a common goal to save our people from being included in the final destruction. So we need to plan how and not fight each other," Rab'k answered, emptying his glass and set it back on the table. "Both of us lose if we fight each other. One other thing, our enemy has magic on its side, very powerful magic. We must be able to offset that or future battles will not be easy to win. "

Monsh'a nodded, walked back to the table and asked, "So what are your ideas?"

They talked for hours and came to some decisions about their preparations for the coming war.

"When should we act on these?" Monsh'a finally stood, stretched and reached for his glass, turned and filled it as he talked. "I can see your reasoning and can also see how we can not only win this war, but we should be able to avoid Baalsa'n's destruction. But where and when are now the larger questions."

"We must wait for these young people I'm talking about. We have to wait for them to feel confident in their actions. Right now, with the few victories they are achieving, they are beginning to gain that. If we wait for that to peak, we should be able to surprise and sweep across the southern part of Aerolan with no difficulty. The surprise is the important part. We must use delaying tactics, small attacks and retreats, complete withdrawals from certain areas and then we will have them believing they can win," Rab'k stood, looked over the maps they had drawn during their discussion and added, "We are almost in a position to act on that surprise.

By convincing Voravia to move her new troops into awkward positions, we should be able to nullify what she is planning. Mano'n has no interest, after all these years of serving Baalsa'n, in any outcome. He just wants it to be over and his personal anguish should make him totally ineffective."

"I can't believe Voravia used me to gain her own army. Where are they?" Monsh'a asked.

"They're below you, literally. For years she has developed an underground tunnel system that reaches from the mountains to the central plain of the southern region. She has long used misshapen characters she learned to create from Baalsa'n, but now she has an enhanced witchcraft to create beings similar to those in your army," Rab'k said, grinning. "I believe you have to admit she was quite crafty about that."

"Hunh. I admit nothing. She coerced, or whatever, my sorcerer into telling her the secret. I would not have done so," Monsh'a spoke bluntly. Rab'k nodded his head and ignored the creature's excuses.

Rab'k, having now retrieved his self-esteem, at least in his estimation, wanted to begin this plan immediately. He waited far too long and, in his respect for Rena'x, he knew he needed to maintain his patience while enduring the wait. Some things he didn't understand along the way. Those led him to commit a great number of mistakes in the past. He also didn't quite trust Mon-sh'a, a creature who was devoted to Baalsa'n in the past.

"Let's call it a night. We both have much to do to prepare. Most of all, we must be cautious. Baalsa'n must not discover our intent," Rab'k added and began to roll their plans, laying on the table, into a bundle. "I'll take these and hide them in a safe place. We cannot risk an accidental exposure."

He briefly recalled the visit of Serlon, Garvan's man, those long days ago. That meeting had triggered his release, a release from having to act out a life he never wanted.

The air was crisp outside when he ducked his head and walked toward his own camp.

Outside the tent sat an old Aerolan soldier, waiting for his turn to be transformed into one of the creatures. He came into the camp with a small captured group and now waited and listened.

After a while, he rose, dropped the bindings wrapped around his arms and legs and walked limping into the night. But the shadows revealed him rising to his full height as he wandered through the trees.

He disappeared into the darkness.

PET'R AND KALBRA'N

Truth. Without truth there can be no freedom. One cannot exist without the other.

Perhaps, the legitimacy of any action is enhanced by the effect these two ideal values have within the action itself. If there are any who doubt this, and who act on the premise these can be dismissed without consequences, then the essence of these values will likely insist on the outcome revealing the validation of the association between the two.

Too ignore these can be deadly.

Our three young heroes are bound by truth. They feel and are compelled to follow the virtues of truth, for they seek freedom.

And, the one who first felt this need was Pet'r. He now has a need to learn more for his own validation. He needs to what the 'gods' – the Al-Es-fer'n – are planning for the future and what they'll be able to do to assist him and his two friends.

Is there to be an ending that qualifies his, and their, effort with any success? Or is there to be only doom?

Simple questions ofttimes require complex answers . . .

Pet'r regretted walking away from Anisah after their argument, but he knew he wouldn't be able to resist her if he stayed.

He insulted her and later, when he learned she left the castle for reasons unexplained, doubted some of his own decisions about what he should do. Maybe he should have given her more attention and listened

When he entered the war room, three of his new lieutenants were waiting. They were sitting around the table, talking among themselves, and jumped up to stand at attention. He waved his hand indicating he had no need for formality. Pet'r was still not accustomed to being someone in command. He attempted to get

359

his work done to support their effort to create a new army. But he was self-conscious about being an overlord, or one of them, as part of his duty.

He walked to the massive table in the center of the room and plopped into place in one of the many chairs. The table was an old dining table when the castle was filled with people, but now they used it for spreading all the maps, reports and other papers he now realized were necessary for a reasonable conversation about what was happening along all the fronts.

The officers were still standing and he finally noticed them.

"Please. Sit down," he asked them to relax. "At ease. Sorry, I forget the formalities." They eased themselves into their chairs.

"Gentlemen, I must be away for a couple of days and it appears Anisah, and the others, are not going to be here during those days so you three are on your own," Pet'r mumbled without looking up.

The others looked at each other and smiled. They were pleased to even be in the room with Pet'r. His fame and prowess were well known and their respect for him was almost adoration. But they tried to keep that feeling from him.

"Yes, sir. I mean. Sorry, sir. Yes, Pet'r. We needed to speak to you about a few things but knew we needed to wait for your meeting with Miss Anisah," one of them offered. But again Pet'r waved his concerns away.

"I appreciate your patience. She had something important to tell me and, considering her importance to us all, I took the time to discuss the issues with her. We have resolved those and I needed to get back to work. So here I am. What is our status?" Pet'r explained without looking up. Those, at the table, looked at each other and grinned again, but none of them let Pet'r see that.

Marja'n, a new face of their forces, rose and delivered his report. He was older than many of the other followers and brought to the battle group an abundance of experience gained from having fought in foreign territories.

Aerolan's wealthy overlords, such as Garv'n, had initiated the use of small escorts traveling with their ships for any event of trouble aboard the ships, and in the ports where they transferred goods to the local businesses. They served as guards for any interference by the locals wherever they might be. Marja'n had been an officer for one those owners. In fact, he had been under the service of Garv'n, and indirectly Rab'k, when he came to their camp. Jond'r was familiar with him from the time when they shared those duties.

Only Borny'a was hesitant in accepting the man, mostly because of the last association. But the man was willing to admit he worked for Rab'k, so their trust was earned. He was enthusiastic about winning this war and was an outstanding training instructor for the close combat routines the fledgling soldiers needed. So they were all glad Marja'n arrived when he did.

"Our main encampment south of here is beginning to fill. We have more space toward the west coast of the peninsula but haven't made plans to include any new areas for an extension of the present camp," Marja'n mentioned, looking around at the others. "We hadn't really planned on there being this many refugees, but the entire eastern seaboard seems to be migrating down the coast and working their way toward us."

"Are there any good areas to the west," Pet'r asked, looking up finally. The others could see he was not well. He hadn't fully recovered from his wounds and he seemed to tire easily. The discussion with Anisah seemed to have diminished him somewhat.

"Actually there are several, but I think we need to stay back from the coastline to avoid potential sea landings. I haven't heard that any of the attacks in the north have included that, but we probably shouldn't try to second guess what Baalsa'n's officers are going to do," Marja'n answered. "I'll scout the area while you're gone and advise you on possible locations. I think we should have some hills surrounding the camp and place guards all along the perimeter."

361

Pet'r listened to the plan and nodded his head, "You seem to have a good plan with what you have explained. I will ask you to reserve some of that land just west and northwest of the castle to accommodate more troops. We are having an increase in volunteers, for some reason, and I need to have them bivouacked until they can be trained.

"Mart'o, have you begun making plans for this new influx of men," he asked one of the other field officers at the table. All had been elevated to the rank of lieutenant since arriving and all had contributed. Certainly with the main members of their effort Geth'n, Borny'a, Jond'r and Acron'n all in the field trying to hold back the enemy, these young men proved to be a boon for maintaining a continuous process for training and care of the new troops.

"You definitely need to work many of them into the west of here as quickly as possible. Leave a gap between this camp and the one already working just north of it. I really don't want the soldiers in the latter to be mingling with the newer groups until we combine all of the them into our standing forces."

"Well sir, I can establish the new camp while you are gone, but, and I hate to say this, these new men and boys seem to be less enthusiastic than the last. I suspect they are only here because they fear being captured at home. They'll need extra attention," Mart'o added.

"I suspected as much. That's one of the reasons I think they should be held separated from the others. I expect a large number of desertions but then they are volunteers and haven't had reason to see how badly they would have been treated had they been captured. We probably need to determine a way to *introduce* them to one of Baalsa'n's Maah'e without actually exposing them completely. We can discuss that when I return," Pet'r added. "Is that all, gentlemen? I do need to prepare for my departure. If there are no other issues, I'll talk to you when I return."

He rose, turned and walked out of the room. The other men

leaped to their feet when he made his last statement because they knew he wouldn't think to dismiss them.

Marja'n gazed out the door a moment, "I suspect he needs to use his magical powers to accomplish something, but he's still seems very weak from his wounds. Maybe he'll get help for those. I wonder where he's going?"

The other two had no idea. Mart'o shrugged his shoulders. "Anyway, we probably need to get back to work."

"Yes, gentlemen. I need to get to the northern camp near Crosspoint as quickly as possible," Lanv'r said as he left the room. "I'll report back later today, if I'm back soon enough."

Pet'r returned to his room and looked around for Anisah though he didn't expect her to still be there.

"Ah, a stubborn woman. But I hate arguing with her," he said to no one in particular. Looking out the window, he was still troubled by the black clouds roiling across the skies of Aerolan. They made him uncomfortable. That hadn't changed much since their encounter with Baalsa'n's original attempt to take control of Narthrae. "Perhaps we can make those disappear soon. Perhaps."

He looked away, picked up his satchel, throwing it over his shoulder. He winced a bit, even that simple movement was enough to bother him. He shook his head and walked to the gate.

The three – he, Anisah and Geth'n – had decided earlier to step outside the castle whenever they needed to teleport, so they wouldn't create a disturbance inside. He paused to talk to the guard a moment, walked across the bridge, stood for a moment then disappeared.

He broke the deep silence of the cavern with a great yelp because of the pain of hitting the floor harder than he expected. He lay there remembering Anisah's statement about a potential injury in transporting and he grinned. But the pain was real and he tried to determine which part of him hurt the worst. He decided some of the wounds on his left side, where a number of the arrows entered his body, were possibly opened again.

She is really going to be difficult with me for this. Got to get up and attend to this problem, before I do anything else.

He rolled to his right, pulling his legs under him so he squatted on his knees with his right hand holding him off the floor. He groaned with the effort, clenching his teeth. He was not going to give in to these wounds.

Well that wasn't graceful, but maybe I can get up and sit instead of just crouching here.

He tried to stand and couldn't. He looked around to determine where, in the cave, he was. The only bench in the great room was on the other side of a stream from him.

Great, even if I can crawl to get there, I'm going to get wet. This just gets better all the time. Of course, I could just sit here on the floor, I suppose.

He tried to turn so he could sit but the pain shooting through his left side almost caused him to fall back on his side. He was barely able to hold himself on his knees and right arm.

Seems I'm in a dilemma here. I'll not be telling Anisah about this. So, crawling is my choice. Great.

He needed to turn a bit to move to the bench. He decided he should scoot around on his knees to get his butt pointed in the opposite direction from the bench. With expectation of pain, he made the effort, groaning a great deal, and was able to work that magic.

Magic. Ha! I'm trapped in a body that wants to be three years old again. This really hurts.

He looked up at the bench, bowed his head and began to crawl. His motion was much like an inchworm. He moved each knee forward until he was almost sitting on his legs then raised and moved his upper body so he could sit up briefly and move his right arm forward.

He determined he should not use his left arm to help. On his first try, the pain of arching his back, lifting his shoulders, raising his right arm slightly and pushing it quickly ahead was almost un-

364

bearable. But he persisted until he came to the stream.

Okay, mighty warrior, this is not going to be fun. How am I going to get through the water? I know it isn't deep, but I'm not certain how rough, or how slick, the bottom is.

He shifted backwards onto his legs and reached as far as he could and put his hand as deeply as he could into the stream. He couldn't feel the bottom and knew he needed to move forward one more time.

This is ridiculous! Surely I can stand long enough to get to that blasted bench. Trying doesn't hurt, I hope.

He used his right arm to brace and tried to move his feet under him. He managed to push them beneath himself, but the pain ripped through him and he almost tumbled over backwards. He held on to his stance for a moment then lowered his knees to the floor again.

Oh! That was painful. Guess crawling is the only option. It's a good thing none of the others, particularly Geth'n, can see him now. This story would get around the camp too quickly.

He sat for a moment, looking at the edge of the stream. He moved his knees forward to prepare to move into it.

"Seems you have had some difficulties, my young friend," a voice from nowhere spoke calmly.

Pet'r looked around the cave then toward the bench. Kalbra'n sat there smiling at him.

"Maybe I can help," the immortal said.

He raised his hand and Pet'r was able to stand. He was still weak but was able to stand, wobbling a bit.

"You should come and sit with me, my son. Tell me why you're here," Kalbra'n said. Without hearing anything else, Pet'r knew there was a touch of amusement in the invitation.

Pet'r looked down at his legs that had failed him only just a moment ago.

"Can I walk?" he asked. He really didn't want to fall again.

"I think you can make it here," Kalbra'n answered. "Maybe

when you have managed that we can determine how to rid you of the pain."

Pet'r smiled, looked at his feet grimly anticipating a first step. He was not wrong in guessing there would be pain. There was a great deal, but he persisted. He was on his feet and was able to continue. He waded across the stream slowly and, with effort, walked the few steps remaining to the bench, groaning and grunting the entire trip. He sat down in an uncontrolled fall, striking the bench with a sudden impact and cried out in pain again.

He looked around at Kalbra'n, sitting calmly, watching him.

"Can you help me with this?" Pet'r asked, imploring the Kalbra'n to help.

"Possibly, you have learned a reasonable lesson. What do you think?" Kalbra'n asked. He rose from his seat and walked to Pet'r. He laid his hand on the boy's shoulder and the pain was gone.

"What do you mean?" Pet'r sat up straight, flexed his arms and shoulders, twisted his torso from side to side. "What lesson?" he asked.

"I would imagine you've learned, with this, you are not invincible. You may feel that way but it isn't true. Not even we can claim that. Centuries ago, Areb'l discovered we couldn't resist death easily and we could experience wounds and pain. So immortality does not provide a protection from pain and death, it just lets us live longer," the older man explained. "You really shouldn't expose yourself unnecessarily. Be cautious and your greater strength will serve you well, but being foolish does not fit into that framework," Kalbra'n explained.

"I suppose I did feel I couldn't be harmed. Obviously, I was wrong. So, did I learn a lesson. Probably. At least, my body has attempted to tell me how foolish I was," Pet'r offered, but smiled at the irony. "But my problems are not the reason I came. We need some advice and some information about the gateways, the *ransect'r*. Borny'a has advised us of their importance.

'Borny'a's a good man, powerful warrior and friend of Areb'l'.

It's good he has agreed to join your group. We have been observing you and the others, and the activities to prepare for war, with great interest. We feel we have chosen well," Kalbra'n explained. "We were only troubled about Anisah, but she has proven to be pure of heart and wishes to avoid the depths of darkness only Baalsa'n and Mano'n would offer her. Hopefully, she'll never move toward that."

"I think she would never do so," Pet'r remarked, feeling confident he was correct. "She is a marvelous person and is dedicated to saving Aerolan and Narthrae as well."

"Be cautious with the word *never*, my young warrior. It is a slippery believe to rely on; you must watch it closely. I implore you to be cautious about many of the people you will be meeting while this war is being fought. There are people, young and old, who might have never been evil, but will be tempted by the power of success into transgressing. Your love for Anisah should not blind you to the possibilities," Kalbra'n advised.

Pet'r snapped his attention to the immortal, "How did you know that? I've told no one about my feelings," Pet'r was surprised by the statement. "Can I bring her here so you can understand who she is?"

"No, I don't think so and it's unnecessary. Remember, my young friend, we watch all of you. We have observed your affections for her. You aren't exactly trying to conceal them. But we have no desire to interfere in that. Our warning is cautionary. She has, by her birth, the capacity to do harm, if she chooses. Just be cautious," Kalbra'n explained. "But now, let's talk about why you are here."

It seemed obvious to Pet'r that discussions about individuals was somewhat uncomfortable to the other man.

"First, you should be able to contact me with a method simpler than having to come to this cave. I suggest we set some pattern no other will be aware of. No hidden words, but an action that will signify to me you have a need to see me," Kalbra'n pondered.

"Possibly something to do with the Ahar'n you always wear, would be the best. A certain touch or disposition of the crystal. It can't be removed from its cage, but it can be touched at the intersection of the cage structure. Let's look at it from the bottom."

Pet'r raised the amulet and held it upside down. There was only one point where he might be able to press his smallest finger through the cage and touch the surface.

"Let me concentrate now while you touch the amulet and I will establish a connection between us through the stone," Kalbra'n became pensive, closing his eyes as he concentrated. "Can you feel my thoughts?"

Pet'r watching Kalbra'n's efforts failed, at first, to realize there was a sensation through his finger.

"Yes, I can. That seems to work and I assume the tingling sensation is a response from you that you received the signal. What will happen then?" Pet'r asked.

"You should remove yourself as quickly as possible from those around you, if you haven't already. Then I will teleport you to wherever I am," Kalbra'n answered. "That is the only way I will be able to do this – only if you are prepared for the transfer. You must remember that anything else could destroy you."

Pet'r only nodded his head and replaced the Ahar'n beneath his waistcoat.

Then Kalbra'n stood and began to pace the ancient floor. The stream gurgled its restless song, stone walls glistened here and there as though watching, and the quiet was only interrupted by his footsteps.

"As for the *ransect'r*, these are often located in very conspicuous places and have a familiar appearance about them. I believe that is part of their magic. I'll tell you their locations, but you must use them with caution. Each time one is used, it takes something from the user's life, a memory not to be regained. Maybe it is an insignificant memory, maybe it isn't. Actually, your friend

Geth'n has traveled through one of these – there is one near Peetle – but I doubt he can recall why, or when, and he experienced what he thought was a dream. It wasn't that at all. He lost a memory and is now unaware of what it was."

"Geth'n? Geth'n traveled through a *ransect'r*? When?" Pet'r was surprised. He thought he knew everything about his childhood friend.

"He traveled to a place he didn't want to remember. Fortunately, he survived," Kalbra'n said. "But I seriously doubt he remembers it. If he does, then Geth'n is more powerful than we had assumed. He is almost as strong, in his abilities, as Anisah."

"Geth'n? I've always thought him one of the brightest guys I've ever known. But magical? It's almost as though you are telling me he is a wizard, a sorcerer," Pet'r marveled at this revelation. Geth'n was his friend and he never would have guessed what he was being told.

"He is," Kalbra'n added. "But let's continue our deliberation on the whereabouts of many of the other *ransect'r*. There are only about 25-30 we know about, but each continent and each country around the globe has at least one. I'm sure Borny'a told you Baalsa'n's forces actually built them but Areb'l, Borny'a and others used them to find allies to defeat Baalsa'n's first effort to conquer this world – so they are useful if used properly."

"Remember this, a memory will be lost each time anyone travels through a *ransect'r*. You must remember that," Kalbra'n added as Pet'r prepared to return to the castle.

Pet'r nodded, turned away and stood in preparation for departing.

"Thank you for this information. Hopefully, we will be able to make contact with the leaders of some other countries and acquire their help," Pet'r said, looking about the cave briefly. "We'll know the answer to that very soon. I think Anisah and myself will be going to Habenlein to meet with their king, or whoever is in charge there. We hope we are doing what will provide us with a sense of accomplishment – we'll only know after all this is over. Until we meet again."

He was walking about while talking to Kalbra'n. He stopped, bowed his head and disappeared.

Kalbra'n sat for a while, looking all about Areb'l's cave.

Will these young people really defeat Baalsa'n? It's a question only time will tell, but we must be diligent in our effort to help. We must be able to anticipate Baalsa'n's plans, and those of his children; his wizards and his minions from other lands. Only the gods can help us if we do not.

He peered at the bare walls through the low light of the cavern. From within them lights glittered as though in answer.

SIARRA'S FEAR

Siarra sat near a lookout post on the upper level of the castle observing a broad expanse of countryside. The land once was an expansive region of farming. She could see to the seacoast in the distance where quiet villages were nestled, plying their fishing trade year after year.

It seemed to her those days must have been serene and good to the people who lived here. She lived not so far away, just north of this region, but the city had drawn her to it. All the young wanted to go and be in Tariny. The city drew them from all around the region and helped it become spirited, youthful and full of enterprise and excitement.

So she felt less of the sense of community of the small city where she was born. So, like the others, she grew to a young woman and left Crosspoint when she came of age and then was no longer involved with the rural areas.

Maybe I, and the others, missed something not knowing of land like this. Not seeing the gentleness of the people who care for it, not noticing those who came from these fishing villages. We lost something by not experiencing those things just beyond our city walls.

Geth'n came from these surroundings, or one that imitated the ideals and provided for the ones who never wanted to leave. But Geth'n too wanted to go to the city. Now too much has changed.

Are we lost somehow? Or maybe we've just forgotten.

She turned away and looked down into the central grounds of the castle. The hustle and bustle of people crowded together to protect themselves, and their loved ones, created a mildly chaotic scene. She looked back across the open fields at the massive encampment of men who prepared for battle, and their women and children who, more importantly, prepared for a war where their

371

loved ones might die.

She was depressed.

What are we going to be, as a community, when all these battles and wars are over. All this conflict happening because one evil being lived and wished to destroy? Will our lives return to what they were before?

Geth'n is so angry now, will he be a good man. Will he want to live in peace, or will he be unable to settle into a life where he no longer hates?

Here am I, my father dead, my brother lost and my family dependent upon me now. What will that mean when we leave the castle — if we ever do?

She turned back to look northward and at the ramparts being built there. Tears flowed easily down her cheeks. She had no one to talk to. All those she felt some comfort in being around were gone, except maybe Pet'r. But he too had changed. Wounded but with his family close by now, he concentrated all his energies on preparing for war.

Geth'n and he had become strangers to her. She held her face in her hands and wept.

"Why did you find me, Geth'n?" she sobbed. "How can we ever be happy with this world in such a turmoil? How will you and I have the time to get to know each other? Is there to be an *us*? I met you and embraced you without thinking. The times together were so pleasant and thrilling. We shared ourselves with each other? Now you're gone from me — in more ways than one.

I hate this war. How can we rid ourselves of this evil that has overwhelmed us and not tear our lives apart:?"

She realized she was talking aloud, stopped and looked around. But the sentry watching from this wall was marching away from her. He showed no sign of having heard. But she bowed her head and wept quietly, mourning her loss.

Can I endure this sadness, this longing, until we have peace, or death? It is so hard to bear.

She stood and turned away from the wall, went to the stairs and walked down onto the main floor. She recognized none of the people on the way to some important activity requiring attention. They flew by her without recognition.

She wanted to scream at the top of her lungs. She, if not for her family needing her, wanted to die. Now, without delay.

She stopped, stumbled into a small alcove and sat on a small bench built into the wall and began to cry again.

Then she sensed a shadow falling over her rather than seeing it. She looked up to see who it might be, but couldn't because of the backlight. She blinked trying to determine who it could be.

"Who is it?" she asked.

"It's me," Geth'n answered and sat down beside her. "It's just me and I'm so sorry I've deserted you, especially now. Can I sit and talk with you.?"

She couldn't believe it; her mouth opened yet she couldn't speak. She looked into his face, his wonderful face, and held her breath. Then she reached desperately for him, pulled him to her, as best she could, sitting in the cramped space and held him as tightly as she could. He sat patiently and waited for her, his arms around her.

She wept into his shoulder. She couldn't contain the spasms she felt with each sob. She couldn't take that breath she needed to, she felt disoriented. Her heart was beating so hard she could hear it. If she didn't breathe soon she knew she would lose consciousness. She didn't want that so she pulled her head back from his shoulder, drew in a deep breath, and looked him in the face and starting crying again, holding him even tighter than before.

Finally, she calmed and pulled back from him.

"I missed you. I've missed my friend. Where have you been? I've been so worried." she rambled. Her questions rolled off her tongue with no way to stop them. She held him again. "Where have you been?"

"I had to arrange some things on the front. I visited Peetle. It was my first time to see what was done. I found my sister and gave her a peaceful burial," Geth'n spoke, as though far away. He looked away from her and she saw the vacancy in his eyes from

373

the sadness and the pain he was feeling.

"But now I'm back and came to find you as quickly as I could. There were some things not going well with all of us gone," he spoke softly, not with the insistent hatred driving his every work as he did before he left. She knew the 'us' was a reference to the leaders, not of him and her. "Now I've found you and want to stay with you for a while, if I may. I don't know how long I have but this time is yours. I promise. Are you doing well?"

She paused and looked at him then turned away to glance across the open, and busy, courtyard.

"I'm doing well, I think. I've just missed you. I needed to talk to someone, almost anyone, about what is happening. The suspense of waiting for a message, or any word, from the areas of war has everyone on edge. We know nothing about our plight. We worry. Especially those of us who have family here. Is there no other safe place?"

"As far as I know," Geth'n answered, "there are no places of safety in Aerolan except this one and the area near Tariny. We are losing much of the lands north and west to the aggressors. We must turn this encroachment around or we will surely lose this war. But I request you speak to no one else about this. We must maintain a vigilant and trusting group of supporters who believe we can win this war, or we cannot hope to have the strength to drive this evil away."

"But how does that give us hope? Isn't that an admission we are standing on a precipice that is crumbling under our feet?" she asked, her brow was wrinkled with inquiry and fear.

He knew she was too intelligent to accept propaganda from him, or anyone. But she wasn't aware of some of the more recent findings of the defenders they thought would aid them. Particularly, the new knowledge about the *ransect'r*.

If we can't convince some of the other countries to come to our aid, and actually attempt to involve themselves in fighting for their own safety, there is not going to be a tomorrow. For anyone. It seems now is the moment of de-

cision and action from our group. We must proceed quickly and leave no lee-way for error. Where is Pet'r anyway?

"Have you seen Pet'r?" he asked her, still holding her close. She raised her head to look at him.

"He left just this morning to go see someone about some new element we need. I didn't talk to him but others told me he was going to see Calibr'a, or something like that," she answered. "Who is that?"

"Kalbr'an is our principle protector, instructor and leader in this fight. He has endured and been involved in these terrible wars before, against the same enemy," Geth'n answered. Now his eyes had that vacant look again. He seemed far away, certainly in thought.

"But I thought you, Anisah and Pet'r were the principles for us. I think everyone does, certainly everyone here," she sat up, looking at him, one eyebrow raised. "Who is this other?"

"He is an immortal. One member of a group, the Al-Esfer'n, who wishes us to succeed. I think the group, and Kalbr'an, is tired of running away as they always have in the past," he answered slowly and deliberately, decided the truth was what Siarra needed. He held some things from her. But those things he openly answered were the truths she needed to rebuild her trust in him. He needed to do that for her and himself.

"Immortals?" she looked away quickly. "We're dependent on someone from a dream?"

I cannot believe he is saying these things. We are lost. How can we survive with only hope on our side? My family, my friend, these people here and everywhere are lost. There is danger from the movement of these monsters across our land. They are going to completely destroy us. We have no way to fight back!

She looked at him, her eyes wide from the realization that there was no hope. Her mouth was opened in shock and she wanted to scream. Scream to everyone here to flee, to run and warn all the people trusting these three young people. There was

375

no hope. The belief in a myth to rescue them was futile.

We all are going to be destroyed.

She couldn't speak. She stood, walked away a few feet, turned and walked back. She stared at this man she thought loved her. She had nothing to say and she tried.

Is he insane? He seems earnest in what he says but how, but why, does he believe what he just told me?

"Please stop pacing and sit down. I can explain," he said, holding his hand out to her. "I can explain. What I am telling you is not part of any dream. I feel I must tell you what has happened to Pet'r and myself over the past few years and tell you who Anisah is and why she is with us – at least, as I understand her reasons.

She only stood and looked at him. She wasn't able to move.

He rose from the small alcove seat, approached her and took her in his arms without saying anything else. He stood with her, not letting go, and held her in the comfort he provided her.

I believe I can trust this man. I feel I can. I have to know about him now. He believes in what he is doing, so can I not listen and discover for myself what he believes. Sometimes that's all we have – our belays. I have to listen to him, for I do love him.

Geth'n began the tale of the adventures of the three crusaders. He told how he and Pet'r had journeyed to various places learning about the people and, yes, the magic that existed.

She pulled back when he mentioned magic, but he held her firmly and she relaxed. He continued.

He told her of the small amulet – the Ahar'n – which Pet'r wears at all times now and what it represented. He told her about the revelations of the abilities he developed, and was still developing, in magic. He told her who Anisah was – the granddaughter of the evil who was trying to obliterate the world.

He told her of the bond between the three that grew stronger with each day and with each trial they experienced during those days of learning about themselves. They could sense each other,

376

in some way. The other two were aware if one of them was in danger.

"But this man Pet'r has gone to meet, what is his role in all this?" she asked, mumbling against his chest. "Is he really immortal?"

"Yes, but he can die. In fact, millions of his people have died on other worlds fighting this one being who, in fact, is one of the Esfer'n. All of them live forever – unless fatally wounded.

He has untold experience fighting this evil during all those ages of hiding and trying to stop the elimination of thousands of worlds throughout the void. But the sad part is that the Al-Esfer'n were a peaceful people and were unprepared for war. Only a few have survived.

Strangely, here they had some success. They drove away this Baalsa'n once before with the help of others like us. Borny'a survived those wars and still lives," Geth'n revealed the history.

"What, he must be centuries old?" she sputtered, pushing away from Geth'n's chest and showing her disbelief.

"He is. I don't know how many years, but he has lived a long life. He was a friend of Pet'r's ancestor during those previous years of fighting. They won. At least enough Baalsa'n had to leave. But now Baalsa'n has returned to complete his original intention," Geth'n patiently explained each time she asked him another question.

"So what do we do now?" she asked, "Just wait for Pet'r to return?"

"We have to," he answered and looked away briefly at the crowd milling about the courtyard. "But there are other things we can do to prepare. Much of what is happening outside the castle is part of those plans. We aren't just sitting and waiting for the sky to fall. We are having some success in the field and we learn from each incidence.

If Anisah isn't here, I imagine and sense she is in the field fighting these monsters Baalsa'n is sending our way. But somehow we have to devise some way to halt their progress so we have time to discover a plan to defeat them. As I said earlier, we will be running out of time too soon."

At that moment, she noticed an older woman, Madifew Cannerty, walking toward them. Siarra began to be concerned, and a little embarrassed, the woman was going to hear their conversation.

"Isn't she a little close?" she said, nodding toward Madifew.

Geth'n chuckled. It was the first time she recalled him laughing at all, since their days in Tariny, at the library.

"Actually, she can't see us," he said casually.

He seemed so certain.

"But how?" Siarra turned quickly to look him in the eye.

"Simple. Magic," he said, not smiling but somehow he seemed amused at her surprise.

"Magic?" she asked. "What are you doing?" She never noticed anything he did to conjure a magic spell. He was sitting, talking to her without any unusual movements or any action on his part she could see.

He laughed aloud this time. She joined him with a small chuckle of her own.

"Magic isn't a mystery actually. But you have to understand what to do. Somehow I have learned that. It can be quietly done, or there can be a lot of noise. Call her name, if you want. She can't hear you."

Siarra spoke to the woman, but there was no change in the woman's demeanor, or direction. Siarra shouted at her as she came closer and there was no reaction at all.

Madifew walked directly toward them and, at the last moment, she veered to her left, pursuing some task and walked down the hall extending to the back of the castle.

"Well, I suppose I have to believe now. How can I help?" she asked.

"There are a number of groups here working on separate

378

parts of the things we have decided need to be done. I fear these things aren't being tied together well. There needs to be someone to coordinate these activities, especially since we, the group of war, have to be away so much. I would like to ask you to do that. I know you have the skills. Anybody who can deal with all the confusion of a large library system should be able to stabilize many things into one.

Besides, people automatically like you. I did. You have a way with people and, sometimes more than the power Pet'r, Anisah and I have, we need to have someone who can manage this place. Most of the men cannot. I think Anisah could but she has larger, and more complicated things, to hinder her efforts," Geth'n explained his concerns, naming several projects that seemed to be losing their direction.

"Would you consider doing this?" he asked. "I can't promise I'll be with you anymore than I have been. But I can tell you I think about you. I care about you. I'm asking you these things because I believe in you."

Siarra was stunned he was asking. The responsibility for bringing together all the activities of a war zone seemed beyond her, but she looked at him smiling at her and decided she could.

She nodded.

"Thank you and we can talk a bit more about my suggestions later, but I need to determine where Pet'r is because I might have to help him," Geth'n looked at her. "I will be back this evening and we can talk more then."

"I also want to suggest you determine how you can get you and your family to safety, in case things do not go well. I suggest you go to the southern coastline, anywhere between here and Farsea, retrieve a vessel large enough and sail back across to Peetle. I cleansed the peninsula there of all danger and placed entrapments for those I do not wish to go there. But, if you can get around to that coastline, you, and anyone you take with you, should be safe.

379

He rose from his seat. She felt, rather than saw, the shield he'd placed around them evaporate. She stood with him and placed a kiss on his cheek.

"I'll be expecting you," she told him, smiled and walked toward the activity section where some of the things they had talked of were being dealt with. She needed to watch and decide what directions to move things. She felt a certain pride he trusted her to do these things and do them correctly.

That was a good feeling to add to what she felt for him anyway.

GARV'N'S MEMORY

Garv'n woke. His eyes opened slowly, expecting to be on the road toward the mountains, in search of the Ahar'n. But he wasn't. He was in a building. Surrounding by people busily running about. He turned his head slightly and noticed there were several younger men lying on cots who seemed to have injuries.

Then he remembered Rab'k stabbing him and grimaced. Instinctively, he reached to touch his neck. But there was no wound. Strangely, there was no scar.

Now he recognized where he was. The castle near Roahan. Ralff'r.

Did Rab'k capture him and bring him here?

But he realized from the bustle of people around him he was mistaken. Rab'k never required this many people. He only had a few soldiers about because he rarely stayed in the castle very long.

One of the young women attending the others came to his bedside. She noticed him moving.

"I notice you're awake, sir. Are you feeling well?" she asked.

He turned his head and smiled at her.

"Yes, I feel fine. But why am I here? Who are you people? Where's Rab'k? Where's Jond'r?" Garv'n, in his surprise, began to ask questions immediately.

Murlena looked at him with widened eyes. Her face showed her shock as he spoke. She stood for a moment and seemed anxious to do something urgent.

"I'm so glad to hear you talking, sir. I have to tell someone. I'll be right back," she stammered.

Then she turned quickly and scampered into the hallway. She crossed the courtyard and into the hallway leading to where the three leaders stayed. Coincidentally, Anisah was there. Her travels along the front, trying to help with the fighting, had exhausted her and she needed to rest a bit.

"Anisah, Anisah, where are you?" Murlena cried out, running through the hallway, looking in every room along the way.

"Murlena, I'm here," she called out to the girl as she ran past the small alcove where Anisah was watching the encampment to the north of the castle. Pet'r was there somewhere. He returned from the meeting with Kalbra'n miraculously healed and went directly to the training grounds without talking to her. She was happy about his health but concerned about his recklessness - a problem that often placed him in danger.

Murlena stopped and ran back to Anisah in a flurry, stopped and waited only a moment before blurting out her news.

"Anisah. Anisah, you must come quickly. Lord Garv'n is awake, talking and asking about Rab'k and Jond'r. He wants to know why he's here," Murlena was so excited when she burst out of the ward, and breathing hard from her run through the castle. "I think his memories have returned! I'm so sorry to bother you, but I thought you'd want to know."

"Thank you, very much. I do want to go talk to him," Anisah said. She rose and walked toward the hospital area.

She wondered what Garv'n remembered, and what he didn't, about the past few months. Voravia's little people brought him to Borny'a's cabin, critically wounded. When she arrived, it was her first opportunity to attempt to heal him, but he was unconscious when she arrived so she used some of her newly discovered, but fearful, skills. She tried to stop the major problems and apparently succeeded. But Garv'n remained in the coma for a time after she took him to Tariny and the hospital, despite her efforts. Later he was awake, but with a loss of memory, when she and Geth'n were with him there. Just after that visit, she decided to transport him to Ralff'r because Mano'n was harassing her.

She walked into the room and noticed the gentleman was now sitting, gingerly touching his neck.

He apparently remembers being stabbed. I wonder who did this to him? He appears to be harmless.

"Good morning, sir. I thought I'd come to welcome you to our safe harbor. My name is Anisah and, I suppose, I'm the one to officially greet you to our home," she said, standing where he could see her without turning his head. She assumed any movement caused pain in his neck.

"Ah, yes. Well, thank you, but, if you're not aware, this is my castle," he answered, looking her up and down in his appraisal of this young woman who thought she was in charge.

Garv'n stretched his arm opposite his wound. He grimaced a bit, but continued to stretch it in several directions.

"Well, at least, that one works well enough. I'm sorry. I wasn't trying to be rude, but what is everyone doing here?" he asked her, now moving his other arm with the pain obvious from his reactions.

"Well, sir. I actually know this place is yours. But we've commandeered it in preparation for the war we're involved in. This was the only place that seemed safe. Many of our supporters have migrated here from several parts of eastern Aerolan. We have camps all about, almost covering this peninsula now.

We are just trying to survive until we are able to forge an alliance with several other countries to fight the people who have invaded," she told him calmly. "Geth'n and Jond'r, my friends, knew the castle belonged to you and that Rab'k used it as a center for one of your policing groups. But Rab'k, we now know, is part of that force trying to destroy us. So, since he wasn't at home we decided we'd make it ours."

Garv'n frowned at the girl. She seemed to him to be a bit prim, but obviously had a strong belief in herself. He wondered who she was.

"You say Jond'r is one of your friends. I don't believe I've met you before," he pointed out.

"But that aside, do you know about my family, do you know

383

anything about their welfare? They live at our villa on the coast south of Tariny," he asked, still trying the muscles on his left side. He was making progress relaying the aches. Anisah was pleased he was making the effort without her asking.

"So far we've managed to protect Tariny and that peninsula. Most of the west coast except in the north region near Voravia's castle has been protected. We were able to ward off the invader. At least for the moment," she answered, without hesitation. "I'm sorry, but you've not met me before now. Well, not while you were unconscious. But, I've been around trying to offer what I could to your recovery. I'm glad to hear you talking. You weren't for a while," she said, pointing the small board he used to communicate.

Garv'n began to notice there was something about the girl, something more than her being a survivor. There was something of the warrior in her attitude he recognized.

Could she be a messenger from the Al-Esfer'n?

"Can we bring my family here?" he asked, thinking how long it had been since he asked a question when he didn't have control over the outcome of the answer.

"I believe that would be unwise, sir. We aren't exactly in control of this area. But it was the one, centrally located, that served our purpose," she explained. "They're probably safer where they are. We can get you to them fairly quickly, if you wish."

"No, I don't think so. For now," he said. He wondered how they could get him there quickly, but didn't ask.

"You are probably wondering who we are. I should explain," she proceeded. "We are very naive and innocent, but we have some expert help. Possibly you could advise us on other resources we are unaware of. There are actually three of us, too young to know very much, too driven to retreat and too sworn to what we want to do, to surrender to the attacks on Aerolan, and actually Narhtrae. Our youth hinders us. But, thanks to the Al-Esfer'n, we do seem to possess some strengths we never expec-

384

ted."

"Al-Esfer'n? You are aware of them? What strengths do you suggest you possess?" he asked.

"We are supported by the Al-Esfer'n though they aren't directly involved. We couldn't do what we've been able to without them, especially my two companions," she answered hesitantly adding the last. "We have discovered we have certain magical powers."

Garv'n looked at her askance.

"You have magical powers?" he grinned. "What powers do you have?"

"We have abilities to modify reality, in a sense. We're uncertain what we do and not fully aware of why it occurs, but, it seems, we can envision a change, some of which can be very dramatic, and those things are changed at our command," she answered, without any indication she disbelieved what she said. "In reference to my companions, we owe much of their new abilities to the Al-Esfer'n. Some, or most actually, of my skills seem to originate from a different source."

Garv'n was a bit surprised by her last statement, but didn't question it.

"But how do you know the Al-Esfer'n?" she asked him.

"I was shown some aspects of the future," he paused to watch her reaction, but there was no obvious surprise shown by the girl. "The Al-Esfer'n came to me, suggested I open my eyes to the changes about us and asked me to help. I wasn't able to do anymore because Rab'k attacked me. I would assume you knew that."

"Actually, I didn't know who attacked you. A small band of Voravia's people brought you to Borny'a, a woodsman and soldier, who lived near where you were attacked, asking for food in trade for you. Borny'a paid that ransom, took you in and gave you safety. You, along with Jond'r and his brother, stayed with Borny'a until the danger was too evident and I brought you both

385

here," she explained. "But I'm not surprised Rab'k was your downfall."

"Jond'r? You know him and Acron'n too," he asked, raising his head to watch her expression. Strangely, he felt no need to question the young woman about her claims. She never hesitated in her statements when speaking of the others. He felt comfortable accepting her at face value.

"Borny'a has been a godsend. As it turns out, he's been around for a while, much longer than one can imagine actually and has skills in warfare. We feel fortunate he wants to help. Also, Jond'r did survive an attack by Rab'k on the same day, apparently, you were struck down. He and his brother, Acron'n, are working closely with Borny'a to try to form our rather makeshift army to fight these villains."

"Jond'r and Acron'n both are well then?" he asked. "That's wonderful news. I haven't heard from Acron'n since I sent him to spy in the desert, north of the mountains. I would assume he discovered some of the problems you speak of."

"I'm not certain of that. He was rescued by Geth'n and Pet'r not so long ago and is a good addition to our decision team. He hasn't discussed what he was doing before, or how he was captured and escaped from the Ravelan. He met Pet'r in the mountains. And then later Pet'r helped him escape. So he's staying, largely because of his brother, I think. But we need more help, these few aren't enough to teach the basics of battle to so many."

So, you, Geth'n and this Pet'r , you just mentioned, are the three. Is that true?" Garv'n mentioned and tried to stand. Murlena, who returned with Anisah and was listening to the conversation, rushed to his side. Anisah stepped forward and held his arm on the side where the wound was. They helped steady him but he sat back down quickly.

"Yes," she told him. "We need your help, if you feel you can and are able. Is it possible you know others who might join us to deal with this horrible menace?"

"Well, my being able physically is obviously questionable. And I'm fairly certain I can't help with your needs for manpower, but I do have a certain fame for leadership and, I assume, for my business dealings.

There is someone who might help who lives just north of Tariny, in Avilan. He's the brother of my sergeant who, I assume, did not survive the attack on my group and me. His name is Turm'l and he's highly qualified as a military man and an officer. I believe he would jump at the opportunity to help you three and he would consider doing that more strongly once I tell him about his brother's demise.

But more than that, I have large economic resources, rather than men. You probably already have, in your forces, most of my men. So let me offer foodstuff, ships to transport men and armament along the coasts and there are other properties about where the people needing to be safer might hide, particular along the coast west of Tariny," he told her. "These things I can offer."

Anisah listened patiently to this man who they all felt would be an important resource. Their hopes were being fulfilled. She was pleased and already making plans for some travel to some of the places Garv'n mentioned to make contact with the people he felt would help.

She was surprised Garv'n was aware of the Al-Esfer'n, but his acceptance of them and her claims about magic helped even more than she expected. This man was a leader of men, a lord in spirit if not in actuality. His contribution would be immeasurable.

So now all I have to worry about is helping prepare for the inevitable, and how to contact the right people. Because I also need to worry about Geth'n and his anger and Pet'r and his brashness. Is it going to be my responsibility to make this all happen as it should?

And what about Mano'n? What do I do about him? I know he still lurks about watching what I do, but what is he waiting for? What does he want? Do I really need to know the answers to these questions about him? Then I have to ask myself why it matters. Or does it?

Why does it matter?

RECONNAISANCE

They assembled where they could. There were a great number of people in the castle now, so Garv'n mentioned the stable had a large tack room and it probably would serve as a meeting hall.

So they traipsed through the mud to cross to the stables. The weather was bad, pushing from the north and east, making the air damp and cold. Rain blew across the grounds, annoying them all.

Most of the men sitting around the room, except Garv'n who was still recuperating and had to lay down to be comfortable, were coming in from the battlefront. Since they decided to drag the enemy into smaller attacks, a number of the officers weren't able to leave their post because of the critical position they held in the field. They would be briefed about the proceedings later when runners were sent to all those posts.

The tactics for the war, so far, were simple and direct. It was guerrilla warfare and seemed to hold the enemy off, for the time being. So except for Pet'r and Geth'n who arrived inside the castle the quickest, the other men were worn and tired from the travel away from their respective battle positions.

There was a new member, Turm'l from Avilan who had only arrived that morning. Garv'n introduced him as Vil'n's brother. Most of the other members, except Borny'a and Jond'r, didn't know Vil'n but trusted Borny'a enough to welcome Turm'l to their counsel. Borny'a and he stood and clasped their forearms for a moment.

"Sorry to hear about your brother," Borny'a said, adding no more. Turm'l only bowed his head.

Once everyone found a seat somewhere, the meeting began. Most of them needed to get back to their post as quickly as possible. Anisah and Siarra, who was surprised she was invited, sat

389

near the front.

Geth'n began the discussion, standing and turning so each person could hear.

"We are now at the point where we probably can actually discuss and plan a way to defeat Baalsa'n. We still have limited resources but Pet'r has verified the gateways, the *ransect'r* exist and was given their last known positions.

Jond'r, Arcon'n and Anisah have been ravaging the enemy, especially along the routes where the Ravelan attempt to bring captives back to their camp. We have to thank Anisah for her special contribution to that effort.

Borny'a and I have been traveling from activity to activity to determine if we are gaining any advantage with what we are doing so far. I want to praise all the field officers for your outstanding work. There seems no doubt we have stalled the enemy. And that gives us some time to negotiate with some other countries. I believe Habenlein will be the first we will talk to.

Also, by way of introduction, we are pleased Turm'l has joined us. That certainly provides those of us learning our leadership roles another tremendous source to develop better skills.

In our training program, we've been training the able-bodied men and boys in the simpler skills of fighting hand to hand. Progress has been excellent, at least in my untrained opinion. Arcon'n and Pet'r have forged a method to train the newcomers to turn them from farmers into fighting members of our force almost overnight.

We need to thank Siarra for her new effort in administering our needs here at our new home, feeding and providing aid to all those people within several miles radius. Most have lost their homes and often family members to this onslaught. It seems her efforts have brought a calming effect to us that was missing before.

Now we need to discuss where we go, or can go, from here. I'd like to ask Borny'a to give us an overview of our military position and make any suggestions he feels we need to concentrate on now."

Borny'a stood, a man unaccustomed to speaking to a group., turning to looked at each face, then he looked at the ceiling momentarily and started.

"I had my doubts when these young people first came to me. No insult, but we were without leadership when there were only four, or five, making the decisions in my cabin, months ago. I'm pleased, but not a little surprised they were persistent and desired to be the best at what each of them does.

One of the chief things we have now, through these young people, we didn't have the last time Baalsa'n invaded Narhtrae. M*agic*.

There was no one to help us fight off the attacks that relied on magic. Areb'l and I were at a loss as to what we could do. We were losing miserably. But, he decided we needed to use the *ransect'r* and contact other nations around the world and convince them to help in our battle against Baalsa'n. The Om-Esfer'n built those for their convenience but never really used to them to visit, or attack, any other country. I assume they thought if they could destroy Aerolan every other country would surrender without a fight.

We decided to use them.

So we started by traveling to Habenlein to talk to them first. Initially, they were uninterested and balked at providing any help. We explained Baalsa'n intent to destroy the entire world, but they saw only that we were being attacked and they perceived no danger in that. They didn't want to help. They were unconvinced. Areb'l and I couldn't think of what we might do to get them to help.

Areb'l then decided to do something drastic. He solicited Kalbra'n to give him a small moment of magic. He asked the Al-Esfer'n to trust him with just that small amount. They were friends for centuries before this, so Areb'l was finally able to convince

391

them we needed just one act of magic to persuade the leaders of Habenlein to join the fight. Areb'l believed once we had one of the countries won over, the others would soon follow.

With that power, Areb'l stood before the ruler of Habenlein and suddenly produced one of the Maah'e from Ravelan forces. He materialized him from nothing and stood him before the king. Of course, the size of the creature overwhelmed all in attendance. The king was stunned by the creature's obvious power and danger. This particular beast was actually a former soldier in our army.

When Areb'l explained the creature was actually one of our own, transformed into this fighting machine, the king rose and declared Habenlein would pledge support. He realized the ability to create such beings endangered Habenlein and potentially other countries.

There was no hesitation from that moment on.

It was that one bit of magic that turned the tide. Here we have, at least, two and possibly three who are able to modify reality a bit.

We need to have these young people use these powers to convince those same countries to join our fight again. We have an agreement with them – the Granoblistia Fealty. But it was established so long ago there is no one else alive, besides Turm'l and myself, who remembers it. It seems probable their new leaders simple aren't aware of the agreement.

We now have knowledge of where there are *ransect'r* available, including the one Turm'l and I personally used in that great fight."

Several of those in the room turned to look at Turm'l with a new understanding of just who he was.

"So Areb'l, a man of great power, and two old vets, from other worlds, were able to forge that alliance and to push the attack to the enemy.

We won with the help of those confederated countries. We

sent Baalsa'n and his people packing. But we need that effort again.

Only this time, we should have a central theme in our pact. We know this time Baalsa'n himself must be destroyed. We have to stop that killer or he will continue to destroy worlds wherever he goes, including us eventually," Borny'a stopped and walked back to his seat.

Geth'n paused for a moment, allowing Borny'a presentation to be absorbed.

"So, understanding Borny'a's account of the past events as revealing, we need to use the *ransect'r* and travel to Habenlein and other countries to warn those leaders and attempt to invoke the treaty we had with them before," Geth'n proposed, looking around the room for approval.

"I would like to request Anisah and Pet'r for this effort. In that way, the two representatives we send will be able to move freely using the *ransect'r*. They also possess magical abilities. And their abilities can be used to impress the foreign rulers. In that way, we show our strength and our confidence in what we are trying to do. I believe those rulers will, in large part, decide to support this cause because of the combination of backgrounds these two offer," Geth'n said. "Does anyone object?"

Anisah agreed immediately by nodding her head toward Geth'n, then she looked to Pet'r to see his answer. He paused a moment then nodded his head while looking at her. She was pleased.

Everyone else looked around the room a bit and no one disagreed with Geth'n's request.

"I would like to offer my fleet for transportation of large groups of soldiers from these other countries, should they agree to come," Garv'n, quiet until now, offered. "That should lessen the impact on those countries who agree to send some, or all, of their force. I've a long standing relationship with most of them and this would go a long way toward relaying any pressure they might feel about getting their troops to our soil and back. We can relay the ships so there is always movement. Does Baalsa'n have any means to attack these vessels?"

Pet'r answered, "I'm not certain. We've seen nothing to suggest that, but we don't know. I think Baalsa'n has not concerned himself because he thinks we have no means, in a military way, to travel away from our continent."

"I see no way for him to have obtained any ships in this short time he's been here. If he is aligned with Ravelan, he has no seaworthy transportation from them. So, we can worry about any problems if we need to. But first, we have to have agreements," Garv'n offered.

"I request either Borny'a, or Turm'l, accompany us," Pet'r suggested. "That's a face which probably fits into the other countries list of heroes. Something along that line offers a stronger suggestion of our belief and strength."

"I agree and suggest Turm'l. I've been involved with the training here and led some of our troops into battle now. I'm probably better known to our people. Turm'l, though a fine officer, hasn't had that opportunity," Borny'a added. "What do you think, Anisah?"

Anisah sat quietly listening during this discussion. Looked up from thinking about the possibilities, "I think it would be a good idea. Turm'l knows these people, and some of their ways, Pet'r and I have little to work with. This addition would help us immensely," Anisah answered.

She would rather Borny'a went, now she had worked with him for a while, but he was right. His leadership was invaluable. Turm'l was still a bit of a mystery, as far as she could tell.

But Borny'a is the one who recommended him, so why not?

'Sir, would you have any difficulty accompanying us?" Pet'r asked Turm'l.

"I understand you, young fellow, may be an ancestor of Areb'l. That alone speaks volumes about who you are and what you might accomplish. I'm honored you asked me. Maybe while we're moving about the other countries; they may remember me. I was the rude one!" Turm'l replied.

Everyone laughed.

"Good. Then I would like to suggest we leave tomorrow. One of the *ransect'r* lays hidden somewhere between here and Farsea. We have to find it first," Pet'r said, standing he turned and looked at his new teammates. They both nodded. "We should probably leave in the morning early."

Geth'n embarrassed Siarra sitting quietly, but she knew he meant well. She felt comfortable with all these people. Except for her father, she met very few she completely trusted around the lands and inside the castle. She marked Turm'l. She wasn't certain about him.

Why hasn't he come forward before now? Why did he wait until Garv'n called him? Is he true to this cause now, or does he have ulterior motives?

Then she stopped herself.

Siarra, you have to trust some people. He's imposing and seems to be a natural leader. But there's something . . .?

Geth'n rose and surveyed the people who would be the winners, or losers, in the long battle to come

"If no one else needs to speak, I think we can go back to work. There's certainly plenty to do. I'd like to meet separately with Borny'a, Jond'r, Arcon'n, Anisah and Pet'r right after we are dismissed. Now that Lord Garv'n is no longer in the kitchen, I think we can meet there briefly. Turm'l. My apologies. You are invited to join that group also."

"Before we go, a word, please," Turm'l spoke up, "there may be the problem of Baalsa'n's awareness of the *ransect'r*. I believe I remember the Om-Esfer'n possessed some way to track a working gateway. Not certain how complex the tracking was, but it's certain he will be pursuing those who attempt to use them. We must always be aware of that possibility. He will not let those gates be a gift."

Everyone stood, walked to the stable door, looked out at the miserable weather and dashed to the castle as quickly as they could.

After they all were back in the castle and started going their separate ways, Anisah watched Pet'r and Turm'l talking as they walked away.

How well will we interact and how do I fit into this situation.

Siarra, walking ahead of Anisah, stopped and asked, "Are you concerned about your trip?"

Anisah, deep in thought about Pet'r, and the whereabouts of Mano'n, jumped a bit with the sudden interruption.

"I'm sorry," Siarra said. "I didn't realize you were so deep in thought."

"No. No, it's fine. I'm just concerned with what comes next. The interesting part is we haven't tried the *ransect'r* yet and, already we're planning on those being an integral part of winning this war. I just wonder how well they work.

As far as I know, we don't have any idea where we will *land* on the other end, nor what kind of trouble we'll have getting to the leaders of each country. A lot of *ifs* to be considered. I'm willing to proceed, but have some apprehension about the trip and its success," Anisah answered. "As Turm'l just mentioned, we have to be careful to watch for signs Baalsa'n is on our trail while roaming through these channels the *ransect'r* offer. I'm thinking I'd rather teleport than run the risks."

"And you will be there to protect Pet'r. Right?" Siarra said, smiling. "That's important to you, I believe."

Anisah looked around at the girl with whom Geth'n obviously was infatuated. She really hadn't been able to talk to Siarra. She knew little about her.

"Yes, it is. What about yourself? Is there no apprehension about Geth'n being here without Pet'r and I being around. Doesn't that bother you a bit."

"It seems you and I read each other pretty well. I hope we're both happy with all these decisions by the men. Hopefully, this war can be finished with all of us still alive. You and I have a particularly important interest in both. Or am I wrong?," Siarra asked, looking in the direction the men were going.

"No, you're not. But we can only hope and fight for our safety and that of our loved ones," Anisah said. "For now I guess I'd better go prepare for this trip." She smiled at Siarra and followed the men to the meeting in the kitchen.

Seems this woman could be a friend. She's right, we have something in common. We want to be happy.

When Anisah arrived, everyone sat down around the table, wondering what Geth'n wanted to tell them. She was thinking whether she and Pet'r would have any privacy to discuss things she felt they needed to reconcile.

Geth'n wanted to be certain he, and any other around with the expertise, would be available to help with these future engagements with other countries. He asked Anisah and Pet'r if they could think of anything more. They could recommend nothing new.

Turm'l reiterated his concern with protecting themselves as they traveled then he added, "I remember Habenlein was one of the more cooperative countries in the past. They probably will make every effort, if they agreed to join with us, to convince other countries to get involved."

"To what extent should you use magic? Turm'l you alone made be able to answer that. These two, particularly Anisah, are quite capable with this, but is it the wisest things to do? Will Baalsa'n, or any of his children, be able to detect this usage," Geth'n asked.

Anisah broke from her reverie, turned and watched Geth'n when he mentioned her name. He was including her, but he probably felt she knew what he was thinking.

Strange how we three seem to think along similar lines.

"I suspect it should only be used as a surprise element, if needed," Turm'l answered. "We probably should implore their

397

help as fellow victims first. If we show too much strength too quickly, they might assume we don't need their help. It is critical we get that last understood. We do need their help."

Pet'r was nodding his head as Turm'l spoke. Anisah was sitting next to him and watched him peripherally. They hadn't spoken about their confrontation since returning. Both kept themselves busy to avoid that.

But, she knew, they would have to determine their near, and maybe, distant future soon. They needed to clear their mind of their personal problems to make certain those didn't interfere with those relevant to saving Aerolan.

"Just wanted to check. We have to be in agreement and communicate more often, if we are going to succeed in this," Geth'n said, then looked directly at Anisah. She knew he wanted her to hold this group together and to allow for mistakes made. But also, as she saw his brow wrinkle, he wanted her to always be the most cautious and use her own judgment about the use of her special magic.

He was aware Mano'n tracked her to almost all her recent locations. That was a serious concern. She knew she broached the subject with Mano'n but still was uncertain he would follow the guidelines of their relationship she dictated at that meeting. So, there was some reason to keep that in mind.

The next morning, Pet'r, Turm'l and Anisah were together early in the small guardroom next to the gate. It was still raining rather hard so they decided to wait just a bit longer before they left. They talked for a while about general things and how much Anisah and Pet'r had learned during their brief time with the awareness and preparation for this war.

"I think we're ready now. We shouldn't have to walk too far to reach the gate and the weather will probably give us an opportunity soon," Pet'r said, looking out the small window of the guard station.

Anisah and Turm'l nodded their head in agreement. The three picked up some things to take along, signaled for the gate to be lowered. When the bridge was available they walked across, looked to the south, turned and began their journey of hope. Only Pet'r looked to the skies. Being a fisherman's son he learned as a youth how to predict changes.

"We should get there without getting wet," he mentioned. Turm'l nonchalantly kept pace with the younger man. Anisah picked up the pace fairly well but it was a little faster than she expected.

"Are there any gaps you young people might need me to fill about what happened before. About why we were successful. At least successful enough to rid ourselves of Baalsa'n and his group for a long while," Turm'l asked. "I visited several of the countries at that time but, as I admitted, I was much younger and not a little headstrong and may have made a few enemies in those places. But, despite that, I agree with the choice of Habenlein as the first to contact. It's the closest to us and they contributed greatly the last time around. You folks are probably correct. It's a good place to start."

After a fairly long walk along the road, Pet'r starting peering off to the side toward the sea, apparently searching for the gateway.

"I believe, according the Kalbra'n, the gate just south of us is the one used extensively before and it takes the traveler within a short distance of the capital of that country," Pet'r offered, "He explained the *ransect'r* look much like a group of boulders. And aged now, they probably blend into the surrounding scenery. Of course this flatland, rolling down to the water, is covered with boulders. We should be questioning every group we pass."

Turm'l made some comment Anisah barely heard.

Anisah was listening to the two men talking, but wasn't interested in the discussion. She was concentrating on determining some precautions she felt they should take for the journey.

399

The element of surprise should be lessened. We aren't there to attack; we're there to make a request. Should we even mention the pact made long ago, the Fealty, or not? New people, strangers to us, often take a great deal of persuasion. The story of Areb'l's demonstration was proof of that. I suspect we need something like that to convince these people we're serious. But what?

Are we in a hurry to lose ourselves in this world.? In this war? Pet'r seems so intense and excited about the arrival of the final battle. I wonder, when it does happen, if he will still want it to be happening.

What is he thinking now? Does he realize we need to be together; does he think about that?

Or me?

CHILDREN BEWARE

Kalbra'n sat high on the ridge overlooking both Aerolan. The deep, desperate desert spread across the northern portion with its people, born of despair, scattered thinly across the almost waterless expanse reaching to the sea along its northern shores. Turning to the south, the lush and fertile land where most of the people of the continent lived.

He stood observing the seemingly peaceful nest of land, knowing there was deep turmoil beneath this facade.

Most of his thoughts dealt with the war to come. He no longer doubted there was going to be another attempt to destroy this world. Baalsa'n's entire being required that outcome. Kalbra'n never quite understood why, nevertheless he had to accept the obvious.

Meanwhile he and the others, trying to find a way to save this world, discovered a precious resource never imagined.

Three young people from southern Aerolan who developed almost unbelievable power within themselves in such a short time. The changes in their personalities, their powers and their desire to save this world astounded him and the others.

They are active, abundantly so. They want to win this, as they must. But desire is the most difficult thing to instill in those afraid to venture forth against their own doubts. I recognize these three, and their accumulated friends, are driven to improve themselves at any, and every, moment.

The strangest is Anisah. How can she be what she has become? It's somewhat fearful to know she's about. What will she want in the long run? Is she powerful enough to achieve it?

He considered these thoughts with some misgiving. He knew about her from the beginning. Even as a young girl she showed, quite accidentally it seemed, powerful extension of her desires.

But, at those times, she seemed to be unaware of who, or what, she was. She undoubtedly could be dangerous.

"Obviously, Mano'n was curious. He almost never left her alone," Kalbra'n muttered. "There can only be one obvious reason. She is his daughter. But why hasn't he stepped forward and carried her into the bond with Baalsa'n. Does he want to spare her?"

Is it possible she is too strong for him to encircle? Has he tried?

She is traveling about, helping Aerolan's front line troops wherever she's able. Yet Mano'n makes no obvious attempt to stop her. Maybe he's afraid of her. Maybe Baalsa'n has a bigger problem than he can imagine. Maybe Mano'n doesn't want to stop her and her friends? That would be a curious direction for him.

Of course, I'm pleased with this development. Never really expected it. But her desires are almost always well intended. Her trip to Varspree was fortuitous. I was able to have the boys be a part of what she will become. Their influence has been remarkable.

I think these children, and we, can win this war.

Baalsa'n paused for only a moment. He paced. He walked to the door of his chambers several times, trying to decide what needed to be done. He stopped each time because he was not quite able to put his finger on what bothered him, nor how to place his concerns into adequate action and force to finish the destruction of this world and move on to the next.

But, the more he paced, the more angry he became with what he perceived as failure - failure of those he was depending on to fulfill his desire and commands. He'd been patient while his own children learned their duties. Now he admitted, his assumptions about the outcome of that patience were incorrect.

Enough is enough.

Suddenly exploding with anger, Baalsa'n completed his trip to the door, grabbed the latch and ripped the great door, taller than 10 men, open. The frame around the door splintered and pieces flew into the room where he stood. He ignored the debris and cast aside the remainder of the door. It slid across the hall and smashed against an outer wall – shattering completely on impact.

He walked into the hallway, looking for someone to use as a messenger, "Guard! Go get the officer of the watch and bring him to me!" The young soldier standing guard, jumped, shocked by this sudden, and unexpected, outburst and ran down the empty hallway.

The sound of his boots striking the floors reverberated through the emptiness above, the dark places rumbled.

When he reached the common quarters, he turned a corner and dashed to the middle door, crashing it open and he charged into the room. The soldiers immediately jumped , grabbing their weapons and bracing for battle. The lieutenant motioned for the guard to come to his desk.

"Sir, the Master is commanding your presence. He wants you there immediately, if his anger is any sign," the guard told the officer., shaking from his experience.

The lieutenant ran back to Baalsa'n's quarters with the guard in tow. He stopped in front of the entry, noticed the door was torn away, stepped through the opening and reported.

"You needed me, sir?" the officer asked Baalsa'n.

"Yes. Yes. Find my children and bring them to me! Now! Tell Monsh'a and his stupid wizard I want them here also!" he turned back into the room, pounded his way to the throne and plopped into it again.

The officer saluted, turned to run back down the hallway and crashed through the door to the barracks.

"Everyone up! Now! We have to find Baalsa'n's offspring! Bring them here – by force if necessary! You two ride hard to Monsh'a's encampment and tell him Baalsa'n wants him and his wizard here. Now!" he shouted. All the soldiers stood for a mo-

403

ment wondering what was happening.

"Now! All of you. Go! Disburse when necessary but do as I say- or we may all suffer the consequences of failure!" the young officer shouted. "Go! Go! There should be some information about where everyone is. Find them and return with them or forfeit your lives!"

The watch, composed entirely of Om-Esfer'n soldiers, realizing they needed to respond quickly, began a great uproar of chatter – brief commands were given, extra information about preparations and quick assignments to groups. Then they began to file out of the room. The lieutenant and his sergeant preceded them as they trotted noisily down the hallway, turned into the correct hall and proceeded to the outer exit. Blasting out onto the bluff overlooking the open desert, they startled the worshipers gathered, marched quickly to the road to the bottom and disappeared over the edge of the cliff.

No sound except the shouted commands of the sergeant and the stomping sounds of the boots could be heard.

When they reached the desert, they turned toward the west moving rapidly. They traveled in a forced march, attempting to cover the ground they needed to travel as quickly as possible. No one opposed them. Most of those in the open ground ran away, trying to find somewhere to hide. Many never saw where they went.

These men were Baalsa'n's elite guard. They broke into a forced march and double-timed through the mountain trail and went directly to Rena'x's camp and commandeered a space for their campsite. Their stay was short – only a few hours – and they proceeded to attack the mountain. At the crest of the pass, they encamped for a few more hours, then they were off again.

They entered Monsh'a's camp and, ignoring or pushing aside any interference, moved directly to the command tent. Several Maah'e attempted to stop them to no avail; the guard simply pushed the irritants aside to deal with and then it only took a moment for certain members of the guard responsible to step from the formation, deal harshly with the intruder and fall quickly back into sequence and rhythm with the others.

They came to a noisy halt in front of the tent. The lieutenant stepped forward, pushed the curtain away at the entrance, asked for no permission to be there and walked directly to where Monsh'a and Rab'k were discussing their plan for the mass attack. Monsh'a looked up to see who had marched into his tent and didn't recognize the officer.

"Who are you and what do you think you're doing marching in here without my permission? Rab'k, is this one of yours?" Monsh'a raised his voice in irritation. He started around the table, but Rab'k reached and grabbed his arm, holding him a moment. Monsh'a looked around sharply, wondering what possessed Rab'k to stop him. Rab'k only nodded toward the entrance.

The first unit of the guard stepped into the tent when they heard Monsh'a's challenge. These men were highly trained, quick to act and held magic from Baalsa'n. They were not interested in excuses – from anyone. Their spears were held forward and all eyes were on Monsh'a.

Monsh'a, recognizing the danger, turned back to the man who had intruded.

"Who are you?" he asked.

"I'm Lieutenant Fern'o of his majesty's personal guard. He requires me to accompany you and Master Rab'k to the palace." the sergeant answered, holding Monsha's eyes though he was at least a foot shorter than the monstrous commander. He didn't turn away, nor glance at Rab'k. He assumed his men were watching both men.

"Why?" Monsh'a asked. If it weren't for the squad, he would have crushed the man where he stood.

"He doesn't explain his reasons to me, sir. But he seemed very adamant," Fern'o responded, he calmly made his demand known. "Perhaps you can ask him when you get there. Sir." The last was explicitly emphasized and, to some extent, sarcastic. Both Monsh'a and Rab'k recognized that.

"Rab'k, what do you think we should do?" Monsh'a turned to his companion and asked.

"It seems apparent that my father is upset about something. I think this is an opportunity to visit and determine what his problems are," Rab'k said icily.

He looked up at Fern'o and around at the guard. Rab'k wasn't happy about this turn of events. He felt he and Monsh'a were making progress in their plans and thought they certainly had the upper hand in terms of overall strength. He saw no reason the Aerolan should be a problem and thought this visit would prove nothing.

"I say these gentlemen have come a long way to extend this invitation. Possibly we can be sociable and rely on their good will. I say we should go."

Monsh'a nodded his head, but frowned at Fern'o.

"We will go with you, Lieutenant. But do not be annoyed about the group who will be following you," Monsh'a said to Fern'o. "I feel uncomfortable being outnumbered."

"Certainly, sir. We expected that," he answered. Fern'o knew what he had to do, without question.

Fern'o raised his hand toward his troops and they parted in deference to the three in the tent. The two guests strode through the line, both a head or more taller than the rest.

As they reached the end of the formed path and prepared to mount the horses brought by Fern'o, Monsh'a quietly signaled his first officer who was standing, watching. His hand was on his sword ready to attack if given the command.

Monsh'a's troops outnumbered Fern'o's and each man was half again as large. But, taking Rab'k's advice, Monsh'a decided he should wait for another day. He wasn't even certain yet he wished to rebel against Baalsa'n. The wrong decision could bring his death and probably that of his own people. The ones he now vowed to protect and the reason he accepted the mixed allegiance with Rab'k.

On the signal, the Monsh'a's lieutenant relaxed, turned to his squad standing in formation behind and barked a few orders. His men relaxed and, without pause, mounted and waited.

Rab'k surveyed the scene around himself as he mounted his horse, held by the bridle by one of Fern'o's men.

I wonder how this surprise is going to affect my loving sister and brother?

Mano'n knew they were coming. He knew when Baalsa'n's squad of specialists cleared the mountain pass. At first, he thought he should leave but then he decided he had no place to run.

Interesting situation, I think. There's no doubt Baalsa'n is unhappy with the results so far in this charade. I've deliberately avoided involvement since Monsh'a's arrival. Rab'k and Voravia, despite her underlying subterfuge, have gained nothing by being who they are. Attempting to subvert Baalsa'n has always been a mistake.

We'll see, I suppose. We'll see.

He waited in his tent. He was in no hurry to stand before Baalsa'n. The last meeting had not gone well and Mano'n fully expected this one to be even worse.

"Ah, Anisah. Can I protect you? Do I need to?" He talked aloud to no one. He felt helpless again. There were other times; other places he night have stayed and been happy. But Baalsa'n had eliminated those opportunities as they arose.

I'm no longer want these wars; these episodes of attack on the Al-Esfer'n are fruitless. But how can I get away from Baalsa'n? How can I avoid this idiocy? Why now, after all these years of working as an integral part of Baalsa'n's armies and his efforts, am I not enthusiastic about being here?

Can it be my daughter? Can it be that after all these worlds with various women, I long for something that is closer to my heart? How strange to admit I'm disillusioned but I think I am. How strange I feel now. I'm without fear and, most of all, hatred. Can I endure not being a part of that and, more importantly, can I help Anisah survive? How can I possibly do that?

Questions. All I have at this moment are the questions I've never asked myself before. For this brief moment, I wonder what is going to happen when I stand before Baalsa'n and his anger.

Maybe I no longer care.

Voravia had her problems. She was running out of room for her secret standing army. She was always busy shuffling all her creatures around to obtain more room to warehouse them, to keep them hidden from everyone else and to try to continue her creation process. She was frustrated by any interruption.

Strange, when I thought I would go crazy because I had nothing to do, I would have welcomed these tasks. But now that time is running away too swiftly, I'm so tired I can hardly hold my eyes open, even at midday. What is this change in Baalsa'n? Why is he calling another sibling meeting after all these years? Why is he sending his personal guard to bring us into this sudden meeting? Does he consider us prisoners?

Earlier, she was bustling about, giving orders and just trying to maintain. Then these troops appeared near the Coma't road and were headed toward her castle. Earlier her people warned her the squad of soldiers was coming, but she didn't know the reason, nor really cared.

But now she had received the missive telling her she was commanded to go to the Baalsa'n's palace.

Back into the desert. Of course, that's something I'm excited about. I've too much to do. I'll not go. I'll just explain I'm too busy preparing for war. Which is true actually, but maybe with a slant I alone know about. This stupid trip will place a delay on what I need to do. I sense the time to act is drawing close. I have to be prepared and be in position to benefit the most from my effort. If I'm not here, I may miss that opportunity.

I would like to turn my Akab'r loose and allow them to destroy these ants. But I can't. I just can't. I'm not ready.

So she was standing now, watching the guard approach. She decided regretfully she must go. She turned from the window and walked through the castle to her dressing rooms. The small Hundr'a were scurrying about trying to pack those things needed for her trip. She barged in and, of course, two of them were arguing about some trivial decision. She had to deal with that and push these idiots to finish before the soldiers arrived.

Strange, I miss Mord and Sesk. They finally became somewhat efficient and accomplished some things without asking me a thousand questions. I wonder what happened to them. I wonder if they're still following Anisah to try and kill her. I wonder how close they have come. If they failed entirely, why haven't they returned. H-m-m-m? Maybe they had no reason.

She shook her head to clear it of these thoughts.

Wasting time with that. Need to think about how I'm going to avoid tragic outcomes in this meeting with my father. As though I really care what he wants; actually never did. But I have to make him believe I'm working on the effort and have the desire to fulfill his.

She watched the preparations for only a moment and then decided she must verify her instructions were going to be taken to her new groups. She needed some certainty they were going to be attended as she commanded. She walked down the stairs to the first subterranean cavern beneath the castle. She followed one of the paths, with the opening to it camouflaged to make it appear unused, until she reached the first chamber.

The chamber was huge, as were many beneath these mountains. It was not much different than the others except it was the closest to her dwelling and was easily furnished with the necessities for what she kept there.

She walked directly to Sumt'r, the old gang leader, who stood rigidly at attention as did all the other Akab'r in this chamber. Their stance had nothing to do with her presence because these creatures maintained this posture as part of their nature. She understood this and felt safe somehow.

She gave Sumt'r responsibility for this battalion because he was experienced with command and felt no qualms about destroying others.

"Are your men aware there is a need to be silent until I return?" she asked. She casually glanced at this large contingent of her new troops. She smiled at the knowledge she had thousands of these creatures at arms length and had them under her command.

"Yes, Mistress," Sumt'r instantly came awake and answered.

"Are there any problems with this group, or any of the other, with understanding what I've commanded?" she glared at him as she asked.

"No, Mistress."

"I will be away from the castle for a short time. I have no idea how long, but my command stands until I release you and the others," she made her pronouncement with deliberation. "See that this and the other groups comply with these orders."

"Yes, Mistress."

Voravia nodded her head, looked around at her troops again, turned and walked back to the simple chamber below her dwelling. She covered the stairs quickly and entered the hallways above. She looked into her personal chambers and noted her items for travel were no longer there.

"Suppose I should make myself available to these pawns of Baalsa'n and allow them to escort me to Esclar'e. Been a while, thankfully, since I've walked those halls," she rambled a bit though no one was about. "This ought to be exciting."

She laughed and walked to meet her visitors.

BAALSA'N'S RAGE

Baalsa'n sat in the darkness, alone. He held his head in his open hand, leaning heavily to help curb his anger. He stood, as he had on several recent instances, threw his great robe around his shoulders and then abruptly sat again. His throne shuddered under the impact.

He was not pleased. He swore softly to the gods he didn't believe in, raised his head and looked around the darkened, great hall. He was disappointed but wasn't going to display that. His anger far exceeded any concern he had for things past. He intended to rectify the problems his spies had told him about and he intended to do that quickly.

Aerolan, and this planet, should have been destroyed by now and they should have moved on to their next goal. He intended to determine why that had not happened.

Someone, or possibly several someones, was going to suffer for this transgression, for this failure.

Yet he couldn't believe, secretly, his own children had created this misdirection. It angered but also puzzled him. On each previous encounter on these accursed Al-Esfer'n worlds, he managed to have some of his offspring assist in the destruction. He thought he'd planned and provided the same prospects for this one.

Yet, he knew. He almost couldn't believe it, but he knew that premise had failed him here. He waited for them impatiently.

What is wrong with my people? Why haven't we finished this already? Who are these others with magical powers? There's never been that problem before — that I can remember. They are so young! Who are they? Curse Kalbra'n and his brood! What has he done? Where did he find these magicians?

I'm going to find an answer even if I have to kill everyone myself. Where

411

are my children? They should be here by now. Why are things not going as planned?

He suddenly stood and strode across the dark marble floor toward the massive doors isolating this room. In mid-crossing, he stopped and held his hand to his forehead a moment, spun around and stomped back to the throne. He pushed back the ferocious desire to destroy. To rip asunder this mountain and personally ravage this land, this planet and these incorrigible people who inhabited this horrid little world. His hatred for the Al-Esfer'n raged through his thoughts and he slammed his fist down onto the arm of the seat, almost tearing it loose.

After a moment he rose and walked toward the door again. Part of the way there, he stopped. Looked up toward the small crystalline windows, gleaming with what little light leaked through into this hall. He had no love for light and had designed this castle accordingly.

He raised both arms with fist clinched and roared, shouted his anger so loudly hangings on walls throughout the mountain refuge shook. The whole mountain vibrated with his anger and his power.

From a short distance away, Kalbra'n, staying as close to Esclar'e as possible, felt the disturbance and smiled. He had done much to surprise his ancient foe and he was pleased he was more effective than he thought he would be. Baalsa'n's anger was a good sign.

These three children, encouraged by the Al-Esfer'n and their will to succeed, were such a valuable addition to Kalbra'n's force; he felt it unlikely the success of this dramatic attempt would be successful without them. He thought it strange their presence had been kept secret this long – and apparently no one knew yet who, what or where they were. Even he lost track occasionally.

Baalsa'n heard his guards marching through the hallways before they arrived.

He, sitting in the shadows, was concentrating on what should be done about the incompetence of these five he summoned. He didn't understand what was stopping the progress they made before the last few periods.

He would have none of this. Not now. Not when he might have Kalbra'n and his group cornered here. Narhtrae wasn't the only planet created by the Al-Esfer'n's efforts, but it was the strongest.

He had withdrawn centuries ago and vowed to return to avenge that retreat. He thought of it as a loss and couldn't allow it to stand. The Om-Esfer'n were counting on him to bring justice by destroying this Al-Esfer'n outrage. The abominations who inhabited this world, and the others still in existence, must be destroyed and the Al-Esfer'n should be included in that obliteration.

He waited and listened, ready to upbraid his leaders for their lack of success.

They walked through the doors. Mano'n and Voravia noticing the doors were missing, turned and smiled at one another. Baalsa'n noticed their humor from his shadowy throne and made note to ask what they thought was amusing.

They all shuffled across and found seats in front of the throne, sat and waited.

"Monsh'a. What is the status of this war? Why haven't you moved more vigorously against the miserably small force I've heard about? What is holding you back?"

"Sir, I must admit ware struggling with these people for some reason. But, Rab'k found the movement of his troops over the mountains hindered by traps set by intruders into our territory.

413

So we were unable to have an opportunity to mesh our troops into a composite unit as soon as we wanted.

We've also experienced difficulty in our recruitment plans. There is some force and a small support group that singly attacks various points of return for our people. Our squads are attacked and the captives liberated. The strangest part of these attacks is the seeming disappearance of the captives and, in some cases, the squad attacking us. We have no answer for those tactics," Monsh'a looked around at Rab'k, who shook his head slightly but nodded his agreement. Baalsa'n could see Monsh'a was hesitant to admit that last bit of information.

"But the overall preparation is almost complete. Rab'k and I now agree this is the best time for an attack. The other force seems as weak as we anticipated but more wily than expected. But, by the sheer size of our troops, we should gain enough ground to completely annihilate these small squads, even if they join together for our attacks. Rab'k and I recommend an assault now."

"Monsh'a, you and Rab'k should follow your suggestion. It isn't necessary to wait for me. You particularly have been here before. What did we do wrong that time?" Baalsa'n asked calmly. Monsh'a didn't expect the calmness and in trying to explain, stumbled a bit before continuing. He hadn't expected a review of the past.

"We delayed too long and the Aerolan were able to recruit other nations, sir," Monsh'a answered, looking again at the others waiting. They gave him an impassive nod. At least, Mano'n did. He was the only one there before.

"What happened? What happened, Monsh'a?" Baalsa'n leaned forward, raising himself so the others could view his face. He was angry and it showed.

"We lost and you, sir, had to leave without accomplishing what you came here for," Monsh'a added, head bowed.

"Exactly! We lost. Does anyone here know whether these

people have found the *ransect'r*? I understand Borny'a is still alive; he would know about them and is probably in league with these upstarts. Has anyone seen to it to rid us of some of these old soldiers? What about Vil'n? What about Turm'l, his brother?" Baalsa'n asked.

Rab'k looked up hopefully. Baalsa'n noticed the movement.

"What? What do you have to say? Baalsa'n growled, glaring at Rab'k, eyes gleaming with malice.

"I killed Vil'n when I retrieved the book from Garv'n, the book that explained where the Ahar'n is hidden." Rab'k spoke hesitantly. "I killed him." He tried to be smug, but he was afraid.

"Well, that's something. Good for you, boy." Are there any other pieces of news you haven't shared with me or my messengers?"

"No, Sir," Rab'k mumbled. Baalsa'n chose to ignore him after that, realizing, once again, the boy wasn't up to the tasks. He needed to talk to Rena'x about why this was true.

I think I should have rid myself of this little nuisance years ago. He's too impetuous and foolhardy. I'll need to see to it he's eliminated in some future battle. Ridiculous waste of good material. A son of mine with no intelligence; just a sense of malice that rules everything he does.

"Voravia, how have you contributed? Lately?" he turned to his daughter quickly, surprising her with the blunt approach.

"I have been raiding some of the villages in the western sector of Aerolan, destroying food reserves, capturing some of the village males for modification to Maah'e and trying to disrupt any use of the people in that area to assist Anisah and her young friends," she answered nonchalantly. She no longer cared about this stupid war and wasn't very elegant in her attempts to convince Baalsa'n. He noticed this change. She didn't seem to have the same eagerness as before and he wondered why.

"Are you actually going to sit there and lay to me?" he shouted at her. Her casual attitude disappeared in that instance, fear evident on her face. "You've done nothing of importance. What ex-

415

actly have you done. My scouts say you have some of your own variety of the Maah'e. Where did you learn the secrets to their creation? How many have you made?"

She sat, her eyes wide, showing how startled she was. She sat, mouth moving slightly, stunned and unable to respond quickly.

"I . . . I have a few. I use them as my bodyguards. They have been on a few forays into the area I mentioned, mostly startling the natives and destroying things I tell them to. Drang'm gave me the secret. It was easy to convince him to do so. I implored him and he relented," she was shivering when she spoke, her voice quavering.

"I could see no harm in that. I felt it would allow me to protect the territory south of my castle, especially since Monsh'a and Rab'k have taken most of the territory just east of there. At least, that's what I thought."

Baalsa'n was standing now, listening to her, saying nothing. His brow wrinkled at the mention of Drang'm, but he said nothing. He knew Voravia used her gender to help her discover things. He knew she was still lying to him. But he decided to let it be. Since he knew what she was doing, he assumed he could commandeer the resources he suspected she was concealing. There was no need to make an issue of that at this meeting. Maybe later he might use it for his own benefit.

But the mention of Mano'n's daughter did arouse his suspicions. He felt that information to be a new wrinkle in an old problem.

"You should be able to contribute a bit more. Your magical skills could be used where the current fighting is the most active. You will start learning where those sites are and go to the points of combat. You can, if nothing else, change men into the Maah'e warriors we need – since you have taken the time to learn that skill. But you can no longer just sit and watch. You will participate, or lose more than you can imagine," Baalsa'n spoke calmly, showing none of his obvious anger. He knew he could use the

416

woman, his daughter, to accomplish many things the men could not.

"Mano'n?" he turned slowly to look at his eldest.

The one who fought for him in the past and was victorious over the Al-Esfer'n and destroyed many of the worlds they found throughout this extended mission. He just stood and looked at him for a moment.

Mano'n didn't flinch or look away, but held his gaze steady, staring back at Baalsa'n with no sign of fear.

"I noticed earlier you find our situation humorous. Is that appropriate considering our current status? Do you and Voravia share an amusing sense of curiosity about what is happening?" Baalsa'n asked, looking toward the two but not incriminating them in anger. Though he was seething.

"Your daughter?" Baalsa'n asked very quietly, turned to find his throne, walked to it and sat. "What about Anisah? Maybe can you tell me what she's about."

"What do you want to know?" Mano'n was more than casual; he was insolent. Baalsa'n found it difficult to restrain himself.

"Do you want to know where she is? I don't know. Do you want to know how powerful she is? I don't know. Do you want to bring her here? I doubt you can do that. I can't. I've tried.

Does that tell you want you want, or do you want me to tell you she may be the most powerful Om-Esfer'n who ever lived, including you. She may be our downfall. I think so," he spoke without anger. He never hesitated. He was being totally truthful. That presented a problem for Baalsa'n and he felt his rage building

"Are you trying to tell me you've lost control of her? Are you so presumptuous as to admit your own shortcomings? Why didn't you bring her to me when she was young and unaware? How could you let her mother influence her to the extent she turns away from what she was born to be and is now defending the Al-Esfer'n? How can you sit there and admit all that?"

Baalsa'n's voice began to grow louder and louder with each question. "You say I probably cannot force her to come here? How can you make such a claim?"

"Because, she isn't afraid of you," Mano'n answered. "Nor of any of us." He nonchalantly waved his hand at his siblings and Monsh'a. "And she has help. Powerful help."

"Who? The Al-Esfer'n?" Baalsa'n almost shouted, turned his head to stare up at one of the openings above, then he laughed.

"No, much worse. She has friends. Two close friends who have developed, somehow, abilities far beyond any of the children the Al-Esfer'n have ever had.

One is another Areb'l, only much more powerful, as Rab'k discovered. Another is apparently a descendant of Kalbra'n. I'm not certain of that. Then there is Borny'a, Jond'r, Acron'n, Turm'l, who recently joined them, and Garv'n, with wealth we can't even approach on this world. Our magic has been nullified.

The most intense part is the worst. They, not the Al-Esfer'n, have decided we will not take this world. They are intent on destroying us now, for themselves and for others who might follow. If they discover, and I suspect they have, how to contact the other countries across their seas and align with them, we certainly will have no more success than before. It probably will be worse.

No, I don't think we have a chance to win now and may lose a great deal more than we ever have," Mano'n finished.

He stood, without budging, looking neither right nor left at the others in the room, staring at the walls behind Baalsa'n, staring at nothing, as he spoke. He showed no fear, nor regret.

He knew he probably had sealed his fate. Death was something he could accept. Deep inside, he was pleased with his daughter and would probably try to protect her if the incident arose where he needed to. He didn't mention that, but he felt it.

"You have deserted our aim! You are a coward!" Baalsa'n was standing and walking rapidly across the short distance between Mano'n and himself. He stopped short of physically attacking his

418

son, but he wanted to. He wanted to slash at him, rip him into oblivion, but he couldn't. He knew if he did it would show weakness and fear on his part. He knew that would make things worse than they were at this point, particularly with the others in the room.

"Not really, father," Mano'n said calmly. "We never had such an aim. It was always you."

With that, Baalsa'n could no longer contain himself. He struck Mano'n across the face. The man offered no resistance, but did remain standing, exhibiting no will to fight back.

Baalsa'n backed away a bit. He wanted to totally obliterate the man. This deserter. This kind of disobedience he never experienced before with his children anywhere else he had pursued the Al-Esfer'n, not even Mano'n was this obstinate before.

Mano'n was always the one he was proudest of. Here he stood in defiance. Mano'n was protecting his daughter. Baalsa'n was not so foolish he didn't realize why. He was just surprised and, strangely, it affected him.

He stood a moment longer staring belligerently at his son. Then suddenly he turned and walked away. Everyone in the room, including Mano'n, was surprised. Baalsa'n sat, placed his chin in his hand resting on the arm and looked at his son, his eldest son. He finally looked away and shook his head.

"You will no longer be my son. You are banished from this moment on and will remain here on this world when we destroy it. You will no longer be involved with what we do, and will have no further say in how we do these things. You will no longer possess any powers to free yourself.

Your counsel and your life are forfeit. But I will not kill you myself. You will watch as death overwhelms this world and you, at the end.

I am going to send you somewhere no one can find you. You will not be able to communicate with anyone where you are because I'm going to send you where there is no civilization. We are

419

through forever," Baalsa'n methodically stated Mano'n's indictment.

"Thank you, father. May you be always in my memory, too," Mano'n spoke softly and bowed his head in deference.

Then he vanished.

At a skirmish on the front near Hang'm in eastern Aerolan, Anisah paused and looked around her. The area was calm at this moment, but she was busy all afternoon and glad when dusk approached and the enemy halted their harassment.

But something had just changed in her world. She felt it, a raw sense of the demise of something relevant to her. At first, she thought of Pet'r, but knew that wasn't what bothered her. Something was different on this small world. Something that affected her more than she would have thought.

Mano'n?

Somehow she knew he was gone.

THERE IS WAR

Decisions. There are choices, many choices, to make in a life. There are multiple reasons to make one, or another, choice. Each choice is unique — but can be undone, both by lack of perspective, knowledge and sometimes chance.

We each are required to make these choices under myriad circumstances, most of these might not be consciously selected at the moment of realization.

War is one of those instances, one of those choices. War is one of the saddest of all choices, yet the decision to engage in conflict is often decided on a whim of some person, or persons, expected to be leaders of people. This choice is not a casual one, but is assumed — by those selecting this one — to be a very natural thing.

It can be undone, for the justification for war involves many more lives than those deciding. But war is often, and sadly, instigated casually, as though there is some rationale that justifies it.

It ultimately is not a game played on a board in some quiet surroundings. It is enacted on a field of death. No one gains by those lives lost. No one can actually justify the outcome. War cannot be entered as a legitimate choice, unless it is a necessary defense against an aggressor.

But now our story has led us to this, an inevitable and irreversible decision by the few to involve the many. Our three young heroes find they must proceed along this deadly path. Their youth leaves them without a perspective, little knowledge and the chance they, and a host of others, will not survive.

But that chance must be taken for this war — because of the persistency of the adversary — cannot be avoided. An adversary in ignorance who knowingly makes a decision - invokes a choice - for everyone who might die.

Many will die and, still, there is no justification. Only hope, thereby chance, exists . . .

Rab'k and Monsh'a, with his wizard, and Voravia returned to the common military encampment, concerned now with their own welfare and the anger of Baalsa'n.

Voravia, wanting nothing more to do with the others, traveled alone to her castle.

Rab'k, knowing his sister was making plans of her own, made no attempt to contact her, nor interfere with what she was going to be doing. He believed her plans were to dominate the battles along the southern and western regions, but he also suspected Monsh'a and he weren't out of the question as far as what she intended to do. He sent spies to watch her more closely.

He did make one excursion of his own to Varspree to listen to the talk in the bars of the city. He, having lived in the south before, was comfortable with being there and felt he could learn something from the gossip.

While he was there, he made a quick trip to the encampment of the Aerolan to determine their status. He did so as a normal village man acting as though he wanted to join their forces.

He saw Geth'n once and managed to avoid him. But, more importantly, he learned the girl, his niece according to Voravia, was away with the strong one, Pet'r. That left the rebel forces with less magical capability and with less leadership than before. There was no detail about where they were, or why they left, but he thought it an opportune time to deal with this rabble and rushed back to his major camp to discuss it with Monsh'a.

He and Monsh'a made a common decision for themselves and recognized they needed to combine their skills and forces to have a chance, now that the south was rising with some strength, to overcome the lesser forces.

Their plan was simple. Now was the time to attack. They launched this without further delay.

Monsh'a and his troops invaded the central plains south of Coma't and east of Varspree with intent to push toward Tariny. Rab'k brought his forces more directly toward the south, entering the prairie country near TrailEnd. The camps were opposite each other just north of the road that ran between Coma't and Valhonal, until Monsh'a main force turned eastward toward Ofan'n.

That portion of Monsha's forces already in the east, previously used to recruit, received their orders and hurried through the night to arrive at the eastern portion of the plains just south of Caliste, while Monsh'a pushed across the prairies and into the hills north of Pull'r. The sound of them marching steadily across the land was thunderous and shocked those from both Ofan'n and Caliste and those near the roads from Safe Inlet, causing more and greater fear than before in those regions.

The troops marching southward finally halted, concealing themselves in a dry area near Hang'm, a village where they could get supplies, and waited. The holding camp was large, covering acres of largely uninhabited, infertile land. It was dry there at this time of the year and it took hours for the dust to settle after the force ended their quick journey and settled in to wait for further orders.

Later, the encampment swelled as Monsh'a's main force arrived and was further stretched across the open fields just north of the low hills that lay from northwest to southeast near Pull'r, to accommodate more unique troops. There were no camp followers, but there were a large number of natives who would become Maah'e, captured earlier and forced to the battlefront along with the rest. A compound for these was quickly assembled in the center of the larger camp. They waited for the transfiguration, most of them unaware of what was to come.

The people of Hang'm, and some from Caliste, rushed away, deserting their towns and fleeing eastward, running for the coast south of Tayrun. Those people caught north of Caliste managed to escape into Doom's Woods and the Forest of Galyd'n. There was nowhere else to go.

Those who arrived at the coast were told they should travel toward the south because most of Monsh'a's troops had been destroyed, or chased away, by someone who attacked not long before. Most of these refugees continued moving that way. They knew so little and there was overwhelming fear and concern for their lives.

It was futile to try to stand against this brutish army. The residents in the area, as well as most small towns just south of Doom's Woods simply weren't able to resist. They were harassed, the men kidnapped and taken away, the women imprisoned and dragged along and the children and older men captured and, often, murdered. So, running was their only answer.

As the day's heat rose and began melting the fog that blanketed the lowlands, the Aerolan scouts began arriving at the Ralff'r castle. Their horses, lathered with foam, walked into the courtyard, collapsing and unable to drink. As they stopped, some of the animals died because they were driven so hard. The men tumbled to the ground and lay prostrate for quite a while.

The guards, and a number of those who tried to help, carried them to the makeshift infirmary. Some took the horses, still standing, away toward the stables. A few of those were eliminated, but most were saved though weakened.

Borny'a rushed to the infirmary to determine the cause for the great haste.

"They're coming!" one whispered. "They've already reached the hills south of Hang'm and are camping there. They've sent out their own scouts and I barely escaped." He mumbled something else but Borny'a couldn't understand it. Under the circumstances, he wished he understood all the young man was trying to tell him.

The others, arriving from other points across the central prairie told similar tales. Borny'a only hesitated a moment after learning as much detail as he could.

I think we don't have enough of an army, just young boys, old men and only a few soldiers, to fight against this kind of assault. But we have to take our people to where they will fight, and possibly die quickly, to save what we have, or we'll all perish.

He had the alarm horns blaring so the other squad leaders

424

would be aware of the dangers surrounding them. He waited impatiently until they arrived.

Geth'n who had been out inspecting the training areas was one of the first to arrive.

"What is it? Why the alarm?" he asked as he jumped down from his horse and walked toward Borny'a.

"They are coming. A massive attack, as best I can determine, coming from more than one direction. The largest, I think, is coming from the northeast directly for here, or Varspree. Another large one is north of Tariny, advancing rapidly. We need to send troops to each location, or they will be on us before we can react," he shouted to his friend, as they came together in the center of the courtyard now bursting with activity. "We need to see if our plans are going to work with the distribution of troops we have. Of course, we all face the consequences if we are wrong."

"You're right, but let's go talk to the rest of the runners who arrived. We need to try to interfere with some of these attacks before this enemy gets too close," Geth'n answered his friend, striding beside him. "I'll take an advance group to the front northeast of Varspree. I can get there fairly quickly with a force sufficient to harass them and slow them down until we can get more of our people into the area."

The air shimmered where Geth'n was standing only a moment before.

Borny'a, without hesitation, yelled to a guard, "Rouse all the military officers here, we need to prepare for an attack on the castle." He ran up the stairs to reach the upper levels around the walls and, on reaching the principal lookout post, burst through the door. All inside jumped to attention.

"Captain, we must intensify our watch. We believe there is to be an imminent attack. Be prepared!" he gave his orders quickly, turned and jogged down a ramp into the castle.

He stopped in the main chamber, commanding a lieutenant of the guard walking by.

"You there! Get the women, children and elderly to safety as we have planned! Do not tarry! There is imminent danger about! Send runners to the settlements to the south and warn them to build whatever defenses they can. An attack will probably begin soon. If they have plans for escape, they should initiate them and begin the work necessary to put them in place. Tell them we'll try to hold the attack back, but we are going to have trouble doing so."

The young soldier was trotting beside Borny'a and listening intently. He nodded his head as he ran.

"Sir, who will be in charge while you're away!" the lieutenant asked as he ran along.

"The captain of the guard unless Anisah returns soon. I'll tell him he's in command. Now be off with you and, when you see Siarra, inform her what's happening. She can also help with the organization, protection of everyone and the evacuation. Now I'm going to the front, with several squads, to help Geth'n."

Borny'a was running toward the stable, while giving these orders, to gather his mount and race to where he thought Geth'n probably was. He left the stunned young officer who paused a moment, then changed directions to find Siarra and the others in charge of the evacuation groups.

Borny'a, leading his horse to the officers' guard post, stopped briefly to place the captain of the guards in command of the castle operations, unless Anisah arrived. Afterward, he jumped onto his horse and galloped out the gate, stopping briefly to give another command.

"Close the gates when I'm gone. Don't open them until the refugees begin arriving," he shouted at the guard at the gate, without dismounting. He watched for the guard's nod he understood, turned his horse and galloped away.

But, on his way, Borny'a needed to stop to confer with Jond'r and his brother. He rode hard, pulled into their most northern training camp, slid smoothly from his mount and pushed his way into the command tent.

Jond'r talking to some of his young officers, turned to see who entered. He stopped talking, excused his charges. Borny'a quickly explained the circumstance.

"The time is now. We've been warned there are troops advancing from Coma't, headed toward Tariny. Geth'n has already taken a number of soldiers to Pull'r to cut off the advance of Ravelan troops there. But I need you and Acron'n to gather the troops who are most capable and take them as quickly as you can to a point south of Valhonal to establish a position for fighting against that attack. The information we have indicates this group to be mostly desert soldiers, probably Rab'k is there.

I'm going to our encampment near Pull'r to help intercept that advance. I'll try to get Geth'n to come help you move the men as quickly as he can – he'll be able to find you wherever you are. You might run to Varspree first and conscript some of the men there – they may be a rough bunch but they know how to fight in close combat.

We've no idea yet of the strength of the enemy, but I've been informed they are organized and quickly approaching from both the north as well as the northeast," he took a short breath, then continued, "But we will, we must, use guerrilla tactics again. We haven't the manpower to withstand a highly trained military force. We have to hope that Anisah, Pet'r and Turm'l are successful and arrive soon with reinforcements. But until then, it's up to us. I've got to continue to the eastern front, but please move as soon as you can to protect Tariny and here."

He looked to each one of the brothers and saw the strength there. These are two good men. They'll get their job done as best they can.

I can only hope that is enough.

"I must leave now. Good fortune to you with those approaching Tariny," He turned, left the tent quickly, jumped astride his horse and galloped away.

Jond'r looked at his brother, "Seems it has begun. Let's get moving."

They left the tent together and rushed to their separate groups.

Geth'n crashed through the entry of the command tent near where the major fight would be. The officers gathered there jumped back in surprise, drawing weapons as they moved,.

Geth'n ignored them and pushed his way to the center of the room.

"This attack can be a small frontal one to determine our strength, or it could be a push to overwhelm us. Prepare your forces. We have the enemy coming from the northeast and the northwest. The forces on the west are mostly desert people and will be more aware of what we can and cannot do, so we'll probably send a third of our troops to stall them; those in training probably with Jond'r and Acron'n.

I, and probably Borny'a, will be here with you and your forces. This Ravelan force here probably presents the greatest danger we will face today, assuming the attack is imminent.

Gentlemen, we seem to be at war. Don't forget all Borny'a and Turm'l have taught you. Don't forget the signals we agreed on. If you fall under extreme situations where you are, retreat. We can fight again another day. Try to stand today and we are lost.

We must maintain our guerrilla methods. We aren't large enough, or capable of holding against the enemy, in this battle. Until we get help from other sources, we are too weak to withstand the attacks to come. Spare your people.

Maybe, just maybe, Anisah will return and she will have some of our allies with her. Maybe then we can rise above this onslaught and push these people back. But, you know, we can't fight in a true battle now.

If you see Borny'a, tell him I have gone toward those eastern hills and will be making some attempts at slowing down the Ravelan. When he reaches me, I will attempt to come to the aid of those in the west. Be strong. I know all of you and I trust you will be intelligent and do the right thing.

Good fortune to you."

He turned and vanished.

He moved to near the top of the hills behind which the enemy camp lay. He lay down and crawled to the top of the ridge and peered over. He couldn't believe the extent and massiveness of the encampment. The Ravelan were walking about, obviously relaxed and ready to go. If these were a sample of the numbers to come, Geth'n knew his people were in serious trouble.

What have we been cursed with? How far does this camp stretch? How many soldiers are about to pour over our poor people? How will we stand up to them and are there any Maah'e with them?

He pulled his head down, rolled onto his back and strangely remembered how he and Pet'r had walked along the roads, not too far to the south, thinking themselves off on a simple journey of discovery.

So little time has passed since then. Look at us now. Are we lost?

He started to rise when a small enemy scouting party galloped to the top of the hill just above behind him and stopped at the ridge. Geth'n rolled beneath some of thicker bushes and hid while listening to what the soldiers were saying. But the language was foreign to him and he couldn't understand them.

Then the riders laughed. He recognized the laugh as belonging to someone who felt confident. They knew this day would be an easy one for them. They sat for a moment longer talking among themselves, finally turned, walked their horses down the other side of the hill, chatting and certainly at ease with the situation.

Our only hope is their attitude they are invincible. How can we use that? Is there anything we have that can stop them? Of course there is. But she's away. Anisah may be are only hope, and she's not here.

He rolled down the hill a little further and, from his vantage point, tried to determine the most protected places down the hill and into the low hills to the south. He was able to discover a few culverts and stands of trees he thought would be protective. He needed to return to his officers to detail what he saw and report honestly what he thought about the situation and what they should, or could, do to make it better.

He disappeared.

Borny'a rode into camp just after Geth'n left. The officers were still in the main command tent as he walked in, noticing the stress already affecting them. It showed in their eyes and on their faces.

"Men!" he shouted as he entered. All of them jumped and seemed ready to flee, but they stood where they were. There were no friendly greetings. Things were much too serious.

"You must not allow the situation to deter you from what you must do. What did Geth'n tell you?"

They explained Geth'n told them to deploy their men, along the ridge but spread throughout the immediate area. They should employ the guerrilla tactics they were recently taught, rather than attacking full force.

"That's correct. Nip at them; tear small chunks away and maybe we can divert their attention until we can get help. There are no more troops, from our camps, coming from the south. There is another attack on the western roads approaching Tariny that must be slowed, or dealt with, by those too young and inexperienced to help here anyway.

Our larger hope lies with Anisah, Pet'r and Turm'l being able to bring some help from Habenlein, at least. We just need to hold as long as we can. Your people have had training from good men. I have confidence you are capable of accomplishing what we have to.

Now! Let's get our people out there and ready!"

At that moment, Geth'n entered the tent. He walked to Borny'a first and asked a few questions. Borny'a revealed the

430

problems in the west and asked if he could help with that deployment before this battle began. Geth'n looked at his friend questioning the request but nodded his head.

"Wait a moment, gentlemen. I have some information I need to share with you before I leave again. There are certain areas where I think we will have enough concealment to be a hindrance to the advance of the enemy. If you will gather just outside, I can point out what I've seen."

He stepped backwards through the tent exit, turned, walked to a small bare area, stopped and drew a circle in the loose soil.

"They are here. There are small hills just this side of them," he drew a line beside the circle. "Those are here." He drew a smaller circle to the right of the first. A small murmur came from the officers. Geth'n waited for that to stop.

"I know this is daunting. I know we are going to be overwhelmed. I won't deny that. But, we have ourselves, our loved ones, our country, and, if I understand Kalbra'n well enough, our world to protect, if we can."

All the officers turned to look at Borny'a who only nodded his head. Then they turned to listen to Geth'n again, faces more somber than before.

Geth'n continued, "I need to go briefly assist our troops sent to blunt the attack of another force advancing on Tariny, but I'll return as soon as I'm able. We should not consider this a suicide mission. We have our own strengths we can use and I, myself, will be at the front protecting you and your people. As soon as I'm back, I will situate myself here," he pointed to a spot on the side of the hill that lay between the enemy and these people.

"I'll be traveling to each of you to give instructions, if I see danger you can't. I believe we can hold here and not allow this enemy to take our lives and homes from us. I believe in you. Before we go, I want to thank you for being here."

Geth'n stepped back and deferred to Borny'a. Then he disappeared again.

431

"Gentlemen, you have your instructions and you have your signal codes for seeking help. Do not try to ignore your dangers. We will support each of you to the fullest," Borny'a added.

"Munc'a, I think your squads and yours, Traci'a, should protect our western flank. Use the forest and cover of the hills there to harass those troops and don't be afraid to retreat if being compromised. We need you and your people more than we need a victory today. Victories will come in the future."

The officers stood nodding. There were no questions. That pleased Borny'a and Geth'n. They felt the training given these men was working better than expected. There was some level of confidence showing through the fear they would naturally feel. Fear was a protector in this case – it made everyone more cautious.

In the distance, a horn blew then more followed. The call to war.

It began.

The enemy moved forward slowly in large bands. The Maah'e, rose , shoulder to shoulder over the nearest ridge in one line that stretched along the top from the north to the lowlands of the south. The Ravelan tagged along behind in lines of men with skills that far exceeded the small force they were attacking.

The thunderous cadence of the drums in the distance, the boots of the leading groups stomping methodically, made the ground shudder with each step. The sameness of the faces of this enemy no one understood. That they marched without fear, without excitement, without concern for the band of fearful soldiers of Aerolan was unnerving and spread the apprehension.

As the line of Maah'e reached the ravines and gorges in the hillsides, they veered around them causing splits in their lines. Borny'a noticed that variation created gaps in the Maah'e line.

We might be able to use those 'breaks' to our advantage.

Then it marching stopped and silence covered the land. The dust fell from the air as though caught by a giant beast, sucking it

432

to back to earth.

A hush settled over it all. A rattle here, an officer yelling there. The field was held in suspension. The heartbeats of the soldiers, in both armies, were almost audible. The tension crackled like quick-fire.

They waited.

Borny'a threw up his right arm and gave a signal repeated along the front line. Suddenly, the Aerolan line broke apart and the soldiers moved obliquely against the enemy, never intending to confront the line head-on. They attacked quickly then scattered into the ravines and into thickly forested areas.

This was not going to be a standard battle – not a battlefield of carnage and waste, or of heroes. The plan was, as it had been for some time, a divisive one. Hit and run was the intent of the deployment. The center and main companies began to move backward with a planned commotion that wasn't clear to the un-trained eye.

But the strategy became obvious as time seemed suspended and only ticked with the beat of the drums that now seemed overwhelming. The Aerolan line scrambled away at the rear as the groups behind retreated first, then the central columns and the front lines.

Behind the hills, the enemy commanders sent the signal to ac-celerate the march. The drums increased the cadence and the ro-botic front line picked up the pace. Now they seemed to pour over the ridges and flow into the valley that separated the two lines.

The distance was decreasing rapidly.

Borny'a faced this force before. Strangely, nothing had changed in all those years. His best guess about what he saw was an assumption the Ravelan, nor the Maah'e, were involved in any new wars in all those years. They seemed slow and immobile though he knew they would remain dangerous. But he recon-sidered methods to use the speed of deployment to the Aerolan advantage.

As the enemy line approached, oblivious of their surroundings, Borny'a raised his right hand again, closed his fist and rotated it while pointing it at the approaching enemy.

From their hidden places, small squads rushed into the enemy line from behind, fighting their way through the first echelons as quickly as possible to attack the second layer of men who were mostly Ravelan troops intermingled from their prior assignments with the Maah'e.

These men, sweltering in this humid land, were exhausted and unable to defend themselves well. The Aerolan guerrilla groups slaughtered them where they stood and then hastily retreated back through the first line. Strangely they had little trouble with that leading group of Maah'e.

Borny'a, watching, realized the Maah'e had their marching orders and wouldn't attack, nor come to blows with his men, until it was time to do so. Their commands were absolute and would not deviate. That immobility would help him and his decisions would use that weakness, as he saw it develop.

But, he had no doubts. When the battle intensified, these forward Maah'e troops would be, for all practical purpose, invincible. Whatever he could do to weaken the remainder of the army following was the only plan that seemed to have potential for his people. He didn't believe his group stood a chance with a direct onslaught.

From beyond the hill, a trumpet sequence started the movement of the Maah'e line.

He gave yet another hand signal and those inside the lines, dived into their hiding places and waited for the Maah'e to pass them. This pattern continued throughout the day.

As dusk approached rain began to fall. Horns sounded from the enemy camp, and there was an abrupt halt of the Maah'e. Those not wounded stood and waited for the next command.

The Maah'e were motionless where they stood, but the

434

Ravelan army behind them began to retreat back over the hills, gathering their wounded as they went. The hillside was littered with bodies, some Maah'e, many Ravelan and, sadly, some Aerolan.

Borny'a gave another signal and his guerrilla forces moved quietly back through the lines and returned to camp. Surprisingly, the element of stealth and quick movement had saved many lives. There were almost no casualties within his smaller groups. He called his officers together.

"Now is when we can take advantage of the moment. These Maah'e are halted on the front line and will stand that way until given another order. I want you, Rawn'a, to take a small group and, moving through the ravines, slip over the hilltops and race through the Ravelan portion of the encampment behind these lines. You need to kill every Ravelan officer you can find, then get out. They are the link that ties this force together, weakening that gives us some advantage.

Meanwhile, we need our death squads wandering through the Maah'e encampments, trying to kill the Ravelan officers and some of the Maah'e there. Many of these creature soldiers will not move without the express command to do so. The only problem I can see will be that certain Maah'e have a sense for preservation – at least, their officers perhaps. If any turn your way during these forays, you should back away. There are enough who will stand until they fall over," he was trying to tell them all he could from those long years before and trying to recall what he and others discovered then that might be effective now.

"Mich'r, you will be in charge of those groups. Pick your best lieutenants and send them out dressed in dark clothing. Try to only use swords, or knives, at close range. Tell your men they must avoid standing in front of the Maah'e, always attack from the back. They are dangerous and unpredictable.

We have few choices here. We are being attacked and this force plans to annihilate us. I doubt if anyone here wants that to happen, so I encourage you to think, to plan and to work hard during this effort. It will be terribly difficult; there will be terror and pain. But, I believe, we can hold these forces back long enough for Anisah and Pet'r to bring us some seriously large forces from our allies. If we can do our jobs, they will help us win this day and this war. So, do your best and use what you've learned to the best of your, and your men's, ability."

He dismissed them and they slowly left the command tent, placed closer to the front line than most of the others previous groups. They were going to be the main element for attack in the early hours. Borny'a, watching them leave, had a heavy heart. He knew many of these men would not see another day.

Watching them deploy to effect the attack, Borny'a smiled thinking of the surprise for Monsh'a and his officers – some of which would also not see another day.

But, he knew, tomorrow was to be a very long day, regardless of what he planned.

Later that evening, Geth'n returned and met with Borny'a and a number of the lieutenants chosen for the forward formation in the attack up the hill.

That was one point that bothered them all. Their people would have to fight going up the face of the hills again. The forces they faced were large people and that height difference would be a factor of importance, unfortunately against the Aerolan troops. The rain was still falling, making the grounds on the battlefield slippery and troublesome.

They talked and planned until late in the night and slowly drifted to their areas.

Geth'n and Borny'a sat and talk about other things than war. They told each other tales of their youth, families and their early life. They laughed a little and were solemn at other moments, but they both found sleep difficult and the night passed with little rest.

With trumpets blaring the call to arms, the morning started

436

abruptly at Pull'r. The fields around were soaked beneath with the mud, churned by the movement of men and animals, flowing with each stream of water. The muffled sound of marching, of horses and other animals calling with voices of their own, could be heard from invisible places. The tension mounted quickly.

As Borny'a and Geth'n watched, their army formed in front of them and stood as a barrier against the Ravelan cavalry they would have to battle to start this day.

Through all this activity, the Maah'e stood and ignored the hustle and bustle. Borny'a and Geth'n could now see the line of these monsters and could only shake their heads.

They knew now they desperately needed the help Anisah and Pet'r would bring, or they hoped would arrive. But maybe that was too late now, those present would have to hold this enemy back.

Trumpets blared a second time from the enemy side. The Aerolan troops began to move slowly toward the line they faced. The Maah'e weren't moving. They stood quietly, watching nothing, only waiting to be released.

As the first of Aerolan front reached these robotic soldiers, a single trumpet sounded from atop the hill just to the north of the main contingency of the enemy. The Maah'e came to attention all along their line.

The Aerolan soldiers were carving their way through these monsters until that moment. Then the Maah'e began to move again, slowly, deliberately swinging their swords, prodding with their spears and the slaughter began.

Now, the enemy, no longer immobile, was annihilating everything in its path.

Aerolan's army was being methodically destroyed. There was no haste on the part of the enemy. The simply plowed the fields of men and animals, cutting great swathes through the line they faced.

Trumpets called out from the Aerolan ranks and the next wing

437

of their army moved forward as a bulwark against the large force pushing them into the mud and blood.

But, to no avail, the battle was being lost, not in inches, but in the length of the enemy's swords.

Mangled bodies littered the grounds, blood flowed from men crying out in their death throes as the Maah'e decimated the ones left standing. There was no mercy and no way to fight back. This enemy was invincible.

Geth'n coldly watched as the overwhelming numbers swarmed toward Aerolan's inexperienced army. Monsh'a's beasts were unforgiving and had no fear of death.

The Aerolan troops fell like grain before the scythe, with almost no enemy casualties. Those, along the front, began to lose their courage and flee back through the lines.

As more and more fled, those behind them turned and followed. Soon the Aerolan force was routed and all began to flee. But the Maah'e forged through them, massacring the Aerolan men at will, no one was spared.

It was over before it really started. The rear of the Aerolan troops began to sag, then to run. Fear overtook them. There would not be a victory on this day. In fact, the Aerolan contingent might be completely destroyed unless something was done and soon.

Borny'a looked toward Geth'n who stood struggling with his decisions. Geth'n turned to look back and Borny'a could see defeat on Geth'n's face. He sent a hand signal to the trumpeter.

Retreat! Retreat!

The bugle blew its mournful sound across the open fields and hills. A moment later and an answer came from the opposite camp.

Cease and Desist!

The Maah'e stopped, some in mid-swing, turned about and began marching back up the hill and over.

The Ravelan forces, or what remained, slumped and ground

438

their way ahead of the monsters. There was no celebration from the Ravelan and the Maah'e uttered no sounds.

Anyone left behind on the battlefield alive, trembled at his or her good fortune. All fighting had ceased.

There was only silence and the cries of the dying. There was no enemy.

The sound of the rain falling steadily was little comfort for either side. It slowly washed the blood through the mud into small streams formed at the bottom of the hill and meandered across the last meadow into the forest.

The land bled.

MANO'N'S EXILE

Mano'n held himself quietly as he flew to his destination. He didn't expect he would be injured, but he did expect to be surprised. He waited patiently and could sense the end as it came nearer.

And he *was* surprised.

It was a cold place, desolate, low flowing hills covered in snow, or ice, as far as he could see. Fortunately, Baalsa'n, at least, had allowed him to retain his ability to keep himself alive and, in this case, warm. So he knew he wasn't going to freeze to death.

In order for him to die, he would have to submit to the anger of his father and allow it to happen.

That wasn't part of his plan. But his plan might be much harder to achieve now.

He shook his head and began to walk across the wilderness toward some higher hills he could see just north and a little to the east of where he was. He decided it would take him a few hours, but maybe a few days, to reach the destination.

He assumed, true or not, there were caverns in the hills where he could take refuge, escape the fierce winds and any snow that might fall. Then he might be able to concentrate on his dilemma and deduce a plan to escape.

At the moment, he was fairly certain there would be no escape without help. So he trudged on through the snow, wondering what might be occurring back home.

Not much, I would think. Baalsa'n has trouble on his hands with my siblings. He now isn't certain of an easy conquest of this world, having experienced a small, but decisive defeat, in the past.

It seems obvious he doesn't trust anyone now — he even dressed down Monsh'a and his wizard, Drang'm. A real surprise for those two.

440

Strangely he directly questioned me about Anisah. I've covered and tried to hide all the information he might receive about her. I think he's not even certain the troublemaker is my daughter. Now I've committed, he will never know from me who is.

This little trip to the hills is taking a long time. Could be I'll need to tramp around a while before I find a place of shelter.

Where is this place anyway? Obviously, it's in the northern portion of the planet. Am I on a mainland area? Maybe the Dome, that's certainly a place where I can't easily be found.

He trudged along heading generally in the direction he picked until he came to a break in the weather. Wondering why, he crept forward cautiously until he reached a place where he could see no land, snow covered or otherwise, in front of him. Then he took one step at a time to test the ground below the snow before shifting his weight to that foot.

Suddenly, the ground seemed to give way. Even above the roar of the wind, he could hear a cracking and crunching sound as a strip of snow, going to his left and right, fell away, out of sight. His foot was at the edge of the land at the break.

He leaned over as far as he could and all he saw was water, as far as he could see into the blowing snow, only water.

He pulled back from the edge of what obviously was a high cliff overlooking an ocean, or bay, large enough he could see no boundaries in the distance. He backed away slowly, not knowing whether, or not, the ground he stood on was fragile enough to break and send him plunging into an almost frozen body of water, from which he might not be able to escape. He squinted into the snow battering him as he stood there deciding what he should do, when he noticed, through the snow, a dim but rising landscape not too far away.

Must have veered from my original path. I'll have to be more cautious walking about. But maybe there will be that shelter up there I've been looking for.

He bent into the wind and pushed himself toward the hill. As he neared the bottom, the wind began to slack and the ground seemed clearer of the drifts he had worked against until now.

He decided to stay on the downwind side of the rising terrain as he climbed. It didn't take him long to reach the top, but he backed down a short distance because the wind was so strong he feared being blown into the sea.

He was very close to edge of the cliffs overlooking the water and became more alert to the possibility he was too close. If he looked to the east, and what he could see of the north, of the land, around all sides was only water.

Obviously on a seacoast which may stretch for miles. I can almost wager this place is not on a mainland anywhere. Too easy to escape. So, it must be an island.

But where? Without magic, I am truly exiled with no help. Because no one, except Baalsa'n, knows where I am.

There might be passing ships out there, but it is unlikely. Those icebergs I see on the water are too numerous for traveling by water.

Apparently, I'm magically lost and only magic can find me.

He trudged a bit further along the top of the hill and spotted a darkened edge near a split in the bluff that dropped into a small crevasse. He walked to the edge of the small canyon and looked down.

No walking that way. I'll have to go inland to find a way around this. But, maybe higher on this ridge, I can find something.

He tried to keep his eyes on where he was going. Though the snow wasn't blowing as hard, he still had some difficulty looking into the wind.

Then he came around a small ridge in the hill and there was the upper extent of the crevasse he ran into before. Just a short way up the canyon, he saw a cave.

It might be shallow, but it's better than standing around in this wind.

So, he walked toward the opening and noticed the wind velocity slowing gradually until there was only the cold.

So I've found my shelter.

442

He moved closer and, though not expecting anything danger-ous, was cautious about entering.

Fortunately, the opening expanded into a larger area. The light from the outside snow, glittered only on stone in the back. There were no animals in the cave and that resolved one of his con-cerns. There were some small nooks and crannies all about the walls.

He decided this was to be his home. Besides he didn't really want to go back out in the wind and he knew any moment there could be more snow. There was no way he could have a fire, but then he didn't need it to maintain warmth.

So now he had to consider the problem of not having any food. Strangely, he never thought of food before. But now he no longer was able to conjure his meals, he would have to find a source. Because despite being immortal basically – or, at least, he thought that was true still – he might feel hunger now. Thirst wasn't a problem, he could chew on the ice, or snow, for mois-ture.

The biggest problem for him, other than food, was going to be boredom. The next one was going to be determining how he might arrange a rescue. That last could be very difficult.

He looked further into the cave. It was larger than it seemed at first glance. He walked around a bend that led into the darkness.

He paused.

It's possible, but unlikely, there are others in this area. Maybe, these oth-ers are not so friendly. I need some way to light my way, if I'm going to ex-plore.

At that moment, there was a flash of light from the darkness. It lasted only a moment but seemed, by its motion, that some-thing, or someone, moving in his direction, carried it.

Interesting. But, now what do I do? Going back to the entrance and step-ping out into the snow seems logical. I have almost no way to protect myself here. Maybe less outside. But I've nowhere else to go.

He turned and walked back toward the entrance. He continued

out, turned up the small canyon and walked carefully to avoid leaving deep tracks. He spotted a large boulder he felt he could hide behind to watch the cave, walked around it and faced back toward the cave entrance. He crouched behind it to be less noticeable and soon was covered with a blanket of snow.

He waited.

In a moment, and much to his surprise, someone walked out of the cave. A lantern swung from a clasp on the utility belt around the waist of what appeared to be a small person, human obviously. It could have been male or female – young or just small of stature. He watched the other walk down the canyon and fade into the falling snow. Mano'n assumed it was a "he".

Who is that? What is he doing here? Where is he going now? When will he be back?

Mano'n moved quickly back to the cave, walked down the dark corridor and eventually, because he was being cautious, came to a large cavern. There were only a few human things scattered about, but those gave proof there were, had been, more than one living there. There was a cooking ring near the middle of the floor.

This is more mysterious every moment.

He was digging about in those items to determine, if he could, something about this person. He heard movement and whirled to check the danger.

A woman, attractive though not young, was standing at the entrance to the room. Her hood was thrown back and dark hair flowed down and bunched inside it. She held a short pole in one hand and a small group of fish on a stringer in the other. She stood without moving; her eyes were wide with surprise.

Mano'n couldn't be considered a normal traveler in this arctic environment. He was wearing a standard uniform of some army, had a light cape over his shoulders. He was dressed all wrong considering. She looked around the cavern quickly and saw no one else.

444

"Who are you?" she asked, not showing an inclination to panic but cautious. "What are you doing here?"

"I apologize for this intrusion," Mano'n answered, "and I think your surprise must equal mine. My name is Mano'n and I'm from – well, I'm from Aerolan."

"And you're here because . . ?" she leaned her head to the side a bit, watching him.

"Because I was left here by someone who doesn't like me," he answered quickly. He felt there was no reason to tell this person too much. Not yet.

"I might ask you the same," he added.

"Ah, yes. Well, we have a similar problem," she answered. "My husband gained one too many enemies and we were banished to this island about a year ago."

"Your husband? Is he about?" Mano'n asked, as he positioned himself to watch the entrance.

"He died," she answered bluntly. "He died."

She looked away, around the cavern and shook her head. "So here I am."

"What is your name, if I may ask?" he said. "Since we seem to be here together now, I'd rather have a name. "'Hey, you' doesn't seem appropriate."

"Yes, of course. Kerina. My name is Kerina." she looked down at the fish she was holding, walked to a nearby shelf carved from the wall and laid the string on the ice. She placed the pole next to them.

"Where are we?" he asked, watching her cross the room. He decided she wasn't afraid of him and, maybe, was going to let things go as they might.

"Xarl'e, an island off the coast of the Dome," she answered, walking to another area where clothing was stacked neatly. She removed her greatcoat and laid it in the appropriate pile. She was still bundled in heavy clothing, but now she seemed much smaller than before.

445

"How did your husband die? You have to be concerned about being here without him," he asked.

"He perished in an attempt to escape. I think the water was simply too cold. He thought he could swim to the Dome, but he was wrong. I stood on the other shore and watched him disappear into the mist. I assume he didn't make it," she revealed. "So, now I'm trapped. We devised ways to gather fish at the base of the canyon. There are shoals that allow for traps. So, we . . . I catch them and that is all I have to eat."

"Though you seem to be doing well enough. Why are you trying to survive? " he asked. He often wondered why mortals struggled so hard to survive. "One would think of giving in to the elements and simply stop their efforts."

"Would you?" she asked quickly.

"Me. Well. I haven't thought about that. It didn't seem important," he casually replied, without thinking.

"That is a strange answer," she looked around at him, one eyebrow raised. "Have you no concern for your welfare? Are you impervious to the dangers of where we are?"

I need to change the subject quickly. This is moving too close to revealing much more than I need to.

"Of course. But I was thinking about your plight since you've been here a while and now are alone. How long since you're husband left?"

"About two months, or more, I think. It's difficult to tell here. It's been a while," she responded, unhooked one of the fish from the string, walked to the cooking ring with it in her hand. She sat down and began to clean it, while still watching him and answering his questions.

"I'd like to tell you I mean you no harm," he said. "I suspect anyone surprised as you were would concern herself with that."

"Maybe," she answered. "Maybe. I do try to survive, but death might be an easier way. Sometimes, when it's quiet here, and it can be very quiet, I wonder why I hold to life so strongly? But lately, my biggest concern has been the loneliness."

"I too thought about the boredom of being here," he agreed. "Not a lot to do, I suspect."

She laughed. He liked the sound of it. Her face formed slowly into a smile that was entrancing. She looked much better without the scowl she wore normally. He liked the change.

"So, we can be friends?" she asked.

"I think we have little choice in the matter. It certainly is better than the alternative.

She laughed again, busily scaling and gutting the fish. She, with or without her husband, found rocks somewhere to cook on, probably from the stream down below,. They were used enough now to not present any danger of exploding with the heat.

The question is the fire. Where did it come from? How does she keep it burning?

He remembered noticing the light tendril of smoke rising from the cooking ring during his initial survey of the cavern.

"How do you keep the fire going?" he said. Walking over to the ring, he squatted down and watched her prepare the fish.

"There is a moss growing under some of the bluffs near the water. I bring that up, allow it to dry. It provides enough heat to cook by. No danger of burning the fish, but they're better just warmed anyway." she said, without looking up. She showed no concern, nor complained, that he was so near. "I have to resupply after a while, but the moss isn't too heavy for me to bring up."

"So, you've been able to exist. Maybe, not without some difficulty, but you will live," he said softly.

"Yes. I survive," she answered without explaining what that meant to her.

He liked she didn't complain about her situation. She was strong in herself and he admired that.

"So, I've now added some conversation for you. Hopefully, we can enjoy that, at least," he added, not wanting to dwell on the survival discussion any longer. He felt, somehow, she didn't either.

She threw the fish onto the hot coals. It billowed steam for a moment then sizzled loudly. She turned it after a moment to cook the other side.

Holding the edge of the fish gingerly, she pulled it from the coals and dropped it onto a small platter, taken from her tools area.

"Now, you can test my cooking skills," she said, smiling at him.

"After you, in case you're planning to poison me," he replied, holding up his hand.

She laughed again, reached and pulled a small portion of the plump fish and popped it into her mouth.

"Not bad. Needs salt," she said, working her mouth around the heat of the fish, pulling a few of the coals from the fire out of her mouth. "Try it. No need to go hungry."

"Thank you," he said, reaching for a pinch of the flesh himself. He wasn't going to reveal he had no need, but he would be cautious about how much he took. "Delicious."

They sat quietly. He mostly watched her as she ate, thinking how nice it was to be with someone who knew nothing about him and wouldn't, if he watched himself.

"Do you have family. . . in Aerolan?" she asked, turning to look at him, juice from the fish sliding down her chin. She reached for a rag laying nearby and wiped her face with it.

A few too many, unfortunately. But you would never believe the stories I could tell.

"Yes, a daughter," he answered. "She's grown now. Really a talented young lady."

"Grown? You don't look old enough to have a adult daughter," she said, smiling.

"Well, grown is not quite appropriate. I think she has some maturing to do before we can call her an adult," he added, chuckling. "Do you have family?"

"Yes, my parents live in Habenlein, in the city of Martur'a, but

I haven't seen them in years. My husband and I lived close by until the army came to take us away," she answered very casually, as though it never happened. "We had no children because we moved about a great deal. But children would be nice, I think. Though it's a little late to be thinking about that now, I guess."

"Ah, we don't know what tomorrow brings. Someone may be on the way to rescue us," he said, trying to lighten the mood.

"True. It is inevitable," she agreed, laughing lightly and taking another bite from the fish. "Have some more – unless it's disagreeable."

"Thanks. No. The flavor is excellent. But I've had a bad day today. Not very hungry. We should be hopeful things will get better, I suppose. That's bound to help our attitude.

"Well, we have little else to help us. I could use a diversion. I've decided you're mine," she turned to him and smiled.

Her eyes were haunting. Mano'n looked away toward the cave entrance.

I really need to take control of this, I think. We could be here a long while.

He stood and walked to the exit. She watched him without saying anything.

"I'll be back in a while," he said as he started out.

"I believe the water's too cold to escape. I'll expect you later - for dinner," she replied, without looking up.

449

TO FIND HELP

They landed a few miles west of a city. A *ransect'r* , as they noticed when they left Aerolan, was a fairly tall monolith, weathered enough to look like the stones scattered about it. This one was located just inside the tree line on a small hill overlooking a valley. In the distance, the city could be seen laying snug against a ridge of small mountains, mainly for protection from the bitter winds blowing almost constantly from the northeast. Low scudding clouds contributed to the foreboding terrain.

The wind was the first thing the three noticed. They quickly searched and found shelter behind some boulders nearby.

"I didn't remember how cold it is here and the clouds seem strange. But I believe I do remember the name of that city being Musragy. It's the capital, of sorts, of this land and empire.," Turm'l said, as soon as he was protected from the wind. "And I recall a lot of wind coming from the humans, but that was mostly hot air. "

Pet'r started to laugh but looking at Anisah, who wasn't laughing, he tried to hold his humor to a smirk.

They stood looking at the city for only a short time and decided shelter was more important.

Looking about they discovered a small cave between the larger boulders. They entered it and found they could walk fairly easily though the men were required to bend their necks to keep from striking the ceiling with their heads.

Pet'r looked out into the night beyond the cave entrance and noticed marks revealed in the shadows along the walls indicating men had formed this shelter. It wasn't a natural cave. It may have been created long before as shelter for this unique site. They decided any other site might also have some sort of shelter nearby.

That information could prove beneficial in the future.

Since they arrived so late in the evening and didn't want to travel the distance to the city to be turned away, they decided it would be wiser to wait until daylight to make the trip. They planned on the cold, knowing Habenlein lay several latitudes north of Aerolan, and brought proper weather gear and some food supplies which they decided to cache in the cave, but they didn't expect the frigid circumstance they were experiencing.

They were also surprised they saw no military about; no small squads of soldiers patrolling this near the city.

"Probably, just waiting for the change of the guards for the evening," Turm'l commented, but decided there was no need to discuss it any further. "So are we going to just walk up to the gate and demand entry tomorrow. Or would it be wiser for one of us to act as envoy and introduce ourselves more formally."

"Formally?" Pet'r asked. "Exactly what, or who, are we supposed to be?" He grinned and looked at the other two.

"We are here for a purpose. So we need to be somewhat assertive and present our request as quickly as we find someone who will make the preparation to send help to us," Anisah insisted.

"We must consider what is happening at home. I think there is a certain air of expectation within the enemy troops I encountered. They seemed to be prepared to go to war in an instant."

But, Anisah . . .," Pet'r started, but was interrupted.

"But what? Are we here to do this or are we just here to determine . . . that the *ransect'r* work?" she flared. She wasn't eager to stay long. She wanted her answers and she wanted them quickly.

"Well, I suspect you're going to discover things aren't quite so easy, Miss," Turm'l said, noticing Anisah flash a look at him.

Well now, the young lady has spirit — best be careful — she doesn't seem to care for the casual approach. Need to take a different tact to explain to these

451

young ones what is probably going to happen. But, I need to tread lightly. As I understand, these two – and particularly the young lady – have some things up their sleeves that could get an old man like me into trouble. I believe I'll avoid that.

"A few of the nuances of a society with a controlled government, especially a monarchy and a common law to rule them under one king., make this a form you haven't seen before. The rulers we worked with all those ages ago were intelligent and honest. We have no idea whether this one is, or not. He, or she, could be forthright or could be looking for subjugation from everyone around them. Or somewhere between. We don't know yet what we may find. So let's talk about kingdoms for I'm assuming the culture here is still based on that form."

Anisah gave him her '*do we really have to listen to this*' look, but Pet'r seemed willing to listen and settled down. He was leaning on some of the packs they managed to bring, holding his hands to warm them at the small fire they decided would make things a little more comfortable. Turm'l was actually surprised the girl was more agitated than the boy. He expected otherwise.

The fire provided the only light, which reflected across the walls of the cave in a rippled effect producing varying patterns. This effect gave one a sense of being under water, if one sat quietly and watched .

"Since you've not lived in a society with a central government, you may find many of the customs to be, quite frankly, absurd and unnecessary. But that part of such an institution has to do with the letter of the law and many of the innuendos of the common society, and certainly the central governance and their acceptance. The officials will assume you understand those nuances. That's where the hard part begins. If we aren't prepared to accept some of those, we may never get to talk to anyone about our problems," Turm'l continued.

He talked more about the significance of understanding the political entity of the countries they visited and taught them a great deal that night about leadership. Some things they thought ridiculous, but others they marveled at.

Anisah, dubious at first, began to realize this expedition was not going to be a simple one. She became more attentive and wondered if she and Pet'r would be able to achieve what they needed to get the help from these people.

Should we have waited for Garv'n, or someone who dealt with people of this sort, to become alert enough to help us before we tried this? How strange to think that these people aren't the same as those she knew and dealt with everyday. Strange indeed.

The morning came quickly. The Aerolan team woke, dressed in the warmest clothing they had, prepared a small meal, ate and were soon out on the nearby road headed toward the city. It wasn't a particularly long walk. The road was flat and took them directly to the gate where they used a small gong hanging to one wall to get the attention of the guards.

"Hallo, may we enter," Pet'r shouted. This was really no different from the major cities in Aerolan where they almost all had gates and required permission to enter at this time of the day.

A man's helmeted head, obviously belonging to a soldier, appeared just over the center of the gate,.

"Where are you from?" the soldier asked, looking out over the terrain for some answers about these three strangers. "How did you get here?"

"We walked," Anisah shouted back. She felt the harsh bite of the cold and wasn't interested in standing in it to talk to this idiot.

Turm'l gave her a harsh look and shook his head. She huffed and turned away to look over the open prairie stretching into the horizon. From what she could determine, from where they were standing, the mountains beyond the city were the only protection from the bitter weather.

"What is your reason for coming this early?" the guard asked, after looking over his shoulder for a quick moment. "Why are you here?"

Simple enough questions, but now even Pet'r was becoming agitated.

"We need to request an audience with his majesty about matters of war?" Turm'l shouted back and turned his back to the gate and the guard. "At least, they should be aware we bring trouble." He smiled at the other two, turned and squinted to look into the neutral horizon to the west.

The land blends colorlessly into the sky. How odd. I had forgotten that. Plays hell with finding your way around, as I remember.

"Do what? For what?" the guard almost stuttered. "Did you say war?"

"Yes," Pet'r answered, but with the sullen voice that could mean trouble. Turm'l was beginning to concern himself with his companions being able to control their tempers.

"You two must control your anger. I warned you the customs here would irritate you. But, if we are going to succeed, we can't allow our differences with them to interfere." he stated. He was blunt but knew he needed to be.

The other two snapped their heads around to glare at him, but realizing he was right, lowered their gaze to look at the ground, or back out over the plains.

"We need to speak to someone in charge, please," Turm'l called up.

In a moment, a new face appeared.

"I'm going to allow you into the secured area inside the gate. But be forewarned, you will be under guard there until we can determine how safe it is to allow you more freedom," a young officer shouted down at them.

The gates began to creak inward and soon the Aerolan were able to get inside the walls and out of the wind blast that were beginning to come from the west as the sun rose. They, at least, could get warm now.

The young officer came down the steps from the tower and

454

walked to them.

"I welcome you to our city and I'd like to ask you to join me inside my office, over there beneath the steps," he said and pointed to a door into a small cabin attached to the great wall.

They nodded their agreement and preceded him to the door. He passed them on the way and opened the door for them to enter, closing it behind.

"I can tell by your accents and your clothing you are not from around here, nor maybe not even from this land," the officer stated. "My name is Hiro'e and I am an officer of the guards."

"I'm . . . ," Anisah started, but Turm'l interrupted her. Hiro'e turned in surprise; he apparently had not realized Anisah was female.

"You are correct, sir and we appreciate your hospitality, but we do have an urgent reason for being here and we need to talk to whomever is in charge. Hopefully, the person in charge of not only this region but possibly the country of Habenlein," Turm'l answered.

"I expect a meeting with the person you are indicating is going to be difficult for you. So, I'll make every attempt to contact one through my commanding officer. I'd like to ask your permission to conduct you personally and introduce you. But first, I'll need to know where you're from and your names." Hiro'e added. "And since you mentioned war, why you are here."

Turm'l noticed Pet'r pushing forward, reached and held the boy's arm.

"Yes, certainly. We are actually from Aerolan. We do bring news of an impending war we believe will not only effect us, but will be brought to Habenlein's door, as well as all the other nations on this world," Turm'l pressed on. "We need to present that information to you and yours, but, in turn, we will be seeking help."

"I see. You do know you aren't expected. A meeting, especially a quick meeting, is likely out of the question," Hiro'e started to

455

explain.

"You mean to tell me you are informed about danger to your country and this world and you have to make formal requests for us to talk to someone about what we know is going to happen!" Anisah could hold back no longer. She felt this young idiot was interfering with what needed to be done to find a resolution to a real problem, a serious problem, and she didn't want to wait – for anyone.

Pet'r looked around at her quickly and could tell things were not going to go well if Anisah became more angry. She had a tendency to act on her *vision* and he realized now was not the time.

"I believe, Anisah," he interrupted her, "the lieutenant is only trying to explain what he is required to do and will try to do his best to help us."

Her mouth opened to say more, but she, looking at both Pet'r and Turm'l, closed it slowly, turned away to stare out the small window overlooking the open area leading into the city.

A unique place, so different from home. The streets, I can see, aren't paved and most of the buildings seem to have only entrances and no windows on the first floor. I wonder why? Must have to do with privacy, but why?

She turned back and decided listening was probably the best thing for her to do at this point. She was having difficulty being patient and now realized any harsh action by any one of them would definitely create yet another obstacle in their path. So keeping her mouth closed seemed a wiser choice.

She noticed the young officer was taking far too many glances at her as he talked to Turm'l and Pet'r.

That could prove handy later.

The men talked a while longer, exchanging details and coming to an understanding about the objectives.

"Let me go discuss this with my commander. I'll return shortly. But I'm certain he will want to meet with you," Hiro'e stated, as he turned toward the door. "Please ask the guard outside the door if you need anything. Anything at all." He glanced at Anisah one last time, opened the door and stepped into the cold. He lingered outside for a moment talking to the guard then trudged across the courtyard to another outbuilding nearer the houses.

"So, you think we will be invited in?" Pet'r asked.

"Probably," Turm'l answered, found a seat and sat, looking around the small office.

Anisah almost jumped in his face. He stopped, looked into her eyes.

"I said., Probably," he almost grunted. "That's all I know now." She backed up and turned away without speaking. She began to pace, occasionally looking out the window.

"Why are they taking so long," she blurted out. "We need to have some action. We need it now."

"I explained to you last night what is happening," Turm'l answered. "I don't remember saying that your temperament, if foul, would be helpful. I've told you both several times now, patience is required. I personally think this young officer will be our ally. He likes you. That is to our advantage.

Anisah blushed and turned away. Pet'r turned to look out the window, watching the people in the courtyard hurrying about and grinned at Anisah's discomfort.

"We actually are doing better than I guessed," Turm'l added. "I thought we'd probably be turned away at the gate. Wouldn't you have been more cautious about strangers appearing at a gate at odd hours?" He pointedly directed that statement at Anisah.

"I suppose," she muttered. "It's just . . ."

"I know. I've been in this situation many times and patience is a difficult virtue when you are harried by the potential death of our society. But these people must hear about that and we have to present it in the calmest manner we have." Turm'l said. "Let's try to maintain a little decorum."

"A good idea," Pet'r spoke up, still looking out the window.

457

"We have to succeed. Here comes Hiro'e and another officer now."

The door opened and the two officers entered. The new officer politely nodded his head at everyone and took a particularly long time when looking at Anisah.

"Hello, my name is Stane'a, captain of the guards. I have listened to your story from Hiro'e. I have decided to try and gain you entrance to speak with one of King Jors'o's counselors. If you convince him of the validity of your story. I'm certain you can win a meeting with the King's High Council to present your evidence to them. They will be the ones who will proffer their judgments to the King to determine whether he will want to hear your plea, or not."

"Thank you, Captain," Turm'l said. "We await the opportunity to meet with the counselor."

"Lieutenant, see to the well-being of these people and make them comfortable. Do you have other supplies you need, or do you need to retrieve any? If so, Lieutenant Hiro'e will see to getting those for you. We offer our hospitality during your visit. Gentlemen. My lady. Until we meet again. Lieutenant." he added, turned, walked out and returned to his office. Both Anisah and Pet'r felt something mysterious about him they could sense but couldn't quite determine what caused their unease.

"Please come with me," Hiro'e turned and said, "and I'll take you to clean quarters where you can relax and enjoy the city during your stay." He walked to the door, opened it and indicated they should follow him. The three looked at each other and Anisah almost blurted something out, but Turm'l's stern look made her hold her comment. The officer followed them out into the cold.

They shuffled across the courtyard to the main street. Looking along its length, they noticed it led through the center of the city and ended near the base of the mountain. The city walls were braced against the mountain, using one of its high bluffs as the eastern border of the city.

They crunched along the street through the snow, much of which was piled against the walls of the buildings and possibly provided more insulation around the ground floor.

They noticed also there were few military personnel, other than Hiro'e and the uniformed guards at the gate. Pet'r was cautious but made every effort to investigate each crossing street as they walked toward their destination. He could see no soldiers, nor local constables to enforce local laws.

Strange. There is no evidence these people need any enforcement officers, of any kind, except at the gate.

About midway across the span of the city, he noticed what was obviously a fortification near the center of the city. Situated higher on a small hill there, it was dark and formidable. But he could still see no sign of the military.

Must be the king's castle. But where are the soldiers? Have we come here for nothing? Is it possible these people have no military? How do they protect themselves? Even in Aerolan we have our small squads scattered about the country as our protectors.

They arrived at a small two story building not too far from the castle. Dull, inhospitable and with a grayish-brown color, as was most of the city, the building wasn't very inviting. It seemed hunched down between its neighbors as though enduring some punishment from its surroundings. Anisah glanced upward and noticed there was only one window on any of the sides she could see.

"Inside you must climb the steps to the upper floor. There are no rooms for guests on the bottom level. But there are several comfortable rooms available above with one central room for meals and communion. I believe you'll find these accommodations quite comfortable. We have these quarters for our many visitors wishing to speak to his majesty. We have tried to provide food, additional outerwear and bedding supplies for your comfort and, of course, you may request other items we haven't supplied.

459

Don't hesitate to contact me, if you need anything ," the lieutenant explained as he opened the door, walked into a hallway. There
were no entrances to any other part of this floor.

He pointed toward the stairs, turned and spoke pointedly to
Anisah. "I'll leave you now. But again, don't hesitate to contact
me." He turned to leave without further instructions, walking to
the exit without waiting for any questions from them.

"Excuse me," Anisah called after him as he reached for the
door to leave. "Aren't you suppose to introduce us to our counselor? How can we contact you?"

He turned back and smiled.

"My apologies. That will come later. But I will have a guard
placed in the small stoop you may have noticed just outside your
door. Also, there will be someone resident in the bottom floor
for your needs. You only have to send a message down from a
small alcove in the central room. If you need assistance in any
way there is a small rope attached to a bell below. The attendant
will come to your room to inquire about your needs, if you sound
the bell.

"How do we make contact with a counselor?" Pet'r asked,
puzzled by the isolation seemingly placed on them. "Are we prisoners?"

"Oh, no," Hiro'e insisted. "We try to treat everyone who visits
the same and this is one of the common areas available today.
You are welcome to visit our city whenever you wish, but both
the guard and the current resident downstairs need to know when
you leave. They take those opportunities to either report to me
of your whereabouts or refresh your apartments. We feel we
should care for your needs whenever we're able. The resident
should be able to answer any other questions you might have
about the city and your needs." He turned to leave again, but
turned back. "There'll be representative of the counselor probably calling on you in the next few days."

With that he quickly turned and left, pulling the door shut behind him.

"What? Where's he going?" Anisah walked to the door, yanked it open, looked up and down the street for Hiro'e and saw him walking toward the castle, not the front gate. She slammed the door in disgust.

"What are we doing here anyway? This is getting us nowhere," she looked around, angry at the inhospitality toward them. "Might as well go upstairs." She approached the steps and stomped upward into the upper level. Pet'r and Turm'l followed, both shaking their heads.

"I don't remember all this severity, or secrecy, from before something must have happened. But then it's been a number of years since I was here," Turm'l said as they rose into the central room.

The room was spacious, but like everything else they had seen, very austere. There was a table centrally located with benches on each side. Around the room were several other chairs apparently intended for relaxation. They were constructed solely of wood with no cushioning.

The alcove Hiro'e mentioned to them was at the back of the room. Anisah walked to the room and looked in. She confirmed, to her satisfaction, there was ample food stock shelved and labeled.

"Well, I see the line leading down to the bell below. Nothing fancy here," she told the others. "Nothing like *home.*"

Turm'l noticed her sarcasm and started to say something.

"Why is there a guard?" Pet'r asked before Turm'l spoke. "This is not a normal lodging for travelers. Are they suspicious of all visitors wanting to speak to the king?"

"This is puzzling," Turm'l agreed, deciding to refrain from re-minding Anisah why they were here. "Makes me wonder if they've had some trouble recently. Possibly an attempt to assassinate someone, maybe the king, or someone on the king's council. All this seems extreme and wary. But I have no idea why we

461

are, in effect, being held prisoner. It's all very strange, for obviously we are being held and diverted from what we need."

"Strange or not. We've come a great distance to speak to these people about helping with Baalsa'n's intrusion – again – into this world, everyone's world. We are representing a country and have made only simple overtures to speak to someone in charge – whether a king, a chief or a rich leader – to get help. If these people want to ignore us, then they should do it now and not waste our time. At this moment, I have my doubts about being able to walk out of this building." Anisah grumbled.

"I want to know when something, anything, is going to happen. Pet'r, why don't you invite our resident up here? Pull the bell," she grunted.

Pet'r looked around at Turm'l who nodded then went to the alcove and pulled the bell cord.

They sat at the table to wait.

"We can ask questions, but I doubt we'll get straight answers from this person. We will probably need to broach the meager hospitality by taking a private, if we can, tour of the city. I suspect we'll be escorted, or followed, by our external guard," Turm'l said.

"I think too we need to do this soon to gain their attention. The rudeness here admittedly is irritating me. But we need to force our hand without creating too much disturbance," he added, pointedly looking at Anisah. She only gave him a false grin and turned to look out the window near her.

She was watching the snow falling gently past the windows when she caught a glimpse of someone looking from the window of the building next door and pointedly pretended she hadn't noticed.

We're being spied upon. Who do these people think we are? Why are they so apprehensive about us? We need to ask some serious questions about how they are treating us.

She casually looked back at the opposite window then away as though not noticing their spy, but allowed herself to catch a quick glance as she looked about their apartment. She saw their unwanted observer was male which didn't surprise her.

She rose and moved across the hall into one of the rooms available for sleeping. This room was even more austere than the central room. There was a cot with a bare and meager mattress, a small table sitting beside it and a candle on the table. There were no chairs. A single window looked out at the taller building next door. On another table in the other end of the room were what appeared to be coverings for the bed – some blankets, some sheets and a pillow.

We'd probably be more comfortable back in the cave at the ransect'r than this and certainly have a stronger sense of freedom. It seems apparent we need to discern the cause for all this mistrust and resolve that before we will be able to talk to anyone. We are prisoners and being watched closely. Possibly I can create a small diversion of surprise to force these people to give us notice. But, I better ask Turm'l and Pet'r what they think about that before I push too hard.

She walked out of the bedroom almost running into their resident, a young woman from below. Anisah quickly looked down the stairs to determine how this person accessed the lower hallway but saw nothing revealing that secret. So she bowed her head, indicated she would follow their neighbor and walked back across to the central room.

"You asked for service?" the woman said. There was no grace about her. She spoke in a monotone and was obviously disgusted with what she was doing. "You rang the bell. What do you need?"

Pet'r was looking out the window when the woman spoke. He looked around and approached her quickly

"Why are we being held in this building?" he asked, looking down at her with a stern look on his face. Turm'l and Anisah looked at him, surprised by his brusqueness. He stood, waiting for the woman to answer, glowering at her. She felt no need to look at him, nor seemed afraid.

463

"You are not being held against your will. You may leave at any time. If you wish escort to the front gate, I'm sure that can be arranged and quickly," she answered his question without hesitation. But the addition of the statement about the front gate aroused Turm'l's suspicions.

"The front gate?" he asked. "I don't believe we mentioned leaving all together. Why would you say that?"

"It seemed a logical bit of advice. It's unfortunate you seemed to not understand the implication. You aren't welcome here, so it would be best if you returned to where you came from – wherever that might be. If you have no further questions, I'll return to my quarters," she said and turned to go.

Anisah stepped in front of her.

"Sit down. Now!" Anisah said, shoving the girl back toward one of the chairs. The girl's eyes widened and stepping back, she dropped into one of the chairs. Anisah noticed she also looked out the window toward their spy watching them before she sat. Anisah moved around so her back was toward the window. Pet'r and Turm'l seemed surprised at her sudden action but waited for her to explain.

"We are being spied upon from next door and we might be interrupted soon," Anisah informed them. "I noticed this when I sat in this chair before. We probably need to use some of the bed coverings to hide us from that – or not. I'd say it depends on what we decide about this trip. This girl is also a spy and will inform the authorities about our habits and any of our objectives she can discover – though she isn't very subtle. For whatever the reason, we are not trusted. They are placing us in a situation of no retreat."

Turm'l listened, nodded and turned to the girl.

"You are foolish to try to intimidate us. We are involved in a war in our homeland that eventually could involve Habenlein if we cannot succeed in defeating that enemy. We have limited patience with interference in that effort. We brought an open mind about whether this country cares or not, but this insidious design fomented by your people concerning our dismissal is unacceptable. We will see your king, or whomever we need to talk to, or we will bring some of our own intimidating elements to the table. We want an audience with the king to ask one question. We will not be turned away until we have his answer," he spoke with authority and strength of a man who meant what he said.

"We aren't afraid of you," the girl said.

"We never asked you to be afraid of us," Anisah almost shouted. She was frustrated by this strange behavior. "What is wrong with you and the others?"

"You are demons! We know you are here to kill the king!" the girl blurted out then quickly looked out the window. She revealed she had spoken out of turn — and was immediately remiss. "You may kill me if you want. But I'll not reveal the whereabouts of the king."

"Demons?" What sort of demons do you think we are?" Anisah sat down in the chair opposite the girl and softened her voice.

"You came out of the *harfer'n!*" the girl shouted. "You came before and tried to destroy us, but we drove you away. Why have you returned? We will not join you!"

Anisah sat back and relaxed.

Now we have something to ask about.

"Turm'l, please explain to this young woman we are not the same people. I need to talk to Pet'r a moment, privately," Anisah said, as she stood up.

"By the way, what is your name?" she asked the girl. Her answer was a glaring stare.

Have to admire her courage.

Turm'l sat facing the girl. Anisah thought of a picture of a grandfather and granddaughter.

"Now, young lady, do we really look, or act, like demons to you?"

465

"Well. No, sir," the girl looked up at Turm'l who smiled, an old, familiar wrinkled face. The girl smiled back.

Well, that's a good start.

Anisah stood and motioned to Pet'r to follow her across the hall to one of the bedrooms where they could be out of sight.

"I'd like for you to find out who the spy is next door, without revealing yourself to our guard. Can you do that?" she asked him. "We need to find out what caused this fear. Knowing that may give us a idea about how to make us friends they'll work with."

"I think so. Shouldn't be too difficult to get over there. What do you want me to do when I find the person watching us?" Pet'r answered. He looked down at her with soft brown eyes. She turned away and looked out a window.

"If you can bring him back over here we can at least talk to someone about what happened and how the *ransect'r* was involved," she said, still looking away.

"I'll be back in a just a bit," Pet'r said and, with that, quickly slid out the window facing out of the back of the house and leaped to the ground below. Apparently, no one was on guard there.

Anisah was going to tell him to be cautious, but he was gone before she could turn back. She only saw him as he dropped out of sight.

Pet'r, please be careful.

She shook her head, turned and walked back across to the communal room, sat in another chair and watched Turm'l talking in low tones with the girl.

Another good step. I think, watching him, he could talk an iceman into buying ice from him. A good man to have on our side. Too bad he would never be able to talk to Baalsa'n. Grandfather would know better than to let this man close to him.

While their conversation was low, Anisah noticed the girl glanced at her occasionally. Without the hooded overcoat she wore earlier, the girl could see she was only a girl too.

Only a girl. How old am I now? Seems years since I thought of that. So busy. So tired. I fear, this war, when it starts, isn't going to end soon. We need the help these people might provide. Have to do something – but what?

While she sat, Pet'r went quickly to the other building. Leaped to a ledge along the back of the larger building, close to a window and slid the covering away. There was something locking the covers, but that gave way easily. The loosened pins flew outward into the yard below without noise.

He stepped into the central room, quietly crept to the hallway and peered around the door facing into the first bedroom. No one was there. He continued to move along the hallway looking into each room. Then he found someone in the third room. The boy was asleep on one of the cots. Pet'r thought the boy was younger than himself – but not by much.

Pet'r walked quietly to the bedside and placed his hand over the boy's mouth. There was an instant response, the boy leaped from under his hand, twirled in the air and landed facing Pet'r with his knife drawn, pointed at Pet'r.

"How did you get in here?" the boy asked. "You couldn't get past the guards without alarming them. Proof. Proof, you are a demon!" he shouted at Pet'r. Then, he attacked.

Pet'r, caught unaware of the boy's intent, just managed to divert the knife before it struck him. He grabbed the boy around his shoulders, spun him about and flipped the knife away.

"Whoa. Stop. I don't want to hurt you," Pet'r whispered in the boy's ear. But the boy continued to struggle.

"You'll not take me alive. You'll not kill our king!" the boy shouted. Pet'r deciding he needed to stop this shouting before it drew the attention of the guard below, pressed down on the boy's throat restricting his ability to breathe and, though he struggled, the boy soon lost consciousness.

"You, tough guy, are a handful," Pet'r grunted and chuckled at the spirit of the boy. "You would have taken me with that first attack – normally. You *are* a tough one."

Pet'r laid the boy on the bed, lifted him to a better position over his shoulder, walked back to the window he entered earlier and leaped to the ground with his new fighter. He soon was back inside the house where Turm'l, Anisah and he were staying.

Anisah wasn't there, so he carried the boy into the central room. The girl, seeing the boy in Pet'r's arms, suddenly jumped up and began to swing her fists at Turm'l who was surprised at the first blow. But he easily managed to grab the girl to hold her off the floor though she was kicking and beginning to scream. Turm'l covered her mouth quickly.

The Aerolan all turned to listen for any traffic on the stairs leading outside. There was none.

"Who are these kids?" Turm'l asked, with a frown. "They seem to the fighting force for this place."

"Yes, I agree and thinking about it, isn't the soldier at the bottom of the stairs a little fuzzy-faced? What about Hiro'e? Really young, don't you think?" Pet'r said. "Are these the defenders of this empire? The very young? If that's true, they are organized."

"We've got to find out what they are doing?" This looks like us," Anisah added. "At least like you and me, Pet'r." She grinned briefly at Turm'l who was still struggling with the kicking girl.

She walked around the flailing legs and touched the girl on her temple. She slumped in Turm'l's arms who placed her gently back into the chair where she was sitting just moments before.

"Should we tie them?" Pet'r asked.

"I don't think so. We have to start somewhere with trust," Anisah answered. "We've got to know what has happened here."

Pet'r, still holding the boy, placed him in one of the other chairs, picked it up and sat it beside the one holding the girl. They waited for them to wake.

The girl woke first and stared around quickly, finding the boy beside her. She jumped up to defend him but Turm'l placed his hand on her shoulder and coaxed her to sit. Anisah moved to a chair facing the girl.

"We are not your enemy. We will help if you can tell us why you two," she said, pointing at the boy," are so intent on driving us away. How did you ever determine you could defend the city against a real enemy?"

The girl sat, pouting. She wasn't going to answer any questions. She kept looking at the boy. Her face scrunched with concern.

"He's all right. Just lost his breath," Pet'r told her. "He should be waking any moment. We all need to relax and wait."

It didn't take long. The boy awoke quickly, as before, and leaped to his feet. But Pet'r, standing next to him, held him in his seat as easily as Turm'l did with the girl.

"Who are you people? Why are you attacking us? We only want you to leave? We want no more fighting! Go away and leave us alone!" the boy started shouting. Pet'r clamped his hand over the boy's mouth again. The girl's eyes widened and she gasped, but didn't scream. The Aerolan once again listened for sound from below.

Anisah was now irritated with these repeat performances by these two and wanted it stopped.

"If you would stop and listen for a moment, we'll tell you who we are. We are not here to harm anyone. In fact, we came here hoping for help from you. We are not your enemy. But I think we know who is. They are the same ones threatening our homeland. We found the secret gateways only recently and are trying to contact anyone who might be able to help us.

I want to tell Pet'r to take his hand from your mouth, but you have to be quiet or we will tie you and gag you while we talk. Do you understand that," Anisah said ,with the sternness of her statement emphasized.

The boy nodded his head.

"Fine. But we will do as I promised if you do not keep quiet," she added and nodded to Pet'r who moved his hand aside.

As soon as Pet'r moved his hand, the boy blurted out, "Why

should we believe you?"

Anisah couldn't believe the boy's obstinacy. But then thinking about it, she realized these young people felt they were protecting their homeland, too.

"I must admit. You're right. Why should you?" she answered. "But think. Pet'r here obviously is strong enough to have already killed you. To keep you quiet, if nothing else and your friend here, she hasn't been harmed. Why, if we were an enemy, wouldn't we just get rid of you, or anyone, who was pestering us, like you two are and look at Pet'r and me. Do we look like soldiers? Well maybe Pet'r, but do I? I'm not much older than you. How old are you anyway?"

The boy glanced quickly up at Pet'r, looked at Turm'l who was now relaxing in his chair, and returned his attention to Anisah. He frowned and looked aside at the girl who only bowed her head to hide her face.

"So, what about the *harfer'n*. You came from one of them. What are you doing here?" he questioned Anisah.

"You're not listening. I told you. We came hoping for help from Habenlein," she answered. She felt calmed now. She was making every effort to show this young fighter she was a lot like him. "We, like you, are trying to save our country from an evil enemy. In fact, we are trying to save the entire world, which includes Habenlein and Musrag'y. You can't help but realize, we have to do so with the same age group as you. The adults seem oblivious to the danger. Or, at least were when we left to come here, though it seemed certain we would be under attack soon. I imagine that will change some minds."

"What do you want us to do?" he asked. He was now listening, probably looking for proof they were the evil ones, but he was, at least, beginning to ask questions instead of shouting threats.

"First, I must ask, who are you?" Anisah returned the question. "Who are you and how did you intend to protect yourself? You appear to have no magical strength, but she said you people

470

drove the evil ones away before? How did you do that?"

The boy looked at his friend and frowned, but turned back to answer Anisah, "I am the king's son. I am trying to protect not only my country, but also my father who is a good man. But he thinks we can hide from our enemies; his council also wishes to hide.

Obviously I disagree. So, I've formed, with my supporters – and there are a good number of them – a militant group to use quieter tactics than war to protect both; we are trying to learn quickly. We fight quietly and secretly but have, so far, lost no patriots in our efforts. There have been two recent attacks, both times we have sent the enemy back through the gateway. But they keep coming back."

Pet'r and Turm'l looked at each other quizzically with that response. Turm'l shrugged his shoulders. There was no way to know whether this was true or not. But the boy was being very forthright and, because of that, they listened to him. Anisah sat back and watched the boy a moment without comment then sat up again to talk some more.

"Thank you for being honest. We have similar problems in our country. We know this enemy will not just go away. Their leader is intent on the destruction of everything. In fact, he came once before, many centuries ago, to do that but my countrymen and the men from other countries, including this one, gathered in defense of our world and drove him and his followers away. For a long while. But now, he's back and intent on vengeance therefore more menacing than before. Your successes impress me and, I think, my compatriots here." She pointed toward Pet'r and Turm'l. They nodded.

"What agreement are you speaking of?" the boy asked quickly. "What agreement between all the countries. It may be I'm aware of what you are talking about."

The treaty was called the Granoblistia Fealty and all the nations swore to uphold it but that was centuries ago," Anisah

471

answered.

The boy turned to his friend, eyes wide and nodded.

"I do know of this treaty. Have you come to help us then?" he asked.

"Well, yes and no. But first, are you keeping your effort a secret then – even from your father?"

Anisah asked the boy.

"Yes. That is unfortunate. But I think he would stop me, if he knew," the boy answered. "There are many rumors going about in the city and, some tell me, in the countryside surrounding. We have no idea what the rest of the country people think. We are a large country with few citizens and are helpless if we cannot do something for ourselves with what we have."

"So you are then the leader of this secret group? Is there no one else?" Pet'r asked, interested now in discovering how this small group had vanquished troops potentially using magic and possibly using the Maah'e.

"I am, but there are others with more experience than me. You've met one. Lieutenant Hiro'e. He was the one who thought we needed to observe your group when you first arrived. He saw the flash from the *harfer'n* when you arrived and sent a message by our carrier. We were waiting for you."

"Good to know that information. Who else is on your team?" Pet'r asked.

"Hundreds. We too are patriotic at heart," the boy answered.

"What about Stane'a?" Is he with you?" Turm'l asked.

"No. He is with the king's council. But he is a good man, just not brave enough to fight," the boy answered.

When the two men backed away, Anisah asked another question.

"What is your name?" she said. "Who is your friend here?"
She pointed at the girl who had not spoken since the boy arrived.

I am Archs'x. She is Rutena, my sister," Archs'x volunteered.
"She actually planned our defensive effort when the others came

through the *harfer'n*. She also volunteered to meet you first."

"You two are the king's children?" Anisah sat back into her chair again. "How can we protect you?"

"I'm sorry I don't understand. We haven't asked for your protection. We wanted to drive you away and we would have. But now you bring us hope and we intend to protect you."

"Wait. Something you said earlier and I need to ask a question about that," Turm'l stepped in front of the boy. "You stated you saw flashes from the *harfer'n* whenever anyone arrived. Does that also include when they leave?"

"Yes, it does," Archs'x answered. "That's how we knew we defeated them the last time."

Anisah looked at Pet'r and Turm'l and raised an eyebrow.

"Something seems wrong about this claim of victory. I suspect those invaders left something, or someone, behind. So we'll need to be cautious. But the information about the flash is something we can definitely use in the future. No surprise attacks. Thank you, son," Turm'l said, showing some excitement with what he thought was unusual and unexpected news.

"So, how can we get to this king's council, or to your father, quickly?" Anisah asked. "We need to determine what your country is willing to do to fight against these people who invaded. Does anyone at high level know about your group? Don't they ask why those men left – without a fight?"

"I don't know actually. We've tried to avoid the high council and my father for several weeks now. But I doubt he knows we are the true patriots here," Archs'x responded. "He's too afraid to face the reality. At least, Rutena and our other followers think so."

"Well. I hate to tell you this, he may know all about your venture. He may be proud of what you are doing. Maybe there's something else in the political world restraining action on your father's part that you're not aware of because you haven't been there in the castle.

But I propose that you two return to the castle – as the king's children – and you help convince him to allow us to speak to him. I'm not saying you haven't performed with courage, but we and the other nations need more than guerrilla fighters. We need all the nations to come together and prepare for war," Anisah explained.

"We need to return to our home for we fear a war has begun there already and we have to help our people. We urgently need to speak to your father, especially without interference from his counselors. Can you two arrange that?"

With her brow wrinkled, Rutena turned and looked at her brother, "How can we do that?"

"I don't know at this moment," he answered, "but we certainly have easier access to him than anyone else. I know he's aware of the Granoblistia Fealty because he's the one who told me about it when I was young. We have to try, I think, and we will." He finished with a bit of confidence and his bravado was evident.

Anisah rose from her seat, smiling about the boy's reference to his age, and walked to look out the window at the wall of the nearby building, partly because she didn't want the young prince to see her grinning. Turning back with a more somber face, she walked to the boy's side.

"We will be patient about seeing your father – at least for two days. But if we think nothing is going to happen, we will leave and not come back. We haven't the time to play politics. We have little knowledge about what we must do to change someone's mind about fighting an enemy in war. But we have to face what we know is happening to us," she spoke with all seriousness for they would have to leave soon.

"But how will you escape what we've put you into?" Archs'x asked. "You basically are our prisoners."

"We have our own ways. Some of which you have no need to know," Pet'r answered. Anisah was tiring of the conversation. Thinking it was becoming circular. She wanted action now.

"You've already seen some of my abilities. We are individually strong, but we may not be able to win our war with just the three of us. What is more important at this moment – and for the next two days – is we will wait here for an answer from you. Or we will depart," Pet'r said, being definite about he and his friends' plans.

Archs'x stood, reached for his sister's hand, nodded and walked to the steps, "We will try to do as you ask. That is all we can do and hope, like you, we are successful. I will send word, probably through Hiro'e, of our success, or failure. In some way, you'll know our answer before you need it for your decision." He nodded his head, turned and, with his sister, walked out of the building.

"Will he do it?" Turm'l asked. "Will he be able to get us to the king?"

"Don't know and can't surmise, but we need to know a little more about what's going on here than what he's told us," Anisah said. "We need to talk to Stane'a. He's the one with a level of authority who would be able to reveal what is happening politically. Pet'r, can you bring him here? Without creating a disturbance?"

"I think so," Pet'r answered. "I think I know a way to get him here willingly. I'll bring him shortly." He turned without another word, left Anisah and Turm'l talking, walked around to his escape route, opened the window and was gone.

"What does he have in mind?" Anisah asked Turm'l.

"I don't know. But the boy has a convincing manner about him," he answered.

"Yes he does. Yes, he does," she replied, turned and walked to the table and sat at the bench. "Aren't you hungry?"

RETURN HOME

They finally were going to speak to the king. His children were able to convince him to meet with the Aerolan. There was considerable help from Stane'a. Not only did he know the young were staging their guerrilla group, but he actually approved.

It didn't take long for Pet'r and Turm'l to convince Stane'a they were there for a better and larger purpose. Stane'a was a veteran military man reduced to overseeing the guard because of political processes out of his control.

But one thing he had not lost. He was a close friend of the king because they grew up in the same village out in the tundra. He was able to meet with him and add his voice in support of the king's children to help convince the king to hear the Aerolan plea – without his council's consent, or knowledge.

Anisah paced the hallway, waiting for entry into the king's hall. She didn't liked waiting but this wasn't any different than all the other times she also didn't like waiting. So she walked mainly to keep her temper in check. But it was difficult. The two with her were no help at all. They were playing their mental war game. Something she had no interest in.

What is keeping this from happening? I never thought convincing these people to help would be so unwieldy. Why can't they understand how serious this is? Why are they not up and about doing the things they need to do to provide us aid in this fight against a common enemy?

She stopped a moment and stood looking at Pet'r, then began to pace even further down the hallway than before.

What is wrong with Pet'r? He's hardly talked to me at all. We need to talk. I don't understand.

Pet'r and Turm'l noticed her walk by them occasionally. They were busy working out the detail of what they needed to ask for, so paid her little attention. For them the larger question, of course, was whether the Habenlein leaders were willing to honor the Granoblistia Fealty written so long ago no one remembered it. There were a number of discussions, but most were disappointing. These people saw no reason to rush into a war with so little evidence of anything happening except in Aerolan – not a place of great concern except in certain minor commercial endeavors.

They certainly saw no reason to anticipate helping militarily. Things just didn't happen that way.

It was difficult for the three from Aerolan to be patient with the leadership here. They acquired one ally when they first arrived.- a young lieutenant, Hiro'e. But Turm'l and Pet'r both suspected the lieutenant was more enamored of Anisah than willing to help Aerolan. Pet'r thought Hiro'e was amusing watching his efforts and he could tell the young man was annoying Anisah.

Now Stane'a, an old friend of the king, was a formidable addition to the effort. But they still had to wait for the never-ending formality of the king's court.

They were waiting in an area beyond the view of the other courtiers so their existence would be kept secret. They had arrived early that morning, well before the movement about the castle began, and were essentially hiding in the king's private chambers. They did get to meet Archs'x and Rutena again and were able to thank them for their help.

But the waiting was still an agony. Especially for Anisah. Her level of patience had diminished over the past year or so. Mostly since she ran away from Caliste and, it seemed, everywhere she turned someone, or something, interfered with what she knew needed to be done before it was too late. She aged beyond her youth though still only a young girl and was not given to forgiveness easily.

Still a girl. How could all these things have come about and how have I survived?

There was movement at the door leading in the king's private meeting hall. It opened and a court minion's head poked out, looked around, saw them and motioned for them to enter the room.

Anisah almost ran to the door but, when she saw Pet'r grinning at her excitement, controlled her exuberance and walked casually into the chambers, head held high. Lieutenant Hiro'e hesitated a moment but was told he was invited also.

The meeting was short. The king's children and Stane'a had already convinced the king the Aerolan could be trusted. He, being aware of the meeting, had recovered copies of the original Granoblistia Fealty and had them brought so they could be discussed.

"So, our young friends, we would like to help and will be able to provide a number of troops," Jors'o stated, making it official.

"But, sir, we haven't noticed any military presence around the city. We've assumed you have little and have very low expectations, but only want to ask for your help in discussing the problem with the other nations who signed the pact to help with troops, if they have them," Turm'l said.

Jors'o turned to Stane'a smiling.

"Well, we have a few surprises of our own. Our military presence is ample, but the view of it is limited. The recent attacks through the gateway, after almost centuries of no activity, surprised us a bit. We weren't totally prepared for it. But we do have a standing army – a large one in fact. They are bivouacked below the castle and, in the mountain behind it in caves, large enough to hold half the population of this city.

When the gate brought new visitors, we were curious and tried to begin talks with them. But they attacked immediately, killing several soldiers at the gates. We weren't able to bring out any of our troops to counter the attack. But when Archs'x patriots attacked, it gave us a small window to recover. We, even in secret from my son and daughter, were able to provide quiet assistance in driving the enemy back through the *harfer'n*. My children were not made aware of the help," Jors'o answered.

"Stane'a was careful about keeping himself and me aware of Archs'x efforts. The one thing that most pleases me is that my son, my young prince, brought our people together as a community again. If it weren't for this terrible weather these magicians left behind, we would be a peaceful land again."

"They used magic?" Anisah spoke up. She was being quiet while everyone discussed what was to happen. But magic was something beyond what these people could do, but not beyond what she could, if necessary.

"Yes, young lady. Particularly in the use of some monstrous man-like creatures I assumed were created by magic. There were a couple of them, almost invincible. But we managed to slay one of them and the other was taken back with the escapees. Why do you ask?" Jors'o answered.

"Pet'r and I are capable of using magic. In fact, I believe I'll be able to remedy your weather problems. In the future, if you need more help, I will try to attend to that part personally," Anisah added.

"You are able to do that?" Jors'o asked. "But you and Pet'r seem children to me. How are you able to handle magic?"

"Not just handle, your majesty, but use," Turm'l said, interrupting. "These two are friends of the Al-Esfer'n."

"Can you be? I haven't heard of our gods in years. I don't know how long before that for others. But they are worshiped here. They are real?" Jors'o was honestly surprised.

"Yes," Anisah answered. "Pet'r on a personal basis; I more in what I'm able to do to help others."

"That certainly inspires us to not only help, but form a more solid bond with the people of Aerolan. We've not been impressed in the recent past with their flagrant absence of moral conduct, but knowing the Al-Esfer'n are trying to assist is ample reason without anything else mattering. We will begin to prepare imme-

479

diately. How many troops will you need us to send?" the king asked. "Stane'a is, in fact, the general of our armies. He's been with the guards to have a first-hand exposure to any other visitors we might have. He reported your presence to me shortly after your arrival. He will be making these preparations and forming a war council to assist him.

Stane'a, is there anything, or anyone, you need to be placed on the council to help begin the preparations."

"Yes, Sire. Hiro'e and your two children, Archs'x and Rutena. They have learned much with our recent crises and more than that, the people know and admire them more than the military. We, in the military command, think they have contributed greatly to our willingness to fight as we must."

"Then let it be done," Jors'o commanded. You begin to assemble what troops Aerolan needs and prepare them for their voyage."

Then turned back to the Aerolan.

"You do understand it will take a great deal of time before we can transport them to you," Jors'o told them."

"We do and we have transport ships arriving shortly for that purpose. We only need to inform the contributor when we return. But I have something to suggest to you," Anisah interrupted. "There is no need for that preparation for a small number of troops. I can provide a means to get them there more quickly."

"You can?" Stane'a asked. "But how many are you talking about? How can you do this?"

"Your men may not like it, but I can transport maybe a thousand soldiers and their officers, in a moment's notice, to several spots I think they would be useful. How good were they fighting the Maah'e – the monster men created by the enemy's magicians?"

"We have strengths of our own, including some large and strong people from the northern regions where Stane'a and I are from. They matched those creatures very well in hand-to-hand

480

combat," Jors'o said.

"Good. Your men should be told there are to be transported by magic, I imagine. I suggest we mention the Al-Esfer'n are watching over us. It should help them relax" Anisah added. "There is nothing to fear and the time of passage in minimal. They only need to be prepared to engage in battle at short notice. But be certain you include some of those larger soldiers, the Maah'e can be expected."

"This can be done today. Maybe later in the day, this afternoon, if that is acceptable. We can meet you in the fields between the city gate and the *harfer'n*. We will be at your command. The officer in charge of the group will be Colonel Trym'a, a good man and strong commander. He will be told to take his launch orders, both for their trip and for the battles where we can help, from you," Stane'a told her.

"You should add Pet'r to that status. He is our warrior. We should meet with the soldiers for the introductions before we begin. Pet'r and I both will speak briefly to them before we leave. By the way, I think we'll probably have a pleasant, and sunny, afternoon to begin our adventure," Anisah was more comfortable now. She was involved again.

"Amazing. The weather has been a burden on our people. One we really don't need. For now, we all need to go to our appointed places and prepare for this afternoon," Jors'o said. "May we know success in this effort. Meanwhile I will send horsemen to those countries south and east of us to prepare for ships leaving for Aerolan. Who should we ask about the best places to land our people, once we arrive?"

"I'll take that responsibility and will stay here while you prepare," Turm'l stepped forward, volunteering. "There are several places and we can plan the attacks properly before we arrive."

Anisah stood, smiling. She knew she could count on everyone in this room. Now she was anxious to begin.

There was something that still bothered her and it was not discussed.

What, or who, did the Ravelan leave behind? It probably wasn't the weather problem. That only seems to be a diversion. So what was it? I'll be certain to ask about anything unusual when I next return.

That afternoon they gathered. The word spread as it always does in a close community. Many of the townspeople, hearing of the event, lined the walls of the city, bundled against the depressing cloudiness, constant rain and the cold. The soldiers stood at attention.

All waited.

Anisah and Pet'r arrived soon. Anisah walked to Turm'l and kissed his cheek. The older man blushed a bit, but held his composure. She and Pet'r walked down onto the field where the small, armed unit waited.

"Today, my friends and your families, we must thank you for your bravery and for your help. We will take an unusual journey to Aerolan and the people there will know you have come to help them. I think there will be success, but only when we have engaged these evil armies will we know. So, let us prepare," she announced. "Furthermore, I'm tired of this weather. We should have a brighter day to send us off."

She raised her hands overhead, looked a moment at the low-flying clouds, mumbled something and the clouds began to dissipate and fade away over the city and for miles about bringing the sunshine many had not seen for months. A cheer went up from the city walls and the soldiers on the field broke their severe military stance and gave a roar showing their approval.

"If you are ready, gentlemen," Anisah shouted to the officers. All nodding their heads, "let us fly."

All disappeared from the field area.

Those on the city wall, including Jors'o, his family, Hiro'e, and Stane'a, gasped at the suddenness of the departure. Turm'l smiled noticing their amazement. He remembered his first instance watching this young woman.

482

It was silent for a moment then a few began to cheer and soon all those along the wall joined in with a roar of astonishment and disbelief.

That same morning, Jond'r and Acron'n were encamped just north of Tariny, near the crossroad at Ransea, with the complement from the training area near the castle. They establish a command center to ward off the attacks from the forces moving in from the north through Coma't.

Geth'n, before he returned to Borny'a's aid, brought the group from their Varspree encampment. They had rushed to that area as part of the contingency they would be needed at the primary battlefield. But when it was discovered Rab'k was advancing along the western side of the war front, it was decided they should instead be moved to protect the attack on Tariny

While at Varspree, they did, in fact, gather, at Borny'a's suggestion, a rather large contingency of men from that city. Most were thieves and killers and would have to be watched, but they were good fighters for the hand-to-hand fighting being used by the Aerolan forces at that moment. These men were happy for a *little adventure*, as they called it.

Jond'r didn't care what they called it but encouraged them with a validation that pleased them.

"You gentlemen," he started, and they all laughed, "need to venture out into the nearby hillsides find anything moving that's bigger than you and do what you do. I expect your presence will be distressing to the command of this desert group. You will be doing a great service to the people of this world, including yourselves."

They gave a shout, rose and walked to the area they had chosen to camp. Before they were settled very long, Acron'n saw some of the townsmen sneaking away from the battlegrounds.

483

This little adventure wasn't enough to hold them all and the pay wasn't enough, it seemed. It would have proven futile to pursue and try to force them to stay, but Acron'n suggested it to his brother. They only looked at each other and shook their heads – no need to waste time.

When they arrived at their location, Geth'n worked with Jond'r to discern the status of the battle area on the TrailEnd road and he suggested they use the tactics Jond'r and Acron'n worked out in their previous encounters with the Ravelan.

"Undoubtedly those tactics will work on these desert people. Rab'k's people are mostly horsemen and villagers who've only fought in brief skirmishes and are unaccustomed to a battle-ground. They'll not understand the lack of a direct attack," Geth'n mentioned. "Take care and you'll succeed. Those, in Pull'r, are facing the worst possible situation and I must leave to see if I can help there."

"You're right. Go help them. We'll be fine. Maybe even successful with this group. I've faith in the skills of our men. Take our best wishes with you," Jond'r said, watching Geth'n express some frustration with having to deal with two fronts.

Geth'n thanked them, bowed his head briefly and disappeared.

Fortunately for Jond'r's forces, they originated the guerrilla tactics in the field much sooner while saving recruits from becoming Maah'e. And they would not have to face the Maah'e.

Just south and not far from the Castle Ralff'r that afternoon, there was a rumbling that many in the castle noticed then there was only a heavy, sullen quiet. Suddenly a small army appeared spread over the landscape. The commands began to fly through the air and the soldiers from Habenlein assembled quickly into a formal bivouac, placing their own tents and establishing procedural processes in an orderly and professional encampment within

484

moments after arriving.

"We await your command, my lady," Trym'a told Anisah as he returned from inspecting his position. "My troops are ready – though I think not a few are a little pale from that trip. Including myself. We should soon be able to deploy as you wish."

"We need to go to the castle first," Anisah said, pointing toward the building isolated just north of them, "to inquire about the current status. Since we've been gone several days, much may be in play now Pet'r and I aren't aware of. Please give us a few hours to determine what the status is now."

"No problem, young lady. You need to have your intelligence updated. We'll wait here while you make those determinations," Trym'a added.

Pet'r and Anisah teleported to the castle quickly. There was panic. The residents were dashing through the hallways trying to reach locations blocked by others running in other directions. It seemed obvious Pet'r and Anisah needed to find certain people who knew what was happening and do it quickly before total panic reduced the area to chaos.

"I'll find Siarra," Anisah shouted. "You go check with your officers to determine what has happened. I'll meet you here in about a half an hour."

"I'll be back shortly," Pet'r answered and disappeared.

Anisah ran against those trying to escape, trying to find Siarra. She passed her room, glanced in, and, not seeing her, moved on through the people carrying their lives on their backs.

How could this be happening? What is wrong?

She pushed on, heading toward Siarra's family rooms, wondering what caused this panic. No one would stop to talk to her. She tried to choose a person here and there to ask, but no one would stop long enough to listen.

She passed one of the outer windows that faced south toward the coast and she could see people moving as quickly as they could toward Farsea. She hoped none of them wandered near where the Habenlein army lay camped. She felt certain the people seeing that army camp would only make the fear greater. The people from the castle were, at least, following the proscribed path to reach safety.

I'll have to make certain I involve the Habenlein people in the escape process, if we need it. I want our people to be comfortable with these people from another land.

She turned a corner down a hallway, near the back of the castle, and spotted Siarra bustling about, helping her family, and others, get ready for their run to the coast. Anisah paused a moment and noticed how calm Siarra seemed, how strong she was in this crisis.

But why this panic? What crisis? What has happened?

She pushed her way along the wall, trying to stay out of the way of those fleeing, until she reached Siarra, busily helping others move along. Anisah looked into the rooms and realized that Siarra's family was not around, apparently they were out on the road to the coast already.

"Siarra. Siarra, over here," Anisah shouted above the fearful noises from those fleeing. The girl turned, looked at her quickly, frowned and turned back to help someone else. Anisah pushed herself through until she could stand by Siarra and began helping those needing assists with their things.

"What's happened?" she leaned over and yelled in Siarra's ear. Siarra looked around quickly, stood up, pushed her hair back. The fear on her face was so strong Anisah almost stepped back a step.

"What?" Anisah mouthed.

Siarra only looked at her an instant and broke into tears. Her hands came to her face and she openly wept. They were standing in front of an open room, so Anisah reached, held Siarra's shoulders and pulled her into the room and out of the traffic of those pressing to leave the castle.

"Tell me what has happened?" she said, only raising her voice to be heard. "Why is everyone trying to escape? What kind of

486

fear is this?"

"War! War. Baalsa'n's people are attacking near Hang'm. Geth'n and Borny'a are there and I don't know how they are doing. Jond'r and Acron'n have rushed to the north of Tariny where another smaller army is rushing to that city. Everything is falling apart."

"Maybe it's not as bad as you think," Anisah said. Siarra snapped her head around and glared at Anisah.

"This is not a game anymore where Geth'n, you and Pet'r can move around solving little problems. This is war! You stand here telling me it isn't so bad. Geth'n is out there risking his life in a real conflict and you think that everything is all right. How can you do that? How can you stand there while the man I love is in danger. I've lost my father and brother to these fiends and you think this is right? How can you? How can you not feel the fear these people have?" Siarra shouted at her, screaming her anger and fear. Her face was livid and harsh as she yelled her condemnations at Anisah. "I say you three were wrong. We are going to die. We will not be able to defeat this evil monster. What do you care. You are part of that family anyway. You can't lose. You are safe. We are not!" She crumpled to the floor, sobbing.

"Siarra, please control yourself. Pet'r and I have brought help. Strong help. We will try to rescue Geth'n. We will fight against these attackers and drive them back into the mountains. But we have to prepare for that attack. We have to gather ourselves and push back against this audacity. We can't afford to hide in fear, or run away. We have to fight back. Please help me. You are one of our strengths. I know, Geth'n would want you to support what we can do to both help us push these monsters back and off our world and to help save him. We have to know what truly is happening. Pet'r and I will go to the defense of our fighting men, and we can surely affect an outcome better than defeat so soon. We will fight until we cannot.

I'll not accept defeat so easily. You're correct. I am a part of that family, but I have no fondness for their leader, my grandfather. He is evil and has been for thousands of years. I will see him stopped in his destructive ways. He should not be allowed to live. I intend to see that come true.

So, please control yourself. Please show these people fleeing for their lives we have the courage to stand against this attack. We must live and destroy this enemy. If we do not. If we are not the ones to stand bravely before this onslaught, these fleeing people will rightfully lose heart and know they are lost. They'll believe their lives mean nothing to us who pretend to be their leaders."

Siarra raised her head. She wasn't crying any longer. She climbed up from her knees and stood before Anisah. Her eyes were leveled at Anisah, but the anger was less.

"Then I will do my best. But, please find Geth'n. I will not be able to go on without knowing where he is and how he's doing," the woman muttered. "That's so selfish of me, but I have to know."

"I can tell you this," Anisah said, "We three have an emotional and mental connection of some sort. We don't know what it is. But I know Geth'n is still alive. I sense it. He is troubled but very much alive."

Siarra's eyes widened and she actually smiled. Then she turned to look at those pushing by the door of the room.

"These people need someone to help them now. I believe that has to be me. Who else is crazy enough to put up with you three?" Siarra said, a mocking look in her eyes. "Forgive me for doubting you. I really do know you care. Now go, make certain we win this day."

She pushed her way into the center of the hallway and began to shout directions to those trying to get out of the buildings.

Anisah saw no reason to push through the masses so she quietly vanished and moved quickly back to where Pet'r was waiting for her. She could see he knew what was about and they wasted no time, but left immediately for the front.

They arrived near Hang'm and were shocked at the disaster surrounding them. The Aerolan army wasn't running away, but dragging themselves away, from what they had experienced. The misery was everywhere, bodies of soldiers lay over one another where the Maah'e tossed them. Blood ran freely and deeply along the paths forming streams to the small branches of a creek that flowed away across the meadows.

"Can you see Geth'n, or Borny'a anywhere?" Anisah asked Pet'r. "Where are they? We know they're somewhere near."

"I can't see them from here. Let's walk to where the command post was on that small hill and search from there," he answered and headed in the direction he'd indicated. Anisah followed.

From the top of the rise, Pet'r spotted both men. They were near the front line, trying to find anyone who wasn't dead. They walked along turning bodies over, or straightening them out, so they could see the faces of the young and old who gave their lives fighting against the enemy. When they found someone alive, they shouted for help from a crew of healers, also looking for others, anyone, who might still be trying to live, following closely behind

Pet'r shouted though there was no need. Even above the line of searchers, the front guard of the Ravelan stood and only watched while this process followed its gruesome path. There was no sign of any of the Maah'e which Pet'r knew probably contributed to this slaughter. The enemy had no heart in using this opportunity for themselves. The Aerolan army seemed totally helpless and the Ravelan felt certain surrender would soon be forthcoming. So they just stood and watched.

Pet'r looked southward and could see the Aerolan soldiers walking away, dragging themselves where necessary, away from the mud and blood of the battle. Then he turned slowly toward the watching enemy. Anisah could sense he was building his hate inside and might possibly launch himself against those watching from above the sodden battlefield.

489

"Pet'r. Pet'r. Stop! Now is not the time. Please leave for a while. Go and see if Jond'r needs help. Determine what we can do on that front. Please do this, we can't afford for you to be embroiled n a private battle. We must have a solid front. We three must be together when we win this thing. We have to rid ourselves of Baalsa'n. Fighting private little wars will not bring us to that day," she shouted at him.

Pet'r glanced around at her. His anger almost reached its peak, but he nodded, looked again at the enemy soldiers above and disappeared.

Anisah ran across the field to Geth'n, and when she managed to get to him through the carnage, reached out to hold him, to comfort him. But he threw up his arm, pushing her away. She turned to Borny'a, but he had no time for her.

Realizing these men had to work out their sorrow, she joined those trying to aid the wounded. By using her talents and her dreams of tomorrow, she began healing the fallen men. She held them, sealed their wounds and filled them with a desire to live. Some seemed to wake with a start, not knowing they were lying in mud and blood, as though fresh for battle. Others were able to rise though having suffered loss of an arm, or a leg, and had to be helped from the field by the healers. And slowly, the army of Aerolan was able to move their people from the battlefield and help them follow the others already walking away.

But, the Ravelan noticed Anisah. They noticed what she was doing. One of them ran to their command post and reported her actions to Monsh'a.

"It's the granddaughter!" shouted Monsh'a. "Lieutenant Rons'a! Form a squad and capture her before she can get away," he ordered.

The officer gathered a small group who jumped to their horses and galloped up toward the hilltop. But when they reached the top of the ridge, they were caught by surprise.

Anisah and Geth'n stood below. Borny'a stood with them,

fully armed. Waiting.

Strangely the ground that was so sodden before was now dried. There were no more bodies, no more people slumped or plodding along on the other side of the hill. It was as though the battle had never been.

The cavalry stopped on the top of the hill, looking at each other and their leader, questioning what they saw and hesitating. Then they charged down the hill.

A mistake.

Anisah and Geth'n stood watching with no indication they planned to run and hide.

Then they reached, held hands and looked toward the attackers and the men along the hilltop who watched.

They waited.

Then quietly but suddenly all those, including those charging toward the three on the field, on the hill vanished without a sound.

Anisah, Geth'n and Borny'a turned away and, following the wounded ahead of them, slowly walked toward the south with the last of their rag-tag army. As they came to the stragglers, Anisah healed the wounds of those who were down, or having trouble walking, and they proceeded on the road toward Varspree.

Monsh'a attending to numerous details, looked around and impatiently inquired about the capture of the girl. No one knew. When he sent a scout to the top of the hill to find his men, there was no one there. All his people who had remained on the hill watching the defeated army flee toward the south and the small cavalry unit to capture Anisah had disappeared, there was no trace of them. In the distance, a scout could see Anisah and Geth'n with Borny'a watching behind them, walking away from the battlefield. He returned to Monsh'a's tent to report.

Monsh'a looked to the top of the hill and muttered, "This is not ended. There will be no surrender. I fear, we are no longer in

491

control." He tried to not say this loud enough for those around him to hear, but the fear that came over his face told most of the story to his people.

They only looked at each other and look up at the top of the hill themselves. Fear passed slowly through the group who lowered their heads, wrinkled their brows and slowly walked away.

ON ANOTHER FRONT

Jond'r moved his men to a point along the road south of Ransea a short distance and planned to distribute them along each side of the road leading to Crosspoint. The area had few trees but was thick with low shrub and heavy growth of tall prairie grass. He knew the desert soldiers, not accustomed to foliage and brush and would be unaware of any danger. He knew his people weren't prepared to withstand a full-fledged assault from trained soldiers, so he was going to use only the guerrilla routines they learned during the rescue skirmishes they were using already. He assumed Rab'k and those from the desert had taken no time to train their personnel for just such a situation.

So he decided to use what he had learned most recently and created a circumstance that the desert soldiers had not been exposed to. His mixture of newly trained people and the criminal element he'd dragged along from Varspree were both eager and both either trained in guerrilla warfare, or were naturally attuned to functioning that way in a fight. Divide and conquer he'd heard someone say and that seemed true enough – and he assumed the only way to achieve a good result.

He knew he had to hold this smaller army while Borny'a and Geth'n dealt with the larger one at Hang'm. His effort was a diversion as best he could tell. The fewer men he lost the better. But a quick victory, or escape, was also a hoped-for addendum.

Rab'k rode ahead of his troops as they marched in time to the drumbeat he used to keep cadence. The stamping feet of the infantrymen thundered through the forest and seemed even louder when they reached the open prairie.

Jond'r and his brother took about half of their men each and spread out along each side of the road for several miles.

493

Their plan intended to have the first of his troops, in this case the group from Varspree, start the attack on the rear of the column marching through and push forward into the center of that mass of soldiers with their success. If anything began to fall apart, they would retreat back into the low-lying scrub and wait there for a signal to attack again.

This following group would attack with stealth, keeping as quiet as possible, but dropping the soldiers from the last rank forward. With that method, Jond'r felt the street thugs would be more effective than any forced army attack and the victims would be down and done before the officers knew what was happening.

Acron'n stayed with the untrained men to attack the rear. He was more accustomed to stealth, having acted as a spy on more than one occasion for Garv'n. The element of surprise was crucial for the attack to succeed.

Jond'r concentrated his men at the center of where he thought about half of Rab'k's men would stretch along the road when he attacked. He had no cavalry to assault this army from the flank. But he prepared his trained group, the largest and fastest of his men, to rush the opponents quickly, darting across the road to the other side, slashing as they went while trying to avoid hand-to-hand combat. If anyone missed an attempt to strike an opponent, he was to keep moving because someone was close behind who might be able to take advantage of the distraction created.

Surprise was the foremost element of such an attack. Jond'r wisely decided he had to use most of his heavily trained personnel at this junction. He meant to cripple the desert people with the suddenness of the attack and using the best was the most economic way to achieve that. But he would leave himself vulnerable if they failed to inflict damage on the troops attacked. And decided he had to risk this.

Then the last were the younger men and boys, placed after the ground attackers who would hopefully inflict sufficient damage, to attack from behind the invaders who, by that time, would have turned to ward off the attacks from their rear.

Jond'r plan basically used hidden soldiers to form a pincer to close in on all sides against an enemy better trained and fully armed for battlefield organization. To make them become disorganized would better fit his under-manned squads.

As the desert soldiers marched by, it was difficult for Jond'r to stay hidden, especially when Rab'k passed by so close. But, one thing he noticed, no one in the marching group was aware of his people. That was his advantage.

He hoped.

When enough time passed, Jond'r walked back into the brush to an open spot where he could look toward the end of Rab'k's column. He waited for a moment then became concerned.

Where's the dust? There must be something happening back there for this to succeed. Is everything going as planned?

It became more and more difficult the longer he waited. But, just when he was about to grab a squad of men to run back to see what was wrong, he heard a low roar from the rear. The muffled sound of weapons clashing, of men shouting and then the columns in front of him began to break apart, despite the officers shouting at them, and the sweep of the fighting flowed over them. The troops were no longer marching in order. They were waiting to be attacked from the rear.

Jond'r ran back up the bank, stood briefly and signaled his squads to attack. The desert soldier's attention was averted just long enough for his few people to dash across, cutting numerous soldiers down before they could react and turn to meet the new attack. His men burst up the other side and then, from across the way, another band swept back across to Jond'r's side, hacking and killing as they ran.

The slaughter in the middle of the column was massive. Soldiers lay on the ground groaning, completely prostrate, dying or already dead.

The front of the column began to collapse to defend itself.

495

The soldiers who were separated from those following began to run back to help. But Jond'r's people were off the road and running along the embankments toward the front of the column to take advantage of the disarray of the remainder in the column.

Jond'r finally saw Rab'k, riding through his men, shouting for them to turn and fight the attackers. Rab'k was so intent on getting his men turned, he was unaware of the smaller attack from where the front of his columns was. That attack burst onto the road and swarmed over the soldiers left behind and, despite their lack of training and their youth, were so effective the desert soldiers began to run from the battle and cut across the fields beside the road where Jond'r's patrolling forces waited for them and cut them down as they ran.

The attackers from the rear continued to push forward, not because they were told to do so, but because of the sheer joy of the massacre. Crazed and hungry, they surged over the hapless soldiers, slicing lives away from close range – often with knives held to kill quickly. They broke the column apart like a pack of wolves taking advantage of the weaker ones.

Ahead, Rab'k couldn't get his people organized. Many of his officers were on the ground, some standing but most lying still, bleeding their life away. He couldn't be everywhere so he was losing contact with his force.

The desert army was finished before they found their enemy.

Rab'k sat watching his troops disappear into the brush, or fall wounded or dead on the road. He could see from atop his horse, his men being snatched down as they ran by men hidden in the undergrowth all along the line of march now.

He knew all was lost.

He screamed out Jond'r's name. He knew, somehow, that was his attacker. He knew he would have been in that position if their places were swapped. So, now he wanted only to kill the man who brought this ruin on him.

Jond'r stayed hidden until one of the men from their frontal attack ran to him with a message that his brother had been wounded and was having trouble with his wounds.

Jond'r felt he had enough of this man, this evil, bullying man who now may have cost him his brother. The man who had cut him down and left him for dead; the man who cut Garv'n and Vil'n down, both good men, in his quest for the death of all southern Aerolan.

He stepped out onto the road. Rab'k saw him and charged, but a number of Jond'r's men stepped into the road with him and thwarted that attempt by shouting and waving their arms to frighten the horse, which jumped aside almost unseating Rab'k. He reined the horse in, jumped from the saddle, drawing his sword. He headed straight for Jond'r, pushing the other men aside with almost no effort, raising his sword over his head as he neared Jond'r and brought it down to kill the man with one blow.

Jond'r blocked the sword as it came down toward his head, dodging aside and tripping Rab'k as he moved. Rab'k fell into the dirt, jumped up, yelled something in the desert language and was preparing to charge again.

At that moment, Pet'r appeared just behind Rab'k. Jond'r and the others saw him materialize and stopped what they were doing. Jond'r was stunned even though he saw Anisah any number of times doing the same thing, he was surprised to see Pet'r.

"Where are you going?" Pet'r yelled at Rab'k and took a few steps to stand directly behind him.

Rab'k spun around swinging his sword with all his might, knowing Pet'r was that near him.

"Die, you coward! Guardian of the Ahar'n! See how easy it is to die," Rab'k shouted as the blade cut through the air, directed at Pet'r neck.

Jond'r and all his men cried out.

Pet'r never moved out of the path of the sword. He kept his eyes on Rab'k's. At the last possible moment, he simply reached his arm up to ward off the blade. It stopped at impact.

497

No harm came to Pet'r. He looked at the blade, grabbed it near the pummel, reached above the open blade, snatched it from Rab'k's hand and threw it away toward the west. It sailed beyond the sight of all who watched. Rab'k's eyes widened. He didn't expect it to end this way.

Pet'r then reached for Rab'k, grabbed the front of his armor and pulled him closer.

"You don't need this either," he reached down into the front of the armor and pulled out the black stone fragment hanging there. "I think you will not need it again." He threw it across the prairie and it too sailed out of sight. Then he spun Rab'k back around to face Jond'r.

"Here, mighty man, you may use my sword to defend yourself," Pet'r said and handed Rab'k the sword he had never used.

Instantly, Rab'k brought the sword up and attacked Jond'r. He tried to pound Jond'r, but wasn't able to swing quickly enough to strike the younger man. Jond'r move back and forth, almost daring Rab'k to come for him. He feinted then retreated, but always he kept his blade in front of Rab'k, making his attacks fruitless. Finally, Rab'k saw an opening and, rushing with all his strength, attacked Jond'r with sword extended to impale him.

Jond'r, having rested and feeling angry about his brother, knocked Rab'k's sword to the side and plunged his own into Rab'k's heart before he could move aside.

Rab'k stood for a moment before looking down at his chest, staggered to one side a bit, lost strength in his legs and they crumpled. He fell on his back in the dirt, wondering why he failed.

He died staring at Pet'r.

The remainder of Rab'k troops, still fighting the best they could, saw their leader fall and began to drop their swords and run toward the mountains.

Jond'r's people, the trained ones, stood back and let the desert

498

soldiers escape. There was no need to follow them. The criminal element from Varspree was not so kind, but soon the area was clear of any fighters other than Jond'r's.

"I have to go see about Acron'n," he said and ran up the road as fast he could. Pet'r was right on his heels.

They asked where Acron'n was as they ran and headed toward where the soldiers pointed. Soon they came to a small crowd gathered around a spot just off the edge of the road and slowed. They walked into the group pushing people aside and came to where Acron'n lay in the dirt on his side.

"Are you all right?" Jond'r asked as he knelt down to examine his brother.

"Well, I think so," Acron'n rolled his head over to look sideways at his brother, "but it hurts like hell.

There was a long pause then everyone around started laughing aloud. They were the victors on this day and felt a certain pride in that.

Later they carried out the odious task of tossing the enemy soldiers to the side of the road to be taken by the wildlife. The desert people would not be attacking them for more centuries than the new soldiers would live. Now Jond'r's troops began their return to the castle at Ralff'r. They had learned much on this day, but most still needed to discover what they could about fighting this war.

Monsh'a had decided to run for the mountains, too. Anisah rushing ahead of her troops straggling home, entered the Habenlein camp, acquire two squads of the top soldiers and return to the lost battle site with them instantly. They marched, with her help, up and over the Ravelan encampment and began to harass them and to frustrate the Maah'e encampment commanders by being faster and more accurate with their weapons than the giants. The Ravelan and their monsters retreated, fighting the new force harassing them from behind. A number of the larger Habenlein attacked the Maah'e, slashing down those trying to lumber away. The contest was uneven and many Maah'e were disabled, or killed.

They didn't chase the departing troops any further than Caliste. Once past that Anisah indicated she would like to stop and wanted to return to Ralff'r. They found one of the Maah'e still alive and brought him to her before she left. She took the prisoner with her.

The Habenlein soldiers immediately ceased their chase, but continued to patrol at the forest edge to make certain no one came back along the path of pursuit.

Monsh'a, his officers and soldiers fled for their lives and eventually disappeared into Doom's Woods.

GRIEF

They gathered in the lower courtyard and out beyond the castle and across the open grounds. Those who returned from the southern coast with their belongings placed them where they were before the scare; those who returned from the Varspree campaign who were able to leave their beds and those who survived the fatal battle at Hang'm were waiting for the three.

The gate was lowered and Anisah placed a spell to broadcast their voices to the crowds of citizens and soldiers from both armies standing outside and beyond to the training grounds and the towns of Roahan and Farsea.

Entering from the hallway together, they walked into full view, stood side by side, and waited for the hum of the crowd to die. There was another with them the people did not recognize. A military officer with a foreign look and insignia. The crowd watched calmly.

"We come before you with grief and with fear, but with hope. Thank you for what you have done and hope what we must do will not endanger any more of you. We can't promise that, but we now know our enemy and his strengths. We have disrupted his plans with these last few days through the efforts of those of you who survived and those who were lost.

Our sadness, as I'm certain you feel it, overwhelms us for we regret we have not fulfilled our promises to you," Anisah spoke, feeling her own sorrow at the loss of so many lives. "But our need and yours, and the desire to help save our country and our world have brought us here. In our failures we are so sorry and we feel your pain for those lost to us; in our victory, we believe we know what we must do to end this desperate life."

Pet'r stood beside her, close enough to touch her garments. Geth'n stood with Siarra, holding her hand, his head hung low in

501

his sense of failure. Borny'a, Jond'r and Acron'n, with his side and arm bound from his wounds, stood with the foreign officer, all holding themselves alert.

"We apologize for all that has gone wrong, but we hope you will stand by us as we push into the future. We now know we cannot wait any longer and we now know the dangers of doing so.

But, this officer," she said, pointing to the foreign soldier, "is the leader of the large company of military you now know is encamped along our shore between Roahan and Farsea. He is from Habenlein and is here to help."

There were murmurs in the crowd. Anisah waited for quiet.

"We thank him for being here with his people and feel they, and many others to follow, will brings us victory against this most evil menace. The people of Habenlein support us. There is promise of others from other nations arriving to further enhance our ability to do so.

This gentleman's name is Trym'a. He is a colonel in King Jors'o's army and has shown his willingness to help as much as he can. He and some of his men were involved in chasing the Ravelan into Doom's Woods after the battle at Pull'r," she finished. The crowd murmured, some even clapped quickly.

"Since our involvement with the enemy ended, we've found one of the monster soldiers we all have feared, wounded at the battle of Hang'm and brought it here to determine how these have come to be. They are a mystery to us, but we can now investigate the phenomenon. We suspect these beings have been changed by magic from all of our men who were being kidnapped before the recent battles. If we can determine what magic does this, maybe we can reverse the spell and bring those men back into our lives.

So, we are working to win. We will make all efforts to keep the battles away from here and, after the colonel's help at Hang'm, we have an advantage and plan to take the war to them.

If anyone. If *anyone* wants to ask more questions, we will all be

502

available, except Colonel Trym'a, to try an answer them. But we will, for obvious reasons, be leaving again soon.

Be strong within and we will have victory. We want to eliminate this enemy. He's been here before but our ancestors only chased him away. This time we will rid our world, and others, of an enemy who should not be allowed to live.

Thank you again," she finished and bowed her head a moment.

The three and their new leaders left the courtyard and walked into the hallway they came from earlier.

The crowd milled about, talking in low voices, expressing hope the time of war would be over soon. They formed friendships with strangers in the castle and now it was like a home for those who wanted only to live in peace again.

Time would tell whether there was to be a future, or not. Time and too many lives.

A lone observer, standing on the distant shore, across the Grac'a Inlet, of the peninsula near Noend, shook his head in sadness, knowing life was going to be horrible for these people, his people.

He listened to the girl trying to bring hope to those remaining and sensed a determination he hadn't felt in many years. There was a possibility. There would be freedom from the tyranny of Baalsa'n. Finally.

And he would be there to help bring victory and freedom to this world . . .

The End

NEXT INSTALLMENT

THE YOUNG SHALL PREVAIL
The Aerolan Saga: **Book 3**

(Coming Soon – Late-2013)

Battles lost. Battles Won. Baalsa'n's forces slowly pushed back
to the mountains.
Will the Aerolan and their allies finally defeat Baalsa'n.
Will Anisah resolve her feeling for Pet'r?
Will she find and reconcile with, or kill, Mano'n?
How does Voravia fare? Is she left to herself or is her fate that
of Baalsa'n?
What about Geth'n and Siarra?
Do Garv'n, Borny'a, Turm'l, Jond'r and Acron'n find their
peace and slowly meld into society? Where will they be after the
war is over?

All questions to be answered in this next story of the war and
its outcome.

Join me next year.

Thanks for reading my story,

Larry Crow

THE AUTHORS

Both authors have tried to work and become authors, but then a great number of people have done that. Of course, we now know how difficult that is. It's took us over 10 years to get the first book – **The Young Shall Inherit** – together and time has indeed marched along quickly during those years.

Larry is a transplanted Floridian having lived here for about 25 years now. He owned a bookstore in the 1980's in Bradenton and then traveled around the US as a computer (Unix) software consultant.- still calling Florida "home". He saw a lot of this beautiful country, as he went and discovered more about people from different places and with different thoughts, he gained a larger perspective and understanding of people and what they like and want.

Jennifer is a native Floridian. She has spent most of her life living in various places around the southern part of the state. She has strong interest in the genre of these books, having devoured thousands of books in her reading everything she could find.

The interest of the two of us meshed. So, I asked her to work with me on the first book. Some of her ideas formed the character of Anisah who eventually proved to be our strongest one.

We started the original book but were slowed by life's circumstances, but then put in another effort later, until it all came together. The typing was the worst – it takes a heck of a long time to type a 400-500 page book. I decided we would self-publish.

Self-publishing is probably the oddest, but most obvious, direction to take and we have control of the work, for better or worse.

I'm proud of our efforts (including Jennifer's help on the first volume) and hope you're enjoying the result.

Thanks for dropping by.

OTHER BOOKS

Aerolan Saga
By: <u>Larry W. Crow and Jennifer L. Ricks</u>
Book One: ***The Young Shall Inherit***
Currently available:
<u>**Printed:**</u>
Amazon
Barnes and Noble
<u>**Ebook:**</u>
Smashwords (in multiple forms)

By: <u>Larry W. Crow</u>
Book Two: ***The Young Shall Endure***
Currently available:
<u>**Printed:**</u>
Amazon
Barnes and Noble
<u>**Ebook:**</u>
Smashwords (in multiple forms)

Book Three: ***The Young Shall Prevail*** (available **Fall** 2013)

Sentoria Saga
Book One: ***The Rights of Man*** *(available* **Winter** *2014)*

Children's Books
By: <u>Nancy F. Crow</u> – *posthumously*
Edited by: <u>Larry W. Crow</u>
Calley's Place

www.ingramcontent.com/pod-product-compliance
Lightning Source LLC
Chambersburg PA
CBHW071629260626
47170CB00001B/25